Merchants

Ghetto **Merchants**

Copyright © 2025 Dre Luv **978-1-953928-59-7**

Belle Publishing
Oklahoma City, OK.

Contact Dre Luv:
IG: Orginaldreluv_
PayPal: PayPal.me/BelicoseEnt
Venmo: @OKCUrbanwriter
Bellicose Investments LLC
2605 N MacArthur Blvd.
Oklahoma City, OK. 73127

GHETTO MERCHANTS

I'd like to thank God first for protecting me
throughout all the years of living life in the fast
lane and delivering me from addiction. Everyone
in the struggle, regardless of which side of the
fence, I hope you can unlock your mind and be
free!

Chapter 1

Sergeant John Hawkins was sitting in a corner booth at Rosie's Diner. There the walls were covered with 1950s memorabilia. He was sipping black coffee while impatiently peering outside at the parking lot. The busy traffic of Northwest Expressway faded into his vision as he waited for his old friend to arrive.

Hawkins was in charge of the Springlake Narcotics Unit of the Oklahoma City Police Department for four years after being a robbery homicide detective for eight. Lately, the responsibilities of running the department have begun to overwhelm him in several different ways. The department was underfunded, and his marriage was on the brink, even more so than when he was working robbery homicide. The harder he tried to get the drugs off the streets more drugs continued to pour in. That, along with the fact that he knew his wife was having an affair with her coworker, was taking a toll on him.

1991 proved to be the most violent in Oklahoma City, with the majority of the problems occurring in Hawkins' division on the northeast side. It was due to the gang invasion from California that began in the mid-eighties. They were looking for untainted turf where they could triple their profits without the old foes to stand in their way. This led to more cash and more guns to help influence the local crews to follow their lead. Hawkins was amazed at how the small city had transformed from a good place to raise children and retire. Now it was nothing more than another urban concrete jungle that the local authorities were losing ground on. They were maxed out, outmanned and outgunned. Hawkins needed help, which was why he was waiting at Rosie's this morning, hoping for a miracle.

Three weeks ago, Hawkins was getting drunk at the Fraternal

DRE LUV

Police Bar on the edge of downtown. He was caught off guard by his old friend Dale Sharper, who was a DEA agent. Sharper now had a head of snow-white hair, which barely made him recognizable. The last time Hawkins had seen him was in 1987, and at that time Agent Sharper's hair was still blonde.

Sharper had taken a seat at the bar on a stool next to him. He ordered the bartender to give him a double shot of Wild Turkey and a glass of Budweiser on tap and whatever my buddy is having, pointing at Hawkins with his thumb. That night, the two lawmen discussed issues with one another, including divorce, marriage, and what was most important in both their lives: their jobs.

The majority of Hawkins' problems stemmed from what seemed to him an untouchable local crew or gang known as the Ghetto Merchants. He had been trying to get these guys off the streets since 1986, when he was still in robbery homicide. Five and a half years later, they were still a thorn in his side, with him working at the Springlake Narcotics Unit.

In winter 1990, he thought the city had the blessing of an early Christmas gift that was going to get them all off the streets. One merchant member was booked into the Oklahoma County Jail for a triple homicide. Unfortunately, the law swayed in the better direction for the criminal instead of the prosecution when it was all over fourteen months later.

Deante Parker, aka Dollaz, was booked into the Oklahoma County Jail on November 22nd, Thanksgiving Day, charged with three counts of homicide. The victims were all murdered with the same 9-millimeter weapon, which was never found. But what was found at the scene was one empty 9-millimeter shell casing with Deante Parker's left thumbprint. The county-appointed district attorney chose to prosecute the case himself for publicity, knowing that he had an easy slam-dunk conviction. Without a doubt, he would seek the death penalty.

Three months after the arrest, during preparation for the speedy preliminary hearing, the district attorney's office was thrown for a loop. The only evidence they had available to convict was missing from the OCPD Evidence Room, and there were no witnesses. If the public caught wind of the mishandling of evidence between OCPD and the district attorney's office, there would be lots of people's jobs in jeopardy. The morning the news discovered that the casing was missing, it was found that it had not been documented anywhere; it had never been logged into the OCPD Evidence Room. This sparked an investigation with both departments' Internal Affairs Divisions. Somehow, nothing was ever solved between the two departments.

After the two continuances the district attorney filed, Judge Thomas Maine granted but set a final date for January 21, 1992. That would be the last day that the prosecution would be able to present their case; if they were not ready, he would be forced to dismiss the case. Although if they decided to refile the charges with credible evidence, Deante Parker would immediately have a warrant for his arrest.

On November 21, 1990, Hawkins and his narcotics team were executing a warrant at 1124 NE 17th signed by Judge Tom Mason. Hawkins was able to get the paperwork signed because of a controlled buy of 56 grams of crack cocaine by a confidential informant. Upon kicking in the door at 6:45 am they found the door blocked by a dead woman's body with two fatal gunshot wounds. One to the neck and one in her chest. A trail of blood led them to the dining room kitchen archway, where the body of a man lay dead as well.

When they swept inside the kitchen, they found another dead man. It turned out to be Hawkins' biggest drug bust because of the 5,521 grams of cocaine that was found in the attic. It also turned out to be his deadliest without him or one of his team members firing one shot. After Hawkins told the story to Sharper and the bar was about to close, Sharper assured Hawkins that he would speak with his superior to see what type of information the federal government had on the Ghetto Merchants.

Before parting that night, they made arrangements to meet later. Close to two weeks had passed since Sharper and Hawkins met up at the Fraternal Bar. Deante Parker had been released for a couple of days and Hawkins was impatiently waiting when he saw Agent Sharper appear out of what seemed like thin air with his usual attire: white cowboy hat, blue denim Wrangler shirt and jeans with black Justin Roper boots. Clipped to his black cowboy belt was a nylon case that holstered his .40 Glock. In his hand, he carried a worn brown leather attaché case.

"Over here, Dale!" Hawkins shouted over the noise inside the crowded diner as he waved his arm in the air from his booth.

Rosie's was so busy with people chattering that nobody appeared to notice the urban cowboy bearing his firearm on his hip as he breezed across the floor. As soon as Sharper sat down, an elderly plump waitress with brunette hair with silver streaks in a bun waltzed over to the booth. She smiled at her newest customer as she commenced to refill Hawkins' coffee cup and Sharper's for the first time. In a snap she was gone.

"Sorry I'm runnin' late John but I'm kinda pressed for time this mornin'. I won't be able to stick around and eat breakfast witcha but I do have a little bit of information for you on them thugs."

Quickly returning from a prior task, the waitress was back with two menus in her hand. Both lawmen declined, leaving her to turn

4

away with a sneer, feeling that with no breakfast being served at the table, the less her tip would be.

"As I was sayin' bout them Ghetto Merchant fellers. I want to add somethin' to their catchy title; them boys are more than just street-level drug dealers. Them boys is gangsters too. I've done some research and feel that when a sum bitch moves with a group and they's constantly gettin' away with crimes such as murder...John, that right there makes em a menace to society."

Agent Sharper stopped to take a sip of coffee as both he and Hawkins looked around the diner, checking their surroundings. They had planned this meeting between the two and wanted to be certain that no coworkers were around because Rosie's was a popular spot. Because of both of their investigative skills, they noticed the two middle-aged couples eavesdropping, two tables over. After both lawmen flashed a smile, Sharper added on a tilt of his hat and they both focused their attention back to their personal business on the Ghetto Merchants. Hawkins then cleared his throat and raised his left hand to his face and rubbing his goatee and beard with a downward motion. "For Christ sakes I'm sick and tired; literally I am sick and tired of these assholes, and I want to get their asses off the streets for good. Dale, our friendship goes back to when I was an Airman, and you were a MP out at the base. I was there for you when you lost your little sister. It was me who supported you when you decided to go to Virginia to join the bureau so don't treat me like I'm some sort of rookie you mother fucker. Tell me what's on your mind and what we can do," Sergeant Hawkins lectured with a plea.

"Relax, John and take a breath. Everything I know is inside the case, even gotta file on Javon Mims. He ain't one of the Merchants but they's connected. A couple fellers at the bureau have enlightened me on him. He's a heavyweight with a California connection. I am almost positive that he is the one supplying the Merchant crew. Now, what I've done is put a red flag on the NCIC Blotter on Mims. If he gets stopped by any law enforcement officer anywhere in the country and an NCIC check is run on him, he will be detained while I'm notified. Now what I'm trying to do is prove that he is their source, and if we can pinch him on anything, I guarantee ya that we'll get em to talk. That way, we'll be able to get them all with a federal conspiracy. Damn a state case, you can see how that has gone. Now, what I suggest you do is some more homework. What I mean by that is press every sum bitch that you bust that works for The Ghetto Merchants and who doesn't and get them to make a deal."

"Believe me when you threaten a mother fucker's freedom they'll consider cooperating at least the weak spineless ones. Those that you feel that can be detrimental on our behalf let em work for ya and that way we can build up enough for a big case to take to the US Attorney, then to the Grand Jury. John, I can't tell ya how to do ya job but that's what I suggest because I wanna see every one of them sons of bitches die in a jail cell."

Sergeant Hawkins looked into the reddened face of Agent Sharper and felt a sign of relief because he believed that he was on his team, and he knew that Sharper was more knowledgeable about drug dealers. He should, he's D.E.A. At that point Sharper pulled a card out of his shirt pocket and placed it on top of the case and chuckled. He patted his friend on the shoulder after he stood up from the booth.

"Listen, John, between the two of us, we can do the majority of the investigative work on our own. Here's my card. Anytime ya come up with somethin' that can help us out, be sure to notify me. When I come up with somethin', I'll be sure to give you a ring over at Springlake Division. As for now, I gotta get downtown."

"Sounds good to me, Dale. Hey...I want you to know that I appreciate your help. The brass at OCPD has cut my budget down to a minimum for my team. They ain't giving a damn about the neighborhoods with crack houses on every block. Their only concern is that the dope doesn't get into their suburban fortresses inside the gated communities. As long as it doesn't affect their children, it's really not a problem. Hypocrites, I tell ya," Expressed Sergeant Hawkins with a serious look on his face.

Sharper's head bobbed up and down, making Hawkins think that he was in total agreement with him, but in reality, he was ready to go. He extended his right hand out to shake Hawkins' before leaving.

"I'm afraid that you're right, John. When the kids on the outskirts of town get affected, it puts a new light on the subject. Unfortunately, we don't make the rules; our jobs are to enforce em. Take care, my friend."

As Agent Sharper made his way to the exit, he tipped his hat and smiled at the waitress when he passed her by. She was pouring coffee at the table with the nosy couples. As he strolled across the parking lot, Hawkins watched him as he opened the door and hopped inside a white late-model F-250 Ford truck equipped with four-wheel drive. Hawkins briefly pondered how stressful the job must be working for the D.E.A. Sharper had aged so much to be just forty years old. Then he reflected on himself because he felt that he had the weight of the world on his shoulders most of the time. Then again, he couldn't begin to understand how Agent Sharper felt because he had lost his only sister to drugs when she was just a kid.

Hawkins pushed his coffee aside and pulled the brown attaché case close and opened it up. Inside were seven files, six of which had names on the outside, and the seventh one was blank. He opened each one.

DRE LUV

MALCOLM PRICELESS LOVE: D.O.B. 10/12/69
7/25/89 Possession of Marijuana;
Oklahoma City Municipal Court # 560148
Disposition: 1 year probation 10/31/89
9/8/90 Felony Eluding;
Oklahoma County CF 90 - 8391
Disposition: 1 year deferred sentence fined 1135.00 plus
property damages 12/13/90

DEANTE LAMAR PARKER A.K.A. DOLLAZ: D.O.B. 4/22/69
10/16/88 Driveby Shooting; One dead, three hospitalized ICU
all survived 12-gauge shotgun blast. No weapon recovered.
No witnesses. Parker was released after a 27-hour
interrogation. No charges filed.
7/25/89 Carrying a concealed weapon 9mm
Oklahoma County CM 89 - 6845
Disposition: 2 year deferred (Supervised) 9/27/89
11/22/90 First Degree Murder 3 counts
Disposition: Charges dismissed at preliminary hearing due to
lack of evidence 1/21/92

BRANDON DARNELL TAYLOR A.K.A. BIG TAY: D.O.B. 6/8/69
5/10/88 Possession Of a Firearm In Commission of a Felony
Possession With Intent To Distribute Crack Cocaine
Oklahoma County CF - 88.5881
Disposition: Regimented Inmate Discipline Program (120
Days) 3 years suspended 3/5/89

8

GHETTO MERCHANTS

GARY ANTONIO TOMSON A.K.A. GOOCH: D.O.B. 6/15/72
7/27/90 Possession of Marijuana (on Oklahoma University Campus)
Norman Municipal Court # 77964023
Disposition: 1 year deferred sentence, 1000.00 fine, banned from NCAA activities for one year 10/10/90

STAN LEE JOHNSON A.K.A. SOLO: D.O.B. 1/7/71
Juvenile Record Kansas City, MO J.J.C.C.
8/30/86 Tampering/Motor Vehicle
Disposition: House Arrest 1 year, property damage of 478.00 11/29/86
12/24/87 Joyriding
Disposition: 6 months Alternative Rehabilitation 1/10/88

DEWAYNE ALLAN ROGERS A.K.A. WAYNIAC D.O.B. 2/18/69
TOMMY DALE SIMMONS A.K.A. TOM TOM D.O.B. 5/11/69
9/26/86 Armed Bank Robbery (First State Bank) 9/28/86 Both Rogers and Simmons were certified as adults
Oklahoma County CF 86 - 1865
Disposition: 25 years Oklahoma Department of Cor-rections 4/1/8

JAVON PAUL MIMS A.K.A. JP MONEY: D.O.B. 8/1/64

DRE LUV

5/13/83 Trafficking Heroin
Oklahoma County CF 83 - 1492
Disposition: 10 years Oklahoma Department of Corrections
2/14/84

GHETTO MERCHANTS

After making it through the third file, Hawkins angrily shuffled through the rest. When he finished, he placed all of the files back inside the attache in an orderly fashion, then took another sip of coffee. Feeling the need to smoke a cigarette to help calm his nerves, he realized that he quit six months ago. All of the information that Agent Sharper brought to the diner was information that he was familiar with already. Even the bank robbery that left Chris Jenkins and Jerry Pratter dead, which led to Rogers' and Simmons' incarceration. Hawkins was the lead detective.

He remembered that breezy Saturday morning in September 1986 when he was called to the scene of the crime at First State Security Bank on the corner of N.E. 23rd and Jordan. In the parking lot on the north side of the building lay the body of seventeen-year-old Chris Jenkins. He had been shot in the face. Ten blocks north, at a right turn only curve on 34th and Jordan, was the body of Jerry Pratter. He was killed instantly in a wreck where he was driving and lost control of the car and hit a tree. Dewayne Rogers and Tommy Simmons were in the car as well, but they lived.

Javon Mims was a factor, true enough, but he was involved with a lot of drug dealers in the Oklahoma City area. Whatever Sharper had planned must be above his level, and Hawkins decided that he would take his advice and play his role as the local drug task force cop who can't get his man.

He slid out of the booth and stood up and reached into his pocket and took his wallet out and pulled out a five-dollar bill. Hawkins tossed it on the table, picked up the attaché, and walked out with his head hanging down. Everything may not have gone like he planned, but something good had to happen sooner rather than later. Hawkins was on his way to the Springlake Division.

Chapter 2

Inside his plush suite at the MGM, Javon waited impatiently for room service as he pulled the last drag on his Newport cigarette. Burning his lips, he raised his back from the couch and quickly stabbed the butt down on the marble coffee table that sat in front of him.

H

e reached over and grabbed the watered-down crown and Coke, swallowing the whole glass with one drink. Javon stood up and stretched while contemplating going to the balcony and getting some fresh air. Instead, he decided to lie down on the tall California king-sized bed. On his way to the bedroom, he lifted his arm to check the time.

T

he hands on his Rolex read 10:05. He paused on his stride to the bedroom and yawned, then he continued on. He couldn't believe that it was ten o'clock already. He knew that he needed to get some rest because he had been up for over forty-eight hours, and inside the casino for almost twenty of them. Now it was Friday. When he made it to the foot of the bed, he dove on top. Just when he got into a comfortable position, he heard his mobile phone begin to ring out in the living area. Javon ignored the ringing, knowing that it would cease and began thinking about the eighty g's he had lost since he walked inside the building yesterday.

Then he thought about the one hundred ten g's he lost last month and felt himself getting a headache. For the past year, he had been hustling hard for what seemed like nothing but his gambling habit and his kilo consignment from his connection in Los Angeles. He was so fucked up in the head that if it was not for Malcolm to come through and help him

12

push his work and make extras, he would have crashed a long time ago. When he actually took the time to think about it, Malcolm was his best friend; in fact, he was his only friend. Although they didn't spend much time together, except when drugs were involved still Malcolm had always been there for him, even when he didn't realize that he was using him.

How could all the time have slipped away, then the answer come to him so simple? It had slipped away just as his money had slipped out of his safe by being irresponsible and taking his life for granted. He was enslaved to an addiction that he had to feed by pushing cocaine across state lines, which had led him to the point where he was getting taxed an extra twenty-five hundred a kilo. All of this was becoming impossible to control; he had to do something fast besides crash.

Javon's backwards hustling was getting everybody paid but him and just when he was about to get five ki's of his own for the first time in over a year he lost the money, since yesterday evening. Javon rolled over on his back and wiped his eyes with the sleeve of his wrinkled long-sleeved Polo button-down. Suddenly, he had a thought. There was still two hundred seventy g's in the back of the Range Rover. That was just enough to pay his connect and get fifteen more on consignment and be right back in the hole again, starting from square one.

He quickly slid off the bed and stepped into the bathroom and stared at himself in the mirror.

"I look like shit."

Smelling his armpits, he decided to just freshen up instead of showering and then head to I-15 and LA.

DRE LUV

While brushing his teeth, he began to let his mind wander again and decided he would give the gaming area one more try. He would go downstairs and get forty more g's out of the Range Rover, flip the money and be right back to where he was when he left Oklahoma City. That way he would be able to stick to the plan of buying his own work, pay the connect off and head back home. His thoughts were interrupted by his mobile phone and a knock on the door. He quickly rinsed his mouth and washed his face and ran to the other room, passing the phone up and answering the door. When he opened the door, there was a clean-cut young white guy wearing a white jacket with his hands on a cart.

"Good morning, sir," he greeted Javon as he rolled the cart inside the suite.

Javon reached inside his front pocket, pulling out thirty-eight dollars. He handed the young man with BRAD on his name tag a twenty-dollar bill.

"Brad, I need you to get my Range Rover brought to the front of the casino immediately," Javon stated firmly.

"No problem, sir; I have a good friend that works AM valet. Let me have your valet ticket, and I can make it happen," Brad responded with a smile as he stood with his arms behind his back.

Javon searched all his pockets, his bag, and all over the suite and he came up with nothing except his nationwide pager which was vibrating inside the creases of a plush sofa. He didn't bother to look at it; he just set it on the table beside his mobile phone. After going all through the suite he paused for a moment and rubbed his hands on his face, feeling the stubble and thought back and tried to calculate his steps.

GHETTO MERCHANTS

When he pulled into the casino and parked, he got out of the front seat to hop in the back of the Rover. Before he could get into the back seat, a valet driver approached him, but he shunned him away because he did not want him to see him getting money out of the bag and putting it in another. The valet driver obliged him and stepped away and back under the portico. At that point, Javon got into the backseat and closed the door and took money out of the Samsonite bag and put it into his small leather duffle. After he finished getting the money situated, he got out of the Rover and tossed the keys to another valet.

"Okay, Brad, I remember now. I gave my keys to a valet driver that was walking towards me when I got outta my backseat. I don't remember him giving me a ticket, in fact I know he didn't...I remember his face too, and he had on a white jacket," Javon explained with an attempt to make Brad understand.

Brad had listened and was observing Javon since he walked inside the suite. He could tell that Javon was scattered; he had seen guys like him thousands of times. He needed to get some sleep and get the hell out of Vegas before he lost his Rolex and his nice chain to a pawnshop in a desperate hope of making it back home. It was obvious that the man had no idea whether he had been given a valet ticket or not, so he cautiously chose his next words, hoping not to upset the guest. He cleared his throat before he began. "Sir, I am afraid that it is not possible that you gave your keys to a valet driver wearing a white jacket. All of our valet drivers wear maroon blazers, as you see I am wearing white. Food service in white, valets wear maroon."

Javon was suddenly feeling his headache again and it was getting bigger. He rubbed his temples, hoping to reduce the pain as he tried to make believe that what he was going through was really a dream. This whole trip was turning out to be a nightmare. Javon paced around in a small circle and dropped his arms down to his side and stopped to face Brad as he took a deep breath.

"Listen, Brad, my truck is a black Range Rover Classic, plate number QXJ909. By the time I get finished with my breakfast, my ride better be up front."

Brad had been scribbling notes on a pad, but after Javon's last statement, he paused and looked at him. Javon was looking at his watch with a facial expression that showed he was serious. Brad clicked the ink pen and opened his jacket, putting the pen and pad inside. He swallowed hard and took a deep breath.

"Uhh, sir, I am going to take this information to security right now. You enjoy your breakfast, and I am certain that we'll have your vehicle out front by the time that you've eaten and gotten yourself together."

Without another word said between the two, Brad opened the door and walked out. Javon looked down at his clothes and took offense to the kid telling him he looked like shit in so many words. Down the hall Brad laughed out loud as he thought about the damn fool in the suite that gave away his Range Rover.

Javon, on the other hand, started looking for the ticket again as he heard his pager vibrating again when he was on his hands and knees looking under the sofa. He raised up and picked up the pager and scrolled the screen to see that his last eight pages were from Malcolm, mobile and home phone numbers, and two of them were from Fats.

"Damn!" Javon shouted as he threw the pager across the room. He watched it shatter when it hit the wall. He stood up and his mobile began to ring again. Javon fell over on the sofa and covered his face and sobbed.

GHETTO MERCHANTS

Malcolm pressed END on his Motorola and laid it down in his lap and wondered why in the fuck this nigga ain't answerin' his phone or his pages. He sighed as he gazed at the traffic while Deziree changed lanes in her Lexus ES 300.

"Where do I get off the highway, baby?" Deziree asked. Malcolm twisted his upper body in the seat so that he could face Deziree.

Just when he was about to answer her, his pager started vibrating. He reached down and unclipped it from his Guess jeans and looked at the screen. Just like he expected it was a sale for four ounces. He shook his head with a sign of disgust as he clipped the pager back on his jeans. A sell for four g's and no work was enough of the ammunition that he needed to vent, not to mention his connect wasn't answering his phone.

"Stop it, Deziree. Why you askin' questions that you know the answers to? You've takin' me or either been ridin' with me to the same shop for years but since your memory is all fucked up get off on S.E. 66th. Cooker's is right across the street from Crossroads Mall."

Deziree took her right hand off the steering wheel after checking the status of the traffic. That was when she poked Malcolm in his temple, making sure that she got his full attention. When he moved his head and looked in her direction, she was looking him in the eye with an evil stare.

"Don't you dare try to take your attitude out on me because you having a few problems with your boys. It ain't my fault that they are not answering ya calls or returning ya pages. Remember this, Malcolm Love, I was minding my own business this morning on my way to your mother's house when you asked me to give you a ride way out here, out of the way. You sho right though, I know where it is, but I was just trying to make conversation with your crazy butt cause I know you're kind of stressed. Hmm, what do you know, S.E. 66th next exit. Let me hurry up and get you there so you can get your ass out of my car."

Malcolm laughed at Deziree's tirade and nonchalantly put his left arm behind her seat and slid it up to the headrest, then grabbed her ponytail playfully.
"Goddamn lil mama...take it easy. You gonna fuck around and getcha pressure all high and shit."

Deziree scowled at Malcolm and raised her arm up, knocking his grasp loose from her hair and scooted over against the door.

"Stop playing, boy! You should have been trying to pull on it last night. Instead, you crawled up in the bed smelling like Remy Martin, talking bout my head hurt. Ten minutes later, you trying to lay up under me, snoring. And you better stop drinking and driving before you kill somebody or yourself, at least stop driving like that in my car. For real though, baby, you can't pay attention to whoever out there that might want to jack you, cause you're loaded."

Malcolm felt the sincerity in Deziree's words and knew that was one reason why he loved her so much. She cared. Now he was feeling kind of bad because he had been acting like an asshole all morning.

"For you, lil' mama, I'll stop drivin' while drinkin' yac."
"Stop lying boy; you say that shit all the time."

As Deziree pulled into Cooker's Auto Accessories parking lot, Malcolm pointed towards his new pearl white Cadillac Seville sitting on chrome and gold Zeniths and Vogues. As Deziree pulled closer to the car, she looked over at Malcolm, who was smiling like a kid pulling into the parking lot of an amusement park. She enjoyed seeing him smile because it made her light up on the inside when she saw him happy, although she seldom felt the same.

When she parked, she quickly reached over and grabbed his hand and squeezed it, and leaned over close to him. As soon as he turned to face her, she began to speak.

"Baby, don't make promises for me, make them for yourself. You must realize that you're going to be a father really soon. Now, get out of my car."

She kissed him softly on the lips and slapped him on his leg as he quickly opened the car door and got out of the car and adjusted his pistol on his waist hidden by his Guess sweatshirt.

"I love you, Deziree," Malcolm spoke genuinely with a solemn look on his face, then he closed the door. Deziree backed her car out and let down the passenger window and stared at Malcolm stepping away from her car to meet what appeared to be a salesman from Cooker's coming across the parking lot.

"Don't let me see or hear about any hoes in that car. You know how you like to act when you get something new. And pull that sweatshirt down crazy ass man, I can see that thing."

Malcolm looked down and made the necessary adjustments with his pistol and his sweatshirt, then he patted his front pockets to make sure that he had his ring with all of his house keys. Finding them there in his left front pocket, he was ready to go. He then looked up at Deziree and winked at her and waved bye with his phone in his hand. That was when the salesman made it to Malcolm and pressed a button on the remote control.

"Disarmed." Sounded the Viper alarm on the Cadillac.

Deziree shook her head when Malcolm flashed her a mischievous grin as the Cooker's salesman handed him the keys. Deziree raised up her window and drove off. No more than four or five minutes had passed; Deziree was cruising at 60 miles per hour going northbound on I-35 approaching the Amarillo/Tulsa junction. She looked into her rearview mirror, seeing a glare of white and chrome coming up behind her fast. Suddenly, she began to feel bass inside her airtight Lexus that wasn't coming from her stereo system. The next thing she knew, Malcolm's white Cadillac flew past her as if she were standing still. At that very moment she prayed to God for the safety of her baby's father because he was a damn fool.

Chapter 3

Deep inside Memorial Cemetery, underneath a life-sized angel made of marble that sat on top of a large headstone, knelt Agent Dale Sharper. He wiped a few tears away as he gazed upon it and read:

MELISSA ANN SHARPER
SUNRISE DECEMBER 25,1959
SUNSET MARCH 18, 1976

"You'd be thirty-two right about now, sis; I can only imagine what you might have grown up ta be. Regardless, you'd still be lil peanut to me. Mom and Dad are still hangin' in there and still missin' you a bunch. Hell, your bedroom still looks the same way thatcha left it so that mom and dad can go in there and hope to see ya dancin' around listenin' to that damn record play, dancin' away. Well, that's all gonna change when mom retires after this school year's up. Her and Dad is movin' down to Jacksonville, Florida and sellin' the house. They say they's got too many memories that they wanna just let go and move on. As for me, I aint doin' too good since Liz and the kids took off. She said she was tired of bein' married to two people...me and my job. I told her good riddance, you know, Peanut, you can't make somebody love ya anyway. Well, I just came by to visit ya for a minute and bring ya a few flowers, I know how ya like daisies. Also, I wanna let ya know that I'm hot on the trail of the son of the mother fucker that took ya away from me. This time I'm gonna do things my way. Don't you worry ya pretty lil head cause your big bubby is gonna be alright and if not, I'll die tryin'."

DRE LUV

Chapter 4

Smashing north on MLK Boulevard, Malcolm looked over at the carwash and saw Dollaz standing beside Cheryl's Jeep. Unfamiliar with the car that pulled into the carwash with the booming system, Dollaz put his hand inside his flannel and put a tight grip on his Ruger 9mm. As the car crept closer, Dollaz asked Cheryl and Dalinda if they knew whose Cadillac that was. Neither one of them knew, but they both acknowledged that they liked the car. Dollaz bent at his knees a bit to try and get a look into the tinted front glass, but couldn't make out a face. Just in case he began to move towards the front of the Jeep to get out of the way in case there were enemies of his behind the tint, bumpin' Ice Cube's 'How to Survive in South Central.'

When Dollaz made it to the front of the Jeep, Malcolm let down the passenger window, revealing his face and letting out the major sounds from all the speakers. He turned the music down and leaned over the console and pressed the gas and hit the brake and threw the Cadillac into park as he laughed at Dollaz looking scared.

"What's poppin' homie?" Malcolm screamed out to Dollaz, who had his Ruger pulled out and was all the way on the other side of the Jeep. Before Dollaz could answer, Cheryl began to run her mouth.

"Is Dollaz all you see, Malcolm? Just cause you showin' off your new car and got a little money, don't mean you better than everybody."
"I guess you heard that, Mr. Big Shot!" Shouted Dalinda from the passenger seat of the Jeep.

Dollaz stuck his pistol back inside his dickies as he walked back around the Jeep toward Malcolm's Cadillac. Malcolm looked over at Cheryl and Dalinda and raised his right hand up and extended his middle finger to them. He thought about letting their comments ride since

22

they were the homegirls, but since it was clear that they were hating he cut in.

"Why you hoes hatin'? Both of ya'll know that if I let either one of you bitches come over here in the passenger seat, you'd break ya neck to come over here. We wouldn't even make it to the highway before you'd be suckin' on a nigga dick, so shut the fuck up."

Dalinda and Cheryl were both caught off guard by Malcolm's comment, but not surprised, as they began to quarrel among themselves. Dollaz leaned into the window of the Cadillac in an attempt to cut off any more words between Malcolm and the homegirls.

"Fuck what they talkin' bout my nigga. You've known since middle school that they don't do nothin' but gossip and talk shit to the homies whenever they can. In fact, maybe you should apologize," Dollaz spoke with laughter in his voice.

"I wish I would," Malcolm held back laughter, too.

"I see some shit ain't changed around here except for the Ghetto Merchants lookin' like they havin' shit their way as usual cause this Lac right here is the bomb my nigga," Dollaz looked inside and backed up and took a good look of the outside admiring his homeboy's ride.

Suddenly, a faded burgundy Honda Accord pulled into the parking lot, scrubbing the tires on the deep dish five stars on its fenders. Once again, Dollaz reached inside his flannel to grip his Ruger and Malcolm grabbed his Llama .45 from the floor, pulled the hammer back and looked over his shoulder. Cheryl and Dalinda got louder as they noticed the car pulled up close on Cheryl's bumper.

"Damn, girl! Here come Ronnell. You know he gonna be trippin, start up the Jeep and let's go before he get out," Dalinda spoke frantically,

DRE LUV

causing Cheryl to panic.

"Bitch, how am I supposed to get out with him right on my bumper and a god damn wall in front of us?"

"Stop bein' so scary and stand up to him, girl!" Cheryl yelled with conviction as she dug in her purse for her cigarettes.

When Ronnell got out of the car, he left the driver's door open and walked all the way around the back after gritting on Dollaz. Making it to the passenger side of the Jeep, Dalinda greeted him with a nervous smile as smoke from Cheryl's cigarette crept out of her nostrils.

Before she could say anything, Ronnell slapped her hard on the left side of her face. Dalinda screamed out loud, scaring Cheryl, making her scream out as well. Malcolm and Dollaz both made a face and made a fist and covered their mouths.

"Shut the hell up and don't even start lyin'. Get yo tramp ass to the crib and tend to them kids. I told you and that bitch I had somethin' to do before y'all left. You told me ya'll was goin' to the store to get some goddamn rollin' papers, that's been thirty minutes ago!" Ronnell shouted with fury.

Dalinda did her best to stop the crying, but she couldn't because she was in pain; Ronnell had slapped her across her ear, still, she tried to explain through her sobbing.

"Ronnell, stop trippin'...I'm sorry, me and Cheryl just so happened to see the homeboy Dollaz walking over here and we stopped to holla at him for a minute. I promise I was on my way back home, baby."

Malcolm continued to observe from the driver's seat as Dalinda did her best to explain. He couldn't help but wonder

24

what Dalinda's buster baby daddy had to do that was so important. It wasn't on him to get involved with his homegirls' business with their niggas anyway because he had seen the same outcome over and over again. They would get smacked around by a nigga, call for help, and get., right back with the nigga that smacked them around the same week. Just when Malcolm was going to tell Dollaz to get in and he let the hammer down on the .45, Ronnell started to pull Dalinda out of the window of the Jeep.

"Getcha bitch ass outta there, come on. I don't give a fuck about a nigga named Dollaz and fuck that bitch Cheryl and fuck the punkass nigga in the Cadillac..." Ronnell ranted as he wrestled with Dalinda.

When he made the remark about the punkass nigga in the Cadillac he sparked a flame inside Malcolm's head. He dropped the Llama on the floor and swung the door open. The next loud noise heard over Ronnell's voice was the sound of Ronnell's hood caving in under Malcolm's feet. Malcolm had run around the back of his car and jumped on top of the Honda Accord in order to get around the Jeep to get up close and personal with the man that called him a punk ass nigga.

The crunching noise caused Ronnell's attention to shift from Cheryl to his car, then to Malcolm when he hopped off it to the loose graveled pavement with his fist balled up and his face twisted.

"Knuckle up bitch nigga!" shouted Malcolm as he walked towards Ronnell.

Ronnell let go of Dalinda, who wiggled back inside the Jeep, and he tried to adjust his feet to get set but was too slow because Malcolm twisted his body and caught Ronnell with a left hook to his right temple. Ronnell stumbled a bit to his left from the blow, then Malcolm brought him back up straight with a right cross to his jaw after he sidestepped. Ronnell's jaw sounded off with a loud pop, and his eyes rolled back, revealing all whites of his eyes. Dollaz caught him before he fell and kneed him in the back, then let him fall on the fender of Cheryl's Suzuki Jeep. Just when Ronnell was sliding down to the ground, Dollaz raised his right leg and stomped down on Ronnell's chest. Dalinda started screaming and pushing on Malcolm, who was holding her door shut so that she could not get out. She watched as Dollaz stomped and kicked Ronnell, leaving boot prints on his Miami Dolphin Starter jacket until Malcolm pushed him, knocking him off balance.

"Dollaz! This nigga through..." Malcolm shouted then he turned around to face Dalinda. "Let this fool ass nigga know who he dissed when he wake up."

Malcolm explained to her while Dollaz tried to catch his breath as he looked around to check the scene. Just when Malcolm was about to step away and let her out, he looked down at his sweatshirt and jeans and saw some blood drops. Dollaz looked down and probably saved Malcolm's life because Ronnell was pulling a /380 out from under his Starter jacket, attempting to take aim at Malcolm. Dollaz reached into his flannel, pulling out his Ruger and slapped Ronnell across the bridge of his nose.

"Malcolm, make him stop!" Dalinda cried out.

Malcolm heard the noise from the blow that came from the pistol connecting with the bones in Ronnell's nose as he turned around quickly to see a chrome pistol on the pavement lying beside Ronnell, who yelled out in pain.

GHETTO MERCHANTS

Malcolm knelt and grasped hold to the pistol and bumped heads with Dollaz as he moved across Ronnell's body and slapped him twice across his eye. Now it was Dollaz's turn to grab Malcolm as he noticed cars slowing as they passed by and some pulling in.

"Let's go Malcolm before we fuck around and kill this nigga. Cheryl, you and Dalinda know what time it is don'tcha?"

Dollaz spoke out with an evil look on his face. Dalinda and Cheryl both nodded their heads with a look of fear on both of their faces as they both climbed out of the passenger door, whimpering and wiping tears. Malcolm and Dollaz ran and hopped into the Cadillac and fled out of the carwash parking lot on the side street heading west on Madison Avenue.

Dalinda held Ronnell's limp body while Cheryl pleaded for someone to call 911.

At the bottom of the block, Malcolm made a right turn on Missouri, shaking his head in disbelief when he noticed all of the blood on his clothes and all over his leather interior. Dollaz was still laughing until Malcolm made the next right on 24th. He accelerated up the block to the sixth house on the left, which was Gooch and Solo's crack spot where Gooch's candy blue convertible, sitting on 15-inch Dayton's, was parked in the driveway. Malcolm pulled in behind the 5.0, parked and killed the engine. He took a deep breath as he looked down at his clothes and his hands, then he leaned back into the leather seat and popped his neck. Dollaz looked over at him for a moment and wondered about the incident that occurred around the corner at the carwash. Something more than Dalinda's man sparked Malcolm's rage—Dollaz knew this to be fact because he had known Malcolm too long.

"Yo Malcolm...I wanna thank you for gettin' me that lawyer. Without him I would probably be on death row right about now or wiped out with a life sentence. The day when they took me outta the pod for a legal visit I just knew it was them punk ass detectives tryin' another shot to get a nigga to tell. Do you know that they tried to tell me that they knew you was the one that put me up to the job of killin' them niggas and that bitch. Them police think you Neno Brown for real my nigga, ha haa. Anyway, you hirin' Chuck Jackson for me and lookin' out for my moms and grandpa means a whole lot. You and the homies are some real ass niggas. I was stressed out like a mutha fucka at first; I had a public pretender, my bitch ran off with my money, my IROC, everythang. The only thang I got now is my Suburban, this Ruger and the two ounces that Solo and Gooch tossed me yesterday when they seen me at the payphone at the hood store on deuce seven. Look here Malcolm, I can see it in your face that you still mad at me for the bullshit I did. All I can do is ask you to forgive me."

After Dollaz spoke his mind, Malcolm tapped the horn a couple of times and looked over his right shoulder towards the post office and MLK to make sure that nobody was creeping up on them. Then there was the faint noise of a siren that was growing closer. When he turned his head back around, he saw the front door opening up behind the bars. It was Solo. He disappeared, leaving the door open. Malcolm raised his steering wheel up and turned his body to face Dollaz with a smirk on his face.

"Check this shit out Dollaz...you chose to remove yourself from our crew because you felt like I was bossin' you around. Don't look like you don't know what I'm talkin' bout homeboy, cause I know you said it. You see what happened was that you started doin' all that mutha fuckin' pillow talkin' with that punk bitch Nessa and you let her send you on a personal mission. I can't even begin to tell you how I felt when you come to my crib that mornin' talkin' bout you wanted your share of the money;

28

GHETTO MERCHANTS

no less than fifty stacks. My nigga that was damn near every dime we had, and I told you that but you was like fuck it. Then three months later your dumb butt was in jail with three bodies on your back and you didn't have nothin'. You went from a dope man to a jack boy in no time flat. And I know you did that shit on 17th Dollaz cause..."

Malcolm was midsentence through his speech when he noticed Solo standing on the porch wearing a wrinkled white tee shirt and some baggy red Girbaud jeans and socks with his cornrows frazzled, waving for him to come inside. Before Dollaz got a chance to reply to Malcolm and before getting out of the car, Malcolm finished.

"To sum the whole thang, you crazy."

Then he got out of the car.

Solo was standing on the porch rubbing his hands together while staring at the newest addition to the Ghetto Merchant's fleet, and then he put on a big smile when he saw Dollaz get out of the passenger side. Solo smiled when he saw the blood on Dollaz's flannel when he shut the car door. Then, when Malcolm emerged from between the Cadillac and the 5.0, he noticed the blood splatter all over his white Guess sweatshirt and some on his jeans. Solo jumped off the porch and ran towards them both, ignoring the fact that he was not wearing shoes.

"What happened?" Solo shouted as Malcolm and Dollaz kept walking towards the house briskly.

"We cool. We just got into a little squab with Dalinda's

big-mouth boyfriend up at the carwash." Malcolm said as he sprinted up the steps and onto the porch.

Solo and Dollaz followed close behind. When they got inside the spot and Solo locked the bars and the door, the sound of the siren had made it around the corner, then it ceased. Malcolm and Dollaz both took off their shirts and dropped them on the floor. Dollaz put his Ruger on the table and sat down on the arm of the couch. Solo shook his head as he looked down and saw the flannel and the sweatshirt on the floor and blew out an irritated burst of air from his mouth, showing his disgust in them. He picked up the items from the floor and walked to the kitchen, where he threw the items of clothing into the trash can, then he returned to the living room. The room was silent except for the TV.

 "'Y'all must have fucked that nigga up. I hear some more sirens comin'. That's crazy...you get your Caddy out in traffic for the first day and got it on the hot list already, ha haa."

Dollaz followed Solo in suit with laughter because what Solo said was true about the car. Malcolm knew he was right as well and he was semi-upset with himself; he gave them both a middle finger.

"Ha ha yaself funny man...is there anythang over here for a nigga to put on?" asked Malcolm with an angry tone.

Solo ignored Malcolm for the moment as he walked over to the door and pushed the towel that covered the window to the side and peeped out.

After what had happened around the corner, it was a

GHETTO MERCHANTS

possibility that the police would pull up any minute looking for the person in the white Cadillac on Zeniths. After gazing through the glass for a moment, Solo turned and walked away from it and approached Malcolm and pushed him playfully. Then he hurried over to where Dollaz was and did him the same way, causing him to fall over on the couch. Solo burst out laughing again as he slid between the table and the couch, where he flopped down beside him.

"There's a bag full of clothes on the bed in the back. I bought it from some booster bitches who was in the pager shop yesterday." Solo answered cheerfully.

Just when Malcolm had turned towards the hallway, he was stunned by Dollaz speaking out of nowhere.

"So, I'm crazy, huh? I could say the same about you, too. What you need to do is stop at the bathroom and look at yaself in the mirror and see who's crazy. Your past is dirty as a mutha fucka too. Shit, look at the shit you did around the corner a few minutes ago. Anyway...after you come back in here, let me know just who's really the crazy one."

After hearing what Dollaz said Malcolm tilted his head back and closed his eyes and thought to himself why is this shit happening to me...why? After he let his question, along with Dollaz's remark, sink in, he took a deep breath and decided to handle this situation immediately with Dollaz, good or bad. Malcolm dropped his head back down and turned around. To his surprise, Dollaz was no longer on the couch; he was approaching him. Quickly, Malcolm set his footing, then pushed Dollaz back with his left and quickly pulled his pants up and tossed the Llama to the floor and raised his hands, revealing fist balled up tight.

"Run up again, homeboy...I promise you I will..."

Before Malcolm could finish threatening Dollaz, Solo jumped up from the couch and got between the two, pushing Dollaz back towards the table in the middle of the small living room. Malcolm never left his ground where he was standing in the hallway, opening with veins popping out of his forehead.

"Goddamn...kill the bullshit! Big homie, grab a seat on the couch. I can't believe you two still trippin' like it's 1990 all over again. We got 92 shit happenin' right now that's way bigger than any one of you niggas egos. Now chill!"

Malcolm looked his little cousin in the eyes, seeing that he was serious, then glanced over to Dollaz, who was standing between the couch and the table, popping his knuckles with an evil grin on his face.

"What's up, Solo? Is something wrong?" Malcolm asked.

Before Solo answered, Malcolm could see the look in his eye that he had when something was fucked up. Malcolm took a knee on the floor, Dollaz reluctantly took a seat on the couch with Solo's encouragement. Then Solo sat down on a metal folding chair where his Polo boots were. He slid his feet inside of them and began to explain.

"It's like this, last night about 8:30 I get a beep from this damn nigga up in North Highland...he wants three zones. And I'm supposed to be pickin' up this lil broad from work at Penn Square Mall and shoot to Brixton Square Theatre out on

GHETTO MERCHANTS

Rockwell Ave to see The Last Boy Scout. I got all my shit planned out just how I'm gonna handle the business. You know we only had six and a half zones left when you got on. Me and Gooch gave two of them to Dollaz. Anyway, I figured that I would just dump the three real quick and have the other one and a half broke down into pieces over here until we got on today. So, this nigga Gooch was sittin' on the phone right there where Dollaz sittin' mackin' on some bitch on the phone when I was leavin' out the door. I hop in my Mustang which was parked in the front yard warmin' up. As soon as I slide in my ride my beeper goes off; it's ol' girl at the mall. I had my mobile, but it was layin' in the back seat with a dead battery."

"Since I hadn't had a chance to get the pussy yet, I decided to run back in the crib and call to make sure me and her was still on. When I dip in the spot, Gooch is hangin' up the phone and tells me that he got somebody that wants the whole four and a half. I'm like cool. I looked at my watch and seen that I had time to shoot by the liquor store and get some Alize' and Remy. But most importantly, I had to drop off sack money at the crib, pull in my driveway, pop the trunk on my 5.0 and pop the trunk on the Grand National and throw the money in there and smash out."

"Anyway, I picked up the phone and hit up ol' girl and Gooch went outside. I start talkin' on the phone and heard my door open because I could hear my music playin' then I heard the door shut again and my shit revin' up. I didn't trip cause I thought that he was movin' my car out the way cause I was blockin' his in a little bit. Man, that nigga smashed out and never came back. I beeped and called the nigga until I fell asleep around two in the morning."

Dollaz and Malcolm's tension had subsided a little bit because both of them laughing at Solo's mishap of getting his date fucked off. Solo maintained a face with no humor as he stood up from the chair and walked around the table and got down on one knee and reached up under the couch and pulled out his Glock and sat it on the table close to Dollaz Ruger. He put his hand back under the couch and pulled out two stacks of cash and stood up.

"I know it's funny to y'all that Gooch bounced out on a nigga leavin' me stuck like chuck with no keys but to the bars, fuckin' off my date and shit. I guarantee you that what I'm about to say next ain't gonna be so funny..."

Malcolm's laugh and smile started to settle after Solo's last sentence.

"You know the eighteen g's that Big Tay was bringin' over here?" Solo started looking towards Malcolm.

"Yeah, where's it at?" Malcolm asked.

"It's in the trunk of my 5.0."

The cordless phone started ringing on the table, breaking the end of Solo's sentence. Solo reached down and grabbed the phone as Malcolm stood up looking disgusted and headed towards the back of the house. Dollaz remained quiet as he leaned forward and grabbed a doobie out of the ashtray.

"If that's Gooch on the phone, tell em to meet us at y'all's crib." Malcolm shouted as he walked down the hallway.
Solo hit the PHONE button and plopped down beside Dollaz and spoke on the phone briefly, saying nothing more than uh huh and nodding his head. When he hung up, he set the phone on the

crowded table and reached over towards Dollaz so that he could hit the weed. Within a couple of minutes, Malcolm emerged from the back, pulling the tag from the sleeve of a green and white long-sleeved Nautica shirt.

"Who was on the phone?" Malcolm asked.

"Big Tay. He said he seen my car gettin' off on Penn from the I-40 crosstown about ten minutes ago. He said he tried to hit me on my mobile then and it went straight to voicemail, Gooch too. He wanted to know if we had any work cause he got people waitin'. I told him to slide by."

"Gooch knows that he's in deep shit with you because of the car thang, but I doubt if his dumbass even know the money In the car...do he?" Dollaz asked even though he knew that it wasn't his business, which is the same thing that Malcolm thought which is why he wanted to handle it away from the spot.

"Solo, let's get over to y'all's crib to see if he over there, if not we gone have to wait for em. Dollaz...you still got that work from yesterday?" Malcolm quizzed.

"Hell yeah, that's why I was at the car wash and the store next door so I could try to get that shit off. What's up...you want it back?"

"Come on my nigga, what the fuck I want two zones back from you for? The reason I asked is because you can dump it right here cause it's rollin' and the other reason is so you can let Big Tay know what's happenin' with Gooch, not to mention we ain't got no work yet. Will you come outside and get the newest throwaway .380 we got? I left it in the floorboard of my Lac, Solo... let's ride," commanded Malcolm.

Solo stood up and knocked fists with Dollaz, then walked around the table and grabbed his Kansas City Chiefs Starter jacket off the back of the folding chair. He pulled it over his head and grabbed his pistol and dropped it inside the front pouch.

"Good lookin' out, homies. I'll be right here, posted up holdin' it down. I'll be sure to put Big Tay up on game. Hey...is there a deep fryer over here cause I wanna be sure to have some hot grease ready to throw my rocks in just in case the po po's hit this mutha fucka."

"That shit's all on the kitchen counter my nigga," Solo answered as they all walked outside.

Chapter 5

Javon had just pulled the handle back on the slot machine when the hostess placed her hand on his left shoulder. When he turned his head around, he saw his casino host, Tabby, who stood approximately five feet tall with a bronze tan and coke bottle shape. Most importantly, she had a beautiful face. She was wearing an off-white linen pantsuit that blended perfectly in color with her shoulder-length auburn hair with blonde streaks.

With perfect composure, she greeted him with a smile as she edged her way between Javon and the slot machine. Suddenly, stepping to Javon's left was a tall, bald white man with a stocky build that he couldn't hide with his black tailored suit. He wore a black tie, shirt and shoes, which gave him the demeanor of being a bodyguard. The bald man approached Javon by nodding his head and extending his right arm for a shake. After getting the silent pleasantries out of the way, he began to elaborate.

"Good morning, Mr. Mims, names' John Smith, head of security. I am very sorry to meet you under these circumstances, bearing bad news."

Javon looked away from John Smith down to Tabby, who had a facial expression that showed the news that was about to be spoken was going to be detrimental. He took a deep breath and prepared himself for whatever they had to tell him.

"Just tell me and spare the bullshit," Javon cut him short as he took two steps back.
"Being that you and Tabby have a certain rapport with each other I will let her explain," John Smith murmured then flashed a bleached white chicken shit smile.

Tabby gave John a go to hell look and ran her fingers through her hair nervously, wondering why the head of security would pass the buck to her for something that had nothing to do with her job. Quickly, she did what she felt always worked—her sex appeal. She put her hands on her hips and looked deep into Javon's eyes with her almond-shaped brown eyes, then she reached forward with her right hand and placed it on Javon's shoulder, stepping closer so the smell of her perfume would help her out. She darted her eyes back towards John Smith to gather courage, then back to Javon, whom she had just concluded was quite handsome. She slightly shook her head and cleared her throat, and began to elaborate.

"Javon, you are one of my favorite guests and you know that I always try to make your stay here as comfortable as possible. Would you agree?"

Javon nodded his head up and down as he spread his legs so that he could get lower and be closer to Tabby's face. She was stunning and to keep from being so tempted to grab her, he put his hands behind his back.

Suddenly, both of them were feeling an attraction, but because of John Smith standing there, it wouldn't happen. After pausing briefly, she continued.

"Therefore, we would like to extend our welcome to you by accommodating you with ten thousand dollars in free play and upgrading you to the Presidential Suite for four additional days."

She paused again and took her hand off Javon's shoulder and crossed her arms over her chest as she pivoted towards John Smith, nodded and positioned herself to face Javon.

GHETTO MERCHANTS

She did her part, which was supposed to come last and maybe there would be more to her part later on inside Javon's suite because she was definitely interested, but nobody could find out. As of right now, the issue of the missing Range Rover still hasn't been addressed, and the way John Smith was stalling, she was going to have to tell him that part as well. Since things were going smoothly, for the time being, although all she told him about were perks, why wouldn't things be going smoothly? Tabby finally said fuck it to herself...she owed him that much. Besides, if he found out she was a procrastinator...Enough was enough, she spat it on out.

"The bad news is that your Range Rover is impounded. Before you get all upset, I want you to know no damage has been done to it. This information comes from a reliable source with LVPD."

"Impounded! Tabby how in the hell did my truck go from right out in front of those doors to a goddamn impound yard?" Javon snapped as he walked and pointed towards the front entryway.

Tabby elbowed John in the ribs with a desperate hope that he would take over the conversation at this point because everyone around could tell there was a problem going on and people were beginning to stare. This time, only John Smith approached Javon. He was prepared for a confrontation because Javon was angry.

"Mr. Mims, will you please calm down?" John Smith firmly requested.

Javon threw his hands in the air aimed in the direction of the security man, signifying that he was waiting for an explanation.

"Calm down...man, are you serious? Do you know how much money I..." Javon stopped himself, almost revealing the information about the cash in the cargo area of the Range Rover.

DRE LUV

Using the moment to his advantage, John Smith pulled a single sheet of white paper folded in half out of his inside jacket pocket and handed it over to Javon.

"That paper was faxed to me from the Las Vegas Police Department; it's a police report. Your SUV was left unattended in a handicap parking space at a truck stop on Cheyenne with the engine running. Before you ask me how your vehicle ended up on Cheyenne and not in our valet parking, it is quite simple. I looked at video surveillance at your arrival yesterday afternoon. It looked as if you shunned the valet driver away and got into the backseat of the SUV for close to four minutes. When you exited the vehicle, you closed the rear passenger door, holding a bag in which you put the strap over your shoulder. At that point, there was a transient that was just escorted out of the casino and was walking towards you. For some reason that I cannot explain, you tossed him your keys. You simply walked right under the portico and inside the casino while the man that you tossed the keys to got into your SUV and drove off."

"The police report shows that they were called at 6:15 p.m. by management at 76 Truckstop. After investigating and finding that the vehicle belonged to nobody there, Barrett's Towing was called. Your vehicle is six blocks away on Commerce at their lot so all you need is identification to match your registration, and you can retrieve the vehicle. On behalf of the casino and your hardship, we will take care of the towing cost. Tabby has already told you about the other free accommodations. Out front we have a driver that will accompany you over there right now."

John Smith led Javon outside to the front portico and beckoned with his hand for a black Lincoln Town Car, which pulled up immediately when it saw the security head with a guest.

When the Lincoln rolled to a stop right in front of them, John Smith opened the rear passenger door, allowing Javon to get in.

"Have a good day, Mr. Mims, and we are truly apologetic for your inconvenience."

John Smith closed the door, turned around and adjusted his tie, surprised to see Tabby had followed behind at a lengthy distance. When he made it to her, she turned and walked with him.

"You realize that if he decides, for some reason, to contact legal representation, we would be in big trouble if this got out?" Tabby stated as she sped up to keep up with John Smith, who seemed to be annoyed.

"Just as long as you accommodate to the fullest, you rest assured that what happens at this casino will stay at this casino, at least on my watch it will."

John Smith replied to her as he walked away, distracted by a pit boss who called for him over the radio.

Chapter 6

After wiping her brow, Deziree unzipped Malcolm's white and black Adidas jacket, revealing her growing baby bump, while she watched the small television as she sat on a stool at the kitchen island. The electronic chime sounded off, alerting that someone just walked in the front or one of two garage doors: one leading to the kitchen and the other to the back door. This time it was the front door. Deziree was at Cecelia's house waiting for her to get back from running some errands.

"I'm in the kitchen, Ms. Cecelia!" Deziree shouted.

To her surprise, it was Malcolm's older brother Kenny wearing a gray sweatsuit with NAVY written across his broad chest. When Deziree saw him, she slid off the stool, both greeting each other with smiles.

"Let me get a hug, sister-in-law." Kenny smiled with his arms open. Deziree opened the jacket showing off her stomach and stretched her arms out to meet Kenny's six-foot one inch two hundred ten-pound frame. Kenny had brown skin with a military crew cut. After he bent down and they hugged, he gave her a kiss on the cheek.

"Look at you, girl, all pregnant and stuff. Go ahead and sit back down and take a load off your feet," Kenny expressed as he held her hand as she got back on the stool.

"Little lady, I think you should be sitting down in a chair instead of sitting on top of that stool. Oh, well, I suppose you know where you want to sit. So, can I fix you something to eat or drink? I'm home now, so I'm going to make sure that we keep my nephew fed," Kenny joked as he opened the refrigerator.

GHETTO MERCHANTS

Deziree giggled as she listened to Kenny, yet her mood changed when he mentioned the word nephew. She had a son and daughter growing inside of her and he didn't know she was having twins. Kenny looked inside the refrigerator and noticed that Deziree had not answered him, so he turned around to see why she had not replied to his question. When he saw her, she was wiping tears from her face with a baggy jacket sleeve.

"What's wrong, sis?"

Kenny quickly moved towards the island, setting the half-empty bottle of cranberry juice on top. He pulled a stool over and sat next to her, putting one hand on her left shoulder and grabbed her hand with the other.

"It's nothing really. My hormones are just going bonkers this morning. I'm okay...really."

Deziree replied through sniffles, then she grabbed the bottle of cranberry juice, twisted off the top, and drank it down with one swallow. Kenny nodded his head up and down with a slight smile on his face, showing comfort to her.

"Anyway, Kenny, your mother invited me over for breakfast, but I was delayed because your little brother had me take him to the southeast side. He had to get his car out of the shop. By the time I made it over here, your mother was gone, but she left me a note on the door telling me she went to the grocery store over on May."

The Armed Forces, along with other training, made Kenny capable of reading people, and looking into Deziree's eyes, he could tell that there was more to Deziree and the hormones spiking because of her pregnancy. Instead of pushing, he decided to let her open up to him, because sometimes patience was the best policy.

"So, when is the baby boy due?"
Deziree jokingly slapped Kenny on his hand and giggled.

"I'm having a girl, too, silly. I'm having twins and they're due
March fifth. I hate to change the subject so soon, but I need
to ask you for a favor, and I need your word that you will not
say anything to Malcolm?" Deziree requested as she squeezed
Kenny's hands tightly.

"Anything, sis, you got my word," answered Kenny as he pulled his left
hand free and wiped tears from her caramel-colored cheeks. The look
in her eyes took his judgment to the point where he felt that if
needed, he just might have to push her lightly to find out what was so
serious that she didn't want Malcolm to know about this
conversation. He decided to strike first to throw her off balance.

"If it's money, we can go to the credit union right now?"

Deziree shook her head no as she reached for a paper towel that was
lying on top of the island. She blew her nose with it, balled it up, and
stuck it in her jacket pocket. She sighed and looked up at Kenny.

"It's not money that I need, yet money is the reason that I feel there's
a problem. Your brother thinks that money is the solution and key to
everything. I grew up with a little money, Kenny, you know that and
I'm telling you that is not what made me happy. I left my dad for that
same reason because he played money games and that's why I fell in
love with Malcolm, because he showed me that I could depend on
him. He showed me what love was, but now it seems as if that is his
whole world. When I ask him what good is money if you're not around
to spend it because you're dead or..."

"Or in jail like our daddy," Kenny expressed with a serious look on his
face.

44

"Exactly. I didn't want to say that because I never want to say anything that will offend anybody when it comes to Mr. Love. But when I think about how his absence has affected everyone in your family, I... well, I just don't want to put my kids through all of that. When I look at your mother at how she lives her life without companionship from the man that she loves, I see me, and I can't want that to be my life or the life of me and Malcolm's children."

"The feeling that I have inside is unimaginable when he leaves the house. I don't know if I'll ever see him walk through the door again because he's gotten himself into something that will put him in jail with a life sentence, or if I will get a call from Ms. Cecelia or one of his friends telling me that he's been killed."

Kenny momentarily let her words sink in before answering. He could tell that she was sincere in heart with what she was saying, so he felt that since she came to him in confidence, he had to make good with her. She wanted him in her corner, and he was going to be there.

"I know my little brother hustles in the streets, but at the level of being scared for his life...I don't think so. Stop worrying about Malcolm so much, sis, the things that daddy was doing, and Malcolm are nothing alike."

"I assure you; Kenny, Malcolm, Stan, and Gary are real drug dealers. I'm talking about six figures. They may not be on the same level as Neno Brown in 'New Jack City', but believe me that they are not riding around town trying to scrape up beer money."

Deziree shook her head side to side in disagreement with Kenny's thoughts of Malcolm's level in the streets. She carefully slid down off the stool and casually walked over to the kitchen door leading to the garage and opened it up, and pointed inside.

"You've been home what, a week or two, so I know you've looked inside of here and seen this new truck and Harley Davidson Road King. This morning, he picked up a new Cadillac that he bought off the showroom floor two weeks ago. Before he even started the car up, he had it towed to a shop and added over ten thousand dollars in rims and stereo equipment..."

Deziree closed the door and faced Kenny, revealing a false surprised look on her face, and walked back to her stool. Once again, Kenny held on to her while she got on top, taking a seat next to her.

"Whewww...now I don't pretend to know a lot about the streets except for what I've seen of it, mostly through Malcolm and his crew. But if they were so petty, why would they all have cars and motorcycles that they hardly drive? Then I want you to factor in Ms. Cecelia. She would be a wreck if something were to happen to her baby." Deziree explained while trying to catch her breath.

Kenny stood up and stretched, then he walked back to the refrigerator as he analyzed Deziree's words while he opened the door and pulled out a jug of grapefruit juice. He twisted off the cap and took a drink from the container. Deziree began to speak again.

"I know that you just got home from the service and..."

"Navy! I am a Navy SEAL," Kenny specified, startling Deziree with his aggressive tone.

"Alright, alright, Navy SEAL, I'm sorry for getting your title wrong. But anyway, your mother told me that you got a Purple Heart and a Congressional Medal of Honor during the Gulf War. Why would you take an early discharge, and you're a hero? I suppose you have your personal views, but I was wondering if you think that you could talk your little brother into doing something positive with his life? All he needs is a good role model around that he will respect then maybe he'll get on the right track. That person is you, Kenny and I really need you to be here. Not for me but for your niece and nephew, along with your mother."

When Kenny looked down at Deziree, she had tears in her eyes again and was holding on to her belly. He walked to the island and sat the grapefruit juice on top and leaned against it and cracked a smile.

"Okay, Deziree, I'll see what I can do. I can't make you any promises because you and I both must recognize that Malcolm is a grown man and has been taking care of himself for a long time. In fact, I can't see my little brother taking advice from nobody, but you have my word that I will try my best."

Quickly, Deziree slid off the stool, almost losing her balance when it slid out. She caught herself by grabbing hold to Kenny's hand that was stretched out, then she walked towards him and gave him a big sisterly hug with a kiss on the cheek.

"Thanks, big brother...I love you. In fact, I'm going to cook my special lasagna tonight and I want you to come over at about seven o'clock."

Before Kenny had a chance to answer, the door chimed again, and the distinct sound of his mother's voice echoed all the way to the kitchen.

"Kenny! Come help me with the groceries, baby."

"Coming, mama!" Kenny replied as he was leaving the kitchen.
When he made it to the doorway of the kitchen, he stopped

and turned around to face Deziree.

"I'll be there, and you have my word that this conversation stays between the two of us."

After Kenny spoke those words, he went to help his mother, and Deziree took a deep breath and smiled, feeling a significant amount of pressure released. Kenny was her only chance, and if he failed, she was not sure just how long she could endure the chaotic life of being a drug dealer's woman.

Solo sped northbound on MLK with Malcolm in the passenger seat of the Cadillac with Ice Cube's Amerikkka's Most Wanted coming from the Alpine. Topping the hill, passing Meyers Place, the light on N.E. 50th came into view, and so did Amy's Soul Food Takeout. Solo reached up and turned the volume down.

"I'm gonna swoop over to Amy's and grab some food real quick. You want somethin'?" Solo looked over to Malcolm.

Malcolm squinted his eyes as he looked ahead to the left at Amy's parking, seeing that it was not crowded from the early lunch crowd. He nodded his head up and down, signifying yes and continued to bob his head to the beat.

"Hell yeah, I'm hungry as a mutha fucka for a catfish dinner with some macaroni and cheese and yams."

Solo slowed down, hit the turn signal, and carefully swung the Caddy to the left, parking crooked, taking up two spaces towards the north end of the building. He turned off the engine, pulled the keys out and grabbed the butt of his Glock that was tucked between the seat and the console. In one motion, he stuck it in the front pouch of his Starter jacket and opened the door and got out. As he stood and scanned the area, waiting for Malcolm to get out, there was the sound of Malcolm's mobile phone ringing. Solo leaned back inside the car and stuck the keys in the ignition and started it up and closed the door. He knew what Malcolm wanted to eat anyway, so he went on his mission while Malcolm grabbed the phone out of the floorboard, pressed SEND and put the phone to his ear.

"What's crackin'?" Malcolm asked with an aggressive tone.

"Not too much out on my end. What's sup with you out that way?"

The sound of Fats' voice threw Malcolm for a loop because he had never called his phone. Suddenly, he realized the reason was that he was probably with Javon at his favorite Denny's spot. Because Malcolm did not reply right away, Fats thought that he and Malcolm's cellular connection had been lost.

"This is Fats homie...can you hear me?"

"Yeah, yeah, yeah, I hear ya, it's just that I was kinda trippin' that it's you hittin' me 'cause I thought you might have lost this number since you never called it before. So, what's up, you over to Javon's crib or somethin'?" Malcolm quizzed him.

Fats was thirteen hundred miles away, having breakfast at a hole in the wall in Compton, California on the corner of El Segundo and Central. He was sitting at the counter with his homeboy Scoob. "Funny you bring his name up but anyway, man I did lose your number, but I got it from Javon the last time he was out here for two reasons. One: I wanted to see if you wanted to sell your 6-deuce rag Impala, but before I had a chance to get at you this one nigga over in

DRE LUV

Gardena came through with a clean ass 6 fo that I couldn't pass up. Second: I needed your number just in case some shit happened again like now. I can't catch up with Javon, have you seen him?"

Malcolm had known Fats for some years now and not one time had he ever sounded like he was beating around the bush, but now he was. This morning was becoming more and more bizarre by the minute as Malcolm's mind raced through every incident that occurred.

"I haven't seen that cat since Wednesday. Matter of a fact, I been tryin' to catch up with him since yesterday afternoon. I've called every number that I got on em and I keep comin' up with nothin'." Malcolm elaborated while finding himself getting pissed off.

"Yeah, man, he got at me yesterday around noon sayin' he was on this side of Flagstaff in Arizona. He shoulda been here no later than five or six o'clock, even with the rush-hour traffic. Last night I had my girl call the Arizona State Police, California Highway Patrol, hospitals all up and down I-40, 15, and the 10, and came up with no Javon. This cat just disappeared into thin air."

"Arizona! Man, that nigga ain't said shit to me about goin' to Cali. Damn, me and him had some business to take care of this mornin' if you know what I mean, just like every Friday. Now me and my boys is ass out until this nigga decides to surface. If I woulda known, he was gettin' ready to shake the spot I coulda just grabbed some extra work...anyway Fats I'm pissed off now my nigga. I'll get back at cha and if you talk to that fake ass nigga before I do tell him I said that was bullshit he pulled on a nigga. I mean that was real fucked up."

Malcolm lowered the mobile phone from his ear and was about to put his thumb on the END button when he thought he heard Fats still talking through the speaker. He pressed END anyway. Malcolm's

50

anger was ignited once again and this time, he knew that he was finally fed up with Javon. For more than a year he had been taking advantage of their friendship and Malcolm had been letting bullshit ride cause he had love for the nigga. That love had been taking chunks of cash out of the pockets of Ghetto Merchants because they had been there to back him up whenever he had a sad story about needing to dump some work fast. After all, Fats was supposedly pressing him. Javon being a manipulator was no news for Malcolm, but still, he allowed it because, regardless of what Javon had said or done, Malcolm made sure that he, along with his crew, got paid. But Javon was still used to having work as a tool to reel Malcolm in, always not letting him forget that he was the one who opened the door for him to get in the game way back in the day.

Malcolm quickly weighed all his options and knew that he and his crew no longer needed Javon for anything. They had money, and with money, they could open up their own doors without Javon's key. The time to execute was right now because their blueprint was already written in stone. No need to procrastinate any longer, fuck putting shit off for later; the time was now.

He had his backup plan from when Javon told him that Fats wanted to buy his lowrider back then, and gave him the number. Malcolm wrote the number down and put it inside his dresser drawer at his mama's house, and he also put it in his pager. He leaned over and unclipped his pager from his Guess pocket and scrolled through the numbers until he got to the numbers that he had locked in. When he got to the one with the 213-area code, his heart rate climbed, and he spoke out loud to himself, saying, 'Have heart, have money.' He grabbed his mobile out of his lap and pressed in the numbers and pushed SEND.

Malcolm raised the phone to his ear and slowly inhaled and exhaled. At the third ring, there was the sound of a fork being dropped on a plate. Without waiting another second for a greeting, Malcolm went for his.

"Hey Fats...you told me a long time ago, one night out here in Oklahoma, that if I needed you for somethin' to ask. Do you remember?"

"Yeah, I remember..." Fats answered with a mouth full of food. "Excuse me for talking with my mouth full, homeboy, but I meant what I said, and I believe in keeping my word. Why don't you tell me what's on ya mind?" Fats expressed casually.

With no hesitation or rehearsal, Malcolm chose to flow from the top of his head.

"What you and Javon have goin' on doesn't have jack shit to do with me except that me and my niggas move the majority of the work. We hustle too hard out here to steadily get fucked around like today. I put it on my mama that we done let a few hundred g's slip from our pockets just so we could help Javon keep the sack right for the sole purpose of you keepin' the work comin' this way. I'm gonna keep it real withcha...the work is always A-1 and that's somethin' a lotta niggas can't deliver on, consistency. I got three hundred to spend right now. Can I get twenty of em from ya?"

Silence fell on both ends of the phone call, yet Malcolm felt confident with every word that he chose. On the other end, Fats did the math in his head and contemplated the g's he would be losing by agreeing to Malcolm's proposal. Javon's price had been set at seventeen five for a while, then there was the thought that he might be taking an unexpected loss because of him. This was a bad time for bullshit to happen especially since there was already too much of that going on in south central. Right now, the feds were picking niggas and Mexicans up all over L.A., handing indictments out like candy. For all he knew, the feds could have Javon detained right now, trying to turn him. Fuck it, Fats decided to deal but to his advantage yet fair to

Malcolm because he had money right now and he admired his style. Fats took a drink of juice, and Malcolm was wondering if it was a bad idea to hang up the phone on him a few minutes ago, then suddenly things changed for the good.

"Okay youngsta, I apologize for the delay, but I think that it was worth the wait...uhh hum goddamn that orange juice is strong as a mutha fucka. Back to the business, I wanna help ya out, but not at that price. I gotta have seventeen, at least. With that three, you can snatch up seventeen, which is still good cause you're gonna win in the long run, and you gotta come and get it," Fats pitched.

"All I need to know is where to go and I'll be out there Monday or Tuesday."

Malcolm relaxed a little and replied without hesitation to the deal. Fats gave Malcolm a phone number with a 909-area code to call when he reached Pomona, California. It belonged to a lady friend who would guide him into the inner city of Los Angeles. He also advised him to rent a Ford van, letting him know that the details would be provided to him once he arrived. Still, he let him know that it wasn't like the old days when you could just throw shit in the back and drive across the country. After explaining a few more details, Fats told Malcolm he had to get off the phone because his breakfast was getting cold.

"Have twenty ready for me when I get there. I'm out." Malcolm hung up with confidence.

Fats smiled a little bit as he lowered the phone and pressed END. As he set his phone down in front of his plate, he could tell that Scoob was staring at him through his peripheral vision, yet he chose to ignore him by picking up his fork. Just when Fats was raising a forkful of eggs and chicken sausage to his mouth, Scoob began to talk. "You been acting shitty to a player since you haven't been able to get in touch with that Javon clown. Now you gonna fuck with his homeboy? For all you know them niggas might be on a fuck you mission together to fuck you. I told you it was something about that nigga that I didn't like...I smell something fishy, dog. I swear that if them niggas come out..."

Irritated by Scoob's irrelevant chatter, Fats placed his fork down on his plate, planted his left elbow on the counter and began to slowly twist to the right on his stool. At the same time, Scoob noticed Fats turning his way, so he eagerly did the same, accomplishing the task of knocking his grape soda over, causing it to spill on Fats' mobile and his plate. Although Fats was quick to react to the accident, sliding off the stool to avoid the purple blue soda, he still got it on his brand-new gray sweatsuit.

"Damn, look what you did you, big clumsy ass nigga!"

Fats shouted in Scoob's face. Scoob looked around to see who was watching him get yelled at, but fortunately for him, only a few people were paying attention to what was going on with him and Fats because of the noise from everyone talking and the morning show playing over the speakers from the radio.

Scoob reached over the counter and grabbed a towel that he had seen the waitress wipe a table with, handing it to Fats. Fats angrily knocked his hand away, causing the towel to hit the floor as he shook his head in disbelief. He unzipped his pocket and pulled out a money roll, unfolded it, peeled off a twenty, and threw it on top of the counter. Then he grabbed a handful of napkins and picked up his mobile that lay in a small pool of soda and dried it off as he headed out the door, leaving Scoob behind.

Feeling at ease in his mind, Malcolm reached up and pulled the sun visor down and flipped open the mirror. Arrogantly, he looked at himself and realized that he needed to get his fade tightened up before he got on the highway. Subconsciously, he looked deeper into the mirror, feeling like he had crossed Javon, but business-wise, he had no choice. There were too many people who depended on him to eat, including two more mouths that were coming in a month, and no friendship was more important than that. Malcolm took a deep breath and closed the mirror cover and pushed the visor back up, then took a look around and began to wonder just where Gooch was and where in the hell Javon had disappeared to and why Solo hadn't made it out of Amy's yet. Then it dawned on him that the reason Solo was still inside was that the place was full of women who worked there.

Malcolm's attention was diverted to his right with the sound of booming bass coming closer. It took about fifteen seconds for a candy blue Cadillac Coupe Deville with a half gray phantom top with dark tint to come into sight. It made a rolling stop at the corner of N.E. 50th, making a right on MLK coming his way. Malcolm reached over his lap with his right hand and grabbed the butt of his Llama stuffed between the seat and the console and pulled the hammer back.

Carjacking was at an all-time high in Oklahoma City and he was sitting in something that jackers wanted. Malcolm was out of sight behind the five percent tint on all four sides of the car and looked on and prepared himself in case anything foul was about to occur. He felt the Coupe pull in beside him, leaving about eight feet between the two cars. Malcolm watched on as nobody got out of the car, it just sat, then suddenly the driver's window dropped down halfway, allowing smoke to bellow out along with earthquake bass and Scarface's Money and The Power.'

When the smoke cleared a little, two familiar faces were

revealed, both staring at Malcolm's unfamiliar Seville.

Out of the passenger side Hoodsta got out and walked around the front of the Coupe stepping up on the curb showing off his white Chuck Taylors with blue strings and all blue Dickie suit with a crisp white thermal and a white beanie on top of his head. As he walked in front of the Seville, he tried to look inside the windshield to see who was inside until he stopped at the payphone. Malcolm laughed at the fact that nobody could see inside while he watched Hoodsta pick up the receiver out of the cradle and tuck it between his ear and his shoulder as he deposited some change into the phone. A gust of wind came and blew his plats around in his face, causing him to pull his beanie down a little further and duck closer to the wall to dodge the cool breeze.

Finally, Solo walked out of Amy's, holding the door for a slim, chocolate female with blonde dookie braids whom he was holding a conversation with until she made it to the driver's door of a black Dodge Shadow parked in front. Solo smiled and waved with one hand and held a plastic bag in the other as he turned onto the sidewalk at the same time that Hoodsta caught sight of someone coming his way in a red jacket.

Slowly, Hoodsta turned to his left to face whoever it was dressed in the red because he was locin' and whoever this was in the red had to be dawgin'. Hoodsta thought that if it was his time to go, let the bullets fly, except that if any bullets would fly, they wouldn't be his because his heater was in the car. Therefore, his only chance would be that Paperboy was watching his back. When he was fully turned around to face the person wearing the red jacket, he was surprised to see that he was who he was paging. Solo was staring at him with a fake scowl on his face to keep from laughing.

GHETTO MERCHANTS

"Hang up the phone nigga and don't try nothing' funny cause I'll blast you right here dawg."
After Solo spoke, he and Hoodsta both started laughing as they gave each other a fist pound.

"I thought you was one of them Eastside Piru niggas tryin' to put some work in on young loc to try and get a stripe or somethin'. What up nigga?"

"Stop set trippin' my nigga and you won't have to worry bout that shit as much although you gonna have enemies for life with your crazy ass."

Solo laughed as he and Hoodsta slowly walked towards the Cadillacs. Hoodsta and Paperboy made eye contact as well as Solo who threw his head up in the air signifying what's up and Hoodsta raised his arm in the air and pointed his finger towards the ground. Immediately, Paperboy turned down his music and Hoodsta turned his attention back towards Solo and pointed at the Seville.

"Fuck what you talkin' bout cuz it's Westside on mine. Annnd, nigga I seen you hittin' some niggas up with the B in the parkin' lot of the club last weekend so kill that. Anyway, I been hittin' you up on your pager all mornin' nigga so why you ain't hit me back. I was hittin' you again cause I just seen your 5.0 turnin' on 55th goin' up in Wildwood Edition off of Kelly. Me and Paperboy need some work nigga. What's up?"

Hoodsta subconsciously scratched the long scar on his cheek, awaiting the answer from Solo, who stepped off the curb heading for the driver's door.

"We ain't got no work homie. Hopefully later on we'll be on deck, if so, I'll beep you or just shoot by the spot." Solo disappointed him as he opened the car door.

"Nigga it's hot as a mutha fucka on 24th. Ya'll got the block jumpin'with smokers; niggas like me and black and whites posted up on the top and bottom of the block. That Caddy is killin' shit off, I shoulda known that pretty mutha fucka belonged to you niggas."

Hoodsta capped as he turned away to walk to the door to go inside Amy's. Malcolm dropped the window and got at Paperboy while Solo was still talking to Hoodsta.
"Yo Hoodsta, if you scared, go to church," Solo spoke out then laughed as he opened the door and got inside the car.
Hoodsta turned around and gritted, then he continued on and opened Amy's door to walk inside. When Solo got inside the car, he heard Paperboy talking.

"Fuck where I got the beanie cuz...when you knock this bitch?"

Malcolm casually put his arm outside and patted the door like the Cadillac was a big white horse as he looked over at Solo and winked, then back to Paperboy.

"I got it right after New Year's. This ain't nothin' but a Seville. Look at you, another Coupe candy painted with the euro clip and molding. You ain't doin' bad at all for yourself, I see ya flossin'." Malcolm smiled as he admired Paperboy's ride, too.

Paperboy stuck his arm out the window, revealing a Rolex on his wrist when the sleeve of his Guess jacket slid up. Paperboy saw Malcolm check out his watch and laughed a little.

"Flossin', stop that shit, Malcolm. This is the same 85 I been havin' I just flipped it and clipped it. What I really want is to be able to ride brand new like you niggas. What it take to get in the Ghetto Merchant program besides just havin' a number and coppin' a little work. I know you ain't gonna let a nigga all the way in unless a nigga family or day one Mafioso right, so what up with a nigga gettin' a whole chicken? Hoodsta been tryin' to get at y'all all mornin'. We been tryin' to get at you niggas since your one homeboy Javon ain't fuckin' with us...that nigga be on some hoe shit for real Malcolm. What's up with that nigga? I be gettin' a whole one here a half of one there and my money is always straight but it's so hard to catch up with the nigga. This mornin' Hoodsta was like fuck Javon and decided that we should get at y'all. We was on our way to that spot on 24th cause..."

Malcolm grabbed the door sill to pull himself forward causing his busted knuckles to leak through the blood that was already dried. This caught Paperboy's attention.

"Damn cuz it looks like you been boxin' a brick wall!"

Malcolm put his hand back inside the car and looked at both of them briefly. He shrugged his shoulders and touched the wounds on his right hand with his left hand, causing him to wince.

"Let's just say I had a lightweight altercation down the street. Check game my nigga, outta no disrespect do you mind me asking' what Javon charges you for a whole thang?"

Just when Malcolm finished asking the question a white crew cab dually truck with OKC WATER DEPARTMENT on the driver's door pulled into the right of Paperboy's car. Inside were two white and two black guys wearing hard hats with all of their eyes locked on the two Cadillacs parked on the wire wheels. Malcolm nodded his head at them with a scowl on his face.

"Come over here and hop in the backseat so we can rap about some real shit without these nosey ass city workers lookin' all in a nigga mouth."

Malcolm raised his window as Paperboy got out of his car and slid into the backseat, taking in a nose full of new car smell.

"Cuz, ya boy been chargin' twenty-five when I get the whole thang and when a nigga short on bread and we can only get a half, he charge thirteen, sometime thirteen five. I know that's right about average around here but goddamn a nigga would think he'd give a nigga some kinda break but he don't show no love. Cuz, you know me and Hoodsta get money on both east and the westside. We fuck off plenty of it too, but we still maintain enough to cop a half chicken once or twice a week. Right now, the shit really got me fucked up cause we supposed to be up in Minneapolis right now. We got Super Bowl tickets and shit."

The sound of Super Bowl tickets made Solo look in the rearview mirror and put his fish down.

"How'd you pull Super Bowl tickets off down here?"

Malcolm asked eagerly as he popped the Styrofoam container.

"I got family in Minneapolis that been tryin' to get me up that way for the longest, that's how. I used to go up there every summer when I was little but I ain't been back since a nigga started hustlin'. That's where my daddy's family is from and every time I holla at them they always tellin' a nigga how sweet it is up there on gettin' money. They payin' somethin' like eight five for nine ounces and thirty plus for a whole thang. One of my uncles wants a nigga up there so bad to bring some work that he bought me and Hoodsta some tickets to the big game to show a nigga what it's like in the field up that way to get a nigga hooked."

"Anyway, that's what me and Hoodsta was gonna do, along with takin' the chicken that we was supposed to get from Javon. We was gonna leave yesterday but since we ain't been able to hook up with the nigga we blew it off. We coulda went on the southside and grabbed somethin' from somebody but if it turned out to be just some alright shit a nigga woulda been mad. So, we said fuck the Super Bowl; Dallas aint playin', might as well flip some money, you feel me cuz?"

Hearing the hunger and sincerity in Paperboy's voice, Malcolm had a plan that began to materialize inside his head that he would be a fool not to take advantage of. Paperboy and Hoodsta were Hood niggas with several neighborhoods that checked dollars. They had the hood throughout the twenties off of MLK and homies tucked in the fortieth blocks, and that was just on the east side.
On the west side, their hood checked from NW 22nd to 50th long and Robinson to Pennsylvania Avenues wide, needless to say, their turf was large. If the Ghetto Merchants put a get money alliance together with Paperboy and Hoodsta, sending them out of town, leaving their clientele with their gang members open to the Merchants. With that alliance, the Ghetto Merchants would have enough manpower to handle any adversary willing to run head-on with a Mack truck. The only thing that Malcolm had to do was drop the prices and fuck the game and the city would belong to them.

It was almost unbearable for Malcolm to mask the excitement that he was feeling when he thought of the power that was close in his grasp and the twenty ki's would turn into forty so god damn quick it was going to be crazy. He had to play his cards right and not let anyone know all of his motives, so he took a breath and gained his composure and closed the lid on his food and set it on the floor.

"So, you niggas got the dough to take the trip or what?"

Malcolm quizzed with the sound of mischief in his voice. The hissing sound of Solo's Coke bottle opening caused Malcolm to look his way, catching a confused look on Solo's face, who was wondering what

Malcolm's angle on questioning Paperboy was. Furthermore, he did not understand why they were not in route to catch up with Gooch at the house before he got away again.

"We got about thirty g's in all cuz leavin' us about...seven to play with. But the problem with that is that bills are right around the corner waitin' for a nigga to come back."

"Malcolm, we need to bust a move my nigga," Solo intervened.

Malcolm raised his left hand chest high, raising it up and down a few times giving Solo the signal to be patient although he knew what Solo was in such a hurry for because it was Malcolm's idea in the first place to find him.

"Okay, Paperboy, I think I gotta plan that can fill up everyone's plate and I mean everybody eatin' for real. Check game, what if you and Hoodsta go ahead and shoot up to Minnesota and see if it's really crackin' up there with the work like your people say it is. You know what, when my girl was goin' to school up at Langston there was this one nigga that was on the hoop squad that used to get a few zones from a nigga to take back to Minnesota when he went home. He got killed in the summer of '90, but I remember him sayin' that it was on up there. Anyway, if it's on for real, we can work somethin' out probably within a week to get somethin' up there to ya. If nothin' else at least you get the chance to go to a Super Bowl and fuck with some outta town hoes with some money from all over the country. And when you niggas get back home I'll let ya'll get a whole one for twenty-three, then we'll negotiate on some other shit. So, what up loc; we gotta roll," Malcolm ended with a foolproof plan.

When Malcolm twisted around in his seat to face Paperboy, all he could see was teeth from his big grin. Paperboy clapped his hands twice and made an impression like he was hitting a baseball with a bat.

"I'm down for that, cuz. Soon as cuz come outta there we on our way to Penn Square Mall, they got a travel agency right across from CHAMPS. We'll be on the first thang smokin' outta Will Rogers. You know Malcolm, there's alotta niggas out here that don't like you, cuz, but it's only because they jealous and can't do the type of shit you do. I wanna fuck witcha so that some of that gift of makin' shit happen will rub off on me, and I put it on the set that me and my niggas is fuckin' with y'all."

"Thanks for givin' me my props my nigga. We gotta roll out for now but when you make it up there and find out the business hit Solo up on his voicemail and let a nigga know something."

Malcolm reached over the seat and gave Paperboy a solid handshake, sealing their deal. When Malcolm turned back around to the front and Paperboy opened the door, Malcolm noticed Hoodsta leaving Amy's with a bag that looked as if it had a couple of dinners in it. Before Paperboy slid out of the backseat, he patted Solo on his right shoulder. As soon as he got out of the car, Solo put the Cadillac in reverse and backed out, tapped the horn, and headed north.

The light on 50th was red, but Solo turned left anyway while turning the music up a little bit.

"Hoodsta told me they seen my car turn up in Wildwood, so Gooch had to be headed for the pad. That's why I was tryin' to bust a move and what kinda shit is you doin by sendin' nigga's on missions all the way to Minnesota?"

Malcolm leaned over to the left a little and reached up and began adjusting the bass. When he finally got the sound that he was looking for he slapped Solo on his arm with the back of his hand, causing him to wince and making Solo laugh.

"I'm sendin' the homie on a mission to Minnesota 'cause we goin' on our own mission to L.A. to cop some work from Fats. I talked to him when you was inside Amy's fuckin' around forever and a day." Instantly Solo started rocking to the beat after he and Malcolm touched fists.
"So, you rollin' or what?" Malcolm asked with a grin on his face.

"Cali...are you serious? Hell, yeah, I'm rollin', when?"

"We gonna do it like Lionel Richie and ease out Sunday mornin'."

Chapter 7

Ronnell lay motionless with a neck brace on as the EMTs rolled him on the gurney through the doors of St. Anthony's emergency room. Holding his hand, Dalinda walked beside him as they bypassed triage and went directly into a trauma station where a team was there waiting. The EMTs briefed them on the extent of his injuries and after that part was over, they left and escorted Dalinda to the waiting room. To her surprise, there was OCPD waiting for her with a pen and pad.

After approximately five minutes of questioning, Dalinda kept her story the same. She insisted that neither she nor her boyfriend knew his attackers. She told the officer that she and her friend Cheryl were at the carwash with her boyfriend, who was washing her friend's Jeep for her. There were some young gang bangers walking across the parking lot, harassing her and Cheryl. That was when Ronnell came to their aid, insisting that Cheryl and Dalinda get inside the Jeep. Ronnell was rat-packed and got whooped bad.

The police officer took her phone number and asked for Cheryl's, and let her know that he would be sure to get back to her so that she could come to the station and take a look at some photos. He gave her a card with his name and number on it, ordering her to call in case she needed him for anything. Just as he was finishing up his report, an old school, seasoned nurse who had her hair pinned up in a bun with a nursing cap and white knit dress all the way down past her knees walked in, approaching Dalinda with a concerned look on her face, causing alarm.

"Excuse me, officer, but my patient wants to speak with the young lady. If you will pardon us for a moment?" The old nurse requested.

"I'm afraid that I'll have to speak to him first."

The young officer replied as he closed his pad and slid it into his shirt pocket and adjusted his belt and his vest. The nurse politely moved Dalinda to the side and stepped directly in front of the officer and put her finger in his face.

"My patient is in no shape to answer any questions from you right now. In fact, you should be ashamed of yourself for suggesting such a thing sonny. Now you go on from here and come back tomorrow and leave them be...go on and get."

The officer stood there looking dumbfounded after getting checked from the elderly nurse who grabbed Dalinda's hand and led her out of the waiting room. Down the hall back inside the trauma area Dalinda peered around the door to see Ronnell laying flat and motionless. She slowly approached his side with tears in her eyes as she gazed down upon his swollen face and head with open gashes that someone had cleaned since he had arrived. Before she entered the room the nurse informed her that he had a concussion that was serious and that they were taking him to get a cat scan within thirty minutes and afterward to get stitched up.

When Dalinda made it to Ronnell she touched his hand. This made him open his swollen eyes and mouth which revealed a large gap where teeth were before the incident at the carwash. When Dalinda noticed that she inhaled and covered her mouth as her eyes bucked showing astonishment of just how bad her boyfriend was beaten up. Ronnell began to talk but Dalinda could not make out what he was saying because his voice was no louder than a whisper. Dalinda removed her hands from her face and sniffed hard with her nose to clear it as she bent down over Ronnell so that she could hear what he was saying.

"I couldn't hear you, what did you say baby?" She asked with concern as she touched him on his shoulder.

GHETTO MERCHANTS

"I said I'm gonna get ya homeboys back." Ronnell replied with his voice sounding a little bit louder than a whisper like before.

Dalinda smiled and bent down a little closer to him and kissed him softly on his busted lip then on his forehead. That was when she raised up and looked around to make sure that no one was eavesdropping, there was nobody around still, so she quickly chose her words and leaned back down within a few inches from Ronnell's ear.

"Baby...you my man and I know you ain't no punk, but I really really think it's best for you to leave what happened at the carwash alone. Them niggas ain't to be fucked with, they got pull around the town and to keep it honest I'm afraid for what might happen if it's not laid to rest. I'm tellin' you this because I love you and I got your back, but I don't wanna see anything else happen. Be-lieve me when I tell you that their crew has a reputation and it's for blowin' shit up." Dalinda elaborated sincerely.

Fighting through the pain and with the awkwardness of the neck brace Ronnell gritted down and rolled over enough to look at Dalinda face to face. When he got where he wanted to be he spit in her face. The shock caused a delay in response which gave Ronnell an opportunity to reach over with his right hand and grab a handful of her hair pulling her close. Dalinda tried to pull away by bracing herself with one hand on the bed rail and one on the mattress but Ronnell's advantage with her hair was too overwhelming. He snatched her down to where her ear was close to his mouth which put her neck in a strain causing her to whimper and wish that the police officer or the stern nurse would walk into the room.

"This shit wouldn't have happened if I didn't have to go find yo tramp ass. How you gonna tell me you got my back but at the same time you takin' sides with some niggas that fucked me up in front of my bitch and got me missin' teeth and shit. I don't give a damn who them niggas is, they ass is mine one day."

After saying his speech, Ronnell gasped for air, causing him to let Dalinda's hair go, still he was able to mush her in the face, causing her to stumble backwards against a wheelchair that was folded up and leaning against the wall. When Dalinda caught her balance, she looked over to the bed where Ronnell was lying flat on his back. She tried to be strong and fight the tears, but she did not have the power to complete that task. She whimpered and covered her face as she slowly backed against the wall and slid to the floor and began to cry.

"Shut up with that cryin' shit and get yo tramp ass home to the kids," Ronnell spoke out loud enough for Dalinda to hear.

She stood up and hurried out of the room with tears flowing down her face, almost knocking the elderly nurse down who was on her way with some help to take Ronnell upstairs.

Chapter 8

Speeding through Wildwood, going north on Everest, Solo turned the music down as he and Malcolm approached the stop sign on 55th. Making a right at the corner, they could see their house up ahead on the left through the naked trees that lined the street. As they got further down the long block, the red 5.0 came into view in the driveway along with the Grand National and a black two-door Honda Civic. Squatted down by the driver's door of the Honda was Gooch, with his muscular forearms resting on his thighs. When Solo whipped the Cadillac into the driveway, it startled Gooch, causing him to rise up from his squatted position and slide his button top off the Civic's hood.

"Watch out!" Shouted the young lady behind the steering wheel. Solo swerved back to the left and parked beside his 5.0 and opened the door. Once out of the car, he headed straight toward Gooch, who was now back standing. Gooch observed Solo and Malcolm who got out of the passenger side holding his .45, staring at him, then stuffing it inside his front pocket, then leaning back against the car door. When the young lady saw Malcolm, she started her car up, and in a split second, Solo was right there pushing Gooch. Being that Gooch outweighed Solo by fifty pounds of muscle and was four inches taller, he was barely able to make Gooch stumble back against the car. Gooch caught his balance and took one step forward, giving Solo a chance to back up while turning to his right to get a glimpse inside the Honda with a look of embarrassment on his face. "What the fuck dawg, is it like that; fuck me, fuck what I gotta do..."

"Hey!" Malcolm shouted, but Solo never turned around to look at Malcolm. Instead, he placed his feet in a seven-stance and rolled his shoulders and raised his hands ready to fight. Gooch put his feet in the same position just in case because he knew that Solo was fast and would take off on him for an advantage against his strength.

DRE LUV

Before that happened, he pointed his finger towards Solo's face. "Chill out, cuz, I don't wanna fuck you up nigga. Give me a minute and I'll explain so back the fuck up. Malcolm...tell Solo to leave me alone."

"Both of you niggas come on!" Malcolm ordered as he headed toward the open two-car garage attached to the beige brick home.

Gooch and Solo stared at each other for a few moments before Solo slowly backed away, never taking his eyes off of Gooch and Martha. When he made it to his 5.0, he opened up the driver's door and looked around inside, finding his mobile phone and beeper lying in the backseat. Instead of grabbing them, he pulled the keys out of the ignition and walked to the back of the car and popped the trunk.

Right in front of his eyes, stuffed between the speaker box and the front of the trunk, was the Nike gym bag, right where he left it. He reached in and pulled it out, and shut the trunk. When he turned around, Gooch was staring at him with a look of guilt. Solo returned the look with a scowl.

"Punk mutha fucka's," Solo spoke out, then he turned and walked toward the house. After Martha and Gooch said their goodbyes and she pulled out of the drive-way, Gooch coolly walked towards the house, stopping at Solo's 5.0, opened the door, and reached into the backseat and grabbed Solo's phone and beeper. The actions that he showed towards Solo, as if he wasn't fazed by what he did, was the exact opposite of how he felt inside. He also felt dumb because he had forgotten about the bag of money that was in the trunk on top of leaving Solo at the spot.

GHETTO MERCHANTS

He had to get his story together fast because Malcolm was going to be on his ass. He walked through the kitchen door and placed Solo's beeper and phone on the countertop to his left, right next to Malcolm's. Sitting at the kitchen table were Malcolm and Solo, splitting the money from the Nike bag to count it. Gooch walked over to the table and sat down, crossing his arms and resting them on the table as he leaned forward. He cleared his throat; Malcolm and Solo both ignored him.

"I got thirty-five hundred for the last of the work, I hit ol' girl for an extra two hun. I had to run her by her granny's house to get the change this mornin'. Y'all know how them laws be sittin' on the southside, that's why I waited for mornin' to run over there."

Malcolm never looked up or responded—he kept counting. Solo, on the other hand, who was still aggravated, stopped counting and slowly turned his neck as if he was trying to release some tension. He dropped the money on the table that was in his hands. He reached into an ashtray and grabbed a doobie and blew it off as he reached in his pocket and pulled out a lighter and blazed it up with one deep pull from his lungs. The cherry ran down to his fingertips and lips, causing him to burn himself and drop the cherry on a hundred-dollar bill. Quickly, he picked up the bill and flagged it, causing the cherry to fall to the floor all while he was holding the weed smoke.

When he exhaled, it was towards Gooch, causing him to break his pose and wave the smoke out of his frowned face. "Come on Solo, I'm sorry. I shouldn't have smashed out in ya ride, I was trippin...shit just got outta hand real fast and I didn't handle the situation right. You've left me at the spot before too." Gooch explained.

DRE LUV

"Trippin...nigga please, like you the only one that had somethin' to do that involved a ho last night. It wasn't about you usin' my ride, it was the thought of you not leavin' me with the keys to your shit. Even if I coulda made it over here, I couldn't get in unless I woulda called Malcolm. Face it, nigga, you left me stranded so you could go trick with ho ass Martha hopin' I wouldn't find out. What's so crazy is that on New Year's Eve she was tryin' to get me to come fuck her at a room she had at the Fifth Season Inn and she fuckin' you two or three weeks later. I blew that janky ass bitch off and now she got yo dumb- ass reeled in hook, line and sinker. All along you so blind to see that she's just butterin' you up long enough to show her cousin and his boys where a nigga be keepin' the work and the money. You so slow that you can't even see that cause you caught up on that ho's looks and a few extra dollars. Where the money at anyway nigga and them extra hun's that you won on are mine for fuckin' my night off." Solo spoke with a serious look on his face.

"Damn cuz...you serious? You on some bullshit for real...Malcolm say some-thing!"

When Malcolm looked up, he was laughing at the sad look on Gooch's face from the tongue lashing that Solo had given him.

"Ahhh man." Gooch spoke out as he scooted his chair back away from the table.

"Gooch, look at how you handled that shit; you was outta line by everythang you did. You puttin' ass over cash and you sleep on the whole environment. You gotta learn to pay attention cause this shit aint no college campus, it's real life or death situations on this field. What if you woulda got pulled over and the police searched the car and found this money? What would you have said if they asked whose it is, and where it came from? Furthermore, what's on your mind for you to bring Martha over here? That broad is scandalous lil cous, she work with her cousin Hector and her job is to get under a nigga and find out where a nigga keep his stash. Once that shit is found out here comes Hector and his boys comin' to pay a visit to the crib ready to smoke somethin' if a nigga don't give it up smooth. You know this shit already but for some reason you don't believe it or either you don't give a fuck what happens to you or us because you like a bitch. On the real tip, I highly recommend that you leave her alone before somebody gets hurt, cause it's only a matter of time before Hector and his boys slide by here and case the joint. I know how they think, so take my word." Malcolm calmly explained while maintaining direct eye contact.

"Fuck them cuz, I bet they don't come over here with that bullshit. They know we got heat and if they wanted to do somethin', why they didn't rob me this mornin' when I was over there on their turf all by myself?"

"For four and a half zones! You stupid for real." Solo shouted as he shook his head in disbelief. At that point, Malcolm knew that he had to do something to change up the program with his little cousins. Gooch stood up angrily and reached inside the front pocket of his 501s and pulled out a wad of cash and peeled off two hundred's and a fifty. He tossed the three bills in front of Solo and dropped the rest of it in front of Malcolm. He then pulled up his sagging jeans a little bit and walked towards the refriger-ator mumbling to himself.

After opening the refrigerator, he pulled out a gallon of milk, unscrewed the top and took a drink straight from the container. Malcolm looked on for a moment, then he went back to his count. Meanwhile, Solo stood and pulled a wad of money out of his front pocket, picked up the two fifties that Gooch had tossed in front of him, wrapped them around the knot, and stuffed them all back inside his front pocket. Solo looked up in time to notice Gooch staring, so he winked at him and sat back down. Gooch put the milk back inside the refrigerator, walked back to the table, and sat down. He resumed his cool pose with his arms crossed as Malcolm and Solo continued to count.

"I think you niggas jealous cause I fucked her and she likes me," Gooch said with confidence in his voice as he looked left to right at Solo and Malcolm.

For a moment, there was silence, then Malcolm and Solo both looked up at one another and burst out laughing hysterically, knocking money on the floor. Not seeing the humor in what he said, Gooch became furious as he watched his cousins laugh at him so hard that tears ran down their faces.

After that, with occasional banter between Solo and Malcolm, Malcolm's mobile phone began to ring. He stood up and wiped the tears from his cheeks, took a deep breath, and hurried to answer his phone. Solo took the opportunity to reply to Gooch's accusation. "Nigga please, Martha's a ho. She been passin' pussy around town since I moved down here in '89. Believe me when I tell ya I don't wanna fuck her."

"Me either," Malcolm said from across the room, then he answered the phone. "Hello...what up, Amber?" Gooch leaned back in his chair and put his hands behind his back while put-ting a fake grin on his face. Malcolm unplugged his mobile from the charger, opened the door and stepped inside the garage.

In the kitchen, Gooch was still determined to get Solo to admit that he wanted Martha, but Solo was headed toward the back of the house.

"Yo Solo, bring back some of that indo you got stashed in your room," Gooch ordered.

Solo stopped just as he reached the archway leading to the other part of the house and turned around. "Was you and your senorita in my room ramblin?"

Gooch stood up with a smile still on his face and walked over to where Solo was and threw his arm around his shoulder and gave him a playful punch in the stomach, hitting the Glock in the pouch instead. Solo looked at him out of the corner of his eye, as if he were crazy, yet they still took off walking together. Within a few minutes, they were laughing and talking loudly to one another, as if nothing had ever happened.

Back in the garage, Malcolm was still on the phone with Amber as he leaned against Gooch's SS Monte Carlo while looking outside at the cars and the street, when something caught his eye inside the garage that he had not noticed when he first arrived. On the far side of the garage, his '62 Impala Convert-ible was leveled out at riding height. The last time he drove it was on Christmas, and when he parked it that night, he pancaked it to the floor.

"Hold on, Amber." Malcolm walked around the back of the SS and immediately began to check for any damage. He knew that he also had put the car cover on it, yet it was now lying on the floor, thrown against the wall. Suddenly, he heard Solo and Gooch's voices again; they were back in the kitchen. When Malcolm stepped back inside the kitchen, Gooch and Solo were both picking up the money that had been knocked to the floor. Malcolm watched them briefly, then he re-engaged Amber on the mobile.
"I'm back."

"Babe, what are you doing; is that Gooch and Solo I hear?"
Asked Amber.

Back in the kitchen, Solo and Gooch were finished picking up
the money, and they sat down. Solo picked up a bag of weed
that he had placed on the table and put his other hand inside
and began to break the weed down, causing the aroma to fill
the kitchen. Suddenly, he and Gooch began to argue again as
usual, as Malcolm sat down at the table with them, causing
them to talk lower when they noticed that he was still on the
phone.

"How long are you gonna be home?" Malcolm asked her.

"I'll be here until I have to go to my 3:30 class. Do you need
something?"

Gooch noticed Malcolm's knuckles were busted up because of
him holding the phone up to his ear. He wanted to know, but
he didn't want to interrupt Malcolm's phone conversation.
"Cuz what happened to Malcolm's hand?"

"Goddamn...bow many times do I have to ask you to stop
cuzzin' me nigga!" Solo snapped at Gooch playfully as he
pulled out a pack of Zig-Zag.

"I need to put my lowrider in your garage," Malcolm told
Amber. Immediately, Solo and Gooch got quiet and looked at
each other nervously. They both knew that some shit was
about to happen because Malcolm didn't like anyone of them
driving it unless he was with them. The last time they took it
out of the garage without his permission, they were at Will
Rogers Park on the south side. They were having a hop off

GHETTO MERCHANTS

with a Mexican from South Side Locos who was in a hot 64 Impala and a solenoid burned out leaving their ass on the ground. They had to have it towed home and Malcolm had it towed to Rowdy's Hydraulics in Dallas, where the lifts were installed when he and Deziree got back in town.

"You've told me time and time again that you were going to bring that car up here, why don't you just get in it and come on? I need to talk to you anyway about that money being cleared in escrow for the restaurant. Everything should be ready for closing within the next two weeks, according to my boss. I am so happy for you, babe. Just think, you and your mother will be the new owners of the old Little Italy Restaurant; finally, you will be able to put your mark on Northwest Expressway. Anyway, I need to get these other papers to Ms. Cecelia so that she can get her lawyer to look over everything before all is finalized. Then there is the thought that I haven't seen you in a week and I need some sex because I'm horny as hell. So will you hurry up and come and tell your little cousins that I said hi." Amber expressed cheerfully.

"I'm on my way," Malcolm replied.

"I love you, Malcolm."

"Hang up the phone, Amber." Malcolm pressed END and set the phone down on the table.

Immediately, Gooch began to explain.

"Big cuz it was all on me. Two weekends ago, when you and your girl went outta town the weather was kinda nice on that Sunday, so I took your deuce out for a spin. Solo didn't know nothin' about it until he seen me up on the strip."

"Goddamn nigga since you bringin' my name in it anyway you might as well tell the nigga who you was with." Solo fired back at Gooch, then lit the fat indo joint.

"Who you have in my car, Gary?" Malcolm asked with a blank expression on his face.

"Martha," Gooch said quietly with his deep voice. Malcolm stood up and walked around the table one complete time and then he stopped once he made it to Gooch placing a hand on his shoulder. Solo looked at them both, amused by the predicament that Gooch had gotten himself into by not thinking.

"After we get this money straight over here, I want you to ride with me to Edmond so we can do some talkin'. Is that cool?" Malcolm asked. Gooch turned his head and looked up at Malcolm and nodded up and down.

"Yeah, why not." Gooch replied. Malcolm patted him on his shoulder a couple of times more then focused his attention towards Solo.

"Okay...Solo get all the loot outta the safe. Somebody gonna fuck around and come over here for real and try to take the shit we been hustlin' hard for. It's obvious that Gooch is ridin' around here slippin' like a mutha fucka so it ain't no tellin' who done followed this nigga home since y'all been livin' over here. How much dough you got out on the street?"

Solo squinted his eyes and tilted his head to the side, giving the impression that he was concentrating. He started counting on his fingers and talking to himself in a low voice while Malcolm reached down on the floor and picked up the

78

GHETTO MERCHANTS

Nike bag and started putting the money from the table inside of it.

"We got about eight g's out but don't trip my nigga cause it's Friday and everybody that gets work fronted will be callin' in fact most of em been beepin' already. They don't know that we outta work, in fact a nigga gotta get at these mutha fucka's before they go to tryin' to flip a niggas money. Hey Gooch, when somebody beeps you that owe us tell em that I'll be by to get at em or have them beep me. That way we can get all that shit in."

"I don't need you to make my moves for me, Solo. Y'all, make it look like I be out here just fuckin' up the business all the time. What's up on the work, Malcolm, cause I got sales that been hittin' me up all mornin?" Gooch asked as he looked at numbers on his pager.

"Ain't nothin' poppin' now, we aint got no work right now cause Javon is on some bullshit so go ahead and handle that shit like Solo was sayin'. When you call the people back that don't owe us tell em that we'll be on next week."

Gooch shrugged his shoulders, stood up and walked to the cabinet where the cordless home phone was located. He picked it up and headed out of the kitchen so that he could make his calls in private. Solo went on his mission to get the rest of the money, and Malcolm headed back out to the garage.

Inside his lowrider, Malcolm sat listening to the high-performance 383 Stroker engine idle as he gathered his thoughts. Within five minutes, Solo stepped through the kitchen door carrying a black duffel bag in his right hand. Gooch followed two steps behind him all the way to the point when Solo put the duffel in the open trunk of the Impala and closed it.

Malcolm put the car in reverse and eased out of the garage to the spot where Solo and Gooch were standing in the driveway. Gooch opened the door and slid in while Solo closed it for him. Malcolm hit the window switch, letting the passenger window down.
"There's ninety-six g's in the back and with that other eight that I'll have in a little while, it will put the count right where it's supposed to be... right?" Solo questioned.

"Yeah, that sounds about right. Check this out, when you get out in traf-fic slide by Javon's mama's house and see if that nigga hidin' out over there. When you finish handlin' up come pick me and this nigga up at Amber's crib."

"Bet...I'm gonna shit and shower first then I'm gone." Solo answered while he backed away from the lowrider.

"You can push the Lac if you want; the keys over the visor, if not, put it in the garage."
Solo nodded his head up and down and put up his right fist, signifying right on. Malcolm popped in a tape in the Kenwood and hit the lockout switch, making the lowrider hop up at all four corners at one time, along with him and Gooch. They backed out in the street with Tupac's 'Soldier's Story' playing low. When they made it to the intersection of 55th and Everest, Malcolm coasted through the stop sign; Gooch tapped Malcolm on the shoulder.

"What the fuck you want nigga?" Malcolm asked after glancing over at Gooch's smiling face.

"Damn cuz when was you gonna tell me bout the road trip?"

GHETTO MERCHANTS

Gooch asked anxiously while rubbing his palms together.

"Road trip, are you fuckin' serious? Fuckin' with you on a road trip we'll fuck around and come outside from a piss break and you been done left a nigga at a rest stop cause you seen a bitch."

"Hold on Malcolm, I understand Solo bein' pissed and you too when it comes to slippin' with that money in the trunk but my sack money ain't never short. Let's keep it real cuz, the count is all that really matters to you anyway."

Malcolm sat quietly for a moment, contemplating on what Gooch said, feeling somewhat offended that he would actually say in so many words that he didn't care about him and Solo. It was obvious that the impression he had of him was misunderstood, and it was time to set him straight once and for all because he had him twisted.

"Keepin' it real huh...you take this lifestyle for granted as if it can't be taken away. Believe me, it can disappear in an instant because I witnessed the F.B.I. and the DEA come to our house and take everythang along with my daddy, just like them people down at Oklahoma University took your scholarship when you got caught with that weed in your dorm room. Just like your position in our program can be eliminated by your absent-minded moves that you tend to make all the time. We can function without you. Check this out, I gotta bigger picture in my mind that's larger than the dope game and worryin' about the count or gettin' busted or even worse shit like one of us gettin' smoked behind a few dollars. Somebody has to stay focused with direction to be able to take this shit to another level for our future. I don't know about you, but I wanna last and the only way we gonna last is for all of us to use our heads as one machine. Otherwise, a nigga gonna be dead or in the pen and I'm not tryin' to be at neither one of those places. Is that real enough for ya?" Malcolm explained calmly hoping that Gooch would understand his sincerity.

"Hold em up Malcolm cause I don't want you to think that I'm not thankful for you involving me in this money game cause it ain't but a handful of niggas around the town my age that have what I got. Give me another chance cuz and be patient and I promise that I won't let you down?"

Malcolm listened as Gooch pleaded his case. He knew that Gooch's intentions were good, yet he was easily sidetracked by the hype of having a little bit of money. Who wouldn't be given that situation but that's why Malcolm had to get him under control now because his responsibilities were about to get bigger. "We'll be pullin' outta here Sunday mornin' so don't tell nobody nigga, not even Auntie Erlene." Malcolm instructed with a firm tone as he checked the traffic coming up on his left while merging onto northbound I-235.

While Malcolm looked over his left shoulder, Gooch looked over his as well, but he wasn't checking the traffic; he was looking in the backseat, reminiscing about when he and Martha were back there getting busy in the parking lot at Taco Bell a few weeks ago. Malcolm smashed down on the accelerator, causing Gooch's head to jerk, bringing his daydream to a halt still yet everything about Martha that he had experienced stuck inside his head like he remembered his birthday.

"What you lookin' at back there?" Malcolm asked while catching him staring in the back.

"Nothin'...hey I was just thinkin bout why would you send

Solo by Ms. Mim's house to see if Javon was hidin'? Let me guess, uhhh would it have somethin' to do with some money he lost gamblin'?"

Malcolm reached down to the Kenwood and turned the music down a little, then he looked over toward Gooch with a confused look on his face. Gooch returned the look, giving off the impression that made Malcolm think that he knew something that he wasn't telling him or that he thought Malcolm already knew.

"Gamblin', what the fuck you talkin' bout?" Malcolm inquired.

"You tellin' me that you don't know that Javon be losin' his ass off at the gamblin' shacks? You don't be out in that mix that much anymore at them spots. Anyway, last Saturday night I was at the Kettle with Solo after we got on from the club. Solo burned out with this little broad he knocked up there and I got a page from this broad that was at Charlie's over on Lottie. So I shoot over to the eastside and fall up in the place to swoop ol' girl up but I didn't see her downstairs in the restaurant area so I go upstairs to the gamblin' shack and make my way to the crap table where I see this broad on the edge of the pool table side bettin' and Javon in the mix. Me and baby hung out for about thirty minutes or so, of course the whole time I was whisperin' sweet nothin's in her ear while I watched Javon lose at least fifteen g's. Yo cuz if you woulda seen the nigga you woulda been trippin' cause it was like he was a whole different nigga."

"Different, how is that?" Malcolm asked.

"It's hard to explain, just different. I been seein' him do the same type shit up at Shy Town's after hour spot doin' the same thang, losin'. I guess he looks different to me when he's gamblin' because I'm used to seein' him when he's around you and he's Mr. Serious Super Baller actin' like he's better than everybody else, cause he got work with his ol Dr. Jeckyll Mr. Hyde personality. You know what, fuck Javon cause when he see me out in traffic he act like he don't know a nigga anyway..."

Malcolm drove along and took in all the information that Gooch spilled for a moment and couldn't believe that he had been sleeping on what he was hearing. Then suddenly it was all clear why Javon's inconsistency and bullshit over the past year had been like it was. Sob stories and drag that pulled Malcolm in to help him make sack money that he had either lost or was making preparations to lose. All of a sudden, Malcolm became enraged again and balled up his fist and hit the steering wheel, startling Gooch while he was in mid-sentence, complaining.

"I bet that bitch ass nigga is down there in Vegas!" Malcolm shouted.

Chapter 9

Martha moved in with her grandparents after a tragic car accident that killed both of her parents in Texas when they were on their way to pick her up after summer vacation. Although she was an only child, she wasn't the only grand-child in her grandparents' home. She had an older cousin named Hector. They lived in a small two-bedroom white bungalow on S.W. 15th, two blocks east of Penn and one block west of Will Rogers Court Housing Projects.

Martha was ten years old when her grandfather passed away from a massive heart attack, leaving his wife in financial strain, causing her to take on two jobs at sixty-five years old. Her absence led to Martha being home alone and eventu-ally hanging out in the predominantly black projects. As for Hector, he started hanging with a gang known as BLM (Barrio La Familia Mexicanos) in which he was later initiated. Within three more years, Martha started skipping school and riding the bus to the malls and stealing clothes. Some she wore and the others she sold and bought groceries and gave money to her aging grandmother for bills.

During this time Martha had been raped twice, once by a drug dealer who hustled at the park down the street from her grandmother's house. This happened one evening when she was taking a shortcut from the bus stop. The first time was by Hector in which he took her virginity at thirteen, one night when she was getting out of the bathtub, and he busted through the door. Scared of what someone may think, Martha never told anyone because she felt that it was her fault because she was well developed like a full grown woman at an early age.

DRE LUV

Hector moved up in rank with the BLM fast, but at the high cost of doing several short stints in state juvenile facilities and breaking his grandmother's heart. As a young adult, he continued with his mischief, although it advanced from stealing cars, vandalizing, and tagging to selling drugs, carjacking, and home invasions. All of his home invasions were developed through Martha, in which sometimes, she was present while playing her part as one of the victims.

Over the years, Hector coached Martha to use her looks and her sex to get close to the dealers so that he and his boys could come and catch them off guard so that he could cash in. Eventually, this left Martha with a bad name all over the city, but still she was spared because nobody had proof of her misdoings, but her and it was getting harder and harder for her to conceal her pain.

The only time that she got to do as she pleased was when Hector was in jail. Since Hector's most recent incarceration, his grandmother decided that she no longer wanted him living in her house. With the help of Martha, she paid a handyman to transform the old, detached garage in the backyard into a space for Hector to stay. This allowed him to do as he pleased in his own space without bothering them in the front house.

On Martha's drive home from Gooch's house, she reminisced on last night and the morning. She had been with a lot of guys before and most for the wrong reasons but Gooch was different from them all. He wasn't complicated or stuck up because he had money and a few toys. He didn't appear to judge her on the rumors that she was sure that he had heard about her, he actually acted like he cared for her and she liked

GHETTO MERCHANTS

him too. She liked the fact that he treated her like a lady and not like the whore that Hector had turned her into and that was the person that she did not want to be anymore.
'.

Just a few months back, Hector instructed Martha to get up under one of the Ghetto Merchants so that he could set up a plan to roll him. Martha agreed, but she knew in her heart that it would be nearly impossible because Malcolm would never fall for her, nor would he allow one of his guys. On New Year's Eve, Martha found out about a big party that was being held at Ebony Club that night, and without a doubt, all of the ballers would be there. That night she made it inside the club and stopped at the bar and ordered cranberry juice with no liquor and checked in her coat. Immediately, she went on the prowl in search for her mark as she waited at the bottom of the stairs by the VIP.

After several frivolous conversations with men leaving the section and some who were going and making offers to her, she finally saw who she was looking for. Solo was walking down the stairs, leaving VIP wearing Cole Haan loafers, Polo khaki pants with a braided belt matching his shoes, and a burgundy, beige striped Polo button down shirt. Diamond studs in both ear lobes, his pinky ring, watch and chain were both Rolex, yet his chain had a large drop with GM paved with diamonds, like everything else, had Solo looking like a million dollars. He spotted Martha off the bat when he stepped over the VIP ropes. She was wearing a tight red, low-cut mini dress with six-inch stilettos and her jet black hair hung below her shoulders with curls on the end.

Solo was coming down the stairs fast, looking past Martha, trying to ignore her, licking her lips while she stared at him. Just when he made it to the bottom of the stairs he looked at her closely and thought to himself that it was a damn shame that she was so fine but poisonous. As he passed her, she reached out and stuck her index finger in his back pocket, causing him to swing his arm back and slap her hand away. This made him spill his Remy Martin on his hand. He stopped and turned around to face her.

"What the hell you want, Martha?" Solo asked with a frown on his face. Martha took a step toward him and put her arms around his waist and pulled his body up against hers, allowing him to feel the heat from her along with the mixture of her Obsession perfume. Solo looked down at her heaving cleavage that moved with her every breath, then he moved up to her pretty big brown eyes, then back down her whole silhouette. He asked himself why does this bad ass bitch have to be so scandalous?

Martha observed Solo, and she knew that he wanted her because there was no way that he could not like what he was looking at, because she knew that she was fine, and she was standing out in a club full of black women. She reached up and grabbed his chain gently with her left hand, being care-ful not to let him go with her right. Martha pulled down on the chain, causing Solo to bend down as she stood on her tiptoes to speak into his ear.

"I want you to come with me. I have a suite at the Fifth Season Inn, and I am ready and able to rock your world all night. Feel me Solo and come fuck this hot wet Mexican pussy tonight."

Martha spoke in a sultry voice that en-ticed Solo...but not enough for him to give in even while being intoxicated.

When she finished talking, she stuck her tongue in his ear,

making Solo pull back, breaking her grasp on his chain and his waist. He slowly backed up and in-stantly knew how she was able to get niggas to slip. She had a way to hypnotize a man with a form of a natural sex potion. Solo looked down at his glass and back to the beautiful Martha and knew that he had to get away and at that moment he shook his head to clear the effects of the alcohol and Martha as he turned away from her and headed toward the bar area where he spotted an old piece of game that he hadn't seen in a while engaging in conversation with some of her friends. Martha's feelings were crushed as she noticed that that was the first time that she had ever been turned down in her life. How could Solo not want to spend the night with her? She asked herself, but subconsciously she knew the answer to that question was because he was not a fool. Suddenly, she felt embarrassed and decided that she was ready to leave as she watched Solo give a female a hug, which Martha was aware of being one of the few females in Oklahoma City who hustled with a few kilos.

Just as she started walking, she noticed another small group of females to her left that were staring at her while two of them were giggling. Right then, Martha had had enough and decided that on top of feeling neglected and cheap by Solo, she was not going to let a couple of schoolgirls who probably got in the club with fake IDs get their laughs off of her misfortunes.

Martha held her head up high as she approached them while she was still getting looks from other men who tried to approach her, but she ignored it all because she was on a mission. When she made it to where the girls were, Martha pointed her finger in the face of all four of them.

"Who do you scary bitches think you are laughing at me? Not

one of you have the heart to even say anything to the nigga but you have the audacity to laugh at me when we all know that each one of you simple little bitches wish that you were me!" Shouted Martha, then she double snapped her fingers in their faces and strutted off, catching the eye of every man who was lucky enough to see the sexy lady in the red dress. Making it to the coat check at the bottom bar Martha pulled her ticket out of her bra in exchange for her black waist-length leather jacket. She reached inside her sleeve and pulled out her clutch, then slid on her jacket as she walked out of the club. As she got closer to her car which was parked in the Pizza Hut parking lot next door she was overwhelmed by a cloud of smoke, bass, and screeching tires. Finally, when she made it to her car, she could see that it was a blue 5.0 Mustang Convertible with a white top doing doughnuts and holding up traffic to people trying to find a place to park as well as her who was trying to leave. Martha attempted to wave the smoke from her face as she unlocked the door of her car, but it was useless because the smoke wouldn't stop coming.

"Stop!" She yelled as she coughed and took in a mouthful of smoke. She got in her car and closed the door. Suddenly the tire screeching came to a halt and the smoke began to clear revealing Gooch hanging halfway out of the window with a grin on his face and arms thrown up in the air.

He mouthed the words 'I'm sorry' and he got out of the car wearing white Adidas shell toes with blue stripes and a blue sweat-shirt with an Adidas sign across the front and original 501 Levis. Around his neck hung the same type of necklace that Solo had on except that instead of having rubies spelling the GM initials Gooch had sapphires. They talked for a moment and got past their introductions—and Gooch's apology, he offered to take her to breakfast. She accepted and followed him to Denny's on 39th Expressway. After eating and talking for a while they realized close to two hours had passed by, which eventually led to Gooch and Martha spending the night together in her suite at the Fifth Season Inn.

After the ride home Martha walked onto the porch, opened the screen door and put her key into the lock and went inside. She wasn't the least bit surprised to see her grandmother sitting in her rocking chair asleep while the sound of the Bold and The Beautiful blared from the television. Being careful not to wake her, she removed her key from the lock, quietly shut the door and locked it back. The heat was unbearable in the house as Martha crept over the hardwood floor headed for her bedroom and the thermostat in the small hallway. She made a left into the hallway then a right where she turned the thermostat down to 70 degrees from 90 and continued to her bedroom where she went inside, closed the door behind her and locked it. She pulled off her coat and threw it on the bed. She walked over to her dresser and opened the top drawer where she pulled out a small digital scale along with the four and a half ounces of crack that she bought from Gooch. She tore open the sandwich bag and almost threw up from the smell of the white chunks that had a beige tint.

"Damn, my baby keep good work." She said quietly to herself. On top of the dresser was a small mirror with a handle on it that her grandmother had bought for her when she was little, along with a single-edged razor blade. She pulled out the biggest chunk and placed it on the mirror, grabbed the razor blade and put the tip of it directly in the center of the chunk. She pressed down, causing a loud popping noise when the chunk split into two pieces and the razor smacked the mirror. Martha nodded her head up and down with approval of the work as she noticed that there were only a few crumbs, as she placed one of the halves on the scale, which read 43 grams.

She remembered Gooch telling her that the sack had 130 grams in it, therefore, she could go ahead and give Hector the forty-three and keep him calm until later. And in the meantime, she still had three ounces and close to an eight ball for herself. Quickly, she reached back into the drawer and pulled out some baggies and bagged three ounces and then she bagged Hector's forty-three grams separately, along with the extra three left over. She blew the mirror and the scale off, then she returned everything where it belonged, except for Hector's stuff and the three grams; she put that in her coat pocket after putting it back on as she headed for the door.

When she unlocked and opened it, Hector was standing there with his arms crossed and a frown on his face, startling Martha, causing her to jump back. "Pinche vato...you're loco," Martha said angrily in a low tone, trying not to wake her grandmother. Hector smirked as he uncrossed his arms and shrugged his shoulders as he stared at Martha from head to toe.

"You tell me bitch, am I?" Martha stepped to him and pushed him in his chest with both hands, then she pointed her finger in his face.
"Let's go out back you fool and be quiet and don't wake grandmother."

She instructed and quietly they crept through the house and out back to Hector's domain. Once inside, Martha sat down on a wooden fold-out chair while Hector flopped down on an old, worn-out plaid sofa. He pulled a cigarette that stuck behind his ear, picked up a lighter that lay on the cushion next to him, and fired up his smoke. Hector took a couple of drags from his cigarette while he and Martha both stared at each other in silence until he offered her the cigarette, in which she shook her head left to right.

"What were you thinking, esse' by bringing that pinche mayate inside grandmother's house?" Hector questioned after he blew smoke toward Martha.

"I don't want to hear that shit from you right now, you wanted me to get with a Ghetto Merchant, and I have..."

Martha paused and reached into her jacket pocket and pulled out the chunk that she had set aside for Hector, and tossed it over to him.

"Now there, are you happy? You always want to question what I do, yet you always want something from me, whether it's money, information, using my car or whatever. So, what I brought him over here. I had to 'cause I owed him money. Besides, this was all your idea, anyway, remember. I'm supposed to get in good standing with him, right, asshole?" You said, "Find out where he lives, then you..."

While Martha had been talking, Hector was examining the yao, basically paying Martha no attention until he heard the words 'where he lives' come from her mouth. Immediately, he cut her off mid-sentence.

"You know where his pad is at huh...tell me where it is!"

Seeing the mischief in Hector's eyes when he inquired about Gooch's house, she knew instantly that she had made a mistake, and it was too late to lie, but not too late to fabricate a story with a slight twist.

"I sure do; he stays on N.E. 24th right down the street from the post office," Martha answered with a sly grin on her face, trying to look truthful as she played her role.

"That's a dope house, stupid. You think those pinche mayates live right there in the hood!" Hector shouted.

Outside, Martha acted as if she was sorry, but inside, she was singing a song of joy and laughing in Hector's face. Most important of all, she had to keep acting.

"Hector all you do is talk shit and call me names, will you be nice for a change and be thankful for what I have done? If that is not where he lives, I am sure that soon enough he will take me to his house, but we've got to be pati-ent if we're gonna hit the jackpot because those guys are having money."

Hector moved to the front of the couch, being careful not to drop the long ember from the tip of the cigarette until he dropped it on the old coffee table that had been burned hundreds of times. He and Martha locked eyes, and she could see the same anger in them that she had watched for years. She swallowed hard, trying not to look nervous. Hector broke eye contact first, giving her a sigh of relief as she watched him reach up under the couch and pull out his tray that was covered with seeds, rolling papers, and a small quantity of marijuana. Hector grabbed one of the rolling papers and sprinkled some weed in it, then pulled a knife from under the sofa cushion and broke a piece of the crack rock off and made some smaller pieces. He then sprinkled the pieces on top of the weed and twisted the joint up. Neither Hector nor Martha said a word to one another. When he finished rolling, he passed the joint over to Martha along with his lighter. She lit it up and took a long drag.

"When you find where he stays, I want to know bitch cause I don't have time to play games with you or them...no pinche games, Martha," Hector spoke in a low serious tone. Martha exhaled the smoke as she passed the laced joint that numbed her mouth as she stared in Hector's direction, feeling like she was looking right through him. Still, she nodded her head up and down, letting him know that she understood that he meant business and she began to feel the room start to spin.

"You keep putting that pretty little snatch on that youngster and believe me when I tell you he will take you to his pad so he can show it off. And if he asks you anything about me or any of my vatos, it will be because his cousin Malcolm is suspecting something. Hey....are you paying attention to what I'm saying?"

Martha nodded her head up and down again.

"Okay, Malcolm is fucking smart and if he knows that you're a do low bitch he'll make sure his cousin dumps your ass. You've got to get close as soon as you can for payday, when I'll have something for you too."

Martha stood up and stumbled a little, then she blinked her eyes and got focused on Hector. Hector began to laugh at her because he could tell that she was loaded, but he didn't expect her to make two fists and point both of them in his direction and extend her middle fingers, then head to the door. After fumbl-ing with the knob for a moment she finally got it open and felt a gust of wind that brought her down from the clouds as she ran across the yard to the gate. She opened the gate and left it open just as she left Hector's door and ran down the driveway to her car. She quickly got in and locked the door in case Hector was behind. She felt the pain that she had endured for years and at that moment it filled her eyes with tears, but she refused to let one fall down her pretty face.

True enough she had made some bad choices where Hector was involved but now was a time for her to make some better decisions that wouldn't cause her to get hurt or possibly bring drama that would affect her grandmother. Some kind of way she had to get away from Hector because if she didn't she would continue to be the person that she had allowed him to make her.

Suddenly her thoughts were rattled clear from her mind by the sound of her pager chiming above her head clipped to the sun visor. Just as she reached up and unclipped the pager, she saw Gilberto and Miguel pull to the curb in Hector's olive green 69 four door Chevy Caprice. She reached inside her jacket pocket and pulled out her keys and stuck them in the ignition and started her car. She quickly backed out of the driveway. Getting out of the Caprice on the driver's side Gilberto tried to stop Martha as she straightened the Honda and slowly pulled forward trying to avoid the back of Hector's car, but she ignored him and put her foot to the floor almost hitting him.

When she reached the end of the block and stopped at the stop sign, she realized that she had been holding her breath. She looked in her rearview mirror, finding nobody behind her that she did not want to see, she cracked her window to let some fresh air inside. Startled by her pager she was still holding in her hand, she turned it where she could see the screen which showed DUPLICATE. She pressed the scroll button and found out that it was her friend that wanted to

GHETTO MERCHANTS

buy an ounce.

"Aint' this a bitch!" Martha shouted out of disgust because she had to go right back to the house and get her work. More than likely she would have to deal with Gilberto now.

Chapter 9

On his way to Midwest City to drop off the broad he had spent the night with at a Motel 6 on Meridian Avenue, Big Tay sped east on I-40 in his root beer colored '84 442 Hurst Oldsmobile. As he glanced to his left while going across the downtown crosstown bridge, he saw Solo's 5.0 going the opposite way. Big Tay lifted his mobile phone from the console and immediately punched in Solo's mobile digits and pressed SEND. He quickly fumbled the phone to his left hand so that he could turn down the music. On the first ring, Solo's phone went straight to a recording, so Big Tay pressed END and decided to call the phone at the spot on 24th. Surprisingly, Solo answered the phone over there and within seconds, they both exchanged information about what was going on with the red 5.0. After they had an understanding, Big Tay announced that he would be there in about an hour, then ended the call.

Big Tay placed the mobile phone down on the console and turned the music back up. He gripped the steering wheel and pressed the accelerator to the floor, making record time to the Air Depot exit, where he got off the highway. He dropped the female off at her apartment complex, which sat next to Heritage Park Mall on Reno. Pulling out of her complex, Big Tay got sideways as he headed westward toward his house in Del City on Scott Street.

As soon as Big Tay parked inside his garage and walked inside the house, he began taking his clothes off pulling his last sock off when he hopped inside the shower. Out of the shower he grabbed some Silver Tabs and a black and blue Dallas Cowboys sweatshirt, and on his feet, he chose a pair of black

Army boots. After getting dressed, he unclipped his pager and pulled out the wad of money from the Girbaud jeans he'd worn yesterday. From the bed, he grabbed his Beretta, tucking it under his sweatshirt inside his waist.

Hurrying to get out of the house, Big Tay made a quick search in the living room and the kitchen, where he found his black beanie in one and the keys to his 89 K-5 in the other. Out the door with business on his mind, Big Tay was headed for the eastside.

It took less than fifteen minutes for Big Tay to pull into the driveway behind Gooch's 5.0, setting off his Viper alarm from the Stillwater Design fifteen-inch Kicker woofers being driven by the Precision Power amps. The windows in the spot, along with the Ruger on the table, were vibrating, causing Dollaz to peek outside after grabbing his table dancing Ruger off the coffee table. Big Tay stayed inside the K-5 waiting for someone to come out, then finally he saw the door open, and a hand inserted a key into the lock on the bars. Suddenly, Dollaz appeared out of the doorway onto the porch and Big Tay turned his music off, leaving the sound of Gooch's talking alarm warning you to stay away from the armed vehicle. When Dollaz got halfway down the steps with his Ruger by his side, he noticed that the man inside the silver K-5 was Big Tay. He looked up and down the block to check for anything or anyone out of character that may wish to cause him harm. Seeing nothing he hopped down the steps and stuffed the Glock inside his flannel into the waistband of his Dickie's and threw his arms in the air.

"What up nigga?" He questioned with a shout and a grin on his face. Big Tay returned the grin with a smile as he opened the door and slid out of his truck and walked around the front meeting Dollaz on the side of the 5.0 where Dollaz was looking bamboozled at the car.

"What kinda shit this nigga got on his load...talkin' alarms and shit?" Dollaz questioned as he and Big Tay gripped right hands and pulled each other in and gave one another a pat on the back.

"Viper shit, everybody havin' a few dollas got it now. What's up with my nigga Gooch and where Malcolm and Solo at?" Big Tay asked with a serious look on his face while heading towards the house.

"They went over to Solo and Gooch's crib to see if he was over there. I just got off the phone with Malcolm about five or ten minutes ago and he said every-thang was cool." Relief showed across Big Tay's face as he pointed towards his truck with his head annoyed by the alarm.

"We shakin' the spot cause this alarm gonna be goin' off for a minute. You doin' somethin' over here why you can't leave?" Big Tay asked.

Before answering, Dollaz jogged back to the spot to turn everything off and in a snap, he was closing the door and locking the bars. He jumped off the porch and ran around the side of the house to stash his work, then he was getting in the passenger side of the K-5 with a smile on his face—glad to be back in the circle with his homeboys.

"Like I was sayin', Malcolm was tellin' Solo some shit about Javon not bein' in pocket. Really I don't know shit except that I'm fresh outta jail back fuckin' with my niggas. What up my nigga, I see you gotta nice truck to floss around town in. You said you was gonna get one of these mutha fucka's the last time I seen you." Dollaz glanced around the inside of the truck

100

GHETTO MERCHANTS

that was filled with leather and wood.

"This ain't nothin' but a 89 model with a few new school upgrades on the inside and under the hood. Really I'm just tryin' to concentrate on stayin' down and get that money in a major way and not do nothin' to crash the program with no dummy shit like Gooch did today and you back in nine 0. There's too much goin' on that keep a nigga's nerves wrecked which is why I'm pullin' over here to get some Remy outta Marsha's."

Dollaz felt the anguish in Big Tay's voice and it hurt him inside because he always gave him inspiration that everything would be okay. He kept him optimistic that one day they would be on top and things were beginning to look as If the Ghetto Merchants were doing pretty good for themselves.

"Tay, I really thank you for lookin' out with the chips you sent a nigga when I was up in that jail house and most important of all...lookin' out for my moms. Thanks to you gettin' her in rehab she wasn't out here trickin' with niggas for twenty-dollar pieces. Now that I'm back, I can do my part on lookin' out for her and my granddaddy. Anyway, my nigga, I heard about you takin' a bigger piece of the action over in the Hall's."

Big Tay wheeled the K-5 into an empty spot at the corner of Marsha's where the winos hung out on the side of the building, panhandling and drinking all day. Big Tay tapped his horn twice, getting the attention of all who were not passed out. Old school Lorenzo jerked his head towards Big Tay's truck and quickly passed his bottle of Wild Irish Rose down to a woman that was sitting on the ground, back against the brick wall. He adjusted his dirty hat and pimp walked towards the truck.

Lorenzo used to be one of the biggest pimps in Oklahoma City traveling nationwide with his stable until the fourth of July weekend in 1981. He took four of his best hoes to the T-Okie Convention down in the country town of Tatums so he could kick back and let his hoes network. Lorenzo hooked up with one of his old classmates that had moved down there in 68 when they were seniors at Kennedy. His friend had been there cooking liquid PCP a.k.a. water and sherm for some years now and had made a name for himself as being a straight up dealer. This particular July fourth Lorenzo smoked a sherm stick on a Kool cigarette dipped to the filter and ever since that day in 1981 he hadn't been the same because the sherm was too powerful for his brain and he never came back after that high. He lost everything he had and turned into nothing but a burned out dope fiend. His friend felt responsible for his mishap because of the way the drug took him away so he looked out for him until he died unexpectedly two years later.

Lorenzo still got respect in the city for being a pioneer in the game by the young and the old but he was too far gone to be anything else but a dope fiend until the day he died.

When Lorenzo approached Big Tay's driver's side door, he had a twenty-dollar bill in his fingers ready.

"OG Renzo, can you do somethin' for me?" Big Tay asked respectfully. With an expressionless look on his face Lorenzo stared at Big Tay then he looked over at Dollaz while trying to focus his eyes on the guy he thought was somebody new in the neighborhood.
"Who's that cat?" Lorenzo questioned Big Tay spreading bad breath that fought with the pine tree fragrance that lingered

inside the K-5. Dollaz leaned over close to Big Tay so that Lorenzo could get a closer look at him.

"Hey pimpin'...don't even act like you can't remember me. Its me, Dollaz." Lorenzo leaned his head inside the truck and squinted again as a smile came across his face revealing yellow teeth along with two gold ones with diamonds on his canines.

"I remember you cat daddy. Ha ha...ol Dollaz, you used to be comin' through here in that blue car with that loud ass music. They said you was in jail for killin' some peoples. When you get out?"

Dollaz's smile disappeared as he sat back in his seat shaking his head in disbelief that a burnt out dope fiend that doesn't know what day it is knows about the shit that happened over on 17th. Big Tay saw the disgusted look on Dollaz's face, so he sat up in his seat and blocked Lorenzo's view and handed him the twenty-dollar bill.

"OG Ren, go in the store and tell Marsha I want a pint of VSOP Remy. You keep the change in fact here you go this way you can get you and ol girl somethin' to eat too." Big Tay spoke out as he reached in his pocket and pulled out another twenty-dollar bill handing it over to Lorenzo.

Lorenzo winked his eye and took off towards the entrance to the liquor store. Big Tay looked around the parking lot to check the scene to make sure there weren't any jackers in sight while Dollaz sat over in his seat biting on his fingernails daydreaming. Big Tay nudged him on his arm with his elbow.

"Yo cuz...don't be spittin' your nails in my truck and what you heard about me takin' somethin' over in Prince Hall?" Big Tay asked aggressively. Dollaz opened the door and bopped out to brush off his lap then he got back inside the truck and closed the door. He pulled down the visor and looked at himself in the mirror, licked his thumb and rubbed his eyebrows down. Big Tay elbowed him again but harder in an attempt to get Dollaz to stop playing around. Dollaz elbowed him back and started laughing, then Big Tay pushed him against the door, causing Dollaz to bump his head against the glass. Dollaz rubbed his head with his right hand and Big Tay started laughing and rocking back and forth in the seat.

"Damn that shit hurt nigga." Dollaz said, then he pointed through the windshield towards the liquor store. Big Tay bit and looked in that direction, unaware that it was a plot to distract him and Dollaz slapped him in the back of the head. Big Tay turned towards Dollaz, rubbing his head now while Dollaz laughed.

"You sho right you ol slick ass nigga." Replied Big Tay as he nodded and chuckled.

That was when Lorenzo came out of the liquor store and pimp walked towards the truck being careful not to drop the liquor in the sack and look cool at the same time.

"Good lookin' out pimpin'." Big Tay said with a smile on his face to let Lorenzo know that he was still a factor in the streets. Lorenzo handed the sack inside the truck and threw up the black fist and he pimped to the side of the building where he was greeted with respect from his friends of his new life. Back inside the K-5, Big Tay handed the liquor to Dollaz, then he raised the console up and reached inside and pulled out a yellow plastic lemon squeezer and passed that over as well. Putting the K-5 in reverse he backed all the way out, turning his wheels all the way to the right until they faced the street.

Suddenly, some females pulled into the parking lot in a Corsica headed towards the beauty supply. They jocked each other, but neither vehicle stopped. Big Tay pumped up the volume with BDP's Love's Gonna Getcha. Dollaz unscrewed the cap on the liquor and squeezed some lemon juice inside the bottle. He took a drink, then passed it over to Big Tay. He boogied while everybody they passed looked on at the K-5 with the boomin system. The song was going off and they had made it only a few blocks away and Dollaz was on his second drink as they headed towards I-35. When the next song started, Big Tay turned the Kenwood down and Dollaz began to tell Big Tay what he wanted to know.

"It's like this homeboy; the word got back to me in S-9 tank when I was in the county that you was the one that killed them Cali niggas they found in that burnt up car behind Northeast High School. As for me...well I'm gonna keep it real witcha, I killed them niggas and that punk bitch over on 17th. Fuck em all, them niggas was rollin' around this mutha fucka like they was better than a nigga or somethin'."

They made it to the I-35 exit and Big Tay jumped over in front of a new Ford truck to get on the southbound ramp. He smashed the accelerator, pushing Dollaz back in his seat as they merged onto the interstate traffic.

"This mutha fucka right here is tight. What's under the hood?" Dollaz asked.

"Balanced and blueprinted 454 Vortec," Big Tay answered with confidence.

"Where we goin?"

"Crossroads Mall, chill out nigga and ride." Big Tay answered. "Anyway, I don't be hatin' on a nigga cause he got more than me or just because he's from outta town. I do demand respect when I give it and that night them niggas disrespected me. That night I went over to 17th to buy a quarter chicken from them niggas for seven g's. I planned on flippin' the money three or four times and then I would've had the money back that I fucked off when I left the crew. That way instead of comin' back empty handed I could put the money back and work with Malcolm on our other differences."

"I went through a whole lot in those few months before I got caught up on that case; my bitch was stealin' money, my moms was stealin' and smokin, then my little brother gettin' ran over while ridin' his bike. I'm tellin' ya Tay that I was fucked up. When y'all came by grand daddy crib before the funeral and followed in the procession I felt like we was still brothers. When the funeral was over and y'all left I wanted to ride out together like old times but I didn't have the courage to come to y'all especially Malcolm to ad-mit that I was wrong."

Big Tay listened as Dollaz spoke and felt his eyes begin to well up then he glanced over when he saw Dollaz wiping his face with the sleeve of his flannel, but he continued to speak after pausing for a moment.

"Back to 17th, I get in the house and follow Mickey to the kitchen where I get my seven g's out and put it on top of the table where he starts runnin' through it to make sure the count is right. His homeboy Buckshot comes to the kitchen door and gets the word from Mickey to grab a nine piece so

GHETTO MERCHANTS

he shoot to another part of the house to grab the work. We ain't doin' no talkin' so I'm on point with my hand on my heater inside the pocket of my big blue and white goose down. Although I've dealt with these cats a few times I didn't trust em because I knew they had got the homie Tim from OGP for fifteen with a staged jack move. That type of shit wasn't gonna happen to me my nigga, no way, and I'm fuckin' with damn near the last of the money that I had."

"Here's where shit starts to hit the fan. Buckshot walks in the kitchen with two sandwich ziplocs and puts em on the table and sits down across from me grittin' and shit. Then Mickey finishes his count tellin' me I'm seven fifty short. So, I run through the stacks real fast and true enough I was short be-cause moms got a nigga cause that was money I had at my grandaddy's crib. So, I tell Micky that I had some moves to make but I would come by later with the change then this nigga Buckshot says I'm a slow ass country nigga that can't count while he grabs the work and pulls it back in front of him. He and Mickey both start laughin' like a mutha fucka at a nigga. I don't even trip cause all I wanna do is get my work and get on so I chill. Then all of a sudden, this nigga Buckshot fucked around and got to boo bangin' too much cause he said why don't you send your mama by here and let her fade the rest of the money on her back and knees. I can't explain it, Tay, but I snapped out cause I just pulled out my heater and popped Buckshot three times. Mickey got up and tried to run but I shot him before he took two steps; he didn't make it outta the kitchen. So, I'm lookin' around for the spent shell casings on the floor when I feel somebody lookin' and when I look up I see this pretty bitch standin' in the doorway with a towel wrapped around her. She was holdin' her hands over her mouth, eyes bucked wide open, tryin to scream but nothin was comin' out cuz. I think she was in shock or somethin' cause I was tryin' to call out to her then all of a sudden all of the shit she was holdin' in by havin' her mouth covered up come out loud for a second when she looked up at me. I plugged her ass too...she caught one in the titty and one bit her in the neck. After that, I grabbed the work and money off the table stuffin' it in my coat pockets. I looked for the last two casings, but I could only find one, I was like fuck it because I'd been in the house long enough, so I stepped over that ho and Mickey in the doorway and headed to the door. I wiped off the doorknob with my shirt and bopped in my IROC and smashed out."

"Pass the Remy and tell me how you got away with a double m four blocks away from where you get money at?" Dollaz asked curiously while reaching for the bottle of liquor.

Big Tay took a drink and frowned as he passed the bottle over, then he reached down and adjusted the bypass to liven up the tweets as he recalled the incidents that brought on the situation that Dollaz was inquiring about. After he got the sound like he wanted it Big Tay gripped the wood on the Fleur steering wheel and took a deep breath.

"After what all you told me, and I look around us right now it's hard to believe that we ain't havin' this conversation in the pen." Big Tay spoke out as he got comfortable in the soft leather.

"Come on my nigga, dont get all sensitive and shit. What's done is done and can't be taken back. When you put yourself in the types of situations that can take you to a point that involves you or them bein' at a funeral believe me when I tell ya that I don't wanna be the one layin' down. You better wake up and see what time it is cause right now the level of game that you niggas have made it to is gonna involve more killin' and jail time sooner or later. There's no way around it cuz, it's already written in the equation so are you gonna give me the spill or what?"

Big Tay stretched and began yawning causing the K-5 to swerve off of the interstate prompting Dollaz to reach over and grab the wheel quickly.

"Good lookin' out homie, damn I'm tired as a mutha fucka. Last night I was diggin' up in my new little broad from Midwest City off and on until about five this mornin'..."

"'Nigga don't nobody care cause you got one of them siddity ass Midwest City broads. Stop stallin' and get to the business." Dollaz demanded with ag-gression after cutting Big Tay off.

"Chill out fool! In real life the shit's your fault cause when you got cracked for that dumb shit our money was already fucked up cause we still had-n't made up for the dough that Malcolm gave you when you wanted out. Then we had to come up with another twenty-five to give that lawyer for your black ass."

Dollaz pointed at himself with his thumb as he scowled towards Big Tay and wondered why everybody keeps tellin' him that everything was his fault. Big Tay and him looked at one another, although he knew that Dollaz wanted to say something he didn't. Big Tay decided to continue with his story.

"Dollaz our friendship goes beyond bein' Ghetto Merchants but rather you look at it like this everybody knows that we're all brothers and here you go and get caught up on a murder beef that carried three bodies in a house that had five and a half bricks in it. That alone could've gotten the heavies involved in it; therefore that woulda gotten us in it because the locals woulda given them information to take to the grand jury to say it was gang related instead of game related. That's why I say it's your fault nigga. We all had to pretty much go underground causin' all of our big sales to go to somebody else while we stayed low hopin' that the feds or OCPD wasn't gonna come looking for us too."

"After a few weeks passed, Malcolm came up with a plan for us that would keep us off the scene but still gettin' paid at the same time. He put himself, Solo and Gooch in different crack spots sellin' nothin' but stones. I went back to the Hall's and got down in the same spot but I got help from a few of my little homies over there to help me pump round the clock. I bullshit you not Dollaz, every spot we had rolled the hinges off the doors cause we had them big ass boulders. At that point of the game the only time we hung out was when we meet up at Solo and Gooch's apartment that they had over on N.W. 48th and Blackwelder. That's where we chopped down and separated the work along with the bill money. Other than that, everybody was on a strict twenty dollar a day spendin' limit. We was able to keep that up because Javon was keepin' us plugged with that good A-1 work that Malcolm was droppin' in that Pyrex on top of the stove. The weight clientele that we did have left we let Javon get them. We did that for six months."

"When Juneteenth rolled around, we was all good and everybody gotta chance to spend a little money. Cuz, I got house payments now on a nice little somethin' over in Del City cause I was tired of bein' over in other people's shit. Malcolm encouraged me to find somethin' and I did he also says that we all need to come up with a plan to get somethin' legit so we can get off the streets before things got bad cause what

goes up has to come down sooner than later. He seems to
think that if a nigga get out the game on top, we can build a
solid foundation underneath to keep a nigga from fallin' back
down too far. Anyway, it was about this time of day and I was
comin' outta Red's store with a bag full of wings, so I stopped
to check a few pages. That's when hood rat Theresa and her
people from outta town pull up high-sidin' in a Lincoln rental.
Them niggas come out here and started puttin' niggas on
their set and then puttin' em down with a little work tryin' to
sew up the projects. I wasn't trippin' cause regardless of who
had work, I was still gettin' mine. All while everybody was
thinkin' the Ghetto Merchants was through because when
somebody would ask a nigga if I seen one of the homies I
would be like I ain't seen them niggas in a grip."
"Anyway, these niggas named Roscoe and Sampson hop oulla
the rental while Theressa stayed in there so everybody could
see her tramp ass behind the wheel. These two niggas walk
up on me, and I put my bag of chicken on top of the phone
box and hung up the receiver—ready to knuckle up with both
of em. What I thought was gonna be some funk turned out to
be Sampson askin' me why I don't cop work from them cause
they knew that I was in the back buildin' of the projects
clockin' a grip. So, I play it cool and say that I'm good with the
connection I already got. He returns by sayin' if the connect is
so good why was I spendin' endless days and nights in the
projects slangin' rocks? While me and Roscoe was talkin' his
boy Sampson was right there eyeballin' a nigga with his arms
crossed like he was the shit. I started feeling like they was
tryin' to put the press game down on me and they had
enough niggas over there followin' them to make somethin'
happen. You know when it comes to gang shit niggas tend to
not care if you was raised over there or not if you ain't down
with the type of shit that they tryin' to do. So, I felt that
before I lost my grip on where I was born and raised by some
weak-minded niggas that been knowin' me their whole lives I

was gonna get rid of the problems before they got any bigger..."

Buzzing from the alcohol, Dollaz was now caught up in the story and began to rub his hands together, anxiously waiting for the action.

"Okay okay, this is what a nigga been waitin' for. Come on with the rest." Dollaz spoke out with excitement written all over his face.

"Damn, I can't believe I missed the exit to the mall. Fuck it we'll keep rollin' and slide up in Sooner Fashion Mall and fuck with some OU broads. So, check this part out, I tell Roscoe and Sampson that my plug was chargin' me eight g's for nine soft and that I wanted to buy a half thang for fourteen. How bout Roscoe says he'll do it? I tell them that my bread is at my uncle's house and he don't get off work until eight o'clock at night. Sampson ask me where my uncle lives cause they'll meet me over there if it's cool. Cuz I gotta be the quickest thinkin' mutha fucka in the world cause I remembered this house for rent on 34th that didn't have a sign in the yard. You know over there on the east side of Prospect where 34th loops all the way back around to Prospect?" Big Tay asked Dollaz then he continued.

"So, I give them the address and we agreed on nine o' clock which gave me plenty enough time to put my scheme in to play. Soon as I made it back inside the projects, I gave one of the little homies on my team a couple grams to rent a smoker bucket for all day and night. Soon as he found one, I tucked the old smoker dude in the back room at the spot with a broad and made sure they had everythang they needed to stay out the way and not needin' to go no place in that bucket. About eight thirty I jumped in the bucket and crept over to 34th and backed in the driveway of the rental property hopin' like a mutha fucka that none of the neighbors trip or call the police. I patiently waited for Roscoe and Sampson to show up cause I had a surprise waitin' for them they never would've expected in a hundred years..." Big Tay laughed at himself for a moment before he continued.

"I hadn't been there three minutes before I got that blessin' in disguise. The Lincoln rental pulled down the block slowly and I flashed the lights on the raggedy Buick Century so they could see me. They pulled into the driveway as I got out of the car holdin' a McDonald's bag, doubled up with a .38 that had a potato stuck on the end of the barrel inside, along with a sixteen-ounce soda bottle filled with gasoline. The only thang that could possibly go wrong would be if they asked me for the money first. I slid in the backseat behind Roscoe; Samp-son was behind the wheel and the car was full of indo smoke with a blunt burnin'. That asshole Sampson said they was in a hurry, so he tossed the yao back to me hopin' that I was gonna do the same with some money. Instead, I grabbed the work and felt around on the gallon ziplock bag to make it look like I was really checkin' the dope out...in the dark. All of a sudden Roscoe turns around in the seat and snaps at me, tellin' me to give up the money or the yao cause they was in a hurry. I play it off by laughin' a little bit and said some ol' bullshit like since I'm spendin' my money, I should be able to take my time so now I'm kinda pissed off cause I felt like the nigga was trippin' out on me."

"So, I calmly put the work to the side and stuck my hand inside the McDonalds bag and pulled out the .38 and put it in Roscoe's face and pulled the trigger cause he was turned around still bein' nosey and pushy. Before Sampson could make a move, I put three in him and two more in Roscoe. I jumped outta the backseat and looked around then I ran around the car and opened the driver's door and scooted Sampson over and I got inside and closed the door. I let the passenger seat back so their bodies couldn't be seen easy. Bloody shit was everywhere cuz, I mean everywhere, even on the windshield. The car was still runnin' so I backed out and smashed up to Prospect and made a left. I smashed down the dip all the way up to 30th and made a right. A coupla cars passed a nigga but I kept doin' me until I got right there by Northeast High and that's when I noticed that they was ridin' with a full tank so I decided to do some shit that I seen on a movie, I pulled in the back of the school to that wooded area past the football field and parked. I got outta the car opened the back door grabbed the work and put it inside the McDonald's bag and took out the gasoline, unscrewed the cap and doused almost the whole thang inside of the car, niggas and all. Then I took my blue rag outta my back pocket and tore it in half where it was still together, popped the fuel door and unscrewed the gas cap and stuffed the rag. I pulled my lighter out lit it then figured that I'd better put some gas on the rag too so I took the rag out and poured the rest of the gas from the soda bottle on it then I stuffed it back into the gas tank. I lit the end, and it started to burn, so I opened the car door tore a piece of the paper from the McDonald's bag and lit that and threw it in and the inside of the car went up in flames. I grabbed the soda bottle and the bag and hit the treeline. Before I crossed 30th I almost snapped my neck turnin' around when I heard the Lincoln explode. When I turned back around there were two cars comin' towards me, so I ran across the street and hit the woods on the other side and ran all the way to the back fence of the projects. I climbed over and made it to my spot and took off all that gas smellin' shit in the kitchen and stuffed them in a trash bag. I took a shower and then went to the bedroom and kicked old school and that broad out to the livin' room while I got dressed. I let them chill with me for a few more hours before I got a ride to go pick up his car. Thank God the car was still sittin' there. Mission accomplished with eighteen ounces of free yao and two headaches gone. You see Dollaz what I've come to find out about street niggas is that they're predictable. I knew Sampson and Roscoe was gonna be high and they would be slippin'. Slippers count, and in their case, it cost them their lives, not mine."

Chapter 11

As soon as Solo stepped out of the shower, he could hear his beeper beeping from the bedroom. He rushed to check it out finding that he had six pages on display. Everybody who owed him he called back letting them know that he was on his way. Those who didn't owe him, he called and let them know that he would get back with them next week. Between calls Solo managed to get dressed and fresh with a Nautica long sleeve shirt with matching jeans. On his feet he slid on Polo boots along with a squirt of Polo cologne.

Admiring himself in the mirror, he realized that he had to get his hair braided before the road trip as he put on his watch and necklace. As Solo watched the colors dazzling from the diamonds and rubies in his GM medallion, he got hyped up thinking about how they were going to shake the city up when they got back in town. After giving himself a wink and a grin he clipped his beeper to his belt and counted out a thousand-dollar stack and slid it inside his left front pocket. In his right pocket, he slid his Glock. Solo then pulled his phone off the charger and headed out in traffic, feeling like he was the king of the world.

Malcolm drove through the alley that led to Amber's garage, surprised to find the door raised. Carefully, he pulled in and parked next to her Nissan Maxima and killed the engine. Afterwards, he walked through the connecting laundry room, which led to the kitchen, where Gooch followed behind Malcolm but managed to stop at the refrigerator. Malcolm kept pushing on towards the small hallway where, if you go straight ahead, there was a half bathroom. If you turn right that led to the living area and left led upstairs to the bedroom. Malcolm checked the living room and found no Amber, so he went back the other way and headed up the stairs. When he got halfway up Amber appeared holding on to the rail taking a step down wearing a short pink robe and a white towel wrapped around her head.

"You're right on time, Mr. Love, I just got out of the shower. Amber spoke in a low seductive tone. Malcolm smiled at her as the two met face to face on the stairwell with him two steps below. Amber untied her robe as she kissed him softly on his cheek. She held open her robe revealing her voluptuous body causing Malcolm to stare.

"Yo Amber, can I use the phone?" Gooch asked, standing at the bottom of the stairs.

"Oh my God...Malcolm!" Amber shouted while quickly closing her robe to get behind Malcolm then peeking from behind showing off her blushing cheeks.

"Go ahead, Gooch, make yourself at home." She replied. Amber playfully hit Malcolm in the chest as he chuckled about the incident, then she turned around and darted back up the stairs. Malcolm walked up slowly as he popped his knuckles.

Inside the bedroom, Keith Sweat was playing, and Amber was standing in front of the bed wearing nothing but a towel wrapped around her head. Malcolm closed the door and began to walk closer as she unwrapped the towel and shook her head and dropped it to the floor. When Malcolm made it to her, he rubbed his fingers through her hair with both hands causing Amber to hold her breath as she pushed her face into his chest and filled her lungs with the smell of his body. After

Malcolm's hands left her head, they drifted all the way down to her butt while he passionately kissed her on the neck.

"Babe, I need you now. Stay with me a while, at least until it's time for me to go to my class." Amber spoke out between moans of desperation to have Malcolm inside of her.

"Way too much goin' on today, Red, besides Gooch is downstairs." He whispered in her ear. Amber broke Malcolm's grasp by taking a small step backward while looking deep into his brown eyes with a plan to captivate his attention. She raised her right hand to her titty and began to rub on her nipple and licking her lips she gradually slid her left hand between her legs. Malcolm looked on as her breaths began to get shorter and her eyelids began to shudder from the pleasure that she was giving herself. Loving what he was seeing with his eyes and his little head Malcolm was not so concerned about Gooch being downstairs. It took only a few moments for Amber to step back to Malcolm. There she grabbed his pistol out of his pocket, knelt down and placed it on the floor. Raising back up she grabbed his hand and led him to the bed turning him around where his back was towards the bed and he faced the door.

"Do I ask for a lot of your time? Do I not do everything and more that you ask of me? Do you like what you see inside my eyes and what I have to offer you with my body and how I respond when you run your fingers through my hair?"

Without saying a word, Malcolm answered her questions with his eyes looking up and down her body. She knew the answers already; therefore, there was no need to talk. Amber took it upon herself and unbuckled his belt and unbuttoned his jeans. Slowly, she unbuttoned his shirt. Reaching under his

118

t-shirt and pulling them both off with his help. After throwing them to the floor, she put both of her hands around his waist and slid his jeans and boxers down. As she went down, she spread her legs apart and squatted in front of him and put his semi-hard dick into her mouth while holding on to the back of his legs. Malcolm grabbed hold to her hair with one hand and put the other on her shoulder as they got into a rhythm as she looked up and he looked down. Amber applied more pressure as she slowed down causing her and him to moan. Within five minutes she had him to the point of exploding but she didn't want him to cum yet because she had another agenda, so she stopped.

"Malcolm you never answered my questions...why?" When Malcolm reopened his eyes, he saw a face that almost looked devilish. Realizing she wanted to play a game he decided to give in and let her have some fun.
"Yeah, is the answer to all your questions, now show me some more of that good shit!" He let out a growl as he responded. Malcolm's authoritative voice turned Amber on making her cum. She stood up and walked around him, sitting at the end of the bed, she leaned back, opening her legs, revealing her shaved monkey.

"Come and fuck me...now!" She commanded and Malcolm grinned before he took a careful step because of his heavily starched jeans hanging below his knees. He grabbed his piece and pulled on it and guided it inside Amber and slowly went in as far as her walls would allow him to. She bit down on her lip and groaned as Malcolm pulled out and went in deeper with every stroke. "Is this what you want...huh...talk to me?" Malcolm asked. Malcolm began to go in harder and harder and Amber's moans became louder, and her face began to turn red.

Malcolm kept going in changing nothing except for putting his hands under her hips and pulling her in with every stroke. This caused him to get to the point of busting a nut when he looked at the sweat beads off his head drop down on her stomach.
"Call me a bitch, Malcolm, call me a bitch...oh shit I'm cumin again Malcolm."

Malcolm held on as long as he could, but when he felt Amber's walls get super-hot and wet, he couldn't hold back any longer. He let his load go inside. After going all the way inside of her for a moment of weakness and ecstasy, he pulled out and jacked the rest of his load on her stomach.

"Oh shitttt...bitch!" Malcolm obliged with his eyes closed. "Open your eyes babe. Amber slowly scooted off the bed holding Malcolm by his sides as he backed up. When she had enough room, she got down on her knees and put his piece back inside her mouth. In no time she had Malcolm's dick back hard as she hummed and smacked on him. When Amber's performance had him about to cum again his left knee began to shake causing him to stumble backwards. She tried to catch him, but he was too heavy for her to stop his fall that made her hit her knee on his 45.

"Shit! Babe, I'm sorry for making you fall."

Amber sprang up from the floor and straddled over him with her arms stretched out to help him up as they both began to laugh. Suddenly, there was an unsuspect-ing knock with the doorknob rattling.

"Malcolm, you cool?" Gooch yelled. Amber covered her mouth and bucked her eyes and ran across the floor to the bathroom while Malcolm raised his back off of the floor. "I'm cool lil cuz...be down in a minute," Malcolm replied. After taking a quick shower with Amber and getting dressed, Malcolm went downstairs, finding Gooch in the living room watching an interview on ESPN with Buffalo Bills quarterback Jim Kelly. Standing quietly in the doorway, Malcolm observed Gooch watching television, knowing that his real passion was for the game of football and not pushing drugs. Finally noticing Malcolm looking at him, Gooch smiled at him, looking like a big kid.

"You miss that shit, little cuz?" Malcolm asked as he walked towards the sofa where Gooch was sitting.

"Hell yeah, so do you." Malcolm sat down on the couch and stared at Gooch for a moment, thinking of the proper words to tell him about the football remarks.

"I miss it too, but it's too late for me to go chasin' a football career. You're pro material—6'2" 230 pounds—come on, man you were gonna be startin' outside linebacker for the Sooners. I coulda went to a small college and got some playin' time, but look how I opted out for the streets. Don't get it twisted, I like havin' you around but I..."

The doorbell rang, interrupting Malcolm and Gooch sprang to his feet, headed towards the door. Malcolm jumped up after him quickly, catching him and grabbing his arm, he cut in front of him and put his eye to the peephole. After looking out for a split second, Malcolm turned around, facing Gooch's smiling face.

"Nigga...you ordered some pizza?" Malcolm laughed.

Gooch flipped his thumb up and over, signaling for Malcolm

to get out of the way.

"Yeah, watch out so I can pay for it." Gooch dug into his pocket and bumped Malcolm out of the way.

After the pizza man left, they stood at the dining table pouring soda and filling their plates with pizza. "Like I was sayin' before the pizza man got here, I like havin' you around, but I think you should consider goin' back to school. You wouldn't have to worry bout nothin' but class and football and let us handle the rest." Gooch listened to Malcolm and chose not to tell him that he had several offers from Division I and II football programs since his 1990 suspension from Oklahoma University and the NCAA. He had to tell Malcolm something to get him off of his back and let him know that he was doing what he wanted to do just like everyone else in their crew.

"Hear me out for a minute, Malcolm. I know I fuck up sometimes, but I promise that I'll tighten my shit up. As far as school goes...I don't wanna fuck with that shit right now cuz. I wanna fuck with you and Solo, I like hustlin' even though I ain't real good at it but one thang I know is that I gotcha back."

Gooch explained with a serious look on his face hoping his reasons would be good enough for Malcolm.

"You sprung on the little money we havin' and the thought of knowin' that we're about to get more. Just think what we could have if you went back to school and dominated that shit and got drafted in the first or second round. This little drug money we havin' wouldn't be shit then and we could clean it up easy. You feel me?"

GHETTO MERCHANTS

Gooch listened to Malcolm while stuffing half a slice of pizza into his mouth and trying to swallow it with half a glass of soda. He chewed for a moment, then he let out a loud belch before answering.

"I' wanna be with you niggas, cuz, unless you puttin' me out the crew? Look Malcolm, what you sayin' is true but if I ain't ready in my head, I ain't gonna be able to focus on class or practice. On some real shit I'll think about lookin' into goin' back in the fall. Maybe by then I'll be ready, and we'll be rich." Malcolm shrugged his shoulders.

"Maybe so."

After leaving the travel agency and Foley's, Paperboy and Hoodsta walked through the food court in route to a row of pay phones. They decided it was best to call up to Minneapolis right now so that someone would be there to pick them up from Minneapolis St. Paul International Airport. Hoodsta stopped at the Corn Dog Depot while Paperboy continued on to the phone to handle the business. He dropped the shopping bags to the floor, picked up the receiver and hit O along with the rest of the phone number that he had known since he was a boy. When the operator answered he gave her his name requesting a collect call in which she patched him through. On the third ring Paperboy's uncle answered and accepted.

"Unc, me and my homeboy are touchin' down at Minneapolis St. Paul Intern-ational on Delta flight 342 at 6:40 this evenin'. Can you pick us up or do we need to catch a cab?"

"Cab...hell naw nephew you ain't gonna take no cab, I'll be

there. Hey boy your daddy just left from over here about thirty minutes ago. We was just talkin' bout cha. I told em that you was supposed to be up here but since you hadn't called, I didn't think you was gonna show."

"Oh really, well let him know that I'm on my way. Unc don't forget to be there to pick us up at 6:40 on Delta flight 342." Paperboy explained. "I"m writtin' it down right now, nephew. I'll be there, bye."

Paperboy hung up the phone and picked up his bags while spotting Hoodsta heading towards a table in the middle of the food court. When he made it out in the open, he whistled, catching Hoodsta's attention while he kept walking towards the escalator that was going to the bottom level.

Chapter 12

Solo checked all the important traps before he made his move over to the Mim's residence in the suburban middle-class and old money neighborhood of blacks, Forest Park. In the driveway was a white Z-24 Chevy Cavalier that belonged to Javon's sister Jazmin. Solo slowed down as he pulled into the driveway, parking behind the car. He put the Cadillac in reverse and started to back out and get on because he did not see Javon's Corvette or his Range Rover. Suddenly, an idea told him to park and get out to check if he was in the house because he could've switched up vehicles trying to stay low-key.

He got out and walked to the front door and rang the doorbell. As he waited for someone to answer the door, Solo glanced inside through the glass door. ·

After waiting a moment for someone to come, he rang the bell again but de-cided to head out to Edmond to finish up the business with Malcolm and Gooch.

Fuck Javon anyway because they no longer needed him.

Solo stepped down the walk, looking across the street at the new house that was being built, knowing that one day soon he would have the finances to do the same if he chose. Snapping back into reality, he heard a noise from the door opening up behind him. When he turned around, he saw Jazmin holding open the glass door wearing black tights, no shoes and a white tank top with her nipples poking and catching his attention. Jazmin had a dark complexion with a face like a doll, complementing her bob hairdo and her body was perfect. Solo stopped and stared at her momentarily.

"Damn you fine!" He unexpectedly spoke out after licking his lips."

"Boy, shut up, you ain't trying to mess with me. Every time I see you out and about, you always got some hoodrats around, and I'm not the type of girl to interrupt your mack game and look like a hater. You must be looking for my brother, huh?"

"Unfortunately, I am, is he here?" Solo spoke slowly with wandering eyes that Jazmin was noticing.

"No, ain't nobody here but me. Mother just went to the bingo hall and my daddy is at his shop. Why don't you come in and kick it for a little while?"

Solo looked around then at his watch as he contemplated on staying. Jazmin stepped out on the porch a little further, putting her butt against the door and crossing her arms up under her chest making it look even more appealing. Solo's contemplation was that Jazmin used to be Malcolm's girl back in the day and she was Javon's little sister. After quickly weighing all of those options out, he stepped across the threshold of the Mim's residence.

Immediately, Jazmin moved in behind him locking the glass door and closing the other one as well, then she headed towards the kitchen switching her ass. Solo stood there and watched her until she stopped and put her hand on her hip and twisted around and winked at him Then she beckoned him to follow her with a head nod. Solo proceeded after her all the while wondering why Malcolm dump this fine ass bitch. Surely not for Deziree, although she was fine as hell too cause she had the long pretty hair and caramel-colored skin with a banging body. Still, she couldn't compare to Jazmin's black ass. When Solo made it inside the kitchen, Jazmin was standing in front of the refrigerator with the door open.

"Can I get you something to drink, snack or anything?"

"Let me get some juice, any kind.'' Solo took a seat at the kitchen table while looking around the newly remodeled kitchen, then he planted his attention back on Jazmin's frame and knew that he had to hurry and get on.

"I been tryin' to catch up with your crazy ass brother for the last couple of days. This dude can't be found nowhere in the city." Jazmin came to the table with a glass of apple juice, handing it to Solo. Before she sat down, she scooted her chair over so that she would be closer to Solo.

"He was over here Wednesday night to get some money. He had some out in the garage in his Corvette and he got some out of my mother's bedroom. They had an argument and mother got really upset with him about something. Anyway, he said he was going to some car show in Texas. And before he left my mother told him that she wasn't going to give him anymore of hers because he messed all of his off..."

Jazmin paused for a moment and played with Solo's braids. "If you have time, I'll braid your hair because it's all frizzy?"

"Yeah, I gotta little time if you can do it now?" Solo asked anxiously as he looked down at her nipples bulging through the tank top—while trying to make sense of what Jazmin said about her mother and Javon's conversation two nights ago. Furthermore, he was feeling a little uncomfortable about the situation that was going on, but he was going with it.

"I can do it right now, follow me to my bedroom where all my hair stuff is." Jazmin stood up and Solo followed her to the bedroom where he flopped down on the bed and Jazmin walked over to her vanity. Once again in the back of his mind Solo thought about Jazmin being Malcolm's ex girl, not giving a fuck about how Javon would feel about what he was thinking. That was when Jazmin turned around and began walking his way swaying her hips while her breast jiggled with every step. Solo put her and Malcolm's high school relationship out of his mind because that was some shit that happened way before he moved to Oklahoma, besides she needed some dick in that moment. For one rea-son, she wanted some, and secondly, she talked too much and he needed to reward her for telling him Javon's business.

Jazmin climbed on the bed with a comb and a small tub with some other products in it. She scooted up behind Solo rubbing her chest on his back while she tried to get in position. It brought a smile to Solo's face and a rise in his jeans.

"Hey girl, why you bring me back here?" Without saying a word Jazmin leaned back and pulled off her tank top. Solo twisted around and leaned back and caught his balance with his right arm. After repositioning himself, sitting on the edge of the bed he leaned into Jazmin's chest with his mouth open. Jazmin grabbed the back of his head with both hands and pulled him in closer, throwing her leg around him getting into his lap. Once in position, she pulled Solo's face up and met him with hers and they began to tongue kiss for a moment.

Jazmin broke free from Solo's embrace and pushed him back on the bed and she stood up and slid her tights down showing Solo her close-cut patch of hair outlining her monkey and the most perfect body that he had ever seen. She bent down untied and took off his boots while he unbuckled his belt and unbuttoned and unzipped his jeans. When Jazmin rose up and looked into Solo's face and at his waist, she knew he was ready. She grabbed both of his pant legs and began pulling them off causing Solo to hurry and grab his pistol placing it on the side of the bed. Once she took his jeans off, she opened the small pink tub that she placed on the bed and pulled out a blackjack condom and a tube of KY jelly. Solo swallowed hard as he observed Jazmin in disbelief that this was really happening. Neither had said a word in minutes. Quickly Solo raised his back off of the bed and pulled his shirt off and tossed it over to the side seeing Jazmin with a big smile on her face while she was looking down at his hard dick.

"Damn, girl, you sure don't believe in wastin' time do ya?"

Jazmin shook her head no and sat the condom and lubricant on the bed and spread Solo's legs apart then bent over, grabbing his dick and pulled on it gently while licking her lips. She braced herself with her left arm down on the firm bed while still pulling on Solo's dick.

"What do you want me to do now?" She teased. It was obvious now to Solo that Jazmin was into the cat and mouse game, which had been demonstrated since he walked into the house. He decided that he was gone play along too.

"You can do whatever you want just as long as you don't bite it."

As if she had been waiting on his consent Jazmin looked Solo in the eyes as she slightly closed her lips and forced her mouth over his dick. Solo tilted his head back and bit his lip, trying to blow off the pleasure that Jazmin was giving him with her head game. It was feeling so good, he almost wanted her to stop.

"Damn, Jazmin this is the bomb girl," was all Solo could mutter out of his mouth besides moans.

Jazmin stopped and giggled as she reached over and picked up the condom, tossing it on Solo's chest. She grabbed the KY.

"I've got something special for you, Solo, with your manish self, put on that condom."

Jazmin flipped the top on the KY and squeezed some of it on her fingers before she placed the tube back in the box. She reached behind her back and began to rub her hand down her ass.

This freak bitch wants me to fuck her in the ass.

Solo was shocked as he watched her while he rolled the blackjack down on his dick.

"I've been wanting to do this with you since last summer when you came down the strip flossing in your new 5.0. Right now, I got the chance to do it so I'm going to, now scoot back on the bed some more."

As Solo complied to her request Jazmin stepped up on top of the bed and stood over him and squatted down until she reached the tip of his dick. She grabbed it and began guiding it into her asshole. Being over-anxious Solo grabbed her hips and tried to pull her down on him, but she resisted and slapped his hand.

GHETTO MERCHANTS

"Boy, let me do this okay." After a few minutes of patience, Solo was in. Jazmin slid down little by little until she got to the point that she wanted, and she balanced herself by leaning back, holding herself up with both arms. She gradually slid up and down until she had Solo's dick all the way inside her down to his nuts. This was Solo's first time having anal sex and he couldn't believe that he was getting turned out by one of Malcolm's old hoes while doing it. As Jazmin began moaning louder and bucking up and down like a wild horse Solo pushed back while looking at her pretty pussy gapped open with his dick in her ass at the same time. Overwhelmed he tried not to cum. Solo decided to take matters into his own hands and put Jazmin and himself to the test as far as he was concerned.

Solo raised up on his elbows, quickly reaching forward, grabbing Jazmin by her hips, pulling her all the way in while gripping her tight with his left hand and hooking around behind her with his right arm. He raised himself up with her pinned against him and flipped her on her back then he grabbed her behind her knees pulling her ass up just enough to start gunning her down. Turned on by Solo's sudden aggression, Jazmin did her best to meet him with every stroke.

"Ohhh yeahh, Solo, that's how I like it baby. Don't stop, don't stop, keep fuckin' that asshole and make me cum some more!" Jazmin shouted out at the top of her lungs. Those words put Solo in the zone making him feel like he was a real-life porno star as he held his nut and closed his eyes and thought about baseball. After what he felt like was five minutes, he opened his eyes and looked down at the penetration of the long stroking he was doing to find out that the rubber was gone. He ignored it saying fuck it and went all the way in and grinded down until he busted off causing Jazmin to do the same because she held onto him tightly.

Then he pulled out slowly.

"Goddamn...look at this shit Jazmin!"

When Amber arrived downstairs, she was wearing a blue sweatshirt with CSU BRONCOS displayed on the front with gold letters, faded Guess jeans and a pair of gold and blue Nike Cortez. She stopped at the dining table, opened the box of pizza and grabbed a slice. then she headed to the couch where Malcolm and Gooch were sitting, watching ESPN. She walked around the coffee table and sat beside Malcolm causing him to scoot over towards Gooch and slide his mobile phone over.

"So, Gooch, do you think the Cowboys got a chance to make it to the Super Bowl next year?" Asked Amber then she took a bite of pizza. Gooch started laughing as he leaned forward, looking around Malcolm to Amber.

"Come on white girl, you don't know shit about football," Gooch stated sarcastically. Finding no amusement in Gooch's statement, Amber quickly took another bite of pizza and touched Malcolm on his arm to get his attention, feeding him the last bite while she chewed. Amber scooted forward to the edge of the sofa cushion and picked up the glass of soda that was in front of Malcolm and took a big drink.

"Dang...babe, why didn't you let me know that was spicy like that?" Amber asked.

"What time do you go to class?" Malcolm asked, never taking his eyes off the television. Amber frowned as she looked at

GHETTO MERCHANTS

Malcolm and tapped him on his leg. She sat the glass back down on the coaster.

"You are such an asshole sometimes and as for you, Mr. Gooch, I'll have you know that I took a course in the theory of coaching football a few semesters back. Now there, I know more than you think. She explained.

"Come on Amber, are you serious, Central State, there's nobody up here qualified to teach shit about football since Pinkey Hurley and K. T. went on to the league," Gooch replied.

"Since you have all the answers about the football program at my school, why don't you come up there and bring your blue-chip All-American skills and help turn our program around? Do you know if you did that, our recruiting would go up because there are lots of high school players that would love to play with you?"

Gooch stood up and gritted on Amber as he walked to the front door, opened it, walked out and closed it behind him. Amber and Malcolm watched in silence until the door closed. She faced Malcolm with a look of surprise on her face, about to say something. Malcolm put his finger up to his lips, signaling for her to be quiet.

"Leave that nigga alone about football cause he's sensitive as a muthafucka when it comes to him and that subject." He explained casually.

"Babe, I didn't say those words to him to piss him off, I meant what I was saying about him coming to CSU to play. Malcolm sometimes they still talk about him on Sports Center when the Sooners get their asses kicked and the analysts talk about what if Gary Tompson was playing in that linebacker position.

Why am I so wrong for trying to motivate him?"

"You're not wrong, but what you have to realize is that Gooch is goin' to have to motivate himself. Not even I can make him go back to school, and he probably listens to me more than he listens to my uncle and my auntie."

"I'm going outside to apologize to him."

"He'll be okay, don't trip, Red."

Malcolm leaned over and kissed her on the cheek, then turned his attention back to the big screen. Amber smiled and put her hand on his, noticing his busted knuckles for the first time. She sighed quietly and decided not to inquire.

"If you say so, oh yeah, I should have all of the paperwork done for your mother and you when I go to work on Monday. I've got to go downtown and get the LLC papers filed then we'll be able to get that money in escrow. I've got another surprise for you, but I can't tell you about it until I know that I'll be able to get it done."

Amber was interrupted by Malcolm's mobile phone ringing. He picked it up and pushed SEND, hoping that it might be Javon. "What up?" He asked.

"Nothing, what's up with you, Malcolm?" Deziree asked on the other end.

"Shittt, I'm out in traffic right now, I had to move my lowrider and do a few other things. Are you good?"

Amber stared in Malcolm's face, causing him to put her on a

mission to get her out of his business. "Go get me that backpack outta that bedroom closet I brought over last week."

"Who are you talking to?" Deziree asked. Amber got up without hesitation and walked out of the room.

"Hold up girlfriend, you askin' questions that ain't none of your business. What do you really want Deziree?" Malcolm asked angrily.

"Damn, Malcolm, I was just callin' to let you know that I was baking a lasagna this evening and I invited your brother over. If it's not too much of a problem, do you think you could grace us with your presence at dinner Your Highness, that is if you have time?" Deziree asked with heavy sarcasm in her voice.

Gooch walked back inside now with a frown instead of a scowl and kept on walking through the living room to the hallway.

"Okay, Deziree, I'll be there, lady, don't trip nigga I just got some shit goin' on as usual. What time is it goin' down?" He asked nonchalantly. Malcolm could hear Gooch and Amber talking as their voices got closer, approaching the dining table where Gooch took a seat and popped open the pizza box again.

"Is that Gary? Who's that girl talkin?" Deziree questioned.

"Hey, stop callin' my phone gettin' at me with some nosy bullshit. I'll see you later on." Malcolm pressed END.

Amber walked back around the coffee table and dropped the

beige Jansport backpack at Malcolm's feet, then she put her left leg back and posed in front of him with her hands on her hips and a big smile.

"Stop frowning, babe and scoot over, everything will be alright," Amber told him as she sat down, forcing Malcolm to scoot over again. Then she threw her legs over the arm of the couch and lay her head in his lap while he punched in Solo's mobile number and hit SEND.

He let it ring until it stopped and went to voicemail. Malcolm pressed END.

"I wonder why this nigga ain't answerin' his phone?" He asked, but not to anyone in particular.

Gooch answered him anyway. "Big cuz, you know if a nigga rollin' in the car, he can't hear the phone ringin', the beats is turned up. Just like you tell me all the time, be patient."

While Amber listened to Malcolm and Gooch's conversation, she devised a way to get Malcolm back to her condo this evening.

"You can use my car if you want, just drop me off on campus and pick me up at the library around seven. I've got some research that I need to get started on." Amber spoke out mannerly with the determination to win Malcolm over from all of the other women in his life.

She was confident that she had the ambition, spark, and determination to make Malcolm happy. All she needed was love from him because she worked hard to get in position to acquire her material needs, furthermore, she had the business mind to match Malcolm's. Together, there would be nothing that they could not have.

"That's good lookin' out, Amber, but I think we'll just wait right here like Gooch said." Amber sighed, with disappointment showing on her face.

She put her arm behind Malcolm's neck, using it as an anchor to raise herself up giving Malcolm a light kiss on the lips. She swung her legs down to the floor and stood up getting a slap on her butt from Malcolm causing her to jump.

"Hey! I guess I'll get going early then."

Amber giggled as she walked away from Malcolm towards the dining table, where she grabbed her Fendi purse and bookbag sitting in a chair. Gooch mumbled something to her as he stuffed his mouth with the last of the pizza and she headed towards the garage.

"Amber, did you get the money outta here like I asked?" Malcolm called after her as he unzipped the backpack.

From the kitchen, Amber turned around and rushed back to the living room.

"Babe, I deposited the money day before yesterday. Stop stressing about the stuff you know that I have under control, I got everything going in the right direction except for keeping you out of situations that are causing you to mess up those magical hands of yours. There's antibiotic ointment in the medicine cabinet and don't forget to set the alarm when you guys leave. Muah."

Amber blew Malcolm a kiss and waved bye to Gooch as she

DRE LUV

headed out to the garage.

Chapter 13

Solo came to Mims' residence looking for Javon a little more than an hour ago and ended up having a landmark sexual experience that he would never forget. Without a shadow of a doubt, he definitely wanted to see Jazmin again for a round two very soon.

Jazmin's initial plan started almost three years ago when she first saw Solo with Malcolm, and she found out they were cousins. She was still hurt from the breakup with Malcolm in high school, so she figured that if she ever got a chance to hurt Malcolm like he hurt her, she would. Finally, after all the years of waiting to execute the scheme, Solo showed up on her doorstep, gift-wrapped today ready to be a pawn. When she saw him in front of the house, she knew that with her sex appeal he would easily be lured into the house. There she had all intention on just sucking his dick and screwing him and telling Malcolm just to piss him off and never talk to Solo again. Instead, she decided that she would keep her and Solo's rendezvous to herself because she was turned on by the way he finished her off. She knew that she and Solo would be nothing more than a booty call because she was young, wild, and reckless and he was in no position to take a relationship seriously. But if he did, she could see herself being first in line for his love when the time was right.

After they got out of the shower, Jazmin hurried to get Solo on her floor between her legs and began braiding his hair. She knew he had things to do because his beeper kept beeping, and his mobile phone kept ringing. Solo ignored both while feeling the heat coming from between Jazmin's legs because she was wearing nothing but a towel.

"Jazmin."

"What Solo?" she asked.

"What put me in the position to be so fortunate to have this pleasure? It's gotta be somethin' cause shit like that just doesn't happen every day." Jazmin giggled as she tilted his head to the other side and put the comb down on his scalp.

"I don't know, well yes I do. It's been about four months since I broke up with my last boyfriend and I was horny. I know what you're thinking...I'm not a tramp Solo just because I let you fuck me in my ass. That's what I like and that's all it is to that. Furthermore, I have only been with three guys, well now four since me and Malcolm broke up April 21, 1987..."

Jazmin paused for a moment, noticing that she was getting teary-eyed and glad that Solo couldn't see her wipe her cheeks.

"I never got over Malcolm although my feelings for him have somewhat gone to a point where I'm not heartbroken over him anymore. I just never understood how he could rid me like he did when we were best friends. I'm the one who helped share the pain when he was down and out about the absence of his father and when he dreamed about someday moving Ms. Cecelia out of the apartments in Musgrave. Would you believe that I'm the one that asked my brother to help him out so he could make some money? I even lied to my mother and father and a homicide detective for him after he killed that security guard that killed his homeboy Chris."

Solo moved forward a little and twisted his upper body around by holding on to Jazmin's knee. The information that she was speaking about was news that he had never heard before and when someone talked about murder concerning his circle, it was no secret. Why was Jazmin telling him this now; was it a setup, or was she in the process of building a new friendship, or was she planning on going to the police?

"What the fuck you talkin' bout girl?" Solo asked her with eyes piercing her soul.

"Turn yourself around, boy and let me finish your hair. You look as if you didn't know, and you're Malcolm's favorite cousin..."

Jazmin calmly stated, then pulled Solo back between her legs and leaned his head over.

"Yeah, Solo, that cousin of yours thinks that he's so smart and I can't take nothing from him cause his clever little plan worked out perfectly for him. I'm gonna take you back to October 86...Ms. Cecelia took me and him out to eat at The Kettle after his football game. Afterwards she drops us off over here around midnight. I lied to Ms. Cecelia telling her that my parents said it was okay for him to spend the night but really they didn't and I sneaked him in because I knew they would be sleep. About six in the morning, he woke me up by giving me a kiss then he went out of the window. I thought he was just trying to get out just in case my daddy came in and caught him before he went to his shop as always at 7:30 Monday through Saturday. I went right back to sleep but before I knew it, I heard my window raising up and Malcolm was coming through it; it was 9:26 exactly on my alarm clock. He was soaking wet with sweat and the look on his face was like a person looks when they get caught doing something wrong, only difference was that Malcolm got away. Of course, I asked him what was wrong and where he'd been, but he blew off my questions and went right in there and took a long shower. When he finished, I was waiting for him with a towel and that was when he told me to go ask my mother to give him a ride home. He made sure to let me know that if I ever was asked, say that he'd been in my room all night since his mama dropped us off. Being the good girlfriend, I went right in the kitchen where my mother was drinking coffee and reading the paper and asked. She did just what he knew she would, she sits both of us down at that table and got on us about having safe sex so that I wouldn't get pregnant. My mother loved Malcolm and still does to this day and in her eyesight, he can't do no wrong, so she ended up fixing him breakfast and gave him a ride home around noon."

"The very next week we had a visit from some homicide detectives, one of them was named Detective Hawkins; the only reason I remember his name is because he was the one asking all the questions. Well, what happened was that they came to the school and picked him, Dollaz, and Big Tay up for questioning about the murder of a security guard. The man who killed Chris in the bank parking lot was gunned down right before the bank opened at nine o'clock when he was getting out of his car. You see, Solo, my mother, along with this house and most important, me were Malcolm's concrete alibi making it where he never spent one night in jail. Beings that Big Tay and Dollaz had nothing to do with it and their alibis were real they all coasted right out of some prison time. I never said anything to him about it and then he turns around and dumps me a week before the prom. For all these years I was wondering how I could get him back and when you moved down here, and it's no secret in the city about how close you and Malcolm are so I plotted on the chance of having sex with you and blabbing it to Malcolm so that it would piss him off and possibly messing up your relationship up. Then you flipped my plan and sprung a bitch today so you have my word that what happened, over here, will remain between you and I. Okay, I'm finished with your hair and the story, now you can go."

Solo stood up and remained quiet for a moment while he put on his shirt and put his pistol in his pocket with the thought crossing his mind he should shoot this bitch in the head right now. It wouldn't be smart because somebody saw him and the flashy Cadillac pulled over to the Mims' residence. "Have you told that story to anybody?" He asked while standing over Jazmin, who still sat on the bed.

"What! Malcolm isn't in jail, is he? You know damn well that if I would have told someone he would have been gone especially since it's him. People don't like Malcolm except those he has a personal relationship with; others hate him or fear him. I'm no snitch, Solo." Jazmin explained feeling uneasy about the situation.

"You ain't a snitch but you'll fuck his cousin, ain't that a bitch." Solo snapped back with a smirk on his face. Solo's last comment made Jazmin stand up to face him. When she did he reached around and gripped her ass making her push him away causing her towel to slip off.

"Get your smart ass out of my house boy!" Jazmin shouted jokingly as she reached down to pick the towel up to cover with. Solo chuckled at the situation while reaching into his left pocket where he pulled out a knot of money and some beeper cards. He peeled off a twenty-dollar bill and a card and handed them both to Jazmin. Unsurprisingly she accepted them both with a smile.
"Thanks for everythang sexy." Solo said with a smile as he

turned around and walked out of the room, thinking that Jazmin could be the downfall to the Ghetto Merchants.

After leaving Forest Park, Solo made a couple of stops consisting of cameo appearances only to be seen flossing in a new car before making it to Amber's front door. He rang the doorbell while holding his phone and the keys in his other hand. Malcolm crept to the door and looked through the peephole, seeing Solo. Malcolm turned around, facing Gooch, who was staring his way with his arms in the air, wondering what was up. Malcolm waved him over, then put his finger over his lips, signaling Gooch to be quiet. When Gooch made it to Malcolm, the doorbell was ringing again and Solo shouted out with a disguised voice. "Dominos!"'

"It's Solo's dumb ass out there playin' and shit. Check game, I'm gonna open the door real quick and you snatch that little yella nigga inside."

"I don't know Malcolm, he'll probably trip." Gooch whispered back. Malcolm scowled back at him while pointing at the door. Gooch then nodded his head up and down, showing his approval. Malcolm eased the lock open then snatched the door open while Gooch reached out with both hands and snatched Solo off of his feet by grabbing hold to his shirt pulling him inside. "Heyyyyyy!

He yelled out while in mid-air with his eyes wide open as he tumbled to the floor and his pistol fell out of his pocket. Malcolm closed the door while he and Gooch both roared in laughter as they watched Solo's reaction when he sprang from the floor with a look of terror on his face. Solo straightened his shirt and balled his fist up as he walked across the floor to pick up his pistol that was lying beside

Gooch, who was rolling on the floor laughing.

"Fuck y'all." Solo picked up his pistol and playfully kicked Gooch in the leg then he found himself starting to laugh as he walked to the couch and sat down where he picked up the remote and changed the television to BET. "Y'all can stop that shit, it ain't that funny."

"We might and might not you cry baby...holdup, anyway I been callin' and beepin' you for two hours nigga. Where you been?" Malcolm asked.

"I been over to your mama in laws house nigga, I got my hair braided." Solo answered as he stood up and pulled money out of his pockets, dropping it on the table, then he sat back down, raised up his jeans and pulled some wads out from his socks. Malcolm, still with laughter coming from his mouth, walked over to the couch and sat down and began running through the bills. After he finished counting, he handed Solo and Gooch both two g's then put the rest in the backpack that Amber had brought downstairs. Gooch stood up from the floor, watching Solo stare at him. He stuck his money in his pocket and grabbed the duffel bag that was in the trunk of the Impala. "Let's roll outta here and do somethin'," Gooch suggested as he looked at Malcolm and Solo.

"You can drop the bag cuz, I think I'll take a cab over to mama's crib. I don't want us to get pulled over with all this money. Nigga lose this and we'll be lookin' sick around this muthafucka, Cali trip canceled. Ya'll can go ahead and push the Caddy today, I'm gonna get all the change together so that when it's time to roll we smashin'. I need to go spend some time with my nosy ass girl too."

"I see you tryin' to do the fam bam thang on big Friday. You

ain't been home on a Friday since you had the flu last winter."
Gooch replied while rubbing his palms together, anticipating
his and Solo's next move.

"Hey funny man, when I went by Javon's mama house wasn't
nobody there but your old bitch. She said Javon was over
there Wednesday night arguin' with his moms about some
money, also that he smashed down to Texas for some car
show. Fuck Javon anyway, we don't need that nigga for shit.
They buildin' some new houses over there by Mrs. Mims' crib,
I wouldn't mind havin' somethin' like that for myself. You feel
me?"

"Texas...that's the drag a nigga usin' to throw a nigga off but you
right, fuck em. As far as what you sayin' about buyin' a crib sounds
like a good idea. When we get back from Cali, you should slide up
to Kansas City and holla at Auntie and ask her if she'll come down
here and put her name on one. I'm sure Amber can come up with
some creative financin' to get a nigga in one." Malcolm spoke as
he leaned back into the plush couch and kicked his feet up on top
of the table.

"Creative financin', what's that?" Gooch asked curiously.

"Creative financin' is a door that opens up when you got cash
money to put in the right hands when a nigga's credit ain't shit.
How do y'all think Mama got in her house? She had a friend at her
job with a son that worked at a mortgage company, and he had a
friend who was a real estate agent. Then I had a few dollars to go
with a few favors and there we was, from Musgrave Apartments
to a twenty-seven-hundred-square-foot flat with white
neighbors." Malcolm explained with confidence written all over
his face.

146

GHETTO MERCHANTS

"Is that how you and Deziree got the crib y'all live in?" Solo asked.

"Hell naw, no creative shit with that one my nigga except for down payment money cause Deziree's fake ass daddy got good credit."

After Malcolm answered that question a light clicked on inside his head when he recalled Kansas City. That would be a good spot to get some outta state money. Also, it would get Gooch away from any type of demo that Martha was setting him up for. With him and Solo gone outta town, there would be no drugs or money at their house so there's nothing for her to feed to Hector and his boys. Big Tay could go with them too and make sure they stayed focused and not get too wild and fuck off the sack. Now that Dollaz was back, the two of them could handle all of the moves in OKC with the help of a few little homies that could be put on the payroll. Dollaz needed and wanted a chance to feel like a man who could hold his own and it was respectable for him to feel that way, so he was going to have his chance to shine and earn his keep.

"Let's roll, Solo," Gooch said while walking towards the door, breaking Malcolm's train of thought. Solo stood and gave Malcolm a handshake, then Gooch rushed over from the door to do the same thing, and they left out.

Malcolm locked the door and walked back to the couch, unclipped his pager, grabbed the cordless phone off the end table and flopped down. He scrolled through his locked numbers, finding Big Tay's and punched in the numbers. In four rings Big Tay answered.

"Who this is?" He asked.

"It's me nigga, what you two cats up to?" Malcolm asked.

"We down her fuckin' off a few dollars in the mall. Dollaz ain't got shit so a nigga had to get this nigga a few fits, kicks and a nice leather piece. Is everythang straight on your side of town?"

"Couldn't be better my nigga, so which mall y'all go to?"

"Sooner Fashion."

"Okay okay, ya'll highcappin' with the college bitches in Norman. That's what's up. Check it out, me Gooch and Solo are goin' outta town for a few days to shake up some shit out on the coast. You feel me?"

"What's up, you want a nigga to ride or what?" Big Tay asked while walking away from a nosy kid trying to eavesdrop while he and Dollaz were headed inside J.R. Riggins.

"I only need you to ride if we don't make it back, you know what it is. In the meantime, keep the homie on point and get him a mobile. I'll probably see you before we leave. Oh yeah, do y'all need some money?"

"We good bro, get at a nigga before you slide outta town." Malcolm didn't bother to reply after Big Tay let him know they were good on cash. Instead, he hung up the phone and called Yellow Cab.

Chapter 14

The cab pulled into Cecelia's driveway, parking beside a black M6 BMW. Malcolm got out with the two backpacks and a duffel after paying his fare. When he made it to the front door, he began to drop the duffel bag so that he could get his house key ring out of his pocket. Unexpectedly, the tinted glass door opened up. It was Kenny. He held the door open while greeting his little brother with a smile; Malcolm nodded his head, signaling what's up as he crossed the threshold. When Malcolm turned around after dropping the big bag off of his shoulder, Kenny was nowhere in sight. Then suddenly Kenny appeared on the other side of the glass, coming inside the door with clothes from the cleaners in his hand.

When he came through the door, Malcolm picked the duffel up and headed back towards his bedroom with Kenny coming up behind him in the hall. "I need to speak with you about something, if you have the time?" Kenny asked.

"You don't say? I need to holla at you too. Do you got any plans in store for next week?" Malcolm asked as he turned into his bedroom.

Kenny, hearing his question, ducked inside his room quickly and laid his clothes on his bed, then he shot back into Malcolm's room.

"I was thinking about going out to put in some applications, it's about time since I've been home for two weeks now. By the way Mama told me to tell you to call her at work, she says it's important. Car insurance, I think. Anyway, why do you ask about my plans for next week?" Kenny waited for a response as Malcolm unzipped the duffel bag, turned it over, and began to empty the cash out on the bed, waiting for Kenny to comment on it. "I was wantin' to know if you'll ride out to L. A. with me, Gooch and Solo?"

"What for and how long will we be away?" Kenny inquired.

"We're goin' out there to pick up twenty birds."

"There are lots of pet shops right here in the city. Why would you want twenty birds anyway?"

"Cut the shenanigans my nigga...I'm talkin' bout kilo's; we call em birds, chickens, bricks and shit like that. Check it out though, we wanna leave outta here Sunday mornin', get down there Monday hang out a little and get on back. I got business to handle up with next weekend." Malcolm explained while he started separating the stacks of money.

Now Kenny was starting to believe some of what Deziree was telling him earlier and was having second thoughts about his promise that he had made to her. True enough, he agreed to look after his little brother, and he always would if he were in danger. Drug trafficking was a whole different page of looking out and it was a page that he didn't sign up for. What had Malcolm been thinking when he patterned his life after their father? Did he want to be like him so much that he wanted to share a jail cell with him, or did he turn out this way because he had no positive guidance during his transition from a boy to a man? Regardless of what happened during those years while Kenny was away, this morning he gave his word to Deziree to look out for Malcolm by any means.

Although Malcolm was Kenny's only biological brother, he had a band of brothers who had a mutual bond with one another. These guys were Navy SEALS. Kenny was the Master Chief Special Warfare Operator of SEAL Team 1 Alpha. For five years, Kenny accelerated and unknowingly recruited for NOC (Non-Official Cover) covert operations work for the CIA, off the books. Unsuspecting, Kenny had found himself conditionally yet unofficially discharged from the Navy by way of the CIA Director via the President because of his ability to be lethal and stealthy, alone, not needing a team to get a job done.

Time still permitted Kenny to spend time with 1 Alpha Team stateside and abroad when they were required to back him up on occasion. Kenny's last mission took place in Baghdad, Iraq. The target was Saddam Hussein. For four weeks, Kenny gathered intelligence afoot and from other operatives, allowing him to put crosshairs on Hussein outside of his main palace. A double agent comprised the mission, with Kenny exposing the potential assassination attempt. Kenny found himself hoodwinked in the middle of Baghdad with Saddam's security team on his tail. Through coms, he reached the USS America Aircraft Carrier located in the Persian Gulf. SEAL Team 1 Alpha, with a new Commander, was wheels up on a Blackhawk helicopter in thirty minutes, en route to Karbala, Iraq, fifty miles southeast of Baghdad.

That was where the extraction for their old leader would be. Three minutes in the air, the Blackhawk exploded, killing everyone on board. A surface-to-air missile was responsible, sparking US Troops on the ground after three days of Kenny gradually making it to the extraction point with two new bullet wounds.

When Kenny made it stateside, there was a private ceremony held where he received a Purple Heart and a Medal of Valor. When he was asked by the President what he had to say, as Kenny shook his hand, and he leaned in close to him.

"Mr. President, I request extended leave with the option of coming back to serve my country. As of this moment, my heart is heavy, and my frame of mind is not in a position to disregard those who wish to play patriot games. Those men who lost their lives in Kuwait were my brothers and they died protecting me in the blind. Right now, it shames me that aristocracy led them into a trap that was set for minions, not for those that bleed valor for our country."

Kenny was granted Executive Discharge leave giving him the option to come back to serve when he was ready. The only stipulation would be to have a psych evaluation. Kenny was a well needed tool for the government to set out to pasture, he had a feel for the job and his job was serving the United States.

Within one week after the ceremony Kenny put his home in Arlington, Virginia up for sale. He packed up some bags for the road and the rest he shipped to Tinker Air Force Base through military cargo to be picked up when he made it to Oklahoma. Upon getting all of his business handled in Virginia Kenny gassed up his M6 BMW and headed across country visiting family from each one of his fallen brothers that perished in the gulf. Afterwards, he headed home to Oklahoma. Malcolm noticed Kenny's silence and the distant look in his eyes that stared blankly at the wall at nothing.

"Kenny, damn bro I see you still out to lunch. So, what's up, you rollin' with us to Cali or what? Hear me out before you say no, I've got a bunch of money, and I know anythang can happen when you least expect it. Straight up bro I need somebody that knows how to shoot if shit gets fucked up and they don't call it killa Cali for nothin'."

GHETTO MERCHANTS

"You certainly have a way with words, little brother but I'm not so sure your words outweigh the danger in your road trip," Kenny replied after pointing at the money and shrugging his shoulders, waiting for Malcolm's persuasion to continue.

Malcolm spread his arms apart in a fashion to make Kenny look at the cash that lay on the bed. "This is what I do, and I like doin' it cause I'm good at it, just like you're good at bein' a soldier, gettin' all kinds of medals and shit. So regardless of what doubt you have in mind, bullshit that mama be talkin' bout and Deziree's constant naggin', I'm gonna do what I do by gettin' out on them streets gettin' it. Right now gettin' it consists of rollin' out to Los Angeles Sunday mornin'. So are you rollin' or what, cause if not we can get on somethin' else."

Kenny now weighed out his options as he paced the floor for a moment. It was evident that Malcolm was prepared to go with or without him. Then he recalled what Malcolm said about having someone with him who knows how to shoot. Stanley and Gary were going with him already, they don't know how to use firearms properly and they're in the streets every day? You would think that someone would take the time to go to the gun range and learn to fire a weapon properly. Kenny concluded that he didn't want to lose the last brother that he had left without him being there with him. It was gonna be Malcolm's way or no way because he was situated in his lifestyle and nothing that anybody said would change how he felt.

"Okay, little brother, you got me for the trip, but before we go, I want to know if I can take that 454 SS for a spin. I seen the keys on the hook in the kitchen the first day I got back and started to take it for ride. Mama almost had a fit."

They both laughed at Kenny's remark while on the inside Malcolm was relieved knowing that he had a war vet riding with him on his mission. Kenny walked around to the other side of the bed where Malcolm was standing, and they gave each other a hug. That was the first time they had hugged each other since Kenny left for basic training in 1982.

"Enough of the sentimental shit nigga, don't come over here fuckin' with me, cryin' and shit. As for the truck, we can roll it when we leave from over here to my crib, but first I gotta get this money together. Oh yeah, I gotta call mama and see what she want, and I need her to get us a rental..."

"Hold em up right there, cowboy, we are not going to involve mama in this shit no kind of way. I have a credit card; I'll get the rental." Kenny interrupted by reaching out and putting his hand on Malcolm's shoulder.

"Okay, bet, my connect told me to get a Ford van, I don't know why, but I believe he knows the business, so I'm gonna follow his lead on this thang. Hertz got Fords so that's who we need to call." Kenny rubbed his chin as he slowly nodded his head up and down while Malcolm opened up the closet door which revealed a black gun safe with a gold tone handle and combination knob. When Malcolm unlocked the safe and opened the door, Kenny saw four cardboard boxes inside, two of them had 100 and the other two with 50 written big in magic marker. Also standing up inside were two AK47's along with a Galil 74 fitted tightly inside the slots. On the top shelf lay a Mac 10, Tech 9, ammunition, and several clips. Malcolm pulled out two boxes, one with 50 and one with 100, handing them both to Kenny, who was standing behind him. Before closing the safe, he rubbed his chin staring inside contemplating on something, then he grabbed two clips, stuck them inside his pocket and then he retrieved the Mac.

By the time he closed the safe and turned around Kenny was

placing the boxes on top of the bed.

"I have to admit that I'm somewhat impressed, little brother, not so much with your lifestyle but the fact that you have managed to put back a little cash. I also like your toys. Now I must know what is your plan for packing all of this?" Kenny inquired while standing with his arms crossed.

"I haven't figured that part out yet, and we're bringing three more pistols, four counting yours." Kenny held up a hand signifying for Malcolm to pause a moment as he left the room. When he returned, he was carrying two military duffle bags half the size of a punching bag. He dropped them to the floor and unhooked each one at the top. He emptied out the contents, which contained desert storm fatigues and boots. Malcolm kept quiet and waited for Kenny to initiate the plan.

"I think this will work out. We'll put everything in these two bags and top them off with fatigues. Second of all; there is a Naval Base in San Diego, I have military identification, if we get pulled over for some reason, we'll be okay. I would show them my id, they'd run it and send us on our way."

After Kenny finished explaining his plan to Malcolm, they began packing one of the green duffel bags. "You know what Kenny, I'm thinkin' you ain't as square as you look. By the way, don't say shit to Deziree about the trip."

That evening at Malcolm and Deziree's house, they ate lasagna, salad with breadsticks and strawberry cheesecake for dessert. For entertainment, Kenny was the star attraction, speaking of his experiences around the globe. When Deziree asked him about his mission that involved him getting the Purple Heart award, he refused to elaborate, telling her that it was classified. Noticing a change in his demeanor about the question, Deziree offered Kenny a cocktail and to adjourn to the den. He accepted the invitation and Malcolm volunteered to clear the dishes from the dining room to the kitchen.

While Malcolm was scraping a plate in the sink garbage disposal, he overheard the sound of his mobile phone ringing over on the kitchen table. He turned off the disposal, grabbed a towel, and dried his hands as he jotted across the hardwood floor, picking up the mobile on the table, pressing SEND.

"Who's this?" Questioned Malcolm, shouting over the loud music in the earpiece.

"Solo, you chillin' at the crib with your girly or what?" Solo replied.

"Turn that shit down nigga..." Solo turned the music down in the Cadillac.

"Yeah, I'm at the crib chillin' with baby, and my brother. What up?"

"Me and Gooch been knockin' hoes all evenin' in the Caddy my nigga. Check it out though...I gotta beep from this sorority broad that said her homegirl is havin' a birthday party at Club 33. It's gonna be poppin like a muthafucka with college bitches from OU, OSU, Langston, and Central State. You want us to pick you up?" Asked Solo as he and Gooch sped up Centennial Highway.

Malcolm looked at the clock on the microwave, reading 8:17. In his heart, he knew Solo was just checking in to see if it was alright to drive the Cadillac to that club because it was on a gravel road down the highway from Langston University.

"Before ya'll roll up there. Bring some of that indo over here. Hey, baby made some of that bangin' lasagna and cheesecake."

"Lasagna! We on our way my nigga."

Solo replied excitedly and pressed END. Malcolm laughed. He decided that he had handled all of the business he needed to handle with it today, except for hearing from Javon.

Suddenly, he felt Deziree wrap her arms around his waist from behind, squeezing him tight, bringing a smile to his face. He grabbed hold of her left hand and slowly turned around so that he could look at her. When he did, he saw a smile that brought new meaning to his life, even more so when he looked further down at her stomach that held his twins. Malcolm loved her but he hated the way she complained about his lifestyle. He never understood why she complained about it so much, being that he was doing the same thing now that he was doing when he met her. She knew from the beginning of their relationship that he was a hustler because he had two sports cars, nice clothes and no job. Furthermore, his mother wasn't rich.

Now, several years had passed by and Malcolm was planning his future with her, his children and his mother along with the rest of his crew. At this point in his life, there was nothing to hold him back and he wished that Deziree wouldn't let his involvement with other women get between them. Although there were others, not one of them had his love like she did.

"What are you doin' in here, I thought you was in there playin' hostess and restin' your feet?" Malcolm asked while bending down, then he placed a sensual kiss on her lips. Deziree kissed him back for a moment, then she slowly pulled away.

"Will you stay home and make love to me tonight?" she asked. The look in her eyes and the innocence written all over her face made him melt deep inside her love...and her love was what he wanted. Forever. "You want some dick tonight lil mama?"

Malcolm replied after grabbing the towel off the table and heading back to the sink.

Meanwhile, Deziree put her hands on her hips, staring at him as she processed the words he had just said to her.

"Is it like that Malcolm or do I have to make arrangements to fit around your other bitches to fuck my man?"

Surprised by her words, Malcolm turned around to face a totally different person than he was hugging and kissing thirty seconds prior. As Deziree approached him with her body language showing anger, he knew he had to check her regardless of her pregnancy.

"Stop the bullshit right now goddammit! Don't ever try to throw shit in my face again about some other bitch. The nosiness and the insecurities are gettin' old Deziree."

Deziree leaned her upper body back as well as taking a step backwards with a feeling of shock because of what Malcolm just said. Her eyes began to well up with tears as she reached out, touching Malcolm's hand. Quickly, he snatched his hand back, wincing from the stinging of Deziree touching the open wounds on his knuckles.

GHETTO MERCHANTS

"Damn!"

"Baby, I'm sorry. I was only kidding around, surely you know that I wasn't trying to hurt your hand. Come here and let me see you, big baby." With a scowl plastered across his face Malcolm took a deep breath as he looked at his hand and Deziree took a step closer to him.

"You'd better chill out. What's got you in such a foul mood anyway, I know it's not what I just said about your bitches, cause we've been past that?"

Deziree reached down and locked her fingers with his and raised their hands up together.

"Listen here, woman, I'm secure within myself and you should be the same. There is nobody that can take your place, just like I know those square ass niggas that you used to fuck with can't compare with me!"

Malcolm kissed Deziree on the forehead then he knelt down and lifted her blouse and kissed her stomach.

"Hello in there...will y'all be okay if I knock y'all up outta there?"

Malcolm spoke joyously. Deziree laughed at him while tugging on his ears, causing him to stand up while showing off a smirk.

"For you to be so smart, you can be so dumb. The only way you can hurt them is to give me an STD, and the only way I can hurt them is to drink. I haven't touched one drop since I found out I was pregnant. Do I not turn you on now because I'm big and fat, or is it that you think I can't satisfy your sexual hunger because of my pregnancy? True enough, I can't move

DRE LUV

like I used to, but you know my stuff is still the best you ever had, and I can still do all the things for you that you like."

Deziree explained while batting her long thick eyelashes. She tiptoed and kissed him on the lips and squeezed his dick at the same time. Malcolm thought to himself, damn I love this crazy ass bitch.

"Go on in the den and chill out with your brother and do some catching up. I got the kitchen right now, along with the red light special later...daddy."

Deziree winked and smiled as she turned towards the counter. Javon crossed his mind for some reason and Malcom decided to power his phone back up just in case he tried to call. He still wanted to give him the benefit of doubt.

Entering the den, he observed Kenny kicking back on the hunter green leather sofa. He was watching Boyz in The Hood on the big screen while swirling brown liquor around inside a brandy snifter. Malcolm walked over to the bar and fixed himself a snifter half filled with Remy Martin then he made his way to the couch, taking a seat beside his brother.

"Kick off ya Reeboks and relax bro, my house is your house. In fact, how bout we toast to a new beginning of havin' long money for our future." Malcolm announced as he and Kenny touched glasses.

After the toast Malcolm sat his glass down on the table next to his Motorola charger where he slid his mobile on. Just as Malcolm and Kenny both reached down and untied their shoes Malcolm's mobile started ringing. Quickly Malcolm reached and grabbed the mobile from the charger and pressed SEND and put the phone to his ear.

"What up?" Malcolm asked as he answered.

"What are you doing babe...you busy?" Asked Amber on the other end.

"I'm tied up on somethin right now with my brother. Is everythang alright witcha?"
"I'm fine...it's just that I was hoping that you would come back over and stay the night with me. All day I've been thinking about you and what we got started on and never finished." Amber sighed and spoke with a sad tone.

The doorbell chimed, causing Kenny to raise and make eye contact with Malcolm as he pointed, signifying that he would go answer the door. Malcolm nodded his head and continued on with his conversation with Amber while Kenny got up and left the room.

"I'm not sure if I'll make it back over there tonight but you can believe that I'll be back over soon to finish that shit. Holla atcha later, Amber." Malcolm pressed END, then he slid the phone back on the charger. At the same time, he heard Solo, Gooch, Kenny and Deziree's voices.

Inside the den, Deziree stepped over Kenny's shoes and sat down beside Malcolm. Kenny came right behind her sitting next to her. Gooch took a seat on the loveseat while Solo walked around to Malcolm and handed him a sack of weed, then he flopped down next to Gooch. He pulled off a brown beanie causing a pinky sized joint to fall down into his lap, which he stuck between his lips. On que, Gooch reached into his pocket, pulled out a lighter and handed it to Solo.
"I was wonderin' when you was gonna give me my lighter

back nigga," Solo spoke out sarcastically while he got comfortable on the leather. Malcolm untied the slip knot on the sack and raised it up to his nose and began to grin while he slowly nodded his head up and down showing that he was satisfied. He scooted forward tossing the sack on the table in exchange for his cognac that was sitting on the table.

"Sit back, silly," said Deziree with a grin as she patted Malcolm on his leg. Everyone in the room started laughing, except for Solo; he fired up the joint. Deziree stood up and stepped over Malcolm's shoes, and made her way over to the fireplace with a smirk as she grabbed an ashtray off the mantle, then brought it over to Solo.
"Take this, cause I don't want any burns in my carpet or on my furniture. I know how you boys get when you're left unattended. I think I'll go to another part of the house, since you're smoking." Solo blew out a cloud of smoke away from Deziree direction while handing the joint and ashtray to Gooch.

"I seen some shit on TV that said weed's good for ya, even pregnant women," Solo replied with a look of mischief.

"I hardly believe that unless you seen it on a episode of Saturday Night Live, Stan," Kenny responded in defense of Deziree.

"Call me Solo big cous, I ain't been called Stan for a while now," Solo responded.

"You ain't gotta go to another part of the house, baby, a little weed smoke ain't gonna hurt. You ain't smokin'. Malcolm told Deziree as he reached across the table to grab the ashtray and joint that Gooch handed him.

GHETTO MERCHANTS

"I take it that you don't smoke bud, Kenny, huh?" Solo asked.

"I don't do dope Stan, I mean...Solo. I believe in keeping my brain cells intact; drugs make the brain slow and cloudy. You know, I would think that in the line of work that you all are in, you would want to be on point." Kenny responded quickly.

It was obvious there was tension, but Gooch broke the chaos before things got out of hand with Solo and Kenny. "Yo Kenny, I heard Mama and Aunt Cecelia talkin' one mornin' at the house. Aunt Cecelia was sayin' that you was in Amsterdam. Is it really like they show on TV? Hoes standin' in windows sellin' pussy, and bars everywhere that sell weed and let you smoke right there?" Gooch asked excitedly.

"There are parts of Amsterdam like that, but remember, when someone else does something, you are not obligated to follow suit."

"Those were very selective words, Kenny; I will definitely think before I just do."

"Anyway, Gooch, Solo, there's lasagna, salad, garlic bread and cheesecake in the kitchen if you guys are hungry," Deziree suggested.

Without saying another word, Solo and Gooch stood up and raced for the kitchen.

Chapter 15

When Javon made it back from Barret's Towing, he was more disgusted than he was prior to leaving the casino. The manager at Barret's would not let him retrieve the Range Rover, nor would he let him look in it or see it, because it was not registered in his name. Being that Javon grew up with his father owning a towing service, he knew there were certain rules they had to follow at a towing lot. The majority of those rules were placed for reasons to avoid lawsuits and insurance hikes.

Back inside the casino, Javon located Tabitha. She escorted him to a window while he explained his misfortune that occurred at Barret's, while she signed off on a tray of chips worth ten thousand dollars and the key to his upgraded suite. Afterwards, they shook hands as she apologized for any inconvenience. They parted and went their separate ways. Javon's first stop was at a craps table where he lost four thousand dollars in under thirty minutes. After that ordeal, he wasn't feeling lucky at all, but he had a feeling that he would get his mojo back soon; he just had to go on to another game.

His next stop on the floor was at a roulette table, where he had some luck for a short while. When he broke even from what he had lost at the craps table he began to feel that he had his mojo back. Suddenly, he had a group cheering him on, a brunette dressed elegantly with the class of a high-priced call girl making her way to his side. Not only did Javon have his mojo back, but he had lady luck standing beside him. He picked up his tray and set it down on the roulette table and contemplated how many chips he wanted to put on lucky number seventeen. He looked over to the brunette, waiting for her approval. "Seventeen, wooo hoooo let's go...yeah baby!" She shouted out over the noise at the table. She had a look on her face that showed Javon that if he hit, she was going to show him the time of his life, with a price no doubt. Javon placed the tray on seventeen. The wheel spun as the tiny ball rolled around the ring, it dropped down and hopped up and danced around while everyone held their breath. It dropped in slot 21—Javon could not believe his good luck had vanished so soon. He put both hands over his face and took a deep breath, hoping to hide everything that showed on his face when he dropped his hands. Removing his hands, he reached for his drink and turned it up, drinking every last drop, then casually set it down on the edge of the table.

Javon turned away, breaking through the crowd, heading towards the elevator with his head down. When he made it upstairs to his penthouse suite, he stopped at a large round marble table sitting in the middle of the first room. On top of the table sat a large fruit basket, along with a sterling silver ice bucket and a bottle of Dom Perignon chilling. After glancing at the fruit and champagne briefly, Javon stepped into one of the bedrooms, contemplating who to call, and he felt like it should be Malcolm. That was his only friend that he could trust, and he would have sound advice on how to tackle the complete situation that he was now in with his life, which was spiraling out of control. That point brought his pride into play, so he decided to call his mother instead. Javon made it to the side of the plushest bed that he had ever seen, looking fit for a king. He climbed on top, then rolled over on his back, suddenly noticing that he no longer had his wallet in his back pocket. "I'll be damned! Thievin' ass bitch got me for my shit at the roulette table. I'm stuck way out here and don't even have ID no more." Javon spoke out in disgust.

Quickly, he stood up after getting his feet on the floor, about to scramble back downstairs to look for the brunette who had clipped him for his wallet. By the time he made it to the front door of the suite, he knew it was useless; she was long gone by now, just like he needed to be. Instead, he looked around the suite for his belongings that he had left behind in the other suite. Inside another bedroom that was grander than the other one, he found his bag and his mobile phone sticking out of the side pocket. He turned the power on, then pushed the number to his parents' house. On the second ring someone picked up but did not say anything.

"Hello, hello..." Javon spoke anxiously until he was interrupted. "Is that all you have to say, son? Yeah...you done got your mother all upset and shit, got her worried that somethin' happened to your ignorant ass. You got people callin' over here from Las Vegas, somebody from a towin' company and then some kind of police investigator from the police department wantin' to know why that Rover truck was left with the keys in the ignition. Ya mama done told those people that you drove the truck to Texas now she thinkin' somebody done robbed and killed ya for that little money you left here with. So, tell me what the hell's goin' on?" Mr. Mims inquired with fury.

"Hold on, pop and let me explain..."

"Let me guess, you was gonna call over here, tell ya mama another lie so you could try to get some more money up outta her. Yeah...she told me everythang, boy and I mean everythang. Where the hell ya at right now?"

"I'm in Vegas."

"Son, why ya lie to ya mama for no reason? You know what, I

told that woman that she was spoilin' ya ass too much but she always wanna tell me to stop bein' so mean. Well, let me tell ya right now, all the fanfare is over with cause we'll be out there tomorrow to get that Rover truck outta the impound. You can ride home if you wanna if not I don't give a damn, but I know I'm takin' that Corvette outta my garage and puttin' that Rover in that spot. It's ya mama's truck now, hell...it's in my name anyway and I'll be damned if I letcha fuck up my credit again like ya did with that Corvette. We'll be flyin' in there on Southwest Airlines at 11:50 in the mornin', so if you leavin' with us ya betta be at the tow lot!" Mr. Mims slammed the phone down, leaving Javon in shock with his mobile at his ear still. Suddenly, he heard the voice that he wanted to hear when he first called.

"Mother!"

"Are you okay, baby? I've been worried half to death since you left from over here the other night. I been calling and beeping you, never getting an answer. Then this evening I made it home from the bingo hall and I found some messages that Jazmin stuck on the refrigerator door. Baby, when I called the number back and spoke with the police investigator and he told me that they had found your truck abandoned at a gas station with the engine running out in Las Vegas. Now that I know you are safe, I feel much better, although you did deceive me about where you were going. Baby, you are a grown man so there is never any need to lie to me about where you go when you leave town. You could have made your mother have a heart attack, baby. Now I know you went out to Vegas just to gamble. Am I right or wrong, Javon?" Mrs. Mims inquired with a calming voice.

"You're right, mother, but I was plannin' on doin'..."

DRE LUV

"Stop making excuses like your daughter. You sound just like her when she gets caught doing something she's not supposed to do only difference is that she is three years old. You on the other hand are not a child anymore. The time has come for you to be a man and take responsibility for your actions. I expect for you to be at Barret's when we get there, also, I expect you to be rested up so you can drive us back to Oklahoma. We have a business out here that needs to be tended to responsibly and that's what you're gonna learn because you're going to work for your father. We will pay your mortgage for February, only because the condo is in mine and your father's name, and we must protect our credit. Good night..."

"Mother, wait, I need you to go to Western Union and wire me about five hundred dollars...please?"
"Go lay down, Javon, you sound pathetic. I love you dearly but wire you money, I will not."

Without giving him a chance to say another word, Mrs. Mims hung up the phone. The only other person that he thought he could depend on to come through for him let him down. Javon pressed END as he realized that his time was critical and therefore calling for desperate measures. In that short amount of time, Javon convinced himself that he had to go back to Barret's, although this time he would not be going through the front door; he had to check to see if the money was still there.

Kenny had got a contact high and raided the refrigerator. Deziree, Solo and Gooch bickered back and forth over dumb shit as usual which turned out to be a good time with the family. When Kenny and the cousins left, Malcom locked up and turned on the alarm because Deziree had turned in a little earlier, feeling a light contact herself. When Malcolm made it to the bedroom, he expected Deziree to be sleeping in the king-sized cherry wood four-post bed. Instead, she was propped up by pillows and covered up to her neck with a thick all-white goose down comforter with lavender sheets folded over. She was watching Midnight Love, and when she noticed Malcolm step into the room, she folded the cover down, revealing that she was naked. Malcolm walked over, then dove on top of the bed and wiggled up close to Deziree and began to kiss her on her chest. She grabbed his head, holding him still and kissed him on his forehead, then leaned back a little bit so that she could look into his eyes, which were bloodshot red.

Deziree smiled and so did he. "Baby, get up and take your clothes off," Deziree demanded. Malcolm sighed and shook his head as he rolled off the bed and pulled his shorts off, dropping them to the floor, then heading towards the master bath. Slowly, Deziree got out of bed and picked up her red silk robe from the stool that stood on her side of the bed. She swung on her robe and followed Malcolm into the bathroom, where he just stepped out of his jeans and socks and into the brass and glass shower stall. Before he closed the glass door, he observed Deziree sitting down on the bench in front of the vanity while staring at him.
"What's on your mind, lil mama?"

"I enjoyed spending the evening with you and Kenny, even your bad ass little cousins. Sometimes I wish that I could just keep you in the house forever, where I know you're safe. Baby, I know I get on your nerves sometimes when I blow things out of proportion, but believe me when I tell you that I mean no harm. One thing that I know is that you cannot contain a free spirit until the spirit wants to be contained."

DRE LUV

Deziree explained.

"I think you say some crazy shit sometimes because your hormones are all crazy and shit. You know what, I seen something like that on Oprah once. She had women on there who were pregnant and thought their husbands didn't find them attractive anymore cause they had gotten swole up. You're my girl, and I think you're beautiful still, now let me finish my shower and I'll be in there to squeeze on ya a little bit."

Deziree stood up and walked back to the bedroom where she lit two scented candles and put on some Public Announcement with R. Kelly to enhance the mood. After those tasks were done, Deziree untied her robe and got back in bed, waiting for Malcolm. Within minutes, he was walking into the bedroom, still drying off.

"Okay lil mama check this out, you bet not worry about no shit like that because you're still the finest thang I ever seen. Not to mention, you gotta be the most strong-willed woman I ever met besides my mama. So, what's up, I see you got the slow jams and the candles goin', you gonna let me have my way with you or somethin'?"
Malcolm dropped the towel as he approached Deziree, whose cheeks filled with color after hearing Malcolm's words. Quickly she pulled the sheet over her face while Malcolm began to laugh as he reached over and pulled the sheet back down revealing a smile that turned into a laugh. With help from Deziree, Malcolm pulled the cover all the way back while the aroma of vanilla filled their nostrils. He got on top of the bed climbing between her legs spreading them apart carefully and went down on her spreading her lips with his tongue, performing just like she liked it. She moaned and rubbed his

waves as he held onto her hips keeping her still while she tried to squirm away.

Malcolm, feeling in charge, moved his hands up under her butt and raised her up, sticking his tongue in and out and around her booty hole. Deziree begged him to stop but he kept going while feeling her wetness all over his face. This went on for what felt like an eternity to both of them until Deziree could not take it anymore. She slid back on the sheet forcing Malcolm to let go then she rolled over on her knees turning around in the bed locking her eyes, hand, then her mouth on Malcolm's dick while massaging his nuts at the same time. Malcolm returned the favor by playing with her pussy. Deziree kept going harder and harder knowing exactly what it took to keep her man because she felt his dick swelling while he tried to break away. She wasn't having it; she went all the way down on him, causing him to blow down her throat. While Malcolm jerked, Deziree sucked everything out of him, never stopping until she got him back hard. Her sole purpose was for him to pound her pussy and put her to sleep and hold her through the night.

In no time at all Deziree had Malcolm's manhood where she wanted it, knowing that it was worth it because her man was going to please her as always.

"Goddamn you got some bomb head lil mama but now I gots to get up in ya. Let me help you off the bed 'cause we gettin' on the floor."

Malcolm slid off the bed and then grabbed Deziree's hand, helping her get off. When she got to her feet, he let go of her hand, then grabbed the white comforter, snatched it off the bed, and spread it out on the floor.

"What are you doing, Malcolm, with your crazy self?" Deziree asked, then giggled. Without answering, he grabbed her hand again and helped her down to the floor. Malcom got down as well, then maneuvered behind her using his knees to spread her legs.

"You ready, lil mama?" Deziree turned her head around and looked at him.

"Yes, baby. I've been waiting for this all week."
Malcolm spread her booty cheeks open and bent down and licked her from her pussy all the way to her booty hole while moistening his drying face.
"Don't make love to me Malcolm, I want you to fuck me nigga...now."

Malcolm obliged her and slid inside. He started slow feeling the tight walls of her pussy gripping his dick like a vice. After working himself inside as far as he could he spanked her on the ass. Malcolm tilted his head back and thanked God that he already busted one nut because Deziree's pussy was too good to hold back. Malcolm looked back down, slowed down and initiated his next move. He began to pump her slowly until she came then he pulled out and stuck his finger in her ass and with the other hand he stuck a finger inside her pussy. Deziree was on top of the world when the song Honey Love started to play and that was when Malcolm made his trick shot. He pulled out his fingers, then grabbed himself and slowly inserted himself inside Deziree's back door.

"Wait baby...don't rush, take it slow," Deziree said as she looked back over her shoulder.

"Shut up and take this dick witcha nosy ass," Malcolm spoke forcefully as he continued to ease inside of her little by little while using one hand to hold her underneath and the other to guide his dick. By the time 'Honey Love' was going off, Malcolm and Deziree were in unison with one another; he stroked, and she backed up. All along, Malcolm was thinking that he wanted this moment to last forever and Deziree enjoyed the feeling of having orgasm after orgasm.

"That's it, daddy, give it to me...fuck my ass and keep me cumming! "
When Deziree said that, Malcolm tried to go deeper and couldn't take it.

"Cum with me daddy!" Deziree burst out, then reached back and grabbed Malcolm's hand, squeezing hard, putting her fingernails into him. Malcolm blasted off inside of her while sweat from his head and chest dripped down on her ass and back.

"Oh Malcolm, you are so good to me, baby, but I need you to get your dick out of my ass...slowly...daddy."

Fats wheezed through coughing on a blunt that burned inside an ashtray on top of his desk as he thought about what was going on in his life, with his money and freedom involved. Javon still hadn't made contact; the feds just made a sweep in Watts picking up a bunch of crip niggas from Grape Street and blood niggas from Bounty Hunters on some cocaine conspiracy shit. Some of them copped work from him, not to mention several of them were on the books because they were consignment. Fuck it, that's just another twist in the game that a hustler from the street has to deal with, taking losses. There's no way to get around it just be sure not to take any losses that you can't make up cause if you can't make it up you need to stay the fuck out of the way.

Fats reached into the ashtray and grabbed the blunt and took a drag while looking outside through the one-way glass at the traffic on El Segundo. There was loud banging on the glass door, causing Fats to drop the blunt and grab his Glock that was sitting on the desk next to the ashtray. Fats looked at the clock on the wall, seeing 10:05 as he stood up and walked to the office door and killed the lights. Who could this be banging on my door? Fats thought as he slowly opened the office door, looking across the waiting area through the glass, seeing Scoob with a big goofy grin on his face. Scoob was a nigga from San Bernardino that Fats met when he was doing time in CDC Blythe. Fats took a liking to Scoob because Scoob had told him some stories about how niggas was fucking him around on the work because he didn't have a proper connection. Fats gave him his information, telling him to contact him when he touched down, which was five months later.

Scoob was a 220-pound muscle bound dude with a bald head with a nice bluff game that got a pass in several neighborhoods throughout Los Angeles. Because of his ghetto pass he sometimes took things out of hand causing gunplay several times when he was in the wrong. Mostly because of altercations acquired from the personal tax that he put on Fats work when he would sometimes make a delivery. Truth be known, Scoob got a reputation of being a slimeball, yet he had a lifeline because of Fats that one day would be cut. Everyone knew that all good things had to come to an end even in the city of angels where even the strong die.

After finding out it was Scoob, Fats took the pistol back to the desk and grabbed the shop keys off of the desk and headed to unlock the door, letting him in along with the cool California night air.

"What's poppin' up in here big homie?" Scoob asked as he headed towards the office while Fats closed and locked the door back. When Fats made it to his office Scoob had his blunt in his mouth puffing while looking on the desk at some of Fat's paperwork. Fats shook his head with a sign of disbelief because he was seeking some time alone to sort out some of his personal issues. Now standing in his office at 10:00pm uninvited was Scoob who had just left no more than two hours ago. Fats walked around his desk and snatched the paperwork from Scoob and laid it down on the desk as both of them took a seat.

"It's Friday night Scoob, why you ain't with your broad or somebody else broad? Anywhere besides here fuckin' with my private time." Fats expressed with a sincere look on his face. Scoob took another pull on the blunt of indo then blew the smoke in Fat's direction.

"Stop trippin' fat ass nigga...I know you're goin' to fuck with some top-flight hoes somewhere. Call a couple of them up and get us a private show, I got a room over at the Travel Master."

"There's a strip club right next door man, go over there and buy you some pussy if you want to. I'm about to get up out of here and shoot to the house." Fats responded.

"You trippin cause that Javon nigga never showed up huh?" Scoob inquired as he passed the blunt over to Fats.

"I ain't trippin' on that shit, what's done is done, if he show he show. I got too much shit goin' on to dwell on one mutha fucka. Don't get me wrong, I need that money just like I need every dollar that belongs to me, but I know the cake ain't always covered with icin' either. In fact, I was just sittin' up here thinkin' bout cuttin' all the old shit off and stickin' with the new. Yeah, I think I'm gonna take shit slow and just fuck with that kid Malcolm. I like him too, cause he got style about himself and most important he ain't scared to roll out here to get what he wants. And the best thing of all is that he doesn't need me to front him nothin' cause he got his own money. That's what I'm talkin' bout, I'm tired of takin' losses around here from niggas gettin' caught up with my work. I swear that if a nigga don't watch out he'll be caught up in one of these federal conspiracy indictments that been floatin' around this mutha fucka. Don't think for one minute that just because they didn't swoop this detail shop and pick our black asses up that we in the clear." Fats warned him.

"I aint got the dough you got to just stop hustlin' in L.A. just because some niggas got caught up in Watts." Scoob cried out.

"I gotcha my nigga, don't trip. Look around, you can run this mutha fucka and push a little indo. What you should do is go holla at old school over in Compton and get a few gallons of that sherm and take that shit out to San Bernadino and give that shit to one of your brothers and let them push that shit. You trippin' my nigga cause they payin' twenty five hundred dollars for a eight ounce bottle. Nigga that's forty g's a gallon you gonna make, you better do the math. I tell you what, think about it and let me know cause if you wanna do that I'll getcha started. But hey I gotta get goin', let's get outta here." Fats told Scoob as he stood up and headed for the door.

GHETTO MERCHANTS

Back in Las Vegas, Javon stared out of the window in his suite at the lights and the people on the strip. He still held on to the empty bottle of Dom Perignon he had just finished hoping it would give him enough courage for his mission. He thought about what his life would have been like if he had stayed off the streets after his prison bid and went to work for the family business. He passed the thought on then reminisced on his time that he spent in the cell with his old friend that he called Pops. Pops was caught on U.S. 87 in the Oklahoma panhandle going north with two kilos of cocaine. The Cimarron County District Attorney chose to prosecute instead of giving him up to the feds. This led to Pops getting twenty years for trafficking cocaine, the biggest drug bust ever in the county, and a slam dunk reelection for the district attorney.

Pops and Javon celled up and kept each other entertained, Pops with stories about hustling in different states and back home in California. Javon mostly talked about what he wished he could do if he had the opportunity to become a big-time drug dealer. Pops took a real liking to Javon and wanted to rest knowing when the time came, he helped him achieve his dreams. Pops was dying of cancer and never let Javon know but he promised him that he would help him out by introducing him to his nephew, Fats. After being cell mates for over two years and Javon was within one year from going home Pops wrote a letter to his sister in Bellflower, California—written in code for Fats. It was to let Fats know that Javon was being trained by him and to look out for him when he contacts him when he touches the streets.

That night after Pops had Javon drop his letter in the mailbox, he gave him his sister's phone number and address, making Javon pay attention to strict instructions about the game. He touched base on letting him know that there's more to making it on top by distributing large amounts of cocaine and collecting the cash. It means nothing if you don't stay on top because if you ever get to the point where you don't recognize yourself, you'll find yourself becoming invisible to the chosen few that love you unconditionally. Pops stressed with emphasis about having a plan put together with the fast money so that one can enjoy life without so much pain. Get money, get legit, get out or get a life sentence and dream about the things that you wish you would have done. To sum it up, don't end up in a jail cell in your forties or fifties telling stories like this but if you do you can rest knowing that you stuck with the GCode. You can hold your head up and walk the yard and look in the mirror when you know that you didn't involve anyone else in your case even when the prosecutors try to scare you with big numbers.

Pops gave Javon the option to use the phone number and address when he gets home if he possessed all of the qualities of becoming a self-made man. Within two weeks Pops received a letter back from his sister with a note inside written by Fats acknowledging the youngster from Oklahoma to call when he makes it home. Pops let Javon read the note from his nephew Fats and was elated that he stumbled up on a righteous connect from the west coast.

Later, after playing chess until midnight, Javon lay in his bunk feeling the aura of power at his grasp until he finally fell asleep with a smile on his face. The next morning when Pop's alarm went off Javon had to climb down to turn it off because Pops was still asleep. That was unusual because Pops always woke him up, so Javon turned on the light after taking a piss and to his surprise Pops was lying on his back with his eyes wide open, glassed over; he was dead. That morning Javon wrote Pop's sister and his nephew, sending his condolences along with all of Pop's personal belongings.

GHETTO MERCHANTS

Javon made it home at the end of spring of the next year and within a week of that he was getting picked up at the Greyhound Bus Station in downtown Los Angeles by Fats who was driving a black Pontiac Trans Am. One week later Javon was back in Oklahoma City bagging up quarter ounces and eight balls of crack inside his bedroom at his mother and father's new house.

Javon snapped back to reality and his past was behind him now along with lots of shattered hopes. The time was now for him to make his move to Barret's, either the money was there or it wasn't but one thing was for sure was that he was not going to wait for his mother and father to see. Javon sat the empty bottle of champagne down on the table, grabbed his jacket and the room key and left the suite. He rode the elevator down to the first floor where he left out the main entryway and flashed his golden suite key to the valet and requested a ride to Commerce Drive. Once again Javon was in the back seat of a black limo for the short drive to Barret's. When they got on Commerce Javon had the driver pull over and let him out at the end of the block, got out, closed the door and commenced walking and the limo took off. When he made it to the side of Barret's which sat on a corner, Javon sized up the eight foot stockade fence, jumped up and pulled himself up and over dropping down inside on a gravel lot filled with cars and trucks. After searching for about five minutes, he found his Range Rover but was unable to get inside because the doors were locked.

Mr. and Mrs. Mims wasted no time exiting the Las Vegas airport with their one carry-on in route to Barret's on Commerce inside a cab. Upon arrival at the tow lot, they discovered information pertaining to Javon being jailed in the Clark County Detention Center. His charges were vandalism,

automobile tampering and trespassing. The vandalism charge
was related to Javon breaking out a window in the Range
Rover. Trespassing came from him jumping the fence and
being on Barrett's property without authorization. In lieu of
professional courtesy, because of the Mims owning a towing
service, they were only charged for the window replacement
along with a hit of embarrassment because of their son's
actions. Before they left the lot, they received directions to
the county jail, where they made arrangements to put one
thousand dollars on his commissary account. They declined a
special visit when it was brought to their attention that he
would not be eligible for bail until he was arraigned by a
judge. Mr. and Mrs. Mims left the county jail, stopped by
Circus Circus, and had lunch, then headed out of town
towards U.S. 93 so they could stop and see the Hoover Dam
before nightfall, back in route to Oklahoma City in the Range
Rover.

Chapter 16

Malcolm and Deziree were awakened Saturday morning by the phone ringing on Deziree's bedside table. It was 9:34 when Malcolm opened his eyes and looked at the clock as he heard Deziree speaking on the phone. After hanging up, she gave Malcolm the message Kenny sent for him to be ready by 10:30 because that was when he would be there. Malcolm knew that the information was for them to pick up the van.

Kenny's day started at 5:00 in the morning with a five-mile run. Making it back to the house, he opened the yellow pages, thumbed through the automobile rental ads until he found the one he needed. He tried calling, but it was too early, as he suspected, but at 8:08, he had a 1992 Ford Econoline full conversion reserved. That was easy, now he had to wake up his mama and Malcolm so that he could maintain a schedule.

When Malcolm slid out from underneath the warm covers and Deziree's body heat, he took a shower and got dressed inside the walk-in closet. There he picked out a lined Nike jogging suit all black in which he never wore. It was a gift from Deziree at Christmas. He slid on the suit along with a pair of black and red Jordans with the Jordan long sleeve t-shirt and the beanie. Deciding to keep his attire downplayed Malcolm chose to put on a black and silver Fossil watch. After that he went to the kitchen and fixed himself a bowl of cereal, taking it to the den where he grabbed the remote and turned the television on.

Switching to the Weather Channel, the highway was clear for the journey to the west coast up until Wednesday morning. A winter storm was coming down from Canada and was due to arrive in the northern parts of Arizona and New Mexico in the a.m. hours on Wednesday. Seeing the forecast Malcolm knew right then that they had no time to fool around in California. They had to get down there, handle their business, and get back. Otherwise, from the information the meteorologist spoke about they would risk being snowbound somewhere in the Great Southwest. Not long afterwards, Malcolm heard the doorbell chime. He glanced at his Fossil, seeing it was a few minutes past 10:30, it was Kenny. Malcolm stood up, grabbed his keys, pager and mobile off the table and headed outside. When he stepped down the walkway to the driveway, he felt the brisk Oklahoma wind cut into his face, making him wish that he had put on something heavier. He sped up to get inside the black SS truck. When he opened the door, he seen his mama for the first time because of the dark tint on all four windows, including the windshield. Cecelia raised up the middle seat console, then scooted her petite body over to let him inside. When she got into her spot, she crossed her arms and locked eyes with her youngest son with a serious look on her face.

"Good mornin' mama. I'm surprised to see you up so early on your day off."
"Good mornin' baby. Cut the bullshit, where the hell you boys goin' and who you goin' with where y'all need a van?" Cecelia inquired.

Kenny kept quiet and focused his attention on the street leaving Malcolm all alone to deal with the questions that their mama had to ask. He'd done enough by letting her know that they were renting a van, adding nothing else to their conversation at the house or on the drive over to Malcolm's. Malcolm pulled off his beanie and tossed it on the dash, unzipped his jacket then pretended to ignore his mama by looking out of his passenger window.

Cecelia's forehead began to wrinkle as her eyebrows slanted inward. She unfolded her arms, then twisted to the right, raising her left hand in the air, putting herself in position to slap Malcolm.

"I know you heard me talkin' to you, boy. Don't make me kick ya ass up in here. First, ya big brother wanna play dumb now you too...I see how y'all do me."

"Damn mama, why you trippin?" Malcolm asked as he turned his head to face his mama.

"You watch that tone with me, Malcolm Love. I ain't Deziree or that big butt redhead white gal that you talk to any way you wanna. Me...I'll kick ya ass for real cause you know I don't play that shit!" Cecelia boldly exclaimed.
Malcolm raised up his hand over his face to block Cecelia's hand while he laughed at her a little.

"Chill, mama, ain't nobody trippin' with you. Me, Kenny, and your nephews are goin' on a lightweight road trip. We ain't even gotta destination, we just gonna strike out and decide where we goin' in the mornin'. Kenny's back home to stay, we ain't ever been nowhere together outta town except when we went to go see daddy that one time in Leavenworth when he first went down. Don't worry, mama, I gotta phone that you can call whenever you want." Malcolm calmly explained.

Cecelia's face slowly turned from a scowl to a smile and her arm dropped down to her patting Malcolm on his leg.

"Okay baby..."

Cecelia used her other hand and patted Kenny on his leg as well and gave him a smile too. She continued.

"When you boys get out on the road why don't y'all try and

talk to Gary about goin' back to school. Erlene told me that some of them colleges are still reachin' out to him to go back to school. They been callin' over to her house leavin' messages and he ain't tried to call nobody back. He's usin' you as an excuse, baby, tellin' Erlene and his daddy that he'll get back to them later. When I see his ass, I'm gonna give him a piece of my mind, I already told his mama and daddy not to be blamin' you for their son out here sellin' dope cause he's all grown up. But you know how my big sister is, she's gonna believe her baby and I'm gonna stick with mine. Kenny, what do you think about the situation?"

"For starters, I don't think you should stress yourself with what Auntie Erlene and Uncle Matt have to say to you about Gary. You got enough going on with your own problems by trying to get the restaurant opened up. It's natural for you to be concerned; Gary's your nephew, mama, but he's old enough to make his own choices. Just for you I'll speak to him about his future." Kenny spoke to his mama, knowing that Gooch wasn't about to give up the fast life to go back to college.

"Mama, Malcolm, what do you guys feel about going to grab something at my favorite restaurant tonight?" Kenny asked.

"Sleepy Hollow can't be your favorite when mama gets her shit open. Oh, yeah, Momma, Amber got some other paperwork for you to sign. You need to meet up with her before Monday if you can. By the way, you haven't told Deziree about the restaurant, have you?"
"No, I haven't, but why are you keepin' it such a secret that you're doin' somethin' legitimate with your money baby? This is a big step forward and I am very proud of you and I'm sure Deziree would be proud of you too. I will say this, when she

184

finds out she's goin' to be hurt, especially because you had another' woman put it together for us and not involve her. You have my word that she will not hear it from me. Don't get me wrong, baby, I like Amber too, but do you really want to hurt either of them?"

"Hurt about what, mama? Everythang I do is for my family, I wish Deziree would get on some bullshit because I have somebody else in my corner that's business oriented. If Deziree wanted to start a business, she coulda been doin' it, it ain't like I haven't given her the opportunity to do somethin' several times. She chose to have a baby and now we ended up with two." Malcolm replied aggressively in defense.

"Shut up, boy, she got three babies with you beln' the biggest one. Yeah, I said it, now whatcha gonna do?" Cecelia joked while getting a laugh out of Kenny.

"Punch this mutha fucka Kenny so I can get outta here takin' this verbal abuse from mama's crazy butt!"

They burst out laughing, still Kenny pressed the gas pedal pulling everybody back in their seats because of the torque from the 454 engine.

Cecelia dropped her sons off and was headed back home while they navigated through the unusually congested human traffic inside Will Rogers International. It was close to 11:30 before Malcolm and Kenny were sitting inside the blue and silver Ford Conversion with Malcolm behind the wheel exiting east on Airport Rd. He picked his phone up off his lap and punched in some numbers plus SEND. After four rings, Malcolm got an answer with the sound of voices and trimmers.

DRE LUV

"Barbershop, this Johnny."

"This Malcolm, Johnny, what up my nigga?"

"It's Saturday and busy, let me guess you wanna get in line with Gooch and Solo?"

"Hell yeah, them niggas up there already or did they just call and make an appointment?"

"Naw they here, I'm lookin' at both of them niggas right now flossin' with their jewelry, killin' em." Johnny smiled as he spoke.

"Check it out Johnny, put me and my brother in line with them niggas. We'll be there in about twenty or thirty minutes." Malcolm spoke like a VIP.

"Hurry up, Malcolm, I gotcha," Johnny told him. Malcolm pressed END as he heard Johnny tell Gooch that he was on his way.

By the time Malcolm and Kenny put the van inside Cecelia's garage, she was gone again, leaving Malcolm's truck in the driveway. Quickly, Malcolm and Kenny made their way to the far northeast side to N.E. 36th and Bartel past Forest Park to the barbershop. When they made it there, the only parking was in the grass on the side of the building next to three vehicles belonging to Ghetto Merchants: Solo's Grand National, Gooch's SS Monte Carlo and Big Tay's 442 Hurst. Malcolm and Kenny got out of the truck, walking past the 442, seeing Big Tay and Dollaz with pistols in their laps smoking a fat joint. Dollaz hit the button and let the window down causing indo smoke to bellow out as he looked at Malcolm, then did a double-take as he barely recognized Kenny. He passed the joint back to Big Tay.

"Damn, Kenny, you got big as a mutha fucka!" Dollaz told him with a grin as he opened the door, gripped the butt of his Ruger and stepped out of the car stuffing the pistol in his waist. He gave Kenny a grip and a pull-in hug.

"Deante, it's good to see you. My mama told me about the incident that almost got you taken away for good."

Big Tay let up the window, killed the engine and got out of the car and walked around to the passenger side. Kenny met him as he came around the rear of the car giving him a hug as well.

"If it isn't Brandon, I see that you're still hanging out with the fellas. I have to say that it's good to see both of you guys. So, how's your people doing?" Kenny inquired as they all gathered together closely.

"Besides havin' sugar diabetes and not wantin' to take his shot my grandpa is doin' okay. My mama ain't on that shit no more either, she's workin' at Albertson's now. Everybody else I don't fuck with cause they didn't fuck with me when I was in jail." Dollaz elaborated, then gave Malcolm and Big Tay a fist pound, crossed his arms and took a pose.
"My people doin' the same thang they was doin' since way back...not a goddamn thang but waitin' on me to make shit happen...hey y'all fuck this shit, let's go inside." Big Tay didn't wait for an answer and headed towards the front of the building, sparking the other three to follow.

When the four of them stepped inside the barbershop, they were shown love from old and new homies as well from those who pretended to like them but in reality, were jealous. Malcolm had a team that had clout in the streets and with that clout came followers who would do anything to get on their good side. This included letting Malcolm or any Ghetto Merchant know when there was a particular group or one person talking loosely about trying to take something. Those people were dealt with by means of a few dollars or ounces of dope.

While waiting for his turn in the chair, Malcolm received a call from Deziree.

She informed him that she knew about the dinner reservations by way of Cecelia. She also said she was bored and wanted to know if he had time to catch a matinee.

Malcolm told her to come pick him up at the barbershop and he would go with her. Deziree agreed, letting him know she would be on her way as soon as she took a shower and got dressed. That would give Malcolm enough time to get in the chair, even if he had to go ahead of Gooch or Solo who only needed a shave.

This afternoon rendezvous would work right on time because he wanted to implement his plan before dinner anyway. Malcolm told Kenny, who sat beside him, that Deziree was coming to pick him up and asked if he needed any money. Kenny sneered and nudged his little brother with an elbow shaking his head letting him know that he had his own money. Malcolm nodded his head up and down then combed the room with his eyes again looking at his crew and how the other hustlers all got into the mix with one another. Then he thought about where all of them would be in a year and what Wayniac and TomTom were doing right now in prison?

GHETTO MERCHANTS

Then he wondered what it would be like if they all were here together, even the homies that got killed the morning of the robbery, how different would things have turned out? But for the ones in the pen, they would be taken care of now and when they get home for their sacrifice of taking the case and not giving up Malcolm, Dollaz and Big Tay. It was time to send them a few g's. They hadn't called in a few months, so that meant they were doing okay and getting their minds together for their parole hearings next year.

The streets had changed in the six years that they had been gone, stakes were high and there were a lot of people who wanted him, along with the other Ghetto Merchants off the scene. This was why he was doing all that he could do to get the crew where they needed to be financially and legally because Malcolm knew the day could come and he would be taken out of the picture. As he glanced around and looked at Solo and Gooch high-siding with all their jewelry on and Big Tay with his giving heart, then Dollaz always possessed by greed, Malcolm knew there was no way the Ghetto Merchants would sustain without his mind. True enough, they all possessed heart and muscle and the knowledge to grind but it takes more than that to run an organization worth six and seven figures besides just looking the part.

After getting out of Johnny's chair, Gooch eagerly hopped in while Malcolm checked out his fade and beard in the big mirror, liking what he saw. He then reached into his pocket and pulled out a short stack of hundreds. He peeled one off handing it to Johnny, who paused after draping the cape over the front of Gooch, letting him know that was for the whole crew. Onlookers stared as Johnny put the bill inside his drawer and Malcolm picked up the shop phone that sat on the shelf in Johnny's station. Malcolm hit Deziree on her car phone, after two rings she answered.

"Hello."

"Where you at lil mama?"

"I'm pulling in beside your truck. It's way too many people in that little building baby. Do you want me..."

Malcolm hung up the phone and gave dap to some of the homies as he made his way out the door. When he got outside and walked around the corner, he saw his girl sitting through her windshield smiling. As soon as he got in the car, he leaned over, and they kissed.

"I'm so excited, baby, I can't believe that you spent last night and today with me. It's been like...forever since you spent a weekend with me. I was thinking that we could go to Memorial 8. What do you think?" Deziree asked cheerfully as she backed out and headed north on Bartel.

"I ain't trippin' where we go, but I wanna see The Last Boy Scout or Bugsy."
"But I wanted to see Hook," declared Deziree with an assertive tone.

"I don't wanna see that dumb shit girl." Malcolm boldly replied.

"But it's..."

Deziree began, but she stopped to think when she saw that he was serious.
"Okay, baby, we can see one of your movies today, but we're

190

going to go see Hook, before it goes to the dollar movie or on tape. Okay!"

"You think just because you lookin' cute and shit that you can get ya way?" Malcolm joked while he played with her neck.

"Stop it, boy, I look cute every day."

Arriving at the movie theater, they decided to see The Last Scout. After getting tickets, they got lots of snacks and seats in the upper middle. Thirty minutes into the movie, Malcolm was asleep on Deziree's shoulder. When Deziree woke him up, the credits were rolling, and music was playing.

"You missed the whole thing," Deziree pouted.

"No, I didn't, I just had my eyes closed. I was listenin' to it." Malcolm lied as he stood up and stretched. Deziree stood up as well.

"Yeah, right, if you were listening to anything, it was you...snoring. Come on, boy, and let's go home and relax before dinner."

Malcolm looked at his watch closely as Deziree led him down the row towards the steps to the exit. The time was 4:18. When they made it outside, Malcolm got the car keys from Deziree. He instructed her to wait while he retrieved the car so she wouldn't have to walk anywhere but off the curb.

When they made it home, they went to the den. Deziree sat down in a recliner, giving Malcolm a sad look when she asked him if he would take off her pink and white cross trainers. Malcolm obliged her, then quickly went on his mission inside the garage. There, he opened the storage door that held the main hot water heater. Malcolm approached the heater, then got down on his knees and reached behind it, where he pulled out a blue velvet box. He stood up and dusted off his knees. Blowing the dust off the box, Malcolm stepped out of the storage closet, closed the door then opened up the box.

His eyes were dazzled by the colors coming from the baguette surrounded by princess-cut diamonds set in white and yellow gold. Malcolm smiled and nodded his head up and down with the feeling that the time was right. When he stepped through the arched doorway, he expected to see Deziree watching television, instead the television was watching her. He walked to her, bent down, and kissed her softly on the lips. Slowly she opened her eyes and smiled when she seen Malcolm's face lit up as she reached up and softly cupped his cheek with one hand. Malcolm then got down on one knee.
"I love you more than you will ever know, and I know that there is no other woman that I wanna spend my life with. Will you spend the rest of your life with me and be my wife?" Malcolm pulled the blue velvet box from his jacket, opening it up to show off the engagement ring.

Deziree's eyes opened wide as she slowly inhaled with her mouth open as the colors from the ring jumped out at her. She was speechless for a moment. Then she looked into Malcolm's eyes, observing his majestic pose of arrogance. Reclining the chair and feeling a dense sign of hope for them both, Deziree reached out with both hands to Malcolm's, which held the box open. She wrapped her small hands around Malcolm's, gently closing the box. She observed the joyful expression on his face turn sour. At that point, she knew that she had hurt him on a day that was to be so special for him.

GHETTO MERCHANTS

"Malcolm, I want you to know that I love you. You are truly the one and only love of my life. You were my first, and I pray to God that you will be my last. Baby, I really don't think that we're ready for marriage just yet." Deziree spoke softly while keeping a grip on Malcolm's hands and the box and maintaining eye contact.

Malcolm leaned back and broke the grasp from Deziree and stared at her with a look that burned all the way to her soul. "Don't be upset with me, baby...I didn't mean anything but the truth, and I most definitely did not mean to hurt you." Deziree stood and walked towards him. Malcolm put the box in his pocket and zipped it up, then held his arm out in front to keep Deziree from getting too close and began shaking his head side to side.

"Naw lil mama...I ain't mad, don't even trip, believe me when I tell ya that it's all good. In fact I agree witcha cause I probably got too much shit goin' on in my life right now so I wanna thank ya for openin' my eyes."

When Malcolm finished, he stepped around Deziree and walked to the table and picked up his mobile and headed for the door. Deziree sped up to follow.

"Malcolm, stop! Let's talk about it, baby...where are you going?"
"For a walk, I'll be back in time for dinner." Malcolm walked down the hallway and opened the designer hardwood door, then the glass one. He continued on across the brown lawn, headed towards the street, unintentionally stepping in a stream of water while stepping off the curb; Malcolm pressed numbers on his mobile, then held it up to his ear. Deziree watched as he turned the corner from the top of their lawn with tears in her eyes.

DRE LUV

Back on his mobile, Solo answered after three rings.

"This Solo."

"Check it out my nigga, can you come pick me up?" Malcolm asked forcefully.

"Yeah, lil daddy, where you at?"

"I'm bendin' the block around the corner from my crib headed towards the Denny's."
"Bet...me and baby leavin' Godfather's, the one close to where you at. I'm on my way..."
"Check it out, is she cool?" Malcolm asked cautiously. Solo knew that Malcolm didn't want to lead anyone to his location.

"Look nigga, baby square...I ain't Gooch, alright. You must wanna go pick up ya Lac, huh?"

"Yeah. Hey, I'm almost at the Denny's, I'll be waitin' for ya. By the way, we pullin' outta this bitch at nine in the mornin'. Make sure Gooch ain't got his senorita at the house when we pick you niggas up in the mornin'." Malcolm pressed END.

That evening at dinner, Malcolm and Deziree played it cool, not one time mentioning his wedding proposal. The tension was obvious to Kenny and Cecelia, although neither one spoke on it. When dinner was over, and they were headed to their cars, Malcolm told Kenny what time to pick him up and told him not to forget the bag.

The drive home was quiet for Malcolm and Deziree. When they got inside, Malcolm went straight in the den and turned

194

the big screen on ESPN. After Deziree changed clothes, she came into the den and sat down by Malcolm. He knew she wanted to talk about their earlier episode. Before she got a chance to begin, he stood up and told her that he was going out of town in the morning as he walked out.

Deziree grabbed a throw blanket from the arm of the couch and covered up, leaving Malcolm alone, knowing that was what he wanted for now. Meanwhile, in the bedroom closet, Malcolm began packing a bag for the road trip as he thought about how stupid he looked for trying to get married and getting turned down. He decided at that point that he would never feel that way again.

Chapter 17

Now on Mission Blvd. Kenny was in the turning lane waiting for the busy traffic to break so he could get over to the Mobil Station. While he waited, he combed the station parking lot, finding no brown convertible Dodge Shadow. Finally, when the oncoming traffic light turned red, he goosed the big Ford across the lanes getting over to the station. There, he pulled up under the canopy where he parked next to some fuel pumps. The jarring from Kenny accelerating the van across the traffic into the station caused Solo and Gooch to awaken in the rear and peek through the blinds. What they saw was early morning sun and cars pulling in with California license plates, while Malcolm and Kenny both got out of the van. Malcolm briefly went inside the station while Kenny walked around to the side of the van, opened the fuel door, then unhooked the nozzle from the pump and started pumping.

While Kenny pumped gas, Malcolm cleaned the bugs off the windshield, when suddenly a brown convertible Dodge Shadow pulled into the station. Kenny was the first to notice, so he whistled, getting Malcolm's attention, then gesturing with his head. The lady driving the Shadow pulled behind the van and parked on the side, blocking the front door of the station. When she got out of the car, there was a tall brown skinned, pretty woman with long, thick braided extensions and huge gold nugget earrings. She was wearing black Keds, black tights and a black leather bomber jacket. This bitch is cute said Malcolm to himself knowing she had to be there for them and at the same time she noticed him looking at her causing her to roll her eyes at him while she put her hands on her hips. Kenny watched the whole scene while the side door on the van opened. Solo and Gooch stepped out, ogling the woman, causing her to step back.

"I saw the Oklahoma plate, now which one of y'all is Malcolm?"

"Shaniqua, no doubt, I'm Malcolm," he said arrogantly.

Shaniqua took her hands off her hips as Malcolm approached her, causing her to wonder how these guys could be from Oklahoma. She expected to see them wearing cowboy boots and cowboy hats, these niggas were dressed like Cali drug dealers. She liked what she was seeing, especially the Malcolm guy.

"So, you're the one I talked to on the phone all early and stuff. Why y'all come so early?" She asked with enthusiasm as she grabbed her braids, pulling them over her shoulder.

"Is it a problem that we're here so early?" asked Malcolm while stepping closer to her.

"Oh no, it ain't a problem boo except that it's gonna take us forever to get to Inglewood from here. This traffic is fucked up out here in Cali. Well, we ain't goin' to make it there standin' here at the Mobil. Let's go, we might be able to make it in an hour or so if we lucky. You wanna ride with me, Malcolm?"

At that point, Gooch pushed Solo aside with his arm and jumped in the front seat of the van. Solo stepped back into the side door while Kenny walked around and got back in the driver's seat of the van. Malcolm and Shaniqua slid inside the Shadow then Shaniqua suddenly jumped out and switched her ass between her car and the van ending up at the driver's window. There, Kenny let down the window for her. She simply told him to follow her closely and if she turns on her signal, for him to do the same and clear the way. Kenny acknowledged her request, assuring her that he was more than capable enough to keep up with her big-city traffic. Shaniqua winked at him and switched back to her car. The Ghetto Merchants, along with Shaniqua, were headed to Interstate 10 West.

In the stop-and-go traffic that sped up for a little while then slowed down to bumper-to-bumper stops, Kenny navigated while Gooch and Solo's faces were pasted to the windows. The van was silent except for the radio. Gooch twisted around in the seat facing Solo.

"Solo...I hope we get a chance to go to the Fox Hill Mall and get some gear that nobody from the crib seen. You already know they got all the new shit out here. Picture the hoes askin' a nigga where'd he get that outfit from and bein' able to say..."

"Cali!" Solo finished Gooch's sentence, showing enthusiasm, causing both of them to start laughing and giving each other a fist pound. The laughing was irritating to Kenny because he felt that Solo and Gooch had a complete misconception of the purpose of the road trip. He turned the radio down.

"I've noticed that you two guys seem to only be concerned with leisure time. The purpose of this trip is not intended for a shopping spree; the purpose is to handle business." Kenny explained sternly.

"Holdem up my nigga. What type of bullshit is you on? How is you gonna tell me and Gooch what all our road trip is about and you ain't nothin' but the driver. Me and this nigga been hustlin' like a mutha fucka for years to get up enough dough to be able to come to Cali and now that we're here we supposed to be all super serious like you. I see what it is with you...you think just because Malcolm calls most of the shots with us that we ain't got no input on nothin' huh? Big cousin or not, fuck what you talkin' bout." Solo expressed while he and Kenny looked at each other through the rearview mirror.

"Chill out, Solo, it ain't that serious. You know, really he's right, cause we really do need to handle the business first. Kenny, don't trip on what Solo's talkin' bout. Hey y'all, let's just get along and hope that everythang goes smooth, so that we'll be comin' back down here soon." Gooch explained to them both in hopes of keeping the tension down between his two cousins. Kenny kept quiet but still he glanced back at Solo several times, debating on kicking his ass, when they got wherever they were going. Solo, on the other hand, was furious.

"Yeah, whatever. " Solo remarked, then he returned his focus to the scenery. Up front in the Shadow, Malcolm and Shaniqua got acquainted in a good way while he observed the freeways. They took the 605, then the 710, and finally the 405. That was when he started seeing planes landing in what appeared to be a neighborhood. He was looking at LAX. At this point, the traffic was more hectic there than anywhere else that morning. It took close to twenty minutes to move a couple of miles where Shaniqua exited on LaCienega with the Ford van directly on her bumper. She made a few turns and then they were pulling into the parking lot of Best Western. After one hour and eighteen minutes, they were in Inglewood.

As Shaniqua pulled in front of the office, she observed Malcolm looking at his watch, then shaking his head. She laughed and playfully slapped him on his leg because she finally had an excuse to touch him without getting out of character. Meanwhile, Kenny was backing the van in an empty spot in view of the motel office. "What are you lookin' at your watch for...you tired of my company already?" Shaniqua asked while putting her hand back on Malcolm's leg as he grabbed the door handle. Malcolm tilted his head to the side, looking at her with a confused expression because he remembered Fats telling him Shaniqua was his girl. Shaniqua was fine and put him in mind of Yo-Yo when she played in Boyz in the Hood. More than likely, she was just one of Fats' broads on the side, but still, it wouldn't be a good idea to plug into her sexually.

Without any more hesitation Malcolm opened the door and walked into the office leaving Shaniqua wondering if she was attractive to him, if he was dedicated to one at home, or was this young nigga out here strictly for business. That mystery just made her like his style even more.

After paying for four singles located upstairs next to one another, Malcolm stepped out of the office where his whole crew was standing outside Shaniqua's car door, talking to her. They had all of the luggage except for the military bags. When Malcolm approached, he interrupted their conversation by handing them their key cards and explaining that there were two rooms behind the one door as he pointed upstairs. Gooch, Solo and Kenny all shook Shaniqua's hand that she offered out of the open window, then they headed towards the outside elevator with their luggage, leaving Malcolm's. Gooch and Solo both called him a hater as they walked away, getting a laugh out of Kenny and Shaniqua. Malcolm paid it no mind and decided to shoot his shot at her.

"Why don't you come up and chill while we wait for Fats to

get back at a nigga, or are you gonna drive off in the LA traffic disappearing outta my life forever?"

Shaniqua smiled at him, then she reached in her back seat and grabbed her purse while Malcolm squatted down, resting his crossed arms on her door sill.

"I don't think that would be a good idea, but here's my beeper number and my house phone. Call me anytime if you can keep it on the under, if you know what I mean? What's your area code?" She asked as she handed him the paper with her numbers.
"405."

"When you beep me, put 405 in for a code. Write your number down for me."

"Check it out, I'm gonna hold out on givin' you mine. You'll get it when I beep ya."
"Be that way then. Well, anyways, it was nice meetin' you. Malcolm but I gotta go. I have some appointments at ten o'clock this mornin'. I do hair, I work at my homegirl's salon back in Pomona. You better call me too." Shaniqua smiled and resisted the urge to lick her lips. She blew Malcolm a kiss as he stood up from her door. Malcolm picked up his bag, winked at her as she started up her car and backed out. He turned and headed for the elevator, then his phone started ringing. He unclipped the Motorola and pressed SEND, thinking it was Fats on the other line.

"What up nigga?" He said cheerfully.

"This is your mama boy. I'm callin' to let you know me and Deziree just made it back over to y'all's house. We been at the emergency room since five somethin' this mornin'"

"Is she alright?" Malcolm stopped walking and dropped his bag.

"She's doin' fine and so are the twins. Look, I'm just callin' cause I don't want you to be in the dark cause you my baby. She told me what happened Saturday, baby, and I want you to know that it'll be alright. So, keep your mind clear and get done whatever it is that ya' doin' and come back home baby."

"Let me talk to her mama."

"She's restin' now, she needs it. Where y'all at anyway?" Cecelia attempted to get some information from her youngest son.

"Mama...I'll call later, bye." Malcolm lowered the phone from his ear and pressed END, then he bent down and picked up his bag and headed for the room. When Malcolm got to the doorway that separated his and Kenny's room, Kenny's door was closed. Malcolm opened his door and dropped his bag and headed straight towards the bed. There he sat down and took off his Jordans and laid back, hoping that Fats would hurry and call because Malcolm wanted to get cleaned up and get a few hours of sleep. He didn't want to miss the call while he was in the shower. Malcolm rose up from the bed and picked up his bag, unzipped the side pocket and pulled out his extra battery for his mobile along with the wall charger. He replaced them with the paper with Shaniqua's number.

Suddenly, there was a knock on the door. Without looking out the peephole to see who was knocking Malcolm turned the knob. Solo pushed the door open and followed Malcolm over to the table by the window. There, Malcolm plugged in the charger while Solo sat down. "Malcolm, I need to holla at you for a minute," Solo spoke while pulling out a small bag of weed and a white pack of Zig Zags. Malcolm pulled the cord and opened the curtains, then he slid open the window.

"Hold up a minute Solo, let me try and call this nigga Fats again. I'm tryin' to see where we at. In fact, ask Kenny if he'll get the heat outta the van?" Malcolm picked up the phone and flopped down on the bed.

"That's why I wanted to holla atcha, it's about Kenny." Solo replied as he untied his weed baggie. Malcolm reached into his pocket and pulled out Fats' number, pressed the digits into the mobile and pressed SEND. As Fats' phone rang, Malcolm was wondering what the hell could have happened for Solo to want to talk about his brother. After about five rings, Fats finally answered.

"This Malcolm, I'm out here in Inglewood at a Best Western. I think I'm on LaCienega or Manchester."

"Alright, homie, that's cool. I see you got in touch with Niqua. How long y'all been there?" Fats asked.

"We just made it to the room after takin' forever in that heavy ass traffic from out in Pomona. Check it out my nigga; my brother, cousins, and me are all tired as a mutha fucka. If it ain't detrimental that we handle the business right now, we need to catch some z's."

"That's cool, I got some shit to take care of anyway. Just call me later on when y'all get rested up. I'll come through there and swoop you niggas up and get somethin' to eat, fuck with some broads and kick it a little. Hey man, did you bring the van?"

DRE LUV

"Yeah, Ford Econoline Conversion."

"Bet, we on track already, don't trip cause I gotcha." Fats and Malcolm both pressed END at the same time with money on their minds. Malcolm took off the low battery and got up from the bed and walked to the table where Solo was just lighting up his joint. He slid the battery on the charger and clipped the hot one on the mobile, then sat down.

"You just gonna smoke in the room anyway even though it's nonsmoking, huh? Shoulda known you would be the only nigga to bring weed to California. Fats said he got some shit to take care of but everythang is cool and that he'll be by to swoop us up to get in traffic after we get cleaned up and get some rest. So, what's on your mind?"

Solo took another hit off the joint and passed it to Malcolm, who thumped the ashes on the table, then he put it to his lips and took a hit. "Me and Kenny had a few lightweight words. I feel like he's lookin' at me and Gooch like we some muthafuckin' peons or somethin' and I don't like the shit. Big cousin or not, Malcolm he ain't gonna be talkin' to me any kinda way he want just because he's a war hero. I'm just sayin' in so many words that I see us clashin'."

Malcolm took another hit off the joint, stood up, and passed it back to Solo. Then he took a few steps over to the window looking down on the busy avenue and gathered his thoughts together for a moment. He had some ideas that came to mind when they were on their way out to the coast. Now was just as good a time as any to tell Solo, hopefully it would boost him up.

GHETTO MERCHANTS

"I need not remind you how much we have at stake with this trip. There's no room for mistakes, nor is there any room for error or tension between us, Solo. It's imperative that you put your ego aside for the time bein'. You understand what I'm sayin'? How you gonna let a square like Kenny interrupt your flow? Get a grip on the big picture my nigga. We thirteen hundred miles from home, we gotta be in sync with one another as soon as we leave outta this room and get out in traffic. This shit is real..."

Malcolm turned around to face Solo because he had been looking out of the window the whole time. "Ain't a damn thang about this trip fake. Now check this shit out, I was kinda thinkin' that since we got Dollaz back on the team it will free up some extra time. Deziree havin' these twins in three or four weeks, she's gonna need some help at the crib. You of all people, besides me know how to handle Gooch and you know how to handle yourself and you know the game so I'm thinkin' about makin' some changes in our program. Instead of goin' to Kansas City to ask Auntie to come down here and sign for a house, why not take Gooch and Tay and see what's poppin' up there on some work. We gotta stack now so that we can push when and how we wanna; prices is high as a muthafucka up in the midwest. That's why Paper Boy made that move, niggas is gettin' paid up there so you can do the same thing in your hometown. The good thang about it is that Minneapolis ain't that far away from KC, meanin' that when Paperboy and Hoodsta need more work, they ain't gotta come all the way to Oklahoma to reup."

Solo stood and walked around the table and approached the window that spread across the entire wall. He glanced over to Malcolm, pulling the joint down to a doobie while absorbing the crisp California air and the game that Malcolm was spitting. Solo liked the thought of returning home to shine on all the people that wanted to see him die in the hospital, all the niggas that dissed him when he was just a little nigga in the hood. And all the girls that wouldn't fuck with him because he didn't have any money. Now he was headed down a path of possibly being a million-dollar baller one day. Malcolm was still talking to him, but he didn't answer so he pushed him on the shoulder, causing him to wake up from his baller dream.

"Hey, nigga, is you listenin' to what I'm sayin'?" asked Malcolm.
"Yeah, I'm listenin' nigga...I'm just hungry as a mutha fucka. I wonder do they got some food spots across the street at that little strip mall?"

"Hear me out for a minute and I'm gonna let you do you. Paperboy left OKC Friday and it's Monday now, I'll bet everythang I own that he on the hustle right now to make that shit crack up there where he at. Is he a more thorough hustler than you? Ask yourself that question then answer and see what you come up with. You knew a little bit when you moved to Oklahoma my nigga but since then I've taught you everythang I know, well damn near everythang. I know you and them two niggas can get some grip off them Kansas City streets. You gotta start thinkin' big my nigga, picture us gettin' paid in three states. Believe me, Paperboy ain't gonna fuck us cause he know we know where his family live and he ain't the type of nigga to fuck a nigga outta nothin' anyway. Only a fool would fuck off a good thang with a nigga frontin' birds to em. Do the math for a minute, let's say they payin' twenty-nine or thirty up there and we payin' seventeen. That's thirteen real quick, so what we do is help him build his bank up and keep pushin' ours. When he finished with his, he ain't gonna be able to get his own until we make another trip to Cali. You

206

GHETTO MERCHANTS

feel me? It sounds dirty but that's just the game. As for Kansas City, we can do the same except it'll be all ours. All ya'll gotta do is fade in some of the old spots and ask a few questions and you'll find some niggas you know, even some of your family on your daddy's side of the family. And that 89 shit ain't gonna happen cause you gonna have two niggas witcha that gotcha back and ain't scared to bust a nigga ass."

"All you gotta do is slide over to auntie's house and ask her to find us a house, slide her a few g's for doin' it and pay our rent up for six months. The only niggas that y'all bring over to the crib should be Paperboy's crew when they come to drop off and pick up. It's that easy, you gonna have to buy a safe and keep it at Auntie's house. Auntie Flo aint trippin' bout a nigga slangin' dope, she like a nigga to hustle and she's the coolest outta all our mamas. So, what's up, you wit it?" Malcolm took a breath and waited for Solo to respond.

"Hell, yeah, I'm wit it, I'm with the whole program, you slick mutha fucka. But what we gonna do bout our house in Wildwood and what about the spot?" Solo asked with a confused look on his face and red eyes ·

Malcolm closed the window along with the curtain and headed back to the bed and pulled some draws and hygiene products
out of his bag.

"Solo think big, you ain't a petty hustler my nigga. We gonna keep your house as long as you want it and we gonna close shop up on 24th. Just focus on playin' your part and keep everythang in position and keep your eyes peeled and stay down. We gotta get Gooch away from Martha because if we don't we gonna end up havin' to do somethin' to her and her punk ass cousin Hector." Malcolm explained.as he headed for the bathroom.

"My phone is dead, let me use your shit so I can call my voicemail. Paper-boy might of left a message by now. We gonna have to get some nationwide pagers now since we gain' to be movin' thangs across state lines for real now."

"Go ahead nigga but you better charge your own shit up too." Solo passed him the phone.

"And tell Gooch to ask Kenny to get the pistols outta the van so we ain't up here lookin' sick in case somebody run up on us and we ain't strapped.

Fats sped northbound on the 405 freeway as he glanced at his Rolex, which read 3:25. It had been a little more than an hour since Malcolm called, letting him know that they were ready to get something to eat. During that conversation, Fats assured Malcolm that he would be on his way just as soon as he finished handling some business that was beneficial to all of them. Now that Fats had the business handled and he was en route to pick up Malcolm and his crew, he wanted to hook something up for all of them that evening with some broads. He reached down and grabbed his mobile from the top of the console and punched in a phone number then SEND. The phone rang six times before there was an answer.

"Hello, this is Chocolate."

"What's up girl, this Fats."

"Hey honey, I was just thinkin' about you. What's up?" she

asked.

"I'm on the 405 about to dip off in the Wood and pick up my homeboys from outta town. We lookin' to have a good time this evenin' and I wanted to see if you had some friends on deck.
"You already know I got friends that I can holla at. How many homeboys do you got and what type of hook up are you talkin' about? If y'all wantin' some pussy from a bitch y'all gonna have to give a bitch some money. A bitch ain't gonna be around here flat backin' for free, especially for some niggas from outta town. Where they from anyway?"

"My niggas is from Oklahoma and they ain't out here ridin' no goddamn horses either. These niggas about that paper, so can you hook somethin' up cause I really wanna see you tonight. Tell me somethin', Chocolate Doll." Fats smiled but suddenly slammed on his brakes and swung over in the next lane to keep from hitting a blue Toyota Corolla in his candy green 92 Chevy Suburban on all gold Daytons. The mobile flew out of his hand and then slammed into the dashboard. Fats missed having an accident by inches.

"Stupid mutha fucka!" He shouted as the big truck came to a halt beside an Asian woman's car. To his surprise, the woman was pointing her finger at him as if he had done something wrong. Fats shouted cuss words at her through the glass, then hit his turn signal and busted a right on LaCienega. After pulling into the parking lot of an AM PM Convenience store, Fats picked the mobile up off the floor and sealed the deal with Chocolate, then continued on his mission to Best Western. Within five minutes, Fats was pulling into the entrance of the motel and calling Malcolm on his mobile. Malcolm answered and immediately came out of the room while talking and spotted Fats in the parking lot. They ended the call while Malcolm commenced knocking on Solo and Gooch's doors. He had knocked on Kenny's first when he left his room.

Malcolm turned around and headed for the elevator, not waiting for anyone to answer the door because he'd already let them know that Fats was on his way, so be ready. By the time he made it to the elevator, Solo and Gooch exploded out of Solo's room, racing to catch up with Malcolm who was stepping inside. He held the OPEN button until they pushed each other around on the walkway playfully until Solo won the shoving match to get inside the elevator first. Once they were both inside, Malcolm continued to hold the button because he was waiting for Kenny. He finally put his foot against the elevator door and peeped down the walkway, seeing no sign of Kenny.

"Cuz, I stepped out on the rail right after you called the room and I seen Kenny walkin' across the parkin' lot towards the van," Gooch stated and Malcolm looked through the wrought iron railing towards the van in search of Kenny. He was nowhere in sight, so Malcolm ducked back inside the elevator and pressed 1 to go down.

"Maybe he's gettin' somethin' outta the van." It was the input that Solo gave while he buttoned the cuffs on his long-sleeved plaid Polo shirt. When the door opened up, Malcolm stepped out first with Solo close behind. Gooch detoured, heading towards their van rental, catching sight of Kenny across the way, up under the vending portico and hot tub area. It appeared that he was staring at them along with Fats' Suburban.

"Let's go!" Gooch shouted while waving for Kenny to come his way. Malcolm paused in mid-stride so that he could see which direction Gooch was looking at Kenny. Noticing what Malcolm was doing, Gooch pointed in Kenny's direction so that Malcolm could see him. Malcolm waved him to come on as well as he took off again, heading towards the front passenger door of the suburban. Malcolm got in the front seat while Solo and Gooch hopped in the back.

"I thought it was four of y'all, Malcolm?" Fats asked while getting fist pounds from all three of the Ghetto Merchants.

"It is four of us, my brother is comin' up behind us right now, hold on a minute. Check it out, Fats, we packin' heat, is it cool?" Malcolm inquired with a nonchalant look on his face as he turned his head towards Fats.

"Hey man, I appreciate you tellin' me, but I really don't think we need that many guns. Fuck it, if we get jammed up, I guess ya'll gotta hop out and run." Before Malcolm could reply, Kenny opened the rear driver's side door where Solo was sitting. Solo instantly gritted on Kenny and tried to kick his legs out to slide out of the truck so that he could put Kenny in the middle. To his surprise, Kenny grabbed his left leg with his right hand and slid him across the leather back seat.

"Hey...what's up with this nigga?" Solo asked, feeling powerless.

"What's up is you're the smallest person in the truck and you want to put somebody in the middle. I think you should chill out, little cousin." Kenny sternly stated after getting inside and closing the door.

Immediately, Gooch started laughing after nudging Solo with his elbow. This made Solo even more upset. At that point,

DRE LUV

Malcolm knew that he had to say something before things got out of hand. Solo was small, but he wasn't going to be pushed over, especially with a gun tucked inside his waist.

"Solo, I know you ain't trippin' bout sittin' in the fuckin' middle. Goddamn will you niggas stop the bullshit already?" Malcolm's voice was filled with anger, along with the look on his face when he turned around to look in the back.

"We can take the van if it'll make you fellas more comfortable." Fats suggested.

Malcolm then turned back around in the seat and slapped Fats on the arm in a friendly way, then he reached over and pulled the seatbelt over his lap and buckled up.

"Naw my nigga, we ridin' with you, let's roll. M&M's is where we goin' right." Malcolm confirmed with confidence.

Fats took heed to Malcolm's seriousness, so he put the suburban in reverse and diverted the tension from the backseat to a situation that was important.

"Is there still no word from Javon?" He asked while edging the candy green Chevy into the fast-moving traffic.

"Hell naw. I left messages on the nigga voicemail; Solo went by his mama's house and they said they ain't seen the nigga since Wednesday. I'ma tell ya some real shit, I'm kinda worried about the nigga but at the same time I'm pissed off cause he didn't keep it real with me. We was supposed to have an understandin' when it came down to the work. It was understood that whenever he got low he was supposed to let us know so that we could stay on to keep our people rollin'.

So, the thought of him gettin' ghost and not tellin' a nigga nothin' really does fuck me up. Because of his bullshit we in L.A. rollin' with you goin' to the famous M&M's Soul Food and gettin' ready to set it off without no middleman. I got love for him but fuck Javon now." Malcolm explained.

"Did you know that he's two hundred g's in the hole with me?" Fats asked. Sitting in the backseat, absorbing the conversation between his brother and the man named Fats. Was it a possibility that he lured Malcolm to Los Angeles with hopes of recouping the two hundred thousand dollars that Javon owed him? That was the reason he got the tag number and called a friend in Virginia to run a check on the plates. That was why he was under the portico waiting by the pay phone. Malcolm had already told him that Fats had a green Chevy Suburban. Now he was able to find out who the vehicle was registered to.

"Check it out, Fats, I hear the words comin' outcha mouth, but I wanna make sure we understand one another. Me and my guys ain't gotta damn thang to do with Javon's bill bein' delinquent because he ain't paid his kilo bill. I buy my shit every time I get somethin' from him even if it's for somebody else. It's always cash and carry with me." Malcolm wanted to make sure they had an understanding.

"It's all good, man, believe me when I say that I wasn't implyin' that you was involved in his disappearance. I trust you Malcolm, I believe that you're a straight up nigga and I ain't on no bullshit either cause I damn sho don't have to pull fast moves on nobody." Fats replied in his defense.

Fats navigated through some back streets of Inglewood until they came up on Centinela Avenue. He turned left, and they headed towards the lowering sun. Malcolm sat back in the captain's chair, thinking about everything that was going on in his life and how it felt like the weight of the world was on his shoulders. It shouldn't feel that way because he was at a point in the early stage of his life where he knew what he wanted, and he had the blueprint of how to get it. He had the key to open up what he felt like every door, he had that cash money to make all of his wishes come true. He also had the weight of his Llama under his shirt just in case shit got shady.

They all rode in silence except for the sound of DJ Quik coming out of the speakers crisply with the bass kicked up just a little. They approached an intersection crossing the 405 freeway, the traffic was even thicker now. Fats grabbed his mobile while merging over into the middle lane and pressed in some numbers. He then asked Malcolm if he would turn down the music a little. Within an instant Fats was talking to someone on the other end of the mobile.
"Is this Xavier?" He asked.

"What's up, Fats? I know your voice anywhere, homes."

"Hey man, I need you to make room inside a Ford Conversion Van. The space has to be big enough for twenty chicken dinners and I'm askin' a whole lot right now, but I need it done tomorrow."
Fats switched the mobile from his right hand and ear to his left side so that he could reach down into his ashtray. He pulled out a half-blunt and stuck it between his lips while Xavier contemplated in silence on the other end. Solo's whole attitude changed when he seen the blunt, so he took it upon himself to reach into his pocket and get his lighter. He tapped Fats on the shoulder with it. Fats shook his head up and down, giving Solo the signal to light the lighter. He did and Fats pulled on the blunt, still waiting for Xavier's answer.

GHETTO MERCHANTS

"I can't start tonight esse' 'cause I'm helping my homeboy with his hydraulics on his six four. Bring it to me in the morning and I will do my best to get it finished. You know for me to make a stash that size is going to cost more than the usual esse'. By the way, I moved to the second building one block west of Alameda on 103rd."

"Okay, you say one block west of Alameda on 103rd, second building?" Fats confirmed.

"Yeah, homes."

"Okay, Xavier, I'll be over that way in the mornin'. Peace." Fats lowered his mobile and pressed END waiting for Solo to pass the blunt back to the front then he tapped Malcolm on the arm.

"We got shit in motion. Tomorrow mornin' we'll drop the van off at the Mexican's shop and hope like hell that he can finish by Wednesday. He'll getcha in cause I stay fuckin' with em, but usually he's backed up because of the good work he does, plus he's got a good location. He's right there by Grape Street and Bounty Hunter niggas and all of them that's gettin' money for real and need stash boxes. Out here LAPD and the Sheriff's be sweatin' the shit out of a nigga lookin' for that dope and guns when they pull a nigga over. Like right now, even though we're in Inglewood if the one time get behind us, I'm takin' em on a chase cause we got guns, which means we goin' to jail so you know what it is. Pass the weed youngsta." Fats explained with convincing words, making them more alert.

After taking another pull on the blunt, Solo passed it forward while blowing smoke out of the corner of his mouth in Kenny's direction. Kenny knew what he was doing but paid no mind because he was aware that Solo was young and immature. Kenny's mission was to pay attention to where they were going,

along with the words that were coming out of Fats' mouth. He was downloading everything inside the archives of his mind. At that point, a phone began to ring up front and Kenny observed Malcolm reach inside his Ralph Lauren jacket where he had his mobile clipped inside. He pulled it out and pressed SEND and raised it up to his ear.
"What's up?"

"Hello Malcolm, your mama told me that you wanted to talk to me," were the words that cracked with Deziree's unusually shaky voice.

"How you feelin' lil mama?" Malcolm asked, feeling as if he was being counterfeit. He knew that if it wasn't for Deziree being pregnant with his twins, he wouldn't care if she was alright or not. She knew that, too. Deziree had stressed herself since Saturday night when Malcolm told her he was going out of town. That night, when she got into bed with him, he turned his back to her, and when she tried to put her arm over him, he slid it off. His rejection of her affection made her feel empty, and at that point, she figured out that that was probably the way he felt when she turned down his wedding proposal. Now she was hoping that he would feel pity for her since she had been in the hospital.
"I'm doing okay...so are the babies. We'll be doing lots better when you come home..." Deziree laughed a little, then she cleared her throat to continue, but first she took a deep breath.

"I apologize for being so inconsiderate towards your intentions and your feelings. If your offer still stands, I would be honored to be your..."

"Kill that shit Deziree, you was right about everythang you said. If you didn't mean it, you wouldn't say it, so fuck it. Check this out, kick back and relax by stayin' off ya feet...I'll be home in a few days." Malcolm lowered the mobile phone and pressed END.

Deziree's eyes began to fill with tears, causing her to hesitate on her reply to Malcolm's words, trying to keep herself in check. "Okay, baby, I'll do that. So, what are you doing?" she asked. She repeated her question twice, waiting for Malcolm to answer her, then she figured out that he was no longer on the other end. She slowly lowered the cordless phone with a look of disbelief, finally letting it drop to the bed. She lay back and turned on her side, and curled up in the fetal position, wondering what she had done. Tears fell down her face onto the cover, and her babies began to kick erratically.

Malcolm laid his mobile in his lap, not bothering to put it back inside his jacket, then he reached over and turned up the flat face Kenwood. He took a long, deep breath and shook his head. Fats could see the disgust in Malcolm's body language, so he tried to pass him the rest of the blunt, but Malcolm declined.

"Everythang straight?" Fats asked.

"Yeah, I'm just tyin' up a few loose ends at the crib," Malcolm told him quietly as he looked out the window at the cars on the side of them.

Chapter 18

Fats, Kenny and Malcolm sat in a booth inside M&M's conversing while looking out at the parking lot at Solo and Gooch mack on two local college girls who were driving a 3 series BMW. The two younger Merchants had finished their food first and decided to go outside so they could take a closer look at a bluff across the street that was covered with palm trees. Just as soon as they made it outside, the BMW pulled up, changing their plans. Now they were busy being young men by exchanging numbers with the first California girls they met besides Shaniqua.

"Look at em, they fell in love with Cali already. When they get a chance to step inside Fox Hill or the Baldwin Hills Mall, them two are gonna go crazy when they see all them pretty broads up in there." Fats said in a jovial fashion while stirring his tea with a straw.

"That's just the kinda shit them niggas wanna do but this trip right here we gotta concentrate on gettin' the business handled. Just as long as thangs go accordin' to plan, we'll be back in Los Angeles before you know it and we won't be pressed for time." Malcolm replied with a calm yet serious expression on his face.

Kenny nodded his head, signifying that he agreed with his brother while looking at Fats, reading his body language. He noticed that Fats had a mellow demeanor about himself, even though Malcolm was not being very social since the phone call he received from Deziree. In fact, Malcolm had been acting differently since they left home. Knowing how important this trip was to Malcolm, Kenny decided to do something he felt was needed. Casually, he leaned over.

GHETTO MERCHANTS

"Don't let your anger ruin your business trip. Relax and leave your problems from home at home," said Kenny in a low tone. Malcolm looked towards his brother and nodded his head, acknowledging what was said. He then sighed and focused his attention back towards Fats.

"Check it out, Fats, that's my bad for actin' funny style. I got shit goin' on at the crib with my girl. She's havin' some lightweight complications with her pregnancy, that's why I need to get this business handled as soon as possible. We gotta get back on the road."

"Hey man, I feel where ya comin' from, so there's no need for apologies. I know how the game tugs a nigga back and forth while you tryin' to juggle family and business. Both of em weigh heavy on ya cause they both a part of ya but regardless a nigga gotta do what a nigga gotta do. We all know that if a nigga don't work he don't eat and neither does his loved ones and right now you workin' Malcolm. Give yourself some credit, there's a whole lotta niggas out there waitin' for a muthafucka to give em somethin', you drove across three or four state lines to make sure your family can eat. You also have to take into consideration that you've taken the game to another level; therefore, your problems are gonna get bigger. Prepare your mind frame to no longer let small shit bother you because the small shit will be what'll knock you down to the bottom, quick. So, from this point on you gotta be extra careful bout who you fuck with cause if niggas was jealous of you before they really gonna be jealous of ya now. Fuck em, keep ya eyes on the prize and ya hand close to ya steel." Fats elaborated with sincerity.

Malcolm and Kenny both paid close attention to what Fats was saying, although Kenny didn't understand what he was saying quite like Malcolm did, but he felt the sincerity. Fats was one step closer to being trusted by Kenny and Malcom.

DRE LUV

Malcolm noticed the waitress coming their way, so he slid his plate over and returned her smile as she picked up the empty plates. Malcolm went back to Fats after briefly deferring his attention to the pretty mixed breed waitress.

"Just what is the prize Fats, in your opinion?" Malcolm asked while picking up his soda.

Fats squinted his eyes and smirked at Malcolm, then slapped the top of the table with both hands as if he were playing the drums, and then he laughed. "My opinion of the prize: to die free, raise my kids, and have enough cash for them to follow their dreams and live happily ever after. It might sound like a dream to some, but for me, it's been my motivation to continue strivin' in this dirty game. Nowadays you got so many niggas tryin' to pull a muthafucka down with them cause they don't have the brains or the determination to get anythang for themselves. Those are the type of people that I do my best to stay away from. You gotta stay away from them too because those the type of niggas and broads that'll get a nigga caught up in federal conspiracy. You know how it go, one nigga get caught up and bring you to jail with em cause you out there doin' good. When that happens, you hit like indo weed. The killin' part about it is that you aint gotta get caught with nothin', but hearsay will getcha fucked off."

"Right now, there's some niggas in federal detention downtown that got picked up right before Christmas, then two weeks ago they swooped up another bunch off the streets. Now I got nigga's baby mamas and grandmas comin' by my shop with they hands stuck out, asses out and everythang else out tryin' to get a few hits. Don't get me twisted fellas, I don't mind helpin' a nigga's kids but it ain't my job to keep holdin' a niggas whole family down just cause he caught a case and he get his work from me. Now if I'm

220

puttin' a nigga down and he gets cracked with my shit that's a different story, like Javon for instance, he's on consignment, I'm responsible to help that nigga if he's caught a case. I know you can relate to what I'm sayin' when I tell ya that if a nigga don't keep butterin' a niggas toast somebody is eventually gonna tell on a nigga. Oh yeah, I wouldn't mind gettin' my fat ass outta Los Angeles before somethin' like that happened."

All the while Fats was talkin' Malcolm listened but for some reason he could not stop thinking about his father. He stood up and picked the tab up off the table along with his mobile.

"There's all kinds of bullshit in the game where we live too. I do my best to keep movin' around the town and crush all obstacles that get in a nigga way. I'm gonna share a little somethin' with ya real quick; our mama and daddy brought us up by instillin' honor, respect and integrity. We was bred to keep our word, because when this shit is old and over with rather a nigga dead, or in jail or livin' the dream of bein' in the land of milk and honey all you have to stand on to be remembered by is your word. I'll always be known for keepin' mine and I'll always be remembered as bein' real and for stayin' down and true to the game. That's been me from the beginnin' and that's gonna be me in the end. I got the tab, fellas, I'm goin' to make a call, catch ya'll outside."

Malcolm left the table without saying another word, heading for the register, leaving Kenny and Fats alone.

"Up until Friday evening, I had never heard a thing about you. All of this just fell into my lap and the only reason that I'm here is to look after my little brother and my knuckleheaded little cousins. You see, Fats I'm not a drug dealer like them, I'm a military machine that has been around lots of things and people, which has given me an insight on reading people thanks to my years of training. First, I had my doubts about this escapade because even

DRE LUV

I know how risky this type of thing is, but for some reason, I believe you are genuine. I trust you to be in my brother's company. He comes off as a real hard nose because sometimes...well, you know him already, it's just that he's pretty much raised himself throughout his teen years because I went away to the service. He's had no guidance as a young man but what he's picked up because our father has been in federal prison since he was ten years old. He's taken it rather hard and that's kinda why he's a straight to the point type of guy, he doesn't do well when it comes to bullshit; I'm saying all of that to ask you to be patient, he'll loosen up sooner or later. Well, probably next time, because now he has his mind set on making it out of California by tomorrow night. There's a big blizzard coming down the mountain range of Arizona and New Mexico, and he's having some problems with his lady." Kenny explained.

"Well, tonight we're gonna see if he can't get loosened up by some midnight California lovin'." Fats returned with some laughter, joined by Kenny. After paying the check and stepping outside the restaurant on the sidewalk, Malcolm paused for a moment and took in the beauty of the bluff sitting across the street. It was beautiful—it looked like a giant cake decorated with trees and flowers. Malcolm had a sudden feeling of serenity within himself that he had not felt in days. Quickly, he was brought back to reality as an older black woman snapped her fingers at two young boys tussling with one another, probably her grandkids. Malcolm smiled at her, and she returned it with a nod as she and the boys breezed by him heading into M&M's.
He turned to his right in route of the candy green suburban to see Gooch and Solo still speaking with the girls that pulled up in the BMW, except now they had gotten out of the car. Both of them were dime pieces. Malcolm pulled his phone up and pressed in some numbers but held off on hitting SEND. When he made it to the front of the BMW, he paused, intending to interrupt.

"Excuse me, do y'all have a friend for me too?" Malcolm asked. Gooch and Solo both looked at him like he was crazy, but both females giggled and then answered in unison with big grins on their pretty faces.

"Sure!"

Malcolm winked as he stepped on knowing it would piss Gooch and Solo off. He stepped off the curb, getting closer to the Suburban when the lights flashed and the alarm chirped, and the doors unlocked. Malcolm opened the door and hopped inside, leaving the door open and pressed SEND on the mobile. In three rings, Amber picked up.

"Hello."

"What's up Red?"

"Not much, just reading a book. What's up with you?" Amber asked.

"Just handlin' a little business, that's about it."

There was a moment of silence after Malcolm answered Amber. She took a deep breath on the phone.

"I think I'm pregnant, Malcolm."

"Are you serious?" Asked Malcolm hysterically.

"Babe...wait a minute and let me explain. I missed my period, although that has happened before, but I've been throwing up in the mornings for the last four days. Hey, don't worry if you feel that way, I made an appointment with my doctor for Wednesday, if you want to come."

"It's just that I thought you were takin' your pills; I ain't trippin'."

"You make it seem as if I did this on purpose, Malcolm. Wait a minute...Deziree is good enough to have a baby, babies by you, but I'm not good enough. Is that what you're saying to me in so many words?"

"Hold on bitch, who the fuck you talkin' to? You got me fucked up...you know what Amber, I ain't got time for this shit right now. I'll see you when I get there!" Malcolm shouted, causing Gooch, Solo, and the girls to look in his direction. He lowered the phone and pressed END, finding himself steaming mad and embarrassed when he looked up to find people staring at him. Thankfully, Kenny and Fats were coming out the door. Malcolm tried to play off the incident by pointing towards Fats and Kenny, causing Solo and Gooch to turn around. Immediately, they began to wrap up their conversations.

When Kenny and Fats made it to the Suburban, they were both laughing until they noticed the scowl painted on Malcolm's face. Fats decided to be the first to cheer him up while climbing inside.

"I just got a call from this one broad. She got us all keyed in with some ass tonight, but it's gonna be at least four or five hours before we hook up with em. They're dancers at this little spot right on the edge of Hollywood," Fats stated, while looking down at his watch, then started up the Suburban.

"That's right up Malcolm's alley, a fast woman." Kenny returned in a joking manner as Solo and Gooch climbed inside and closed the door. Solo was so happy that he didn't mind getting in the middle.

"So, what's up with these ho's, Fats?" asked Malcolm while buckling his seat belt. Fats put the Suburban in reverse, checked the mirrors and backed up with the help from Solo and Gooch. After getting backed out, he put the SUV in drive and slowly pulled off. He looked over to Malcolm and chuckled.

"Now that's the Malcolm I remember. We gonna have some fun tonight and get some business handled too, but we'll get everythang else handled tomorrow my man. Just kick back and let me drive this shit out here, y'all my guests and I'm gonna show ya what it's like on a typical night in Los Angeles. I got this broad named Chocolate; pretty black mutha fucka, young, long ass legs, and a money-makin' bitch. Tonight, she and four of her girlfriends are leaving work early to come fuck with us. We gonna meet em over at Chocolate's spot later on over in West Hollywood. We gonna sip on some yac and Alize', blow some good weed and let them broads choose up and have a good time. You know what I mean?" Fats explained boastfully as he crept out on Centinela, barely escaping an accident from a Jaguar heading westbound. Fats paid no mind to the close call with the Jaguar in which the driver was riding his horn as he passed by; Fats leaned forward, putting his finger on the volume button. He paused before he turned the volume up for the drive.

"Hey y'all, we gonna roll over to my shop and grab some indo first, then we'll go next door to this little hole in the wall strip club. That way we can eat away at the time and weigh our options and rap while we look at some more broads. "

"Yo, Fats...can we slide by the room real quick so I can grab my mobile?" Gooch asked.

"No problem, Gucci, we goin' that way." Fats answered.

"It's Gooch, Fats," corrected Solo, causing everyone to laugh.

"My bad lil' homie, I always thought it was Gucci." Fats nodded his head as he looked in the rearview mirror, seeing Gooch looking at him with a grin. Fats turned up the music and showed off what he had in the back with DJ Quik's song "Tonight" jumping out of the speakers.

"Thank you for choosing Leisure Flight Private Jet, ladies and gentlemen, this is your pilot speaking. If you look out your windows, you will see Saint Louis shimmering lights and the Gateway Arch on your left. We'll be touching down in Terre Haute in about thirty minutes. Hope you all enjoyed the flight."

It was the sound of the pilot talking over the PA system while cruising four hundred miles per hour at thirty thousand feet inside a Gulfstream Jet...

PART II

GHETTO MERCHANTS

Chapter 19

It was freezing cold, and the ground was covered with snow outside J Building inside the Terre Haute Penitentiary in Indiana. Chance Love was enjoying his favorite card game, casino, when the unit officer called his name for a visit over the intercom.

"Did ya hear that Archie... a visit? Must be the gamble god tryin' to rescue your janky ass since I'm up on ya ten books of stamps." Chance roared with laughter after "casinoing" his cellmate again.

He scooped up his cards showing Archie all eleven points then he dropped them on the desk and picked up his Hard Time mug and took a sip of coffee. While Archie began to reshuffle the deck, Chance shuffled over to the toilet and took a leak. After he finished and washed his hands the correctional officer was calling his name over the intercom again asking him to come to the officer's station.

"You needsta take yo ass down there and see what they want. We damn sho don't need them comin' up here to da haus lookin' round and findin' the brew cause you didn't go see what them white folks wanted." Archie spoke while he continued to shuffle the cards.

"Shut the fuck up witcha country ass. Too goddamn late to be gettin' scary, what they gonna do, stack another life sentence on top of the ones we got already?" Chance joked while grabbing his pressed uniform from behind the rest of his clothes that hung on his personal hook on the wall above his locker.

GHETTO MERCHANTS

"Just when I get to the point that I's forgotten that I gotta life sentence, you's always seems to remind me somehow." Archie replied with his deep southern accent as he stood up and stretched then headed out on the tier so that Chance could get ready.

While taking a quick shower Archie informed the officer that Chance was on his way. After he finished and changed clothes then made it to the officer's station the C.O. informed Chance that he was going to an attorney visit. He was let out of the block and entered the hallway corridor en route to central control which was located beside visitation. All the while he was on his way he was puzzled by the whole situation of having a visit by an attorney, it was sure to be a mistake of identity no sooner than he entered the room. Besides there was a long eighteen years left before he came up for parole on his life sentence; there was nothing else to do today besides kicking Archie's ass in the casino. He may as well waste some time with the visit being that he hadn't had one for twelve years.

Chance made it to central control, and he was met by the day shift lieutenant who began to escort him to a hallway past the visiting room door. As they made a right down the glassy waxed hallway the seasoned lieutenant spoke.

"Mr. Love...you must be one of the lucky ones who still has ties to the streets. S.I.S. was informed about this visit close to a month ago, they did a little investigating and found that you seldom use the phone, yet you get money sent in every month and you have close to eleven grand on your books right now. I think you're slowly getting your money sent in from the streets old man so you can be in control of paying the team of lawyers behind this door."

DRE LUV

The lieutenant stopped and Chance looked amazed at what the lieutenant was saying.

"Cut the bullshit LT, what the hell's goin' on here?"

"Because the room we have reserved for attorney inmate visit ain't big enough but for three people along with the table, beings that you got a team of lawyers the warden approved you all to use one of our administration meeting rooms..."

The lieutenant unhooked his keys and unlocked the door waving a hand for Chance to enter. The lieutenant locked the door behind them then they proceeded down another hallway; this one was shorter with a stairwell at the end. Now Chance was beginning to have butterflies because he knew that when he got into a room with a team of lawyers he was going to look like a fool when they asked him who he was. Finally, what felt like what some may call a last walk to the lethal injection table they made it to the meeting room. The lieutenant tapped on the door, twisted the knob and stuck his head inside and announced to the visitors that their client was present. In an instant he ducked his head back out and smiled at Chance.

"Good luck Mr. Love, and I hope that you get outta prison before me because I got ten more to do before I retire."

After speaking what he felt were words of upliftment the lieutenant pushed the door open for Chance then he quickly pulled it back.

"I'm supposed to handcuff you, that comes from the captain. Fuck him, I personally don't think you're a threat."

He patted Chance on the back and reopened the door allowing

him to pass. Upon entering the room, he was greeted by friendly faces consisting of two men and two women. All four of them stood up and carouseled around the table. Each one gave him a firm handshake as they passed. One of the men was a tall white man with a beige cowboy hat that matched his tailored suit along with custom boots.

"Good morning, Mr. Love. The name is J. D. Coxel, these two lovely ladies are Shawn Davis and Carla Mosley."

"And I'm Jeffrey Morgan, pleased to meet you, Mr. Love." He identified himself with intense zealousness.

"It's nice to meet all of y'all as well, but I gotta tell ya right now that there has to be some kinda mistake. I got life with at trial back in 1980. I think someone got me mixed up with somebody else, believe me when I tell ya that someone screwed up. There's no need in me wastin' y'all's time or mine. I'm Chance Love outta Oklahoma City and I ain't hired no lawyer, let alone four of em."

After casually grabbing onto Chance's arm and coaxing him to take the seat at the head of the table J.D. signaled for the rest of the team to take seats. He took his seat last and began explaining the purpose of their visit with his deep Texan drawl. Chance placed his arms on the sides of the chair and crossed his legs while focusing on the man who appeared to be in charge.

"I assure you that you are the correct Chance Love. We were retained by a firm outta Oklahoma City, Jackson and Jackson. This came about approximately six months ago. Since then, our investigators have been goin through your discovery, transcripts, hell...we even acquired some undisclosed notes that were thought to be thrown away by the government. We have a wide array of resources to work with."

"I must tell ya that there was no way that you shoulda been indicted under the Rico Act. The cooperation from two of the Nigerians, one being the actual head of the continuing criminal enterprise was the only reason your name was brought to the grand jury. The U.S. Attorney used you as a scapegoat for another conviction knowing that any jury would find you guilty because you were the owner of the gas station which was the hub for the heroin ring. Although you were being paid considerable amounts of cash for the use of your property you should not have gotten a life sentence. I don't give a damn if it is with the possibility of parole, you should have gotten no more than five to life for your minimal involvement. You were never identified by any of the informants as ever being around any drug activity, nor were you ever identified by anyone but the Nigerians during their deal cuttings."

Chance was puzzled by the whole ordeal, the representation and everything that went along with it. One thing that he knew for sure was that his case truly evolved from his small gas station that sat on the corner of N.E. 38th and Lincoln Boulevard. It was no mistake of identity that brought the team of lawyers to the federal prison that he had been at for more than ten years. Suddenly Chance shivered, finding his forearms covered with goosebumps as he thought about the day he was sentenced to life with parole. Cecelia's scream shrieked throughout the courtroom from the time the judge handed down the sentence and the U.S. Marshals ushered him out.

To this day the vision of his wife's tear-soaked face was still a vivid picture in his memory, and there he was helpless, unable to help her in a time of need. Finally, there was a dim light in his darkness that could take away heart wrenching pain. Chance briefly closed his eyes feeling a burning sensation behind his eyelids. When he opened them back, he quickly wiped two individual tears, one on each one of his chubby cheeks. Noticing everyone looking at him, he cleared his throat and took a moment to get his thoughts together without interruption from the law team. They knew that the news Chance Love was getting would be overwhelming for anyone. After about thirty seconds of silence Chance covered his face with his hands and took a deep breath, then he lowered his hands from his face and placed them on the table making eye contact with each person at the table.

"Who's payin' for this cause I know this ain't no pro bono job?" Asked Chance with a look of seriousness, showing that he wanted to know answers now.

Shawn Davis, who was sitting to the right of Chance quickly thumbed through the stack of files she had sitting in front of her as if her job was solely to stay on point. Within seconds she was handing Chance Love one of the rust colored files with a white label that read FINANCE. Chance opened the file and began to read while Jeffrey Morgan began to elaborate. By his appearance he was a typical conservative successful black man with a black suit with black wingtips to match, along with the white button-down oxford and the black tie.

Judging from his balding salt and pepper hair plus the round gold wire framed glasses he was no doubt in his late forties or early fifties. "Our firm has been paid seventy thousand dollars plus travel expenses. We've also been guaranteed a bonus of ten thousand more upon your release. It seems that you were unfortunate enough to have a public defender that misrepresented you throughout your court proceedings along with your trial. In my opinion he should be barred from law and face criminal charges for what he did to you. Several public defenders cut corners and close their eyes when they see a crack in a case that can set their client free or at least

reduce charges to allow their client to get a smaller sentence.
The reason they don't is because they want to keep their
rapport with the prosecutor pleasant. They trade off wins to
those clients that they like, the ones they don't, they let the
government have their way, especially if they don't
cooperate. The same practice goes on with private firms as
well; they lunch together, sleep together and party together.
This type of crap does not happen at Coxel Morgan and
Associates, we work for our clients and do whatever it takes
to make things happen in their best interest."

"Furthermore, we do not work with people that cut deals for
a lesser sentence by snitching. Our main priority is
winning...we like to see our people go home from the
courtroom because of the good job we've done to represent
you. For these reasons, Mr. Love, we are the most sought-out
law firm in Texas; corporate, civil, and criminal..."

As Jeffrey Morgan continued to present the integrity of their law
firm, Chance was still thumbing through the file, reading only
certain parts. Finally, he ran across the part he was looking for. It
was documentation of six payments made to Coxel Morgan and
Associates by Jackson and Jackson by way of his son, Malcolm
Love. Suddenly Chance's reading and Jeffrey Morgan's speech was
interrupted by the buxom blonde with green eyes and pants suit
to match who was introduced as Carla Mosley.
"Excuse me Jeff, Mr. Love...do you mind if I call you Chance?"

"Go right ahead sweetheart." Chance answered while visioning
Carla naked as he finally realized that he was sitting in a
comfortable chair, the first one since he was snatched out of his
house Christmas Eve in 1979.

"Okay, you should be in Oklahoma City within two months, we're going to try and get you a bond but it's highly unlikely. We didn't come up here to lie to you and say that this is going to be easy because we have a fight on our hands. What you have is our word that we will do our best and things are looking good on your behalf because we've found out how the U.S. Attorney broke several rules. We've submitted a 3582 motion to the courts that is going to give them no choice but to rehear your case. If all goes well, we will be getting you freed by getting your life sentence removed where you will be free to go by having time served. I want you to know that my colleagues along with myself will be giving you one hundred and ten percent to make sure you get home to your family because you've been gone long enough for this bullshit. I apologize for my language but that's the truth."

"Now we're going to take a few hours to brief you on our strategy, we're also going to be asking you a lot of questions about what was going on in your life back then. I know you may not want to go back to then because I can only imagine how difficult this has been but it's all in your best interest. By the way we have made arrangements for you to lunch in here with us if that's okay with you?"

"Listen here Ms. Carla Mosley, you can keep me in here all day as long as it's gonna help me get outta this joint." Chance responded, noticing Carla Mosley was not wearing a wedding ring.

Chance's response caused a round of laughter from the whole law team including himself. At the same time when everyone was laughing, he thought about his baby boy. The story was true about him being a hustler, he couldn't help but feel responsible and if anything happened to him it would be his fault for doing what he felt his father had done to get ahead in life. His second thought was about his good friend who had turned out to be like a big brother. Archie would be left alone after being Chance's cellie for the last eight years.

Meanwhile back in Inglewood, California, Malcolm was slowly awakened by the sound of a honking horn from a car alarm. When he opened his eyes, he saw the bright red numbers showing 7:42 inside the pitch-black motel room. He rolled over and put his arm over Gabrielle's waist and pulled her in close. The feel of her warm body next to his caused him to get aroused as he began to slowly grind and she began to moan. Feeling Malcolm's stiffness Gabrielle decided to seize the moment by flipping over to face him and grab his dick and began stroking it until she got it rock hard while kissing him on his stomach and chest.

Gabrielle felt as if she had Malcolm captivated by her intimacy; she got on her knees and straddled him then tried to stick him between her lips. Just as she readjusted her body by placing one hand on his chest balancing herself while having to raise her knees off of the bed to get on him, Malcolm, who had been holding on to her waist decided to lift her off of him. One reason was that he didn't have any more rubbers and regardless of how fine she was he couldn't run up in this stripper bitch bareback. He didn't need another baby and he damn sure didn't need something on his dick that wouldn't ever come off. So, without saying a word he slid to the edge of the bed and switched on the lamp then stretched. Gabrielle crawled up behind him and started kissing him on his neck while holding onto his muscular shoulders.

"What's wrong sexy?" She asked with her seductive Hispanic voice that purred. Reaching down to the floor broke Gabrielle's hold on his shoulders nearly causing her to flip over while he pulled up his underwear out of his jeans. Malcolm stood up then turned around and put his underwear on feeling her breath on his stomach while looking at her perfect body and pretty face. She swallowed hard as she gazed at him from head to toe thinking about how bad she wanted him right now, but it was looking like it wasn't going to happen because something was seriously bothering him.

Outside the horn continued to blare, making Malcolm wonder why nobody bothered to turn off their alarm. Finally, he couldn't fight his curiosity any longer. He walked to the door and opened it up letting a cool blast of morning air flow into the room causing Gabrielle to get under the cover. Although he was cold and covered with goosebumps Malcolm walked out on the walkway. To his surprise the honking horn was accompanied by flashing headlights on his rental. Before he was able to react the alarm stopped and Kenny stepped up beside him, rubbing the sleep out of his eyes.

"Something told me to bring the bags up to the room last night. I did, last night shortly after we made it back here me along with the help from the young lady in my room. They're safe little brother..."

Kenny took a few steps to the left so that he could see the other side of the van. That was when he noticed the broken glass on the pavement from one of the side doors.

"Looks like some snake broke the glass to get in." Kenny calmly told Malcolm as he walked back towards him. Coming out of the doorway that joined both Kenny and Malcolm's rooms were both women that spent the night with the brothers. Gabrielle was wearing the shirt Malcolm had on last night and the other woman was wrapped up in a blanket. Malcolm noticed the change of expression on Kenny's face, so he turned around to see what had caught his attention.

"Hey, y'all go back inside. We got this out here!" Malcolm

commanded with a mean expression on his face that surprised both women.

Before saying another word Malcolm waited for the women to go back inside.

"Somethin's up with this shit, I might be trippin' but one thang I know is that a nigga can't underestimate a mutha fuckin' thang. I gotta call Solo and check on them niggas, and we gotta shake these hoes. They might be in on this shit, who knows. I'd rather be safe than sorry."

"Sounds like you got the right idea. We also need to hurry and get away from this motel..."

Malcolm's forehead began to wrinkle, and he started to grit his teeth.
"I know that look little brother, relax for now and don't jump to any conclusions cause I know what you're thinking. Go on inside and wrap things up with the lady and I'm gonna do the same. I know you think that Fats had something to do with this but before we get things taken out of context, we need to see how the morning pans out. This is Los Angeles therefore anyone could be responsible for the glass. Just be thankful you still have your money, now once again go in there and call Stan and Gary." Kenny spoke quietly.

Malcolm was first through the large doorway then into his room. When he walked inside and closed the door behind him, he could hear the shower running. He wanted to go in the bathroom and shower with Gabrielle, but he knew he had business to tend to that was more important than a bitch. He walked past the bed and snatched up the blanket and threw it over his shoulders on his way to the table where he had his mobile phone. He sat down, picked up the phone and punched in Solo's number. After about five rings Solo answered with a voice that let Malcolm know that he had been asleep.

"This Solo..."

"Solo, wake up my nigga!"

"I'm up, what the fucks up Malcolm?"

"You and Gooch still at that bitch Chocolate's crib?"

"Naw, we in Hawthorne with those sisters. Somethin's wrong aint it?" Solo asked while his piece of game from last night began to stir in the bed as he got up and swung his legs over the edge of the bed.

"Check game...get one of them hoes to bring you niggas over here. Don't be bullshittin' either nigga, get up. Oh yeah, whoever bring you niggas over here let her know that we need directions on how to get to 103rd and Alameda. We also gonna need another place to stay because we might be here a few more days anyway. Shit might get tricky, so be careful of them hoes too, we can't trust nobody." Malcolm pressed END leaving Solo with a task to handle.

Malcolm sat the mobile back down on the table then he walked over to the bed and picked up the room phone and called next door letting Kenny know that Solo and Gooch were safe, and they were on the way. After hanging up the phone Malcolm walked to the bathroom and got inside the shower with Gabrielle.

Back in Hawthorne, Solo got up and put on his clothes as soon as his phone call ended with Malcolm. He shook Brenda, waking her up then giving her a quick rundown on what he needed her to do for him and the crew without giving her too much information. She willfully agreed to help them out and let Solo know that she knew where he needed to go and where a good hotel was in the same vicinity.

Once Solo had that underway, he went to the bedroom where Gooch was and knocked on the door and yelled for Gooch to come out. When he finally came out and Solo gave him the rundown on what Malcolm said he frowned like a child being told to stop playing and go to bed. He didn't say a word, he simply reopened the door and walked back into the bedroom and closed the door in Solo's face. Just as Solo was about to go into the bedroom after him Brenda's door opened, catching his attention. She stepped out into the hallway wearing nothing but a short t-shirt barely covering her pussy and ass cheeks. She smiled at him as she stared while going across the hall to the bathroom that was right across from her sister's bedroom.

When she stepped inside, she nodded for him to come inside with her. Solo began to grin as soon as he made a move towards her. He closed the door behind him, and Brenda reached down and pulled the t-shirt up and over her head revealing a perfect thick body and a shaved pussy. Inside his mind he thought about all the years that he had dreams of California. So far, his dream was starting off good, but he knew that since the phone call from Malcolm the possibility of the dream turning into a nightmare could happen. Brenda stepped to him and began unbuckling his belt so Solo figured that he might as well enjoy the dream as long as he could, besides what's another thirty minutes or so.

Paperboy along with Hoodsta had gotten everything in line that they set out to do in Minneapolis. They partied all weekend, on top of going to the biggest game of the year to watch Washington beat Buffalo. Most importantly they got a chance to network through family with guaranteed clientele from Detroit, Chicago and the metropolitan Minneapolis Saint Paul area. The game plan was set and the only thing they were waiting for was the Ghetto Merchants to get back at them on the route of getting the work up there, and a price. Now it was Tuesday morning, and they were sitting on the couch at Paperboy's cousin's apartment in south Minneapolis. The complex was situated on Bloomington Avenue just off of 27th. This was a high traffic area that was the heart of where they would be dumping all of their work. The area was perfect, there was a store on the corner and a small strip mall on the other corner plus a church.

"Yo cuz, now that you got the plan set up how long is it goin' to take for you to get the work up here?" Questioned Paperboy's cousin Neeko while he was rolling up a joint of skunk weed.

"My nigga told me it would be sometime this week. I believe in him, he's a real muthafucka. The thing that makes me know that it's gonna crack is because he came at me with the proposal. So as soon as he get back at me I'm sure it's on cuz. Last night I left a message on his voicemail so I'm expectin' to hear from him today, tomorrow or never. A nigga gotta be patient and wait, you feel me?" Paperboy answered, then Neeko passed him the joint.

When he stuck it to his lips and pulled, he felt a sense of confidence as the smoke filled his lungs. He knew that Malcolm would reach out and come through when Solo checked his voicemail. Hoodsta stood up and walked over to the window that looked out on Bloomington.
"I'm diggin' this town cuz. The bitches up here are choosin'

like a mutha fucka and all the niggas is just doin' they on thang just like they do at the crib. Not to mention there's a lotta niggas up here crippin'. Yeah, I'm gonna like this shit." Hoodsta spoke out as he left the window and headed back to flop down on the couch. Neeko knelt down and tightened the laces on his Timberland boots while he looked towards the couch. The look on his face showed that he was in disagreement.

"Yo cuz, I'm gonna tell ya right now. It's easy to blend in up here and it's easy to get fucked off too. It's evident that you's a loc'd out nigga, but if you gonna be up here you gotta put that shit aside. The reason I say this is because if you don't, we'll be in some gang shit, that takes away from gettin' money time. I ain't tryin' to be caught up in all that, especially since I been waitin' for a opportunity to make some real money for years. Now I got the chance to have my cousin up here with some work that I got access to, shiiitttt...I ain't gonna let nobody get in the way of that. I'd be a fool to let you or anybody else fuck that up Hoodsta. Now listen to this shit, if a nigga stay on some laid back playa time we'll last and get rich. All I need you niggas to do is keep them birds flyin' up this way."

Hoodsta didn't like what Neeko had said because he felt like he was being checked, and he wasn't used to nobody checking him except Paperboy and his mama. Here he was out of town with his day one homeboy and they was both crips and now they were in his cousin's crib and he was a crip too, but he was talking about being a player. Paperboy watched Hoodsta's facial expression when Neeko was lacing them with the game in his town. Paperboy knew that Hoodsta did not like adhering to anyone else's agenda especially when it came to the point of him hav-ing to lay low with his crippin'.

GHETTO MERCHANTS

He handed Hoodsta the joint and picked up his glass of Kool-Aid and broke the tension that was heating up.

"So whatcha sayin' is that a nigga don't need to be wearin' chucks, khaikis and shit, no powder blue?" Paperboy inquired to what Neeko was saying. He just wanted Hoodsta to understand for all of their safety.

"You damn right...it's enough niggas up here gang bangin' as it is. Why come all the way up here to be on some extra bullshit that's gonna draw unnecessary attention by havin' blue flags hangin' outta ya pockets. Don't get strikes against ya for dumb shit cuz when all y'all gotta do is sit back and count money. Let us niggas from Minnesota handle the rest." Neeko explained so there would be no misunderstanding.

Hoodsta stood up and walked over to Neeko with his perfect strut, swinging his arms in rhythm to his skip-like walk and gave Neeko a fist knock. That was his way of acknowledging his g status in his town, still he wanted to make himself clear on where he stood.

"Alright cuz, I know a nigga gotta be smart if we gonna last in this shit. I ain't gotta problem with fallin' back if that's what the program consists of but believe me when I tell ya that if some funk jump off, I'm gonna bust on the first thang movin' and get outta town on the first thang smokin'. Yeah, my nigga, I put that on my hood cause we get it on down our way too. We sendin' niggas home in body bags where I come from."

Paperboy stood up and rubbed his hands together after he listened to Hoodsta's rant. "Fuck some talkin', let's go grab somethin' to eat and then let's hit the mall and get some Timberlands so we can blend in with the rest of you niggas. I'm all for not havin' to do nothin' but count money and fuck with bitches." responded Paperboy.

They all laughed amongst each other while grabbing their coats as they headed out the door.

After getting in and out of the shower in a hurry to get away from Gabriel's exotic sex appeal Malcolm got dressed quickly and impatiently waited for her to do the same. He watched her moves from twisting up her long curly hair and pinning it up with a pencil from her purse, to pulling her skin-tight dress over her head without panties or a bra. Since he met her last night, he had spent countless minutes looking for a flaw on her five-foot curvaceous body along with her Asian and who knew what other ethnic background she was from. Here it was the morning after and the only flaws he could come up with were that she could be involved in what could be a move against the Ghetto Merchants' cash and the fact that she was a stripper/hooker. But the biggest flaw of them all was that she didn't live in Oklahoma City. It was probably best because she was so fine that she would have a nigga fucked up and off trying to keep up with her.

"I can't believe that you're actually kicking me out." Gabrielle stated, then she sat down next to Malcolm and put on her shoes that were on the floor.

Goddamn this girl is fine. Malcolm thought to himself. But now wasn't the time to be putting ass over business, getting out of Los Angeles with all that he came for was priority.

"It's nothin' personal young lady, it's just that I have some things to do that are more important....you probably ain't

used to a nigga tryin' to rush you off cause..."
Gabrielle raised her head up and batted her thick eyelashes
exposing her big almon-shaped brown eyes and smiled briefly
before cutting Malcolm's speech off.

"You are most certainly right; this is the first time ever that a
man asked me to leave before I was ready. It's something
about you, you're different than most guys that I've been
with, or should I say...that I've been around."
"You don't say huh, so how much do I owe ya for last night?"
Malcolm asked nonchalantly while reaching into his pocket.

Instantaneously Gabrielle's smile turned upside down to a
frown and her forehead wrinkled up while she rose to her
feet and stuck her hand out putting her finger In Malcolm's
face.

"Owe me...nigga I ain't no hoe! I don't know what kinda game
you and Fats think y'all playing but I ain't the bitch you think I
am. Just because I take my clothes off for a living doesn't
mean my pussy is for sell. I swear I can't believe that I actually
thought you was different. Every last one of you drug dealers
that have a little bit of money turn out to be all the same..."

"Holdem up girl, chill out. All we have is a simple
communication problem. I was under the impression that we
was all hookin' up for a few dollars. Goddamn, you done took
this shit way outta proportion."

After listening with her arms crossed and tapping her foot
Gabrielle went over to the table and snatched her purse then
strutted towards the door.

"I'm leaving. Will you call your brother's room and tell my girl
that I'm waiting for her in the car, I've had enough of this

shit."

Just when she was reaching for the doorknob Malcolm grabbed her by the arm with his right hand while he held her jacket in his left. When she stopped, she turned around and stumbled backwards, Malcolm caught hold of her arm firmly and held her up against the wall causing her to be startled.

"Look woman, you can leave outta this room with an attitude if you want, but I want you to know that your reasons are all wrong. I'm not here to judge you by what you do for a livin', neither did I ask you to come to this room to disrespect you. If you's a stripper you's a stripper, if you's a hoe you's a hoe, I do not give a damn just as long as you give me my respect. You do that and I'll do the same for you."

Gabrielle was suddenly turned on by Malcolm's vicious tirade. She dropped her purse, letting it drop to the floor then she tiptoed and threw her left arm around Malcolm's neck and kissed him on the mouth. Gabrielle's actions caught Malcolm off guard causing his reaction to pull away, breaking the brief embrace.

"Hold em up little lady, I thought I told you last night that I didn't do any kissin'." Malcolm told her as he headed back towards the bed, turning his back to her.

Gabrielle was in an embarrassed state of mind hating herself briefly for being such a silly heart because she realized that she had suddenly found herself having a crush on the out of towner. Quickly she bent her knees and picked up her purse from the floor all the while her and Malcolm stared at one another. "I apologize for springing that kiss on you, I...I don't know what came over me. I've got to know something; did you mean what you said before I attacked you?"

Malcolm was just about to sit down on the bed, instead he turned around to face her finding her approaching fast while reaching for her jacket that he still held in his hand.

"Oh yeah...now I'm trippin', this jacket ain't gonna look half as good on me as it does on you. Malcolm handed her the jacket and smiled, she smiled back and giggled at his humor while she put the jacket on.

"As far as what I said about not judgin' you for what you do for a livin', you damn right I meant it. I think you're a cool chick Gabrielle, who knows, maybe one day we'll hook up again and do somethin' besides hang out at Chocolate's crib and a motel room."

"I'd like to hang out with you too, in fact, how about the next time you decide to come to L.A. let me show you around Hollywood. I think you'll like it because you're the type of guy that likes flash, I can tell. As for now I'd better go. Ohhh, do you need help finding a place to fix your van?"

"Naw girl, I'll get it handled. Don't worry, let me walk you to your car and we can knock on the door for your friend."

"You are such a gentleman, by the way...I wrote my beeper number down plus my house phone. I put it in the drawer over there, use it sexy and let's go so we can handle our business." Gabrielle explained as they both headed towards the door.

It took almost an hour for Solo, Gooch and Brenda to make it the motel. As soon as they all made it upstairs, Solo let Brenda in his room while he and the rest of the crew discussed their situation along with their game plan. They met up in Kenny's room and there Solo let them all know that Brenda was down to help them out any way that she could. Gooch was loading his extra clip with socks on his hands while Kenny checked out the Mac.

"What's up cuz, I mean what we gettin' ready to do?" asked Gooch, noticing the disarray in Malcolm's behavior that was usually noticeably collective.

Malcolm picked up his blue steel Smith and Wesson by the wooden grip off the table and pulled the slide back to check the chamber. He was unsure if he had chambered one or not. Malcolm was on edge, and he didn't like being in this situation, yet he was, but he had family with him that he trusted that had his back. He had to get his mind right and come up with a plan, and it had to be executed quickly, allowing little to no room for error.

Malcolm wanted Fats to be his number one suspect, but in order for him to be sure he had to know what happened last night after he and Kenny left them all at Chocolate's house. Too much was on the line to have a misunderstanding that could cost them their lives; the money came second.

"I'm not quite sure what we're goin' to do yet...how bout you tell me what happened at Chocolate's after me and Kenny got on?" Malcolm asked while looking in Gooch's direction. He was excited because Malcolm asked for his input first.

"Okay...not long after you and Kenny left me and Solo agreed that we was goin' to spend the night with Felicity and Brenda at their crib. After we had that settled and Fats found out that he wasn't gonna have to bring us back over here he went to the back of the house with Chocolate. Right when we was gettin' ready to leave with the girls some nigga come over, his name was Scoob. How bout this nigga come in the crib tryin' to push up on Felicity. She wasn't havin' it, so they end up arguin' and shit until Fats shows up and tells the nigga to shut the fuck up. Fats apologizes to us; the nigga sit down on the couch, and we leave out the crib. On our way to the car Felicity and Brenda both tell me and Solo that nigga been tryin' to hook up with both of them since they met him through Fats. They say that since neither one of them ever gave him the time of day he just be on bullshit when they see one another."

"So, is that all that happened?" Kenny asked, looking in Solo's direction.

"What...we left and went over to their house and got some pussy, what do you think we did?" Solo responded with a smirk on his face. Kenny's body language suggested that he was fed up with Solo's smart mouth. Malcolm noticed.

"Hey! You two niggas are gonna have to let y'alls egos go someplace else because this ain't the time or place. I'm serious, cut that bullshit out, Solo, Kenny."

Malcolm chastised them, they both nodded their heads in agreement. That was when Malcolm's mind let him come up with a plan. He stood up and paced the room a few times in silence, then he looked out on the busy street out the window. After he looked out at the traffic and the rest of the scenery he turned around and leaned back on the window seal and began to explain. "This is what we're gonna do. We'll get Brenda to drive the van cause the first thang we gonna do is find the Mexican's shop that's gonna put in the stash. We got the cross streets bein' 103rd and Alameda, all we gotta do now is find Xavier. Solo, you ride with her, and we'll follow behind in the car. We get the van dropped off then we go check into the hotel she was tellin' Solo about that's in Compton. Then we go check on Fats, we'll surprise the nigga by showin' up at his shop. If he had anythang to do wlth what happened, it'll show all over his fat ass face. Who knows, it may be just coincidence for someone to break in a van with Oklahoma plates. Fuck it, it's done and over with now, let's get in traffic."

Everybody stood up and grabbed their bags, Kenny and Gooch grabbed the two military duffles as well. Just when Gooch was heading out the door he turned around and asked a question.

"Why let Solo and Brenda drive the van?" Malcolm almost snapped then he thought about what Gooch said. "You know what Gooch, you got somethin'. Kenny it might be better for you to ride because the van is rented in your name. Who knows, the van looks like it could be stolen, if the police pull it over it would look better if you was in it. Solo go tell baby what that part of the plan is real quick and meet us downstairs."

After Malcolm rearranged the plan quickly, they all left out of Kenny's room. Malcolm made a quick stop next door at his room and slid open the bedside table drawer. Inside sitting on top of the Bible was Gabrielle's number on a piece of folded stationary folded sealed with a kiss from her lipstick.

Chapter 20

Kenny drove with Brenda giving directions from the passenger seat of the van while Solo followed with Gooch and Malcolm riding shotgun in her Accord. They stayed on the freeway until they exited off on Alameda, on the eastern edge of downtown Los Angeles. At the light at the bottom of the ramp Kenny turned right and they traveled south until they got to the intersection of 103rd. Needing no instruction from Brenda, Kenny pulled over to the curb as soon as they drove through the green light. Right there on the sidewalk stood an old Mexican man wearing blue and white pinstriped jean overalls selling roses and oranges.

Everyone got out of the vehicles meeting up on the sidewalk except for Brenda who stayed inside the van. Malcolm reached inside his pocket for money and when he pulled his hand back out, he peeled one twenty-dollar bill from his wad. Everyone from Kenny, Solo and Gooch wondered just how they were going to find the shop owner named Xavier, including Malcolm. When he saw the old man hustling on the curb, he had an idea that would possibly work. Malcolm approached the old man, both with grins on their faces except the old man's grin revealed a couple of missing teeth. Malcolm handed the old man the money while checking out the location, they were virtually surrounded by warehouses. This particular area was mostly all industrial, therefore they would need help from someone familiar with the area and knew Spanish because all they saw around were Mexicans. To Malcolm's surprise the old man spoke English.

"Senor, would you like oranges or roses?" he asked with broken English while stuffing the twenty-dollar bill inside his pocket on the bib of his overalls. Malcolm kept his hand extended until the old man noticed that he was holding it out for a shake, then he obliged. After the shake Malcolm turned around and pointed at the van with the broken window which was obvious with it being a new vehicle. Malcolm turned back around to face the old man who was still leaning to the side from looking around Malcolm along with Kenny's large frame. At that point Malcolm made praying hands and put what he felt was a sincere look on his face.

"Sir, if you could please help me and my family find a shop that is owned by a dude named Xavier. He's supposed to do some repairs on my van, but I don't have his number anymore because he just moved his shop over here not too long ago." Malcolm spoke with conviction, making the old man interested.

The old man paused before answering by tilting his head to the side and putting the palm of his left hand on the side of his face before his face lit up along with his index finger pointing straight in the air.

"You say Xavier, eh?"
"Yes sir, in fact if you can find him, I'll give you an extra fifty dollars."

That was the time that Solo shook his head in disbelief at what Malcolm was trying to do and walked over to the van to talk to Brenda. Gooch reached down and grabbed a bag of oranges after making eye contact with the old man and pointing towards the bags and roses in his cart. Instantly he popped one of the oranges free from the plastic and started peeling it with his teeth. As for Kenny, who was standing within arm's reach of his little brother, he was watching the traffic coming towards them from the west on 103rd and the cars and trucks going up and down Alameda. It seemed as if everyone driving by was looking in their direction.

GHETTO MERCHANTS

The old man, he squinted his eyes when the sun in the east suddenly rose above the van hitting him in the eyes while he dug deep into his memory in hopes that he could make an extra fifty dollars this morning. After about a minute of contemplating he began to nod his head and grin showing his yellowed jagged teeth.

"Senor, you give me three, no five minutes and watch my things here. Me know who you look for. I be right back."

In an instant the old man spun around and trotted down the sidewalk headed west. Malcolm rubbed his hands in the air hoping that he didn't make a wrong choice and that the old man wouldn't return with a gang of Mexicans strapped with AK's. From inside Brenda's car he heard his mobile ringing, so he went to go answer it.

"Hey fellas, I'm gonna need ya to get on point. We don't know what's going to come around the block, the sidewalk or from behind one of these buildings. For just a few minutes I need your undivided attention...please. Kenny requested to Gooch and Solo.

Malcolm reached inside the open window and pulled out his mobile, pressing the SEND button. He turned around and edged over and sat on the hood of the Honda giving himself a clear sight of everything coming in his direction on 103rd.

"What's up?"

"Hey man I'm sorry I'm runnin' late. I had some last-minute supply pickups that I had to get for my shop. Give me about an hour and I'll be that way, right now I can't get away my man." Fats explained with the sound of seriousness in his voice.

DRE LUV

"Are you gonna be at the shop?" Malcolm asked firmly.

"Yeah, well at least until this last delivery gets here then I'm on my way to you." responded Fats unassuming that there was a matter.
"Cause I'm already on my way over there." Malcolm answered not knowing what was in store with his destiny in the next five minutes let alone in the next hour. Malcolm pressed END. Just as soon as he lowered the mobile phone, he heard a loud whistle.

Kenny was the whistler getting his attention over the noise coming from a freight train on the east side of Alameda. When Malcolm looked towards Kenny he nodded his head towards the west. Sure, enough it was the old man walking in their direction with another man, this one was Hispanic as well. He wore faded green coveralls with a black bandana tied around his head Aunt Jemima style with the swagger of a gang banging Mexican. The closer they got to the corner Kenny could tell that the younger guy wasn't strutting because he was only swinging one arm, he was walking that way because he had his right hand inside his pocket holding on to something. The old man was smiling when they met up, but the younger man was looking serious as he observed four black men, two of them were spread apart with their hands under their shirts.

"Who's looking for Xavier?" he asked as he stopped about five feet from Malcolm and Kenny.
"Yesterday evenin' I was with my homeboy, his name is Fats, do you know him?" Malcolm asked.

Xavier swallowed hard and cut his eyes left then right trying to get an eye on Solo and Gooch who had now made it ten feet from him on both sides. Nervously Xavier nodded his head up and down acknowledging that he knew a Fats.

254

GHETTO MERCHANTS

"Okay esse' that means we're gettin' somewhere. The van he spoke on is the one parked behind me." Malcolm explained, then gave Solo, Gooch and Kenny a stare down look. The old Mexican man had already backed up ten feet away while Xavier still held his ground knowing that he didn't stand a chance if some funk jumped off.

"Yeah homes, I remember but he didn't say anything about a window." replied Xavier cautiously as he watched Malcolm reach into his pocket.

Malcolm pulled out his wad and peeled off a one-hundred-dollar bill and handed it in the old man's direction who came forward when he saw the money along with a slight grin on Malcolm's face. When Malcolm handed it to him, he nodded.

"Muchas gracias, señor."

"Good lookin' out old school, we couldn't of found homie right here if it wasn't for you." Malcolm expressed gratitude as they shook hands again ending their business once and for all. The old man nodded his head and waved at the other Ghetto Merchants and at Brenda, he then stepped to his cart and began pushing it towards the north. He was headed towards downtown or Southgate.

Malcolm refocused his attention back to Xavier who had now taken his hand out of his pocket and struck a pose with his hands locked behind his back.

Check this shit out esse', somebody broke in my shit last night in the parking lot of the motel over in Inglewood. I'mma keep it real witcha, all I want is to get the stash spot put in and the glass put back in the mutha fucka. We gotta be on the road this evenin' homie." Malcolm explained while going after Xavier, who ended his pose and headed towards the van.

"How big do you need the stash spot homes, cause if I have to do lotsa work it's gonna cost you some extra bread, especially if you want it by evening...today".

"Check this shit out esse', I ain't trippin' bout no extra bread. I need a job done and I need it done fast, can you handle it or not? I need a spot big enough to put twenty ki's, plus I need some extra room for some guns. If you can do that, we got business to handle, if you can't we gettin' ready to push on down the road?" Malcolm asked aggressively while Xavier was looking at the door with the busted window.

Xavier listened to Malcolm while he picked out pieces of shattered glass that was stuck in the rubber seal. When Malcolm stopped talking, he turned around to face him.

"Be cool homes, let's go around the corner to my shop and I'll give you a price. I'm gonna have to get some help if I'm gonna finish today. I'm tellin' you this because most guys don't like extra people knowing where their stashes are located. I guarantee you that my friend is solid, you don't have to worry about him, okay. Well let's head around the corner, I'll drive the van..." Xavier laughed as he and Malcolm gave each other a soul handshake, then he headed around the back of the van, there he saw the license plate.

"Damn homes, you brothers are from Oklahoma? Where is Fats at anyway, that fucker owes me three hundred.''

Malcom opened up the passenger door, Brenda got out and went to her car while Malcolm waited for Xavier to get in. Kenny was still standing next to him.

"Brenda...hold on a minute..." Malcolm told her as he walked towards her and Brenda stopped and turned around when she heard his voice.

"How far away is that motel you was tellin' Solo about?"

"It's straight down this street that way. It's the Compton Hilton and it sits on the corner by the 91 Freeway, it'll only take about ten minutes to get there."

Hearing Brenda's statement Malcolm quickly explained his plan to everyone. First, he had Kenny go ask Xavier for directions to his shop from where they were standing. Secondly, he asked Brenda if it was okay if they used her car for a little while after she took Solo and Kenny to the hotel. She agreed just as long as they were going to be able to take her to work tonight. Malcolm assured her that she would make it to work on time, and that she would be compensated for her help. She declined to take any money for helping them. That made things run a little bit smoother, having a local on their team that appeared to be real. Brenda went ahead and got in the passenger seat of her car while Malcolm explained to Gooch and Solo. He let them know that Solo would stay at the room with Brenda with all of the luggage and the money, Kenny would drop them off and come back and pick him and Gooch up at Xavier's shop. From there the three of them would slide by Fats' detail shop on El Segundo.

Without a doubt Xavier would be able to give them directions. The last thing that Malcolm instructed Solo to do was get a suite so they would have enough room for everybody to get some rest when they all made it back to the Hilton. By the time Malcolm was finishing with his game plan Kenny walked up and all Malcolm said was, come and pick him and Gooch up at Xavier's and grab the rest of the bags out of the van.

After Kenny and Solo grabbed the other bags from the van Malcolm and Gooch got in and Xavier drove them through a maze of warehouses after turning off of Alameda into an alley. They ended up one and a half blocks away from the corner where they first met the old man that introduced them to Xavier. Once they made it inside Xavier's shop, he and Malcolm struck a deal to get all of the work done for five grand. After the deal was dealt Malcolm raised the stakes and made what he hoped was a guarantee of getting the work done on time by offering Xavier an extra thousand if he could be finished by six o'clock. Xavier agreed with the terms, liking the way the young dope boy from Oklahoma did business. Malcolm reached into his pocket and pulled out two stacks and handed it to Xavier. Then he surprised Gooch by asking him for a thousand. Gooch looked at Malcolm in disbelief when he asked him, but he gave Malcolm the money anyway. Malcolm took it and headed towards the office where Xavier had walked to. When Malcolm stepped into the office, Xavier was making a call; he held his finger up in the air for Malcolm to hold on. He put the phone on speaker, sat the receiver back in the cradle and sat down on the edge of his desk when someone on the speaker said,

"Hola."

"Voy a pagar sus mil dólares para que me ayude en la actualidad (I'll give you one thousand dollars to come help me today)." Xavier answered, then hit the off button without waiting for an answer.

"Mi relative will be on his way to help, believe me when I told him I'd give him a thousand dollars all he seen was pesos in his eyes," Xavier explained with laughter in his voice while Malcolm passed him the money he got from Gooch, who just walked into the office and sat down.

"Say homes...you are spending a lot of bread for a stash in a rental. You should probably invest in your own van or truck. That would save you lots of bread, man instead of doing this every time."
"I gotta 454 SS." Malcolm stated arrogantly.

Xavier scooted back on his desk and began to market his skills.

"What I can do with your truck is put a dummy gas tank on the passenger side. It is double lined all the way around where if the police tap on the tank, it sounds like there is fuel inside, but really it is water, except for in the filler neck. The filler neck is sealed at the bottom, and it's filled with fuel to give the illusion that the tank is full. Take my word, it will look as if Chevrolet put the extra fuel tank in at the factory but really you'll have a fake tank that will hold forty kilos and some artillery. I tell you what, bring the truck out here and I give you a deal. Give me two days and forty-five hundred dollars and it'll be ready for the highway. Hey, homes, it's just an idea, think about it. For now, write a number down that I can reach you at when I finish your rental...here is a pad and pen. I have to get to work." Xavier told him, then he slid off of the desk, handing Malcolm a notepad along with a pen. He walked around his desk and sat in his chair.

While Malcolm wrote down his number, Xavier shuffled through some papers on his desk until he found the one he needed. He reached forward and grabbed the phone and made a call to get a replacement for the broken glass. Being on the phone for no more than thirty seconds, he got up and headed for the shop area, then paused right before he made it to the doorway and turned around.

DRE LUV

"What's your name homes?"

"They call me Love," Malcolm responded quickly, not wanting to give Xavier his whole name, knowing that he would assume Love was a street name.

"Okay, Love, you guys kick back in here while I get started."

Xavier walked out of the open doorway to the shop and got to work on the van on his own while Malcolm and Gooch waited for Kenny to return. About twenty-five minutes passed by when the outside office door swung open. Just when Malcolm thought Gabrielle was the prettiest woman on the West Coast, he found himself to be mistaken. A woman with light brown skin walked in with dark brown hair with blond streaks, pink lips and what appeared to be no makeup. She wore a long-sleeved beige and red paisley silk blouse buttoned up just enough to make you wish the button would pop loose. Her pants were khaki and, on her feet, up to her knees were dark brown riding boots that matched her belt along with her Fendi purse that hung over her shoulder.

Both Malcolm and Gooch were speechless as she passed through, only acknowledging them with a slight head nod and a fake smile. When she passed, Malcolm leaned forward, watching her hourglass frame strut towards the Ford van where Xavier was working on inside the rear doors, making noise with some power tools. When she made it to the van, the only words that Malcolm and Gooch could understand were when the woman shouted Xavier's name; everything else was spoken in Spanish with a loud, high-pitched voice. The pretty woman's tirade went on for about two minutes while Xavier stayed inside the van. Finally, he slid out, still she gave him no room to explain whatever it was she was upset about. Suddenly, the woman reached inside her purse and pulled out a chrome revolver that looked like a 38.

Before Xavier could budge, the woman slapped him on the side of his face with it, causing him to grab his left cheek. Surprisingly to Malcolm and Gooch, Xavier didn't defend himself; instead, he took more verbal abuse from the woman who pointed the gun at his forehead twice during her rant.

Finally, she walked away, headed towards the office. Malcolm and Gooch both casually put their hands on their pistols but not showing them. When she made it halfway, she dropped her heat back inside her purse and used the same hand to get her hair out of her face. That moment was the sexiest thing Malcolm had ever seen a woman do; he wanted her bad. As she walked through the office, she passed them this time as if they were invisible and went out the front door. Malcolm hopped up from his seat and dashed to the door and looked through the glass. The pretty woman was getting behind the wheel of a late-model E-Class Mercedes-Benz.

Just as she was putting her key into her ignition, she looked towards the front door of the shop in time to see Malcolm staring through the glass. She realized that she was frowning when she looked into the mirror and put the car in reverse. Before she backed out, she turned around to see that Malcolm had come out of the door, approaching her car. She smiled at him, but still she backed out onto the street and drove off. Gooch came outdoors to see what was going on to find Kenny driving up.

"Go ask that muthafucka is he still gonna have the van ready...never mind, I'll go ask. I'll be right back." Malcolm said before he walked back inside the shop.

When Scoob stepped inside Fats' office, Fats was sitting behind his desk, looking over some paperwork.

"Big homie, what's up?" Scoob asked as he took a seat in front of the desk. "I'm tryin' to get some figures straight in this ledger before Malcolm and his crew get over here." Fats replied without raising his head up to look at Scoob.

"Them Oklahoma niggas are coming over here...when?"

Hearing the change in Scoob's voice, Fats raised his head and dropped his pen when he saw the unusual, frightened look on Scoob's face.

"What's wrong man?" Asked Fats as he scooted forward and placed his arms on top of the desk giving Scoob his full attention.

"Nothin', I was just askin'. Where they at now, still in Inglewood?" "If nothin's wrong why the fuck you askin' all the questions then? What the hell you up to man, cause I can tell you up to no good?"

Scoob nervously rose up from the chair and walked to the corner of the office where the compact refrigerator sat on the table. He opened it up and pulled out a can of soda.

"Damn Fats, chill out my nigga. I was just asking because I wanted to know if they still buying that work today or not?"

"Get me one of those sodas outta there..." Fats stated then he waited for Scoob to bring him the soda. When Scoob turned around to face him carrying the soda Fats could tell that he was holding something back.

"Yeah, they buyin' the work, why wouldn't they? Them young niggas are havin' a few dollas and they ain't bullshittin about gettin' some more, that's why I like em. They should be pullin' in here anytime now."

GHETTO MERCHANTS

When Scoob passed Fats his soda, Fats noticed that his hands were trembling.
"Damn Scoob, you shakin' like a mutha fucka...you been doin' that shit again?"

"Hell nawl!" Scoob answered while looking at his hands and back to Fats.

Fats shook his head as he stood up and stretched and walked over to the window looking out on El Segundo.
"Yeah, whatever nigga...I gotta take a shit real quick, why don't you go out front and look out for the homies."
Scoob hurried out of the office before Fats could dissect him anymore. As for Fats, he was wondering why Malcolm got up this morning and got on a mission on his own without waiting for him. Then he dismissed the idea because he knew that Malcolm wanted to get his business handled so that he could get home. But on the other hand, could it be possible that they're in route to pull a jack move?

"Hell naw," Fats answered himself out loud with a chuckle to follow, then he thought about how weird Scoob was acting.
"Something's up, but I can't quite grasp on to what it is."
Regardless of if anything fucked up was going on or not Fats would have his nine double m close at hand just in case anybody was on some bullshit.

"I gotta stop blowin' that good weed in the mornin', it's startin' to make me paranoid." Fats continued talking to himself as he sat down on the toilet and grabbed the Lowrider Magazine off the sink.

On his way outside Scoob stopped at the cashier counter and bummed a cigarette from Fats' cousin Teila, who hesitated because she didn't like him. Now, as he leaned against a pole that held up the portico, he began to think of the move that he pulled earlier that morning, which turned out to be worthless. Last night, after he had the incident with the girls at Chocolate's house, he and Fats discussed business involving the Ghetto Merchants. Unsuspecting of any ulterior motive from Scoob, Fats let him know that he had to meet up with them in the morning at their motel in Inglewood. He also let Scoob know that he needed him to make some moves that were important as far as transporting some ki's from his Mexican connection to the detail shop. Afterwards, they would need to wrap the work up for Malcolm and his crew so they would be safe on the highway from a routine traffic stop on the road from a drug-sniffing K9. Scoob agreed with Fats' plan and assured him that he would be on deck to help in the morning.

When Scoob left Chocolate's house, he had a whole different plan than what he and Fats had discussed. His plot was going to change his life for the better, being that it was obvious that he was going to have to look after himself before too long. Fats was pretty much finished providing work for niggas in Los Angeles; therefore, his position would be eliminated. Instead of taking the long drive home, Scoob slid from West Hollywood down to Inglewood and got a room at the same Best Western where Fats' out-of-town guests were staying. He was going to rob them for the drug money, but how, he wasn't certain because his plan was short notice, and he was by himself. Second of all, he didn't know what room or rooms they were in. Then he thought that it was a possibility they left the cash inside the van. They had a large sum of money, so there was no way they would've left the money in the room while they were out and about with Fats, because everyone knows that housekeeping bitches go inside rooms and steal every day.

After getting his nerve up, Scoob left his motel room and got inside his Taurus that was parked right in front of his room on the first floor. From there, he looked around through the dimly lit parking lot, finding only one van that did not have a California plate on the front. He started up the Taurus Wagon and pulled out of the parking lot and drove directly across the street where there was a twenty-four-hour laundromat in a strip mall. He parked over there and walked back across the street and slid through the darkness, where he made it to the back wooden stockade fence. He crouched, although he wasn't worried about being seen by anyone but the receptionist behind the desk, because they did not have security. When he made it to the van, which lacked a California license plate on the front, he noticed it had an Oklahoma license plate on the back door.

Scoob pulled his pistol from his waist, then crept up to the side doors where he stood up and looked around. He didn't notice anyone stirring around so he focused on the proper spot on the glass on one of the side doors and used the butt of his pistol like a hammer busting the glass. Quickly, he crouched down again for a moment as he edged to the front passenger side, looking up at the rooms facing him, still there was no sign of anybody aware of what was happening in the parking lot. He crept to the back door, where he rose up and used his elbow to bust out the window, enough for him to reach in so he could unlock the door and open it up.

As soon as he opened the door, he set off the factory alarm, which caused the horn to blow and the headlights to flash. Scoob didn't hesitate to jump in the van, hoping he would catch the Oklahoma boys slipping. After rambling through the van quickly all he found was an ice chest with snacks, a case logic cassette box, and some trash. Scoob was furious, but he couldn't do anything about what was not there for taking so he knew he had to flee.

When he dashed out of the side of the van, he saw an Asian

woman come out of her room, checking to make sure that it wasn't her alarm going off. When she saw the flashing lights on the van, she waved her hand in the air, showing no concern because it wasn't hers, then she stewed back into her room and closed the door. As for Scoob, he was gone across the street in a hurry so that he could get out of Inglewood without going in the back of a police car.

Now standing outside the shop, Scoob could see to his left, pulling into the parking lot that was connected to an alley, was Chocolate's friend Brenda's burgundy Honda Accord with tinted windows.
"There's the nigga that was trippin' at Chocolate's crib. Hurry up and park this mutha fucka so I can take a look at this nigga, he was actin' all cool last night." Said Gooch as soon as he saw the dark bald headed cock diesel nigga named Scoob standing underneath the portico to the entrance of Fats' detail shop.

"Oh yeah, well check this shit out...right now he's suspect, so therefore the same rules that apply at home apply out here. He might of just been trippin' on some pussy he can't get, and it might be somethin' else. Don't get outta the car flexin' over some bullshit cause we out here on somethin' else for now. Ya hear me?" Malcolm warned while turning around in the seat, talking to Gooch. Gooch smirked at Malcolm then turned his head the other way and nodded.

"Alright let's go." Malcolm commanded as he opened the car door.

When Scoob saw the three guys, including the one from last night and two of them tucking pistols in their waist under their jackets, he was suddenly afraid. The seriousness in all three of their faces showed that they were there for a reason other than what Fats was aware of. He wondered if one of them saw him running away from the van. If so, he was fucked, but just in case they didn't he took a deep breath and tried to remain calm as the big youngster from last night approached him with a grit on his face.

"What's up cuz...is Fats here?" Asked Gooch while standing arm's length away from Scoob, sizing him up, letting him know he wasn't ducking no funk. Scoob cleared his throat and gave him a fake grin and stuck his fist out for some dap while beads of sweat began forming on his bald head. Malcolm walked up behind Gooch and casually pushed him to the side, then gave Scoob dap, and so did Kenny. Gooch took turns rubbing each of fist with his hands, contemplating.

"Hey fellas...Fats is in his office; I think he's taking a shit. He's expecting y'all, so he sent me out here to look out. My name is Scoob."

Scoob kept darting his eyes back and forth to each of the out-of-towners, trying his best not to look guilty, but he knew that he was doing a horrible job. He decided quickly that he needed some help to get the cheat off of him, so he reached for the door and opened it.

"We can go inside, come on, fellas," Scoob casually invited.

Malcolm walked in first with Gooch trailing right behind him. Kenny opted to go in last behind Scoob once everyone was inside the small reception area, where there was a counter with a cash register on it to the left. Sitting on a stool behind the counter was a cute redbone chick with long cornrows with red, black, and green beads lying on her shoulders. She had been filing her fingernails, paying no attention until the office door over in the right corner of the reception area opened up and Fats started talking.

"Well, well, well, I see y'all made it over here..."

Back in the doorway, Scoob stumbled over Kenny's foot while backing up in a hurry to get back out of the door.

"Excuse me, homie...Fats, I'm going to the ARCO. I'll be right back," Scoob nervously spoke after he smiled and patted Kenny on the shoulder.

"Ya'll want anythang from the store?" Fats asked while waving them to come inside his office. Gooch, Kenny and Malcolm all shook their heads no.

"Hurry up and get back, man, we have a whole lot to take care of," Fats ordered as Scoob backed out of the door while he and Kenny stared at one another until he was out of sight, heading towards the side of the building.

Kenny didn't like the vibe that Scoob was giving off, so he decided to do what he felt was right, and that was take precautions for his brother. To the left of the cashier's counter was a dim hallway that had a sign hanging from the ceiling: RESTROOM/ SHOP AREA. Kenny sped up and touched Malcolm on the shoulder causing him to pause before following Fats into the office.

"Gary, I want you to wait out here and keep your eyes peeled. If you see anything that looks out of character, come in that front door or down that hallway, I want you to call my name..." Kenny reached inside his windbreaker and pulled out his Sig. The redbone receptionist yelped and covered her mouth, dropping the fingernail file to the floor. Fats stepped to the side in an attempt to be a shield between Kenny and Teila.

"Hold on man, what the fuck is this shit? What's the problem, fellas?"

"We're just bein' safe, Fats, that's all," Malcolm answered while Kenny took it upon himself to take a quick look inside Fats' office to make sure there was not a trap waiting for them. If it were, he was the one who was trained to handle it.

Fats turned around and let Teila know that everything was okay and not to be alarmed, but inside his head he was pissed off because he wasn't aware of the sudden strange behavior from Malcolm and his crew. In less than thirty seconds Kenny came out of the office letting Malcolm know that it was all clear. Fats showed anger in his face as he walked past Kenny into his office and Malcolm was right behind him and Kenny was last. As for Gooch, he played it cool and walked over to the cashier and pulled up the extra stool and introduced himself so that he and Teila could get acquainted while he looked out.
Back inside the office Fats walked around his desk and took a seat then he gave Kenny and Malcolm a hand gesture for them to do the same. He then picked up the can of soda and took a drink before saying a word.

"Kenny, Malcolm, I gotta tell ya that I don't like it at all how y'all come inside my place of business scaring my little cousin to death by pullin' outchea pistol and shit; I thought we had an agreement that we was gonna be business associates for a while but here y'all go with this bullshit. I'm not the type to get rattled, ya feel me but there's gotta be an explanation for this shit. I don't do business like that; you should know that Malcolm cause I'm the reason you gotcha foot in the door right now and this is how you repay me. That shit was real disrespectful man."

"Kenny, let me holla at Fats by myself. We cool, don't worry...just keep ya eyes open." Kenny stood up and kept his eyes on Fats as he backed out of the door, leaving it open. He stood in the corner of the reception area so that he could keep an eye on Fats because he knew that he had a pistol inside the top drawer of his desk. If he made the wrong move, it would be his last. Showing a disgruntled look on his face, Fats leaned back in his chair and held his hands behind his head with an attempt to relax before he continued his conversation with Malcolm.

"I gotta know what happened with our trust between now and last night, and don't tell me nothin' else that's gonna fuck up my high any more than y'all already have."

"I woke up this mornin' with the sound of the alarm goin' off on my rental."

Immediately, Fats dropped his hands down to the sides of his chair with a look of devastation showing on his face now as he thought about Scoob acting strangely this morning. As he briefly tried to fathom the thought of Scoob having a role in that, Fats slowly shook his head, showing disgust as he reached forward, grabbed his soda, and took a drink.

"It just seems kinda strange that outta all the vehicles in the parking lot with outta state plates somebody would pick mine. Why? I mean, what's really weird is that only you and ya girl Shaniqua knew where we were stayin'. The hoes from last night never left outta me and my brother's sight neither did they make any phone calls. As for the comment you made about bein' the reason I got my foot in the door is fucked up too. My foot is in the door because I got my own cash Fats, not because of you, homeboy. I'm a hustlin' mutha fucka and I got a team that has helped me get here. True enough you got what I need but if there's gonna be a problem I'm sure I'll be able to find somebody out here that ain't gonna try to fuck over a nigga." Malcolm commented with an above-normal voice.

GHETTO MERCHANTS

"I apologize for the remark Malcolm, but the part of you thinkin' I had anythang to do with some bullshit over in Inglewood last night you're wrong. Take a look at this picture, you come out here to buy twenty birds. My purpose for you and your crew is to get where I'm at 'cause I got money already and I ain't gotta get more by fuckin' a nigga around by breakin' in a goddamn van. Malcolm, I ain't got no reason to steal from you even if I wanted to. What I need is for you to keep comin' out here spendin' three, four, five hundred g's so you can see that mil. Once you see that mil, that means I'm seein' major green too, so can you tell me why I wanna fuck that up?" Fats spoke with conviction, then he kicked back in his office chair while putting his hands behind his head again, showing a sign of arrogance.

"Everythang you sayin' sounds pretty good, but somethin' is tellin' me that your boy Scoob ain't on the same page with me and you. He was actin' weird as a mutha fucka when we pulled up, you seen yaself how the nigga was actin' when we was out there..." Malcolm explained while pointing behind towards the reception area with his thumb.

"Look...where he disappeared to. I tell ya what, just ask him for me and see what he say. If I'm wrong that's my bad but if I'm right you'll know you gotta mutha fucka in your organization that's bad for business, yours and mine. That's the kinda homeboy a nigga don't need around."

Fats took in Malcolm's request and carefully kicked his K-Swiss boots up on his desk.

"I'll do that just for you Malcolm and you got my word that if he had anythang to do with what happened to your rental he will be dealt with. Now that we're on the subject of homeboys, what do you suggest we do about Javon?"

"Javon, what about em?" Malcolm questioned bluntly.
"What I mean is how do you feel about takin' care of his two hundred g debt. You know what I'm sayin, since we're takin' responsibilities for our homeboys. Two hundred g's is a nice piece of change to be blowin' off, I mean it would be such a shame if somethin' happened to sweet moms or that fine ass sister of his..."

The position that Fats was putting Malcolm in was unexpected, yet it was all part of the game, whether he liked it or not. The rules of the game sometimes extended to family when certain circumstances were involved. The possibilities were high now that Javon had crossed the line in the rules of the game when it came to the part of owing money. Something was definitely wrong for Javon to not call anyone, but until it was justified that it wasn't his fault, and it was found out he was in deep shit. Because of the stakes and accusations that were made by Malcolm, Fats was ready to stroke his own ego by making it clear to Malcolm that he had power.

Malcolm briefly pondered on the situation of what Javon would do if he was the one sitting across from Fats and Cecelia and Chance's lives were on the line. He didn't like the conclusion because it was evident that he and Javon were cut from a whole different cloth. Fuck it, he couldn't let anyone hurt Javon's family when he had the power to stop it, being that he prided himself for having principles. It was time to strike a deal, which was what Fats had wanted, but he would have to deal on Malcolm's terms or there wouldn't be a deal at all.

Malcolm focused his stare on Fats once again while lifting his back from the chair and placing his arms on the edge of Fats' desk.

"For all we know, Javon could be somewhere with a hole in his head, dead and stankin' in a ditch somewhere between here and Oklahoma City. For all I know it, this could all be part of your plan to get me for more of my bread. One thang I know for sure is that whatever happens in the darkness will eventually come out in the light. Anyway...what I propose for now is for you to toss me two extra birds. I'll pay you fifty g's for them, plus I'll throw in an extra dime of mine off the top. That'll be twenty-six g's knocked off Javon's bill. But first, I gotta have the tab dropped down to one fifty. You do that and take the scope off of his people, and we can knock the bill down every time I cop work."

"I like the way you conduct business. You gonna be a rich mutha fucka one day Malcolm because you got somethin' that a whole lotta other niggas lack...integrity. We gotta deal."

Fats took his feet off the desk and chuckled as he stood up. He then leaned across the desk with an open hand. Malcolm extended his, and they locked grips. Kenny moved closer to the door, observing and listening to the whole ordeal, not liking the position his brother put himself in with Javon's debt.

After the firm handshake, Malcolm leaned back in the swivel chair showing his cockiness by crossing his legs and rubbing his nose showing off his usual smirk.

"Now that we got all that settled, can I see the work?" Malcolm questioned seriously.

"Let me show ya somethin', hold on. I'll be right back."

Fats stood up and walked into the bathroom. He had some work that he was waiting for somebody to pick up at noon, but he was gonna show Malcolm anyway just so he could high side. Within seconds of Fats entering the bathroom, Malcolm could hear the sound of something heavy being moved over with a screeching noise. In under a minute, Fats emerged from the bathroom with two brown Dillard's shopping bags, one in each hand. To no surprise to Fats, Kenny was standing beside his brother, who was still sitting down.

"Malcolm is lucky as a mutha fucka to have a brother like you cause you ain't gonna let nothin' happen to that nigga huh," Fats stated as he maneuvered around the desk and dropped the bags beside Malcolm. "We're safe in here, but go ahead and close that door, homie."

Malcolm leaned over to the side and peered inside both bags after Fats walked back around the desk, wearing a grin on his face. The bags were filled with at least ten to fifteen birds each. Malcolm felt like jumping in the air with the same excitement as someone who just won the lottery. When he looked up, Kenny had stepped back over to where he was, looking inside with a face that showed he wasn't impressed. Standing up on the other side of the desk, with a big grin and his hands rubbing together eagerly, was Fats. He understood Malcolm's joy, unlike Kenny, who knew nothing about hustling cocaine. Malcolm started slowly shaking his head side to side, unable to hide his excitement. Fats took a seat again.

"Goddamn Fats, I ain't ever seen that much work in real life except for on the TV."

"Just keep ya head in the game and learn to dismiss that little shit, Malcolm. I promise ya that if you trust me and keep that ambition that you got, there is no end to the possibilities of how big you could get."

Right then, Kenny knew that Fats was trying to reel Malcolm all the way in with a dream that may be unreachable with certain sacrifices. Surely Malcolm was not that naive to fall for a line like that. Malcolm broke his attention from the shopping bags and put his serious face back on and faced Fats while leaning back in his chair, locking his fingers together resting them across his stomach.

"That is what I'm hopin' for homie...but anyways we're gonna push on. I'll be callin' when Xavier finishes up with the van, that's supposed to be sometime before six. He's been paid a few extra dollas to get the job done before nightfall because we gotta get to the house and put the town on lock."

Malcolm stood up and adjusted his pistol on his waist under his jacket. He stepped around the shopping bags and headed for the door; Kenny let him pass him up so that he could follow behind.

"Hey Malcolm!" Fats shouted. Malcolm and Kenny both stopped and turned around to face him. "My cousin out there with Gooch can take him and Solo around to the mall or somethin' while y'all waitin' for the van, that's if..."

"Not this trip Fats, maybe next time," Malcolm replied, cutting Fats off before he could finish his sentence then he opened the door and walked out.

Inside the reception area Gooch had Teila's full attention when Malcolm beckoned for him to come on. Malcolm and Kenny passed through and on out of the door while Gooch waited for Teila to write down her phone number. Outside Kenny and Malcolm both were thinking what happened to Fats' partner Scoob yet neither said a word about it until they got inside the car waiting for Gooch who was now walking towards the Honda Accord.

Back inside the detail shop Fats came out of his office and asked

Teila if Scoob had come back. She informed him that he had left right after him and the other two guys closed the door when they were in his office.

Two hundred miles away, inside a Clark County Courtroom stood Javon, standing beside him was his public defender.

"Your honor, I represent Mr. Mims. We have come to agreement with the state for my client to accept a guilty plea today and ask for sentencing as well. The agreement with the state is for six months in the Clark County Jail along with one year of probation. Judge Gray, my client has written a letter of apology to Barrett's Towing expressing himself how sorry he is for the burglarizing and vandalism on their property..."

Special Judge Marshall Gray was on the bench looking through his bifocals which were barely hanging on at the tip of his nose as the public defender passed the plea agreement to the bailiff.

"Uhh your honor...also if you'll take notice to the fifteen hundred dollar fine agreed upon along with damages."

The young rookie prosecutor with the bad haircut, cheap suit and scuffed black wingtip shoes spoke again before the judge could respond.

Judge Gray pretended not to pay attention to what the prosecutor was saying. He began reading the plea agreement that was handed to him by his bailiff and occasionally looking to the disheveled-looking defendant. After he read the plea agreement, the old silver-headed judge rolled his chair over towards his clerk, where she stood and leaned over the rail as he whispered something into her ear. The secretary giggled as she and the judge both looked over at the defense table. After the giggling ceased from the young secretary and the googly eye looks from the judge, she nodded her head up and down to confirm whatever it was that he confided in her about. He watched over his glasses at the young buxom beauty as she sat down smiling at him, then he rolled back over to the bench where he unzipped his robe partially and pulled out a handkerchief and blew his nose loudly before he moved on.

"Does the state feel that this is sufficient punishment for...uhh Javon Mims?" Judge Gray inquired of the prosecutor. The slim prosecutor quickly rose from his seat, making a banging noise from hitting his knee on the table leg. He gritted his teeth while the sign of pain showed across his face. To cover his accident, he straightened his tie and rolled his shoulders back, then took a deep breath.

"Yes, your honor. The defendant has waived all future hearings, including pre-lims and wants no bond. The state can save time and money by accepting this today," Explained the prosecutor.

Judge Gray leaned back in his big black chair and observed everyone who sat inside his courtroom while he thought about his lunch break with his secretary as soon as these proceedings were over.

"Mr. Mims, I want you to consider yourself lucky that the prosecutor, along with your represener, have come together to get you out of my courtroom in a hurry. I want you to know that I have a strong mind telling me that I should not accept this plea agreement. Although you have no extensive record, and none at all in the state of Nevada. Factor in a phone call to my clerk this morning from your mother asking for leniency for you because you have a gambling addiction. What I'm going to do for her is accept this plea along with some added stipulations with your probation. I'm adding a twelve-step program for you to apply along with two years of probation to take back to Oklahoma when you get out of our jail. This is gonna be the time that the saying what happens in Vegas stays in Vegas isn't going to apply. You'll be taking two years of probation home with you, and I don't want to see you in my court again. Do I make myself clear, Mr. Mims?"

Javon's public defender nudged Javon with his foot and whispered for him to stand up with him. Before they were both standing, Javon answered.

"Yes, your honor, I agree with your terms and thank you, sir."

When Scoob left the detail shop, he thought he was made, and he was terrified. He didn't go to the ARCO on the corner; instead, he walked around the detail shop and collected his thoughts for a moment. That was when he decided that he needed to get away from there, so he came around the north side of the building where the overhead doors were. He saw a clear path to the brown Taurus wagon, and he took it. Once inside the car, he started it up and jetted out of the parking lot en route to his crib in Lakewood. On his way home, he sped eastward down the 105 Freeway, all the while keeping his eyes in his rearview, thinking that someone was following him. When he made it safely inside his living room, he locked the door behind him quickly. He turned his attention to a half-empty bottle of tequila sitting on his black lacquer coffee table. Scoob walked aimlessly around the chair that separated him from his bottle and his couch. He picked up the bottle and dove onto the couch all in one move. Once his body was stable, he unscrewed the top off the bottle and took a drink. The bitter taste caused Scoob to scowl making him not want any more for the moment, so he screwed the top back on and sat it back on the table. He looked at the time on his gold nugget Seiko, then he leaned forward and rested both of his arms on his knees while he slumped over. The same question came across his mind again; why and how had he let himself get into this situation, but at this point it didn't matter.

From here on out, he was no longer going to let his loyalty dictate his future. Ever since he and Fats had become friends, he had always been there for him with every beck and call. There was never a favor that was asked that was too big, including getting blood on his hands. Years later Fats began using his friendship as a tool now, suddenly, he wanted to bow down from hustling in Los Angeles because some niggas got caught up by the feds. To make matters worse he wanted him to run the detail shop and sell weed while he's out living the high life spending his millions and collecting more with the Oklahoma niggas along with other business ventures that he had acquired.

Although it wasn't Fats' fault that Scoob fucked off all his money and depended on the extras that he charged when he made sells, Fats never offered him a deal to where he'd be set for life like him. While all of this was going through Scoob's mind, he was disturbed by the ringing of his home phone. After six rings, the answering machine picked up because Scoob didn't want to. The greeting on his machine finished, and the sound of Fats' voice began.

"I don't know what kinda bullshit ya pulled after leavin' ol' girls house late last night but I gotta idea. Don't fuck up a good thang, I mean that shit. When you get this message get over here so we can go pick up that other work..." The answering machine beeped, giving Fats no more time to talk.

Scoob reached for the bottle again for a drink, dreading the thought of how Fats was going to act when he saw him again, and it wasn't good. Then Scoob got to thinking after he turned the bottle up. Fats got work at the shop already, so he was trying to trick him into coming back over there to confront him in front of the Oklahoma niggas and make him out to be a spectacle.

"This nigga Fats think he got all the sense in the world...I'll show him, I'm gonna slide on them niggas at the shop around six this evenin'. That big mouth fat mutha fucka done forgot he told me that they was tryin' to get outta town this evenin'. Yeahhhhh, I'll be there with a surprise for that ass..." Scoob spoke out loud to himself, then broke off into an evil laugh as his Pac-tel pager started vibrating on his hip.

Scoob pulled the pager off his belt and looked at the number on the screen. It was the number from the detail shop. He tossed the pager to the side and almost spilled the rest of the liquor in his lap. Scoob placed the tequila back on the table, then he kicked his feet up on the coffee table that leaned over from the weight of his legs. He no longer gave a damn because he was planning now to be headed somewhere far away where nobody knew him. There, he would start a new life with plenty of money and dope to sell; it was his time to shine.

Over in Compton at the Hilton Hotel, Brenda was channel surfing while Solo was checking his voicemails. The most important one was from Paperboy letting him know that Minnesota was all good for the picking. After running through the rest of his messages, Solo called Paperboy's beeper voicemail, leaving a message for him to know that they should be seeing each other before the weekend, and he left him his mobile phone number.

Chapter 21

The Ghetto Merchants, along with Brenda, were posted up inside their modest two-room suite at the Hilton when Malcolm received the phone call from Xavier. He was calling to let him know that he was finished with the van. Malcolm took a peek at his watch, seeing that it was 5:37. Immediately, Malcolm informed him that he was on his way. With no other words to say to Xavier, Malcolm pressed END. He stood up and stretched. Kenny, who had been asleep on the other end of the couch, had opened his eyes when the mobile phone rang, hearing Malcom's side of the conversation stating that he was on his way. After stretching, Malcolm went to the suite's separate bedroom. In there, he knelt beside his travel bag, unzipped it, and dug his hand in the compartment where he kept his emergency cash and pulled it out along with his pistol. He stood back up and tucked his pistol in the waist of his jeans, and he stuffed the cash into his front pockets. He heard someone come into the room. When he turned around, he saw Kenny and Gooch.

"Check it out, the Mexican is finished with the van, so it's time to get the show on the road. Get the fully outta the bottom of that green bag and put it in your bag on top of the clothes so a nigga can get to it quick..." Malcolm said while looking directly at Gooch.

"Solo!" Malcolm yelled to the other room to wake Solo up, who was asleep on the chaise lounge with Brenda in the other room. The yelling startled Solo as he woke up, causing him to jerk violently and accidentally knock Brenda to the floor just as Malcolm entered the room, seeing the incident.

"Damn nigga...look what you made me do!" Solo yelled angrily as he pulled Brenda to help her up from the floor while Malcolm grinned.

"My bad, Brenda, it's time to roll up outta this joint. We need to use your car again; Kenny can come back..."

"Fuck that, we all goin' Malcolm, besides..." Solo responded, still frustrated from being startled awake, not giving Malcolm enough time to finish his sentence.

"And I have to get home and get ready for work." Brenda interrupted as she sat on the chaise, putting on her shoes. Solo sat down beside her to do the same, putting on his Jordans.

"It's gonna be a tight squeeze in that little ass car but we gotta move together from here on out Malcolm," Solo suggested.

Without saying a word, Malcolm nodded his head, showing that he agreed with what Solo said. At that point, Gooch and Kenny walked into the room, both were carrying their personal bags along with a military duffle as well. Solo quickly tied his shoes and followed suit hurriedly to get his belongings. This time, Malcolm shook his head, signifying no.

"All we need is the money and the weapons. We can come back and pick up the clothes on our way out. Let's go." Malcolm ordered.

Within twenty minutes, they were parking in front of Xavier's shop. Gooch got out of the car, looking at the sinking sun towards the west as he walked to the door. He banged on it heavily just in case Xavier was way in the back. After banging on it a couple of more times Xavier appeared through the door glass, coming from the shop area. Xavier opened the door, and Gooch went inside along with Kenny. Malcolm and Solo waited outside with the money still in the car. Malcolm reached into his pocket, pulled out some money and peeled off four hundred dollars, and handed it to Brenda, who was behind the wheel. At that time, Gooch was waving for them to come in from the door of the shop.

"You didn't have to give me any money, it felt pretty good to help you ol' country boys out. Thank ya. Solo, you betta call." Brenda clowned while giving them her best impression of a country girl.

Malcolm laughed as he opened the door and got out, pulling out both bags. Solo got out right after Brenda gave him a kiss on the cheek, then she backed out on the street and drove away.

Once inside the office, Gooch, who had Xavier's keys, locked the door behind them, then the three of them joined Kenny, who was in the shop area, talking to Xavier, and there was another Mexican inside the van cleaning it out. When Malcolm got closer to the rear of the van, where Xavier and Kenny were, he laughed to himself when he thought about the pretty woman who had slapped Xavier with the pistol earlier in the day. When he turned around, he had a big bandage on the side of his face. All Malcolm could do was shake his head and wonder if Gooch was thinking the same thing he was since he saw it.

When they got to the van and saw the back floor compartment, Malcolm, Gooch, and Solo could not believe their eyes. There was a compartment almost as wide as the van and one and a half feet wide and at least ten inches deep. Xavier showed them how it blended into the carpet when it was closed and how to open it. Ready to keep moving, Gooch and Solo put the money in the stash box while Malcolm paid Xavier, along with making arrangements with him to bring his truck out soon, since he was satisfied with his work.

With the van loaded with everything and everybody, Xavier opened the over-head door and Gooch pulled out. At the same time, Malcolm pulled out his mobile and called Fats. After only two rings, Fats answered, and Malcolm let him know that they were on their way to his detail shop. Fats assured him that he was ready for them and to come on. When Malcolm and Fats ended their phone call, they headed back south on Alameda. They had four pistols, a Mac 10, and extra clips; they were ready for whatever.

The sun had almost completely set as they headed westward on El Segundo while passing through the light crossing Avalon. As Gooch signaled to the right and slowed down to pull into the detail shop, Fats was walking Teila to the car when they got there. Quickly, he rushed her into her car and slapped the top of the roof after closing her door. She slowly pulled off while staring at Gooch, but he paid her no mind because he was on a mission. Fats and Malcolm made direct eye contact as Fats crossed in front of the van so he could talk to Malcolm on the passenger side. Malcolm admired the way that Fats' demeanor was always calm, but he was hard to read. Still, after all that had occurred between them earlier, he managed to have a pleasant look on his face. Malcolm was no fool; he was aware that looks could be deceiving. When hundreds of thousands of dollars were on the line everybody was a suspect when it came to some bullshit. Therefore, if Fats was trying to put a move down on them, he would be telling the story in heaven or hell because today would be the day he would die. Just as Fats almost made it to Malcolm's window, Malcolm pulled his pistol out from his waist. He then released the safety and placed it in his lap as Gooch let his window down for him.
"Check it out y'all, I ain't gotta tell none of ya that before we leave this mutha fucka in a bag don't hesitate to bust first."

Malcolm's words were from the heart, and everyone in the van knew it, and they also knew that he would get down first if they were in danger. Fats stepped up to the van window seeing the pistol in Malcolm's lap as well as Gooch's, along with the Mac between the two of them. He could see it in their eyes that they were on edge and were not there to play games. Fats chuckled as he took two steps back while straightening his all-black Dodgers hat with both hands.

"So, I take it that you're satisfied with the Mexican's work. You must've buttered his toast pretty damn good for Xavier to get finished like that."

Before Malcolm answered, he opened the door and gripped his pistol before stepping down out of the van. He looked down the alley to his left and towards El Segundo, seeing nothing out of the ordinary. He put his pistol inside his front pocket covering the butt with his jacket.

"Now you know the only way to get shit done fast is with the persuasion of a few dollas," said Malcolm.

Inside the van, Kenny quickly gave Solo and Gooch instructions on how they were going to look out. Gooch's assignment was to watch the front alley, Solo's was to watch the street behind them along with the back wall. Kenny's task was to watch Malcolm and Fats and anything that came out or around his shop. Once they were clear on what everyone had to do, for now Kenny opened up both of the side doors. When Fats looked his way, he saw the Mac was now lying on the floor beside Kenny's captain's chair, which he swiveled around to face the front of the shop. Fats nodded his head up, saying what's up to Kenny without saying a word, then he put his attention back on Malcolm.

"You know what Malcolm...I've said this before, but I believe in givin' credit when it's due. You know how to keep business business and playtime separate and that alone gives a man a certain type of style that has to be in him; never can that be copied, my man."

Just as the two headed for the front door on the detail shop, Kenny unholstered his Sig from inside his windbreaker and hopped out, passing Malcolm and Fats by stepping in front of him.

"Change of plans, fellas. Malcolm, you get back inside the van. I'll go in to check the place. Fats, I'm sure you can understand my concern for my little brother..."

"Me too," were Solo's words as he got out of the van as well.

"Come on, man...are you kiddin' me?" Asked Fats as he looked at all three of the men who had him semi-surrounded. Beings that Kenny was trained for shit like that Malcolm let him have his way and turned around and got in the same seat that Kenny just got out of.

"You heard the man Fats, them two will go in witcha. Me and Gooch will be out here waitin' until it's time to pull the van inside." Malcolm stated.

Suddenly Fats' calm demeanor was looking different as if he was getting irritated, yet he agreed.

"Okay fellas, we can do it y'all's way..." Fats spoke as he started walking towards the shop with Solo and Kenny on both sides of him.

"All these precautions are gettin' crazy now, we doin' all this for three hundred g's. I'm gonna need y'all to trust a nigga." Fats slowed down for Kenny and Solo to take the lead inside the shop then he stopped and turned around to speak to Malcolm again.

"Y'all can pull on the side. We'll open the garage door from the inside as soon as your goons sweep the building." Spoke a sarcastic' Fats while pointing towards the northwest corner of the building. He then wheeled back around to find Solo holding the door open while Kenny was edging towards his office with his pistol extended in front of him.

Back inside the van Gooch pulled a cigarette from behind his ear that he bummed from Brenda. He stuck it between his lips and fired it up, then he put the van in drive, and slowly crept to the side as he focused on the alley, and Malcolm watched the three inside the shop through the glass until they were out of sight. The clock was ticking, and the California sun had disappeared.

"Let me hit that square, nigga," Malcolm said while reaching for Gooch's cigarette.

Inside the shop Kenny crept towards the office while he kept his eyes peeled to the hallway on the left. He looked over at Solo and pointed two fingers at his own eyes then he pointed towards that hallway giving Solo the insight to look out. Solo nodded his head and Fats shook his in disbelief as Kenny edged into the office. After being in there for no more than fifteen seconds, same as before, he came back out, giving Solo the signal that it was clear. He then walked across the reception area and put his back on the wall once he made it through the railway opening. In the hall were two doors, one was straight ahead with an EXIT sign displayed over the top and EMPLOYEES ONLY displayed on the door. The other door was on the right, it had RESTROOM with black and gold stickers. Kenny grabbed the knob on the bathroom door and pushed it open while brandishing his firearm. Once again, there was nobody lying in the cut behind closed doors. He then waved Solo to follow him as he headed through the last door, which revealed a large four-bay shop with only one car inside. Kenny was surprised at the size because it wasn't noticeable from the front or the side of the building that faced the street. He continued to do his thing by sweeping all the visible blind spots in the shop in the dim light, causing Fats to tap Solo on the shoulder.

"Goddamn, he got moves like a mutha fucka man...a nigga don't wanna be on his bad side cause he comin' to get that ass like a smooth assassin." Fats whispered.
Solo nodded his head while gripping his Glock tighter, then he slowly walked out into the shop area in case there was some bullshit, after edging Fats to go ahead of him.

Meanwhile, back in Oklahoma City, inside Malcolm and Deziree's den, Cecelia was lying down on the couch watching a taped episode of The Young and the Restless. Out of nowhere, Cecelia heard Deziree screaming for her from the rear of the house. She sprang up from the couch and ran to the back, where she found Deziree on the floor on her knees holding her stomach. When she saw Cecelia's face, she reached for her as if she were a child, reaching for her mother to pick her up, crying.

"Here I am, baby...what's wrong witcha?" Cecelia asked as she got down on the floor with her.

"I've got to go to the...oh God, Ms. Cecelia, I think the babies are coming." That was when Cecelia noticed that Deziree was wet; her water had broken.

Cecelia jumped up and got the phone, and called 911, giving the operator directions to the house. While she was still on the phone, Deziree began screaming Malcolm's name as tears flowed down her face.

Kenny finished sweeping the work area and observed Fats and Solo approaching one of the garage doors. When the door raised, Malcolm was staring at them with the Mac-10 in his hands, crouched down on top of the closed stash.

"Gooch...back it up," Malcolm announced as he hopped out and walked inside.

Fats turned around and headed towards an old gray metal desk. There he got a half joint and lighter off the top and fired it up. By the time he blew out some smoke, the van was inside, and Kenny was still on point until the door lowered all the way to the floor. Malcolm's attention on the business was sidetracked when he noticed there was a '61 rag Impala parked next to the wash bay. He set the Mac down in the van and walked that way. Fats did the same. The all black and chrome Impala had Malcolm's full attention as he looked through the passenger window. Fats stepped to the rear of the car and pulled his keys out of his pocket, and popped the trunk. With a devilish grin on his face, he clapped his hands together, then he looked at the time on his watch. Malcolm met up with him as he reached for a large gray duffle bag that was sitting between two hydraulic pumps.

"Shut the trunk for me...." Fats handled the duffel and turned to face the others. "Let's get the show on the road fellas, cause I gotta be someplace after I lead y'all outta the city. We're gonna take the I-15 Freeway until we get to the 10, from there ya on ya own. I'm tellin' ya right now that I watched the news, and they said the winter storm is coming down between the mountains and will hit northern Arizona and New Mexico by daybreak. So, by the time the shit get bad y'all should be damn near outta Arizona at least. We need to get the work wrapped and the money counted fast," 'Fats instructed while on his way towards Gooch, Solo, and Kenny.

"Get the money out," shouted Malcolm from across the shop, still admiring the car. Fats set the duffel of cocaine on a metal table that had folded shop towels on it. Then he pulled all twenty-two kilos out with Solo right beside him to make sure the count was right while Gooch got the money out of the van. As for Kenny, he put his Sig back inside his jacket in the shoulder holster and found himself a seat. Malcolm made his way to the van, opening up the door and getting a small black plastic case from the storage bin on the lower part of the door.

When Malcolm emerged from the side of the van, Fats was explaining to Solo how to wrap the ki's with the axle grease and plastic wrap that he had on the bottom shelf of the table. Gooch was at the desk, emptying the money out of the bags, when he saw Malcolm with the small black case that was the size of a portable cassette player. Malcolm placed the case on the table and opened it up, revealing the contents inside. There were eight small vials with clear liquid inside them and a precision knife. "What the fuck is that shit?" Solo inquired, immediately ending the conversation with Fats.

"It's a cocaine test kit. Put a little bit in a vial and shake it up, if it turns blue it's real yao…" answered Fats as he squatted down. When he rose back up, he had a handful of latex gloves that were on the bottom shelf of the table.

"Show them how to do it, Malcolm, while I go up front and grab some duct tape for the holes cut in the birds by the knife. Somebody grab that bucket of soap in the wash bay and bring it over here to the table. I'll be right back."

Fats took off for the doorway that led to the customer area along with his office and Kenny jumped up from his chair and followed. Fats started laughing, showing that he was no longer irritated by the Ghetto Merchants being cautious as he and Kenny began talking as they went through the door.

Malcolm pulled out the knife and cut open the first bird by making a small X. Solo was right there with Gooch, looking from the other side of the table. Solo had already unscrewed the top off of the first vial and had it waiting for Malcolm to drop some of the fish scale-looking cocaine into it. With about a quarter gram on the blade, Malcolm made the first drop. Solo screwed on the top and shook it up; the liquid turned blue purple. Malcolm was pleased, but he would not be satisfied until he saw the blue liquid seven more times.
By the time Malcolm reached the third one, Kenny and Fats returned, engulfed in conversation. Without hesitation, Fats took charge as he stepped to the table by putting on a pair of latex gloves. He then showed them all step by step how to wrap up the kilos so they would not be detected by a drug dog on their trip back to Oklahoma. After he did two of them and observed Gooch and Solo do one a piece, he was cool with it, as well as Malcolm. Fats peeled off the gloves, and he and Malcolm headed to the desk and got on their mission of running through the cash to make sure it was right. Kenny took his spot back in the seat, overseeing everyone handling their business. His experience of the drug-dealing game had already shown him that trust was a rare jewel. Everybody wanted it, but everybody didn't deserve it, and that applied to every aspect of life, whether it was drug dealing or decisions made at the White House.

Malcolm and Fats were busy. As soon as Malcolm took a rubber band from a stack of money and counted out one thousand dollars, he put the rubber band back on and tossed it to Fats. He recounted everything Malcolm tossed to him, then he dropped them in the same bag he had the kilos in. It was 7:11 on Malcolm's watch when he reached one hundred thousand dollars. As if it were planned, the phone started ringing from a horn that was rigged up on the wall. Fats kept counting, ignoring it while he and Malcolm continued to rap about their future plans outside the dope game. Fats was lacing Malcolm with game on real estate and other legal business ventures when his mobile began to ring. Fats paused from talking and counting and looked down to his right side, where his mobile was clipped to the side of his Cross Color Jeans. That was when he noticed he had gotten some axle grease on his white and blue Dodgers jersey.

"Fuck!" He shook his head and unhooked his mobile and pressed SEND.

"What?" He shouted into the phone, then he paused as he listened for a moment. Without warning he snapped out on whoever was on the other end.

"Come on man, you know where the fuck I am. I'm where you supposed to be helpin' me at...what...there you go askin' a nigga twenty-one questions...you outside, then come to the front door then."

Fats pressed END and placed his mobile on the edge of the desk exchanging it for his keys.

"Hey...Linc from the mod squad..." said Fats while looking towards Kenny. "Will you go up front and let my man Scoob in?" Fats asked while grinning.

Malcolm busted out laughing because he, Kenny and Fats were

292

the only ones that knew Linc on the show Mod Squad was a black cop: Kenny got up with a smirk on his face and grabbed the keys by holding onto the one single key for the door. Solo and Gooch could tell that Kenny didn't like being the blunt of Fats' joke even though they didn't know what the punch-line was not to mention who Linc was either. They continued with their assignment.

"Malcolm, slide me about thirty stacks from that side of the table. I'll run through that real quick so we can get on cause I'm tryin' to get y'all out on the road."

Scoob looked as if he saw a ghost when he noticed Kenny come from the hallway entrance holding the keys. Instantly Kenny could tell that he was up to no good because he flashed a fake grin and raised his right hand showing the peace sign. Kenny put the key into the lock, unlocked the door, allowing Scoob to pull it open. Kenny blocked the majority of the doorway forcing Scoob to turn to the side to get in. Looking at the parking lot, which was dimly lit, Kenny noticed nothing different except for the brown Ford Taurus Wagon that Scoob was undoubtedly driving. While Kenny locked the door, he could see Scoob staring at him in the glass, but when Kenny turned around, Scoob turned as well and headed towards the shop area. That was when Kenny noticed a bulge from the butt of a pistol under his shirt above his right back pocket. Kenny quickly got behind Scoob before he made it to the hallway.

"What's up with you, man? Get from behind me like that, and where my homeboy?" Scoob questioned after he spun around to face Kenny.

Kenny could tell he was nervous because after he spoke, his bottom lip was quivering. Without saying a word, Kenny pointed down the hall. Scoob turned back around and stepped, feeling a bit of inspiration from his fake courage that he displayed, which showed him that he could continue with his plan by himself.

When Scoob entered the shop, he saw everything happening in plain sight. Fats was sitting at the desk counting money with the shot caller for the out-of-town niggas who gave him a fuck you stare. Then Scoob saw Gooch and Solo standing at the shop table, both of them gritting on him with a stack of kilos in front of them. After pausing for a moment Scoob proceeded on to the desk where Fats sat. With cash in hand, Fats looked up and back down after seeing Scoob's face. Scoob knew Fats was pissed off because he never returned to help him out since he left that morning when he was supposed to be going to the ARCO on the corner.

"What's poppin' Fats?" He asked nervously with sweat beading up on his brow. Kenny held back at the doorway, his hand gripping his Sig inside his jacket. Malcolm stared at Scoob while Gooch and Solo continued to wrap the work with the axle grease, soap, and plastic wrap. "I'm workin', what it look like? It's obvious that I can't depend on you for shit. I told you I needed you to help a nigga out today cause if you woulda' these niggas would be on the road by now cause the work woulda been ready to put in the stash."

Scoob stood there looking dumbfounded for a moment while trying to come up with the right words to say while fidgeting.

"Scoob...I don't know what kinda fool you think I am..."

"Hold up Fats, I had some family shit to take care of. I had to take my granny to the hospital and shit. I forgot that you needed me my nigga, you know how shit goes sometimes when a nigga get sidetracked."

"Shut the fuck up with that lyin'. You was so busy that you

couldn't answer your beeper? Hold up, you lost it, I bet or you forgot to put it on today or somethin' like that huh? You know what...fuck ya and get away from me. I ain't tryin' to rap withcha right now."

Fats never stopped counting while talking to Scoob. Scoob merely dropped his head and turned around and walked out of the shop feeling embarrassed like never before. He paid no mind to Kenny who had stepped to the left of the door where there was a corner that was dark.

"Damn Fats', is everythang cool?" Malcolm asked.
"Yeah, it's cool, I'm just kinda pissed off that when I need somebody to do somethin' important, they always got somethin'...it's always some bullshit Malcolm. Somebody always gonna take advantage of a nigga's kindness. You know what, I'm finished with this shit homie." Fats spoke then he began putting the rest of the money in the bag.

"Yeah...I know exactly what you mean." Malcolm agreed as he glanced over at Solo and Gooch.

Scoob was pacing the floor in the reception area trying to strum up the courage to go back down the hall putting his plan in motion. Without a doubt he would have to kill everybody even Fats. Then a sudden rush of adrenalin came over him when he thought about being a big shot in another city along with watching the clean-cut weirdo named Kenny die. People would be looking for him when it's found out that Fats had been killed along with four other people. Scoob was ready to take the chance. He walked to the water cooler and got a cup of water and drank it down. He took a deep breath and whispered to himself, "I can do this," and took off down the hall. When he got halfway to the shop doorway he reached back and gripped the Ruger 9mm and brought it around with his right hand then used his left to pull the slide back. He did not know that Kenny was standing in the cut, and he heard the sound of the pistol being chambered.

Kenny stood erect and pressed his back to the wall in the dark, just around the corner from the doorway. He tried to get Malcolm's attention, but he and Fats were facing the opposite direction. Solo and Gooch were facing each other by standing on both sides of the table, laughing about something while they worked. The only way to warn them would alert Scoob that he was made, and he would probably come through the door with the gun blazing. Kenny got his footing together to give him the push from his legs for the attack he would have to make to disarm Scoob. Kenny knew that with his training, Scoob, nor any average man, would be a match for his hand-to-hand combat skills. Then it happened just as Kenny suspected, Scoob walked through the door and shouted.

"Getcha goddamn hands up...everybody!"

Kenny peeked around the corner to look and was surprised to see Scoob had his pistol down by his side. Instantly, Kenny wondered how a man could tell them to get their hands up and he's slipping by having his firearm to the side. He looked over at his family and Fats, only Solo and Gooch had their hands raised. Malcolm leaned back on the desk and crossed his arms while Fats twisted around in his chair to look at Scoob, who was behind him.

"Hey, man, put that gun away. What the fucks up because I know you ain't ready for this move Scoob? Believe me when I say, you don't wanna go there...I know you ain't that big of a fool..."

That was when Scoob raised the gun and aimed it at the black lowrider and fired a shot in the door, which drowned out the rest of Fats' sentence.

GHETTO MERCHANTS

"I aint playin' Fats...put all the money in the bag and you niggas over there, get over here!" Scoob shouted with a deranged look on his face.

Before he could fire another shot, he saw someone to his right out of his peripheral vision, and with no time to react, Kenny chopped down on Scoob's forearm, jarring the pistol free from his hand. Then with precision Kenny grabbed his wrist and twisted his arm, dropping his forearm down on Scoob's elbow causing it to snap and him to scream out in pain. Kenny spun around the front of him and delivered a solid blow with the palm of his hand to his sternum which knocked the rest of his breath out of him that he didn't lose when he screamed out because of his elbow. As Scoob began to drop to the floor holding his chest with his right hand while his left arm hung loose Kenny crouched and caught him by putting him in a front chokehold. With one quick twist Kenny broke Scoob's neck then let him drop to the floor. Everybody was shocked, unable to believe what they just saw. Kenny disarmed Scoob and killed him in seconds with his bare hands.

"I told ya that nigga was foul. Now what...what we gonna do bout this shit?" Malcolm addressed Fats who stood up and walked over to Scoob's body without saying a word.

Malcolm walked behind him but to his flank towards Kenny while Solo and Gooch hurried across the floor to see Scoob close up while Fats knelt down by Scoob's body and closed his eyes for him while shaking his head in shame.
"You alright, Kenny?" Asked Malcolm as he placed his hand on his brother's shoulder.

"I didn't want to kill him, it was just...well it was just when he fired the weapon, I knew he was going to do something stupid. I've got to protect my brother; you guys go ahead and finish your business, and I'll call the police."

Fats raised his heavy body up from the floor, tears flooded his eyes as he turned to face the four men.
"First of all, I wanna apologize for this nigga. Second of all, we aint callin' the police man. I don't give a damn how you explain this shit, we all goin' to jail if we call one time so kill that," Fats explained.

"Ya see, before we left home, we knew there was a possibility of somethin bad happenin' because plans don't always go as expected. I hate this shit had to happen Fats but if it wasn't him on the floor it woulda been all five of us. So where do we go from here?" Malcolm spoke with a look of sincerity on his face.

Then out of nowhere Solo kicked Scoob's body. "Bitch ass nigga, that's whatcha get."
Gooch cosigned and spit on the corpse.

"Hey...chill out!" Malcolm shouted.

"Come on Gooch, fuck this shit," Solo took off back towards the table with the work. Gooch followed right behind.

"All I can say is that I hate all this shit happened and now I believe he was responsible for breakin' in y'all's van too. When he asked me where y'all was stayin when he come over to the girl's crib last night, I didn't think the nigga was plottin' to gank you niggas. Anyway, I wanna extend my deepest apologies to all y'all and I hope we can still do business together. In fact, for my life, I'm clearin' Javon's debt to y'all, but I'll get back to that in a minute. I'm gonna knock forty g's off today, and the two extra ki's are extra. It's the least I can do, shittt my life is worth way more than just forty stacks and two ki's. Now back to Javon, Malcolm...you got my word that I won't fuck with his family but if I find out this nigga is out there fuckin' off my money...I'm puttin' his head to bed. As for Scoob's body, I can handle it, don't worry bout it. I do need some help wrappin' him up and puttin' him in the back of the Taurus. Is that cool?"

Before Malcolm could answer he heard a mobile phone ringing from inside the van. He looked in the direction of Gooch and Solo, who were closest to the van. They paid the ringing phone no mind because they both left theirs in the suite.

"Catch that phone for me." Malcolm yelled.

"I'm doin' somethin' too...damn," Gooch said with a frown on his face as he headed for the van peeling the gloves back off.

The door was still open so all he had to do was reach into the console. He pressed SEND and put it up to his ear. After he said hello, he heard a voice that he'd heard his whole life, and she sounded upset. He set the phone down on the seat and headed back to the table.

"Aunt Cecelia is on the phone."

Malcolm started to question why he didn't bring it to him, but he knew it was useless because he would come up with some bullshit excuse why. He opted to hurry over to the van to see what was going on.

"What, Mama?" He asked with an aggressive tone.

"What, Mama? Who in the hell do you think you're talkin' to, little boy?"

"Okay, okay...I'm sorry mama, what's up cause I'm tryin' to finish something up real quick."

"Hush up lyin' talkin' bout you sorry. Listen, you need to get your black ass home right now because this girl's in labor. We on the second floor at Baptist Hospital."

"Mama, let me talk to her?" Malcolm asked anxiously. Malcolm waited for his mama to hand Deziree the phone but after waiting for a few moments heard nothing. Malcolm realized that his mama had hung up the phone or he got disconnected some other way. Malcolm stood holding the phone for a moment staring at nothing, lost in the zone. Then all of a sudden, he snapped back to reality, a dead body, babies being born a month early, and twenty-two birds that needed to get to Oklahoma and the upper Midwest. Not to mention the issue with Amber saying that she was pregnant. There was no doubt that Malcolm had a lot of things on his plate. He unplugged the phone from the cigarette lighter charger cord and walked back around the van with a puzzled look on his face which Solo and Gooch noticed. Before any one of them could ask him what was the matter he hurried passed them over towards Fats. Fats and Kenny were over on the other side of the black lowrider getting something to wrap Scoob's body up in when Malcolm spoke out.

"I gotta go to the airport...my girl is in labor."

Fats along with everyone could hear the urgency in Malcolm's voice. Fats broke into a brisk walk leaving Kenny holding a car cover as he headed to Malcolm's aid.

"Let's go to the office so I can get a cab over here. I gotcha man, don't worry but you need to look in the phonebook and call the airlines so you can catch the first thang smokin'." Fats told him and Malcolm walked past Scoob's corpse as if he never existed.

Chapter 22

Martha was in the middle of trying to conduct some business when she had to stop and come back because of Hector blowing up her pager with 911's. He had been on it nonstop to get updated on her mission of finding him some sherm (liquid PCP) to smoke. After networking from almost every side of town and having to laugh and smile in a bunch of niggas faces, she finally met up with someone who had it. A brief phone call later, they agreed to meet each other in Bob Davis' parking lot at the fish market on N.E. 34th and Kelly.

There she spent fifty dollars on a vial and because of her sex appeal he gave her an extra one along with his home number just in case she needed anything else hoping he would get a chance to fuck.

When Martha walked through the front door at home, her nerves were wrecked, and on top of that, her grandmother had the heat turned up to an unbearable degree. She quickly took off her coat and tossed it on the couch, and headed for her grandmother, who was sitting in her rocking chair watching television while knitting. Martha stepped in front of her grandmother and bent down, causing both of them to smile then, she held her hair to the side and kissed her on the cheek. Suddenly, her grandmother frowned when she saw the blouse that she had on that exposed a large portion of her full chest.

"This is for you, nieta. You need this to put around your neck to help cover up your chest. In fact, you need to change because it's going to be cold for the next several days. You go around with your goodies, showing you'll surely catch a cold or something worse if you know what I mean." Her grandmother looked at her while handing the scarf to her.

DRE LUV

"Gracias, Abuelita, it is beautiful like you...are the boys still here?"

Once again, her grandmother's face winced with sourness as she made a shooing type of wave towards the kitchen door.

"Yes...they are in the back house drinking Cerveza and who knows what else. I seen Hector and Gilberto leave and come back with a bag full of it after they come in here and took the phone with them out back. Listen, can you not hear those fools laughing and shouting like little boys that don't have a care in the world? Then I look at you, my precious nieta, if you do not be careful, they will destroy you and doom you to hell as they are. The path that you all are on is not righteous and it leads to going nowhere fast. You must get your life together and find yourself a good man. He doesn't have to be a Mexican boy either he can be that nice black boy you brought over here Friday morning. I could tell that he likes you through his eyes, I seen the way he looked at you when you came from out of there. You like him too, huh? He is big and strong...all that is for you if you want it, get him baby and be happy..."

Martha listened to the words that her grandmother spoke, and she wondered if it was possible that Gooch really did like her because she did like him. But it would be impossible for them to be together because of conflict with people in both of their families. Malcolm despised her and knew about the skeletons that she possessed inside her closet. As for Hector, he wanted to rob everybody, so what was she to do? Her grandmother couldn't protect her from him; she never had, although she never knew what all he had done to her. Just when Martha was about to leave her grandmother's presence, her grandmother grabbed her by the arm in an attempt to get her full attention by bearing down with a piercing gaze from her gray eyes.

GHETTO MERCHANTS

"Dios tells me that Hector and Gilberto may get you hurt or involved in some...mischief that you may not be able to handle. Always remember that if you play with a snake, you will eventually get bitten. Now go...bring my phone back with you and before you leave, take off that blouse."

Martha knelt and gave her grandmother a hug after the heartfelt talk that was food for thought. Her grandmother was a wise woman, so she knew that she should take heed to what she said, and before long, she would give it a try. When she made it to the back of the house, Hector was in his usual spot, the broken-down couch, and their other cousin, Gilberto, was sitting on an old, tattered chair. Gilberto was from Texas and had just been released from prison and caught a bus to Oklahoma from Huntsville early that morning.

"So, where's the sherm at punta?" Hector questioned Martha cheerfully by trying to put on a front in front of Gilberto.

Martha reached up under her blouse and pulled the vials from underneath her bra, wondering how she was ever going to be able to deal with both of them?

Fats had stood in the doorway watching for the cab while Malcom made reservations. On his third call, he found his best option, it was Delta flight 304 leaving LAX at 9:05, arriving at DFW at 1:30 Central Standard Time. In Dallas, there would be a layover for his connecting flight at 5:10 a.m., leaving Dallas and arriving at Oklahoma City's Will Rogers International at 6:00 a.m. Just as soon as the reservations were made, Fats continued to watch out for the cab while Malcolm went to the back to have a quick talk with his crew.

DRE LUV

Solo and Gooch were loading the stash with all the work and the weapons, except for Kenny's, along with the other money. Kenny, on the other hand, was wrapping Scoob's body up with the car cover and duct tape. All they were waiting on was to pull in the Taurus wagon and load Scoob up, and while they waited for Malcolm to leave and that's just what they did. After that was done, Malcolm walked up front to chop it up with Fats, who had a long face while looking at his watch.

"You alright, big homie?" Malcolm asked as he approached Fats and patted him on the back.

"Yeah, I'm good man, hey look...here's ya cab pullin' in right now. Don't worry bout them, cause I'm gonna lead em way out where they can bypass a lotta traffic. As for me...shittt I'll be okay, it's just hard to believe that a dude that I looked out for all of these years would turn on me overnight. I'm gonna tell ya right now, get ya money up and get in the game and make it work, cause I'm gettin' out as soon as you get us both rich, now go on and congratulations on the twins, Malcolm."

They shook hands, then Fats unlocked the door, letting Malcolm out. As he watched him get in the back seat of the car, he knew they would be cutting it close, but they'd make it.

As Fats locked the door back, he turned off the light, and in his mind, the man who tried to take his life was never his friend, and he would feel no remorse in the morning when he took the wagon to the steel crusher with Scoob in the back. He would never be seen again, but still he'd be stuck to pay for the nigga's funeral because Scoob's family didn't have shit. In the back of the shop, Fats closed the door after Kenny pulled the van out with Solo in the passenger seat and Gooch in the back. They were all going to follow Fats in his Suburban to the Hilton, where they would get their luggage. from there, they would follow on the 91 Freeway with the cruise control set at 64 miles per hour.

Inside the Suburban, Fats listened to the SOS Band at a moderate volume while the Ford Econo-line followed behind at a safe distance. He contemplated on how every day he woke up to do the same thing. He made a pact with himself that he would spend more time with his family because they had unconditional love. Money brought out evil in Scoob and he let his greed take him under. Fats was determined that would not be him. Before Fats knew it, he was approaching the I-15 junction, and he slowed down for Kenny to go around to make sure that he exited. Kenny took the I-15 Barstow Las Vegas and Fats got off on the next ramp and turned around, knowing that he would see them again, sooner than later.

It had been close to seven hours since they left LA. Solo climbed behind the wheel in Flagstaff, where they got their first bit of snow. Gooch was in the back sleeping again while Kenny stayed awake in the passenger seat, making sure Solo was capable of driving in snowy conditions. There wasn't much conversation once they left. Without a doubt, everyone was dealing with the downside of the trip in their own way, although Solo was trying to grasp his future duties. He was on his way back to his hometown in a few days with a small crew. Big Tay being with him was assuring, and so was having Gooch, even though he takes life as a joke more often than he should. Solo was hoping that the mishap that happened in LA would bring Gooch back to reality. He also knew that when it came down to it, there was not one person on earth who was down for him as much as his little cousin Gooch.

Kenny restlessly moved around in the seat while watching the steady snowfall. He glanced over at Solo, noticing that he had somewhat of a grin on his face. After all they had been through over the last two days, Kenny couldn't imagine what he could be so amused about. If he hadn't been there, all three of them would have probably lost their lives, not to mention that the snow was getting heavier. Perhaps he had been a little rough on him. It was obvious that he did have Malcolm's back to whatever extent he could. From the looks of things, they would both be around each other more, so it made no sense for them not to try and get along. Kenny decided to break the ice and see if the two of them could talk civilly to one another while Gooch was still asleep.

"It's going to be sort of hard for me to continue calling you Solo. When I look at you all, I mainly remember is a bad little red boy with braids running around with asthma. I've got to ask: how did you get the nickname Solo?"

Kenny could see the smirk on his face through the dim light from the gauge cluster in the dash.

"That was a long time ago, Kenny. I remember when my mama would take me, my little brother, and my sister down to y'all's house way before Uncle Chance got locked up. Damn...those was the days back when my pop used to be around too...Well, anyway, that's kinda where I picked up the nickname Solo when my pop left us. I felt like I was alone except for mama and my little brother and sister. That's how I come up with the name Solo, I had to make choices on my own as a kid. Check this shit out though, there was this one Thanksgivin' when Malcolm and Aunt Cecelia came up to our house, it was right after grandaddy died. Malcolm was braggin' bout you bein' on a big ass ship, out in the Pacific Ocean. The next time I seen you again was when I moved to Oklahoma City back in 89." Solo explained.

Solo's memory brought a smile to Kenny's face when he heard

him open up about family issues.

"I suppose it's safe to say that you didn't miss me that much?" Kenny inquired.

"Hell, yeah, I missed you, you my big cousin. Man, you used to be chasin' me, Malcolm, and Gooch around and sockin' us up. I missed you for real, man; we all missed ya. It was like you never came to visit; I mean damn...this only the second time you been home in three years. Malcolm used to always talk about it when we would be gettin' high; he'd be sayin' he wish he knew why you didn't come home to visit more..."

Solo's voice trailed off into something else inside Kenny's mind, which took him to other parts of the world when he was enlisted in the Navy. Back then, there were things that he had done after he left his Navy SEAL team. There were so many skeletons in his closet that kept him away from his family. He stayed away. He felt as if it was keeping them safe because he never knew what agency from another country would find out who he was. After Kenny had zoned out for a few minutes on Solo, he realized that Solo was waiting for a response. The only thing Kenny could reply to was what he heard at the start of their conversation.

"I did miss my family, all of you, but when you are a soldier, there is a certain duty that you must uphold. That duty is to protect the United States of America by any means necessary. In my mind, I was taking care of all of you by doing what I could to protect this land that people take for granted. If regular citizens only knew the threats that were posed on the United States. Every hour of the day there is a group, whether it be organized or not, someone is plotting some type of terrorist act against our country. My job was to make sure that never happened, and I was damn good at it. Anyway, Solo, that's enough about me. Could I persuade you to inform me on the incident when you got shot? I was only told the story vaguely."

Solo took his right hand off the steering wheel and grabbed his cup of coffee and took a sip, and set it back inside the cupholder. He then picked up the cigarette pack that belonged to Brenda, took out a cigarette, and lit it. He cracked the window before speaking.

"It was bout this time of the year. I didn't go back to school after the Christmas break because I was stuck in the city jail for some unpaid tickets. Mama was trippin' and shit talkin' bout she didn't have no money, so my day one homeboy caught a robbery case tryin' to get up some bread to get me out. I got out about two weeks later to find out this nigga had a high ass bond, sittin' in Jackson County. I was on some bullshit back then; you know stealin' cars, rims, systems, booty's, and grills. So, one night I went to this club on Prospect and stole this niggas Fleetwood and sold it at the Amoco on 75th and Troost for eight hundred. I went and bought a half ounce of crack and posted up at these two eight-plex apartments on Lockridge, right off Benton. There was this old woman who knew my pop's side of the family over there, she smoked."

"She'd let me stash my shit in her place and crash when a nigga got tired and shit. One day I ran down the back stairs from her place to make a sell and when I got down there, there was about four crip niggas I was familiar with. They used to hang out at this park on 27th and Cypress. So, these niggas short stopped my sell and they wanted to shoot some dice. I was like fuck it; I'll buck these niggas down for they little ol change they made off of sellin' they fake ass rocks."

"There we was, me and four of them all in a circle down on a knee. I was trimmin' the shit outta them niggas with my dice lockin' game. So, I ended up hittin' em up for about nine hundred. I went to pick my money up from under my shoe and here these niggas go talkin' bout they wanted they money back, and I got my dumb ass down there with no heat. My only chance to get away was to try and make it up the stairs or scrap with all of em and get beat down. So, I faked like I was gonna break em off, but instead I broke for the back stairs to get up to Ms. Kim's apartment. By the time I leaped up to the fourth step one of em told me to stop, and another one said shoot that nigga cuz. Before I could make it to the second-floor back porch, I heard two shots. I collapsed and fell back down the stairs, and my back and leg felt like they was on fire. Muthafuckas took my money and was gonna kill me cause they had a gun to my head but some of the tenants came outta their back doors of the buildin'. I ain't gonna lie my nigga, I thought I was gonna die. I was cryin', prayin' and everythang before I passed out."

"I woke up in the hospital with Mama holdin' my hand with tears in her eyes. She hopped up and asked me how'd I feel, I asked her am I gonna be able to walk again. She told me, yeah of course, and that if the bullet in my back woulda been a little further over, it woulda hit my spinal cord. If it woulda been over a little more the other way, it woulda fucked my kidney up. The bullet in my leg is still there. Just the thought of thinkin' how my life woulda been if I woulda got paralyzed...damn."

"I can only imagine..." said Kenny, acting as if he hadn't been shot. "What kind of gun were you shot with?"

"Nine-millimeter, thank God it wasn't a hollow point. So, after bein' in the hospital for six days my doctor went ahead and released me, and mama had a surprise for my ass. She took me straight to the airport and put me on a plane to Oklahoma City to live with Aunt Cecelia and I didn't have no choice. When I got picked up from the airport, she put down all the rules that I had to go by and the main one was goin' back to school and no gang bangin'. We got to ridin' and she pulled into this neighborhood where I was diggin' these nice cribs. Then she pulled into the driveway of one and the garage door opened up and I seen Malcolm's Grand National inside. I was all excited and shit, I said Aunt Cecelia when did y'all move, and she told me they moved right before Christmas. She helped me get my bags and showed me around the house, my room and shit. When we made it back to the kitchen so I could grab some food, Malcolm and Gooch came through the door..." Solo's voice began to crackle.

"Are you alright?" Kenny asked while reaching over and turning the radio down a little more.

"Yeah, I'm cool."

"Okay then, you wanna go on and finish the story then?" Kenny joked after playfully punching Solo in the arm.

"Anyway, Aunt Cecelia got to talkin' shit about me and Malcolm, warnin' Gooch not to be like us. You know she blamed herself for Malcolm not goin' to college by takin' a partial football scholarship. She felt like Malcolm was raisin' himself when she was workin' and goin' to chef school and that was when he came off the porch and started hustlin'. Shittt back then Malcolm was what, nineteen years old when I moved in with them back in 89. He had a '86 Grand National and a '89 Super Coupe Thunderbird. It was too late for her to stop him."
"I can remember the spring of '87 when I was home on leave for a few weeks. Me and mama took Malcolm up to Langston to take a look at their Football program. They were having an inner squad scrimmage if I remember correctly. We were at the football field, sitting in the bleachers, and Malcolm was down there on the sidelines, messing around with some of the players. I seen him

flash a gang sign to some guys that were approaching him, but when they met up, they began talking and laughing with one another. I didn't make an issue right then, but later on that evening, when Mama went to bed, I confronted him about it. I explained to him how kids in bigger cities are getting killed every day over colors. He just looked at me crazy and never said a word, and finally he got up and went to his bedroom. Look...the moral of my story should be clear to you. You were almost killed because of gang violence. We as a race of blacks need to stick together and not separate ourselves from one another by the color we have on or the neighborhood we live in."

Solo shook his head with the sign of disbelief at Kenny's perfect picture of society that did not exist, forcing him to defend himself.

"Holdem up, soldier boy, first of all, I wasn't shot because I'ma blood, I was shot because I was in the wrong place at the wrong time. And on Malcolm's behalf, he wasn't gang bangin', he was part of a click called the Mafioso Seven. Niggas at that campus knew that nigga, he was probably just hittin' em up with the M for Mafioso. Gang...yeah right, the only gang was Dollaz, Big Tay and the rest of his homeboys that you've known since they was kids...You funny as a mutha fucka Kenny, you know that. Now what Malcolm is, is a gangsta and my hat is forever off to him because of some shit he did for me. Don't get me wrong that was some gangsta shit you did back in LA, but it couldn't compare to how Malcolm handled these bitch ass niggas. That shit you did out there you learned in the army; Malcolm got that shit from the streets..."

"I'm not gonna tell you again, I'm a Navy SEAL." Kenny angrily remarked, cutting Solo off.

"My bad..." Solo laughed, Kenny didn't, but Solo continued his story.

DRE LUV

"Okay big cousin, anyways you gonna have to teach me some of that shit one of these days. Now, back to 89 in Aunt Cecelia's kitchen after she went to work. Malcolm rolled up a fat joint of some hydroponic weed, and we smashed out in his Thunderbird. We got high as a mutha fucka on our way to the east side to get some barbeque at Leo's and to drop Gooch off. The shit was crazy cause it's like that nigga was a ghetto celebrity way back then, ho's and niggas jockin' this nigga. So, we all go up in Leo's and get a table in the back. While we was waitin' on our food, Malcolm's whole frame of mind changed and it wasn't from the weed. Off the rip he asked me if I knew where the niggas be at that shot me? I was like hell yeah, I know where them niggas hang out. Then he asked me if I wanted to do somethin' bout the situation and I immediately knew what time it was. I nodded my head up and down; at that time this sexy ass broad brings our drinks to the table. As soon as she left Malcolm said road trip while slamming the table with his fist. Gooch's young ass spoke up and asked when was we leavin'. Malcolm gave Gooch his props on wantin' to go with us and ride on them niggas. He just couldn't let him go cause he knew that any thang could go wrong, and he didn't want him caught up in case we got fucked off. Needless to say, he was mad as a mutha fucka and didn't wanna talk, he pouted like a big ol' baby until we dropped his ass off and peeled out. By the time we made it to the house and smoked another joint, we had plotted a plan. When Aunt Cecelia made it home that night, we was both in bed sleep. Before the sun come up, we was on I-35 headin' north to Kansas City in the Grand National with an AK-47 stuck inside a pillowcase in the trunk with two fat ass revolvers."

"We got up there and took the I-70 around to the east side and got off on Van Brunt and checked into a bullshit room on Linwood. I stayed up in the room with the 44-Mag while Malcolm pushed on down the boulevard on foot to keep the plan executed. The nigga was dressed down in some faded 501's, old tennis shoes, sweatshirt and black parka with a hood. Right down the street, he found what he was lookin' for in the McDonald's drive-thru, an old late 70's model Delta 88. This mutha fucka was a straight bucket. Malcolm bought it from this older broad with a bunch of kids in it; he paid her fifteen hundred dollars. She didn't ask no questions, but would he drop her and her kids off."

"When he showed back up at the room, he had some food and a full tank. We chilled up in the room til right after dark, that's when we got in traffic. I was sore as fuck, bandages wet as a mutha fucka and every thang but fuck it, we was on a mission. I got behind the wheel with the 44 in my lap, Malcolm in the passenger seat with the K still in the pillowcase, butt stickin' out the end between his legs and his .45 layin' on the seat. We hit Van Brunt and turned back left and headed towards this Church's Chicken on the corner. I made a right turn, then turned up in the parkin' lot that hooked up with the alley. I swear I don't know what made me go that way first, but I swear to ya right now that right up under the street light walkin' towards the alley probably headin' to this little mom and pop store for some drinks was three of them niggas. I told Malcolm there them niggas go right there. He looked around and didn't see any threats or really I don't think he gave a damn cause he jumped outta the car with that AK and let that mutha fucka spray after he yelled at em makin' em to turn around. When them niggas hit the ground, he walked all the way up on em and finished the job just in case there was any sign of life left. I ain't gonna lie, I was scared as a mutha fucka. When he jumped back in the car he had to tell me to drive. How bout I punched it straight forward and ran over the niggas. We made it outta the alley and hit Hardesty and busted a right and come all the way down to 27th and busted another right towards Van Brunt. There's a police station right on the corner but we made it right there and had to pull over to the right cause them cops was pourin' outta the parkin' lot. As soon as we got a break, I kept goin' straight all the way to Lister, then I made a left. Once I got on that street, I put my foot to the floor all the way to 30th. I made a left and smashed all the way to the corner of Quincy, that's where Malcom made me get out and head for the Grand National. The motel we was at was right down the street, another block. What Malcolm did was stick a rag in the gas tank, light it up and throw the AK down in a big storm drain on the corner. By the time I was walkin' in the motel parkin' lot, Malcolm come runnin' down the street. He unlocked my door, and I hopped in the GN and all of a sudden, a nigga heard an explosion. Malcolm jumped in on the other side, started the car and we was rollin' with the 44 and the .45 with NWA bumpin' in the two knob Alpine. We smashed down to Van Brunt, then got on I-70 West until we made it to I-35, exiting south. Shiittt we was in the clear with nothin' in front of us but highway and street dreams. Now you know why I owe my loyalty to your little brother. He didn't have to do what he did, but he did, and he did it for me."

"Since that day, my life has changed. If I woulda stayed up in Kansas City back then I'd probably been dead or in jail. Instead with me movin' to Oklahoma it made me into a nigga that a whole lotta niggas wanna be like and a lotta of em want a nigga outta the way. There's not too many niggas my age havin' the kinda shit that I'm havin'. I put a whole lotta muscle in my hustle but the one that got the shit poppin' for me was Malcolm, fuck a flag, red or blue when it comes to him and when it comes to gettin' that cock suckin' money. That's the type of shit that's got this world turnin' along with help from the Ghetto Merchants."

Solo let off a sinister laugh while he reached for his coffee. Then he and Kenny were both surprised by hearing an unexpected voice from the back.

"Yeah," Gooch spoke out of nowhere.

Solo laughed, and Kenny turned around in his seat, catching Gooch stretching and yawning. When he turned back around and looked out of the windshield at the snow, which was getting heavier, he felt more at peace. His two little cousins really did believe in Malcolm, and they'd do anything to protect him if they had to.

"Thought you were sleeping Gar...I mean Gooch?" Kenny joked.

"Ha, ha very funny, Rambo, I mean Kenny." Replied Gooch.

All three of them laughed together, but Kenny knew the joke was mainly on him. He quickly cut off the banter and got back at Solo.

"Okay, guys, that's enough laughing at good ol' Kenny. Solo, I've got to know what Mama had to say when you guys made it home?"

Solo settled his laughter and got back to the scenes in his mind from 89. "Well, we strolled in later than expected cause we stopped at the Waffle House out on 122nd. That whole day was like glue because so much came together on that particular day. That was the night Malcolm met his redhead broad. Amber. She was a waitress over there and ever since he's been fuckin' with her. In reality, he in love with her..."

"I don't want to hear about who Malcolm is in love with, I want to know what happened at the house?" Kenny cut him off.

"Chill out nigga, this my story. Anyway, we talked about everythang on the way back, especially how he felt that his life changed after the feds come and got Uncle Chance on Christmas Eve. Come on man, Christmas Eve...that'll make anybody bitter to lose their daddy on Christmas. See y'all did shit with Uncle Chance, my daddy wasn't shit. He never did a damn thang with a nigga. When we got home and crept up in the house, Aunt Cecelia was sittin' in the den waitin' and she was mad as a mutha fucka. She asked where we'd been, Malcolm lied, talkin' bout we been ridin' and was hangin' out up at Langston chillin' with Deziree. Hey man outta nowhere Aunt Cecelia slapped the shit outta Malcolm and told him that was for lyin'. Before she gotta chance to slap the shit outta me I apologized and told her I wouldn't do it again. Malcolm was hot as a muthafucka when she sent us to our rooms. How bout before we even made it part ways down the hallway by the den, she told us to come back. She gave both of us a hug and a kiss, and she had tears in her eyes. She apologized to Malcolm, but she said she was so worried that somethin' had happened. She talked a little more shit then she ended up changin' my bandages in my room and tried to get me to snitch on us. She popped me on top of the head playfully and called me a little fucka and walked out when she got done."

"The next day,3 she took me to get enrolled at Putnam City High so I could finish my school year, although I had to go to summer school. But as soon as I graduated, Malcolm had Amber to rent us an apartment on N.W. 48th and Blackwelder. He plushed the crib out and tossed me the keys to the Grand National and I got on my grind with him, Big Tay, Dollaz and this fool sittin' behind us, although he was really in the way. But one thang he did do was give our crew our title of bein' called the Ghetto Merchants. He said he learned in school that a merchant was a person that buys a product and sells it for profit..."

"Hey, cuz I gotta take a leak," Gooch interrupted again.

At the next stop, they pulled over and everybody used the bathroom; they were in Holbrook, Arizona. Solo got in the back, and Gooch got behind the wheel. Within no time at all, they were back on I-40 heading east, and the only sound you could hear was

GHETTO MERCHANTS

Jodeci and Gooch singing along. Kenny observed Gooch's driving and was comfortable and felt like he could handle the weather. He decided it was time to get some rest. Just when he closed his eyes, he began to reminisce on the Christmas Eve when his life changed. He was fifteen years old and was thrown into manhood overnight when his daddy was taken away. All that his family had been accustomed to for so long was taken away overnight, except for their dignity. Their money and their home were gone, but they had each other.

Three short years later Kenny enlisted in the Navy and went to Great Lakes, Illinois. From there he went to San Diego, California. Later he went to Coronado, California where he endured Navy SEAL training at the Naval Amphibious Base. From there Kenny's career excelled in Black Ops. Out of all the things that Kenny endured on missions thousands of miles from home, he always felt bad about leaving his mother and brother. Suddenly the sound of Gooch changing tapes caused Kenny to open his eyes. The windshield was blurry, not from the snow but from tears.

At Dallas Fort Worth Airport Malcolm was fastening his seat belt. He was sitting next to a businessman in a gray double-breasted suit. When the pilot took off down the runway, he informed everyone that the weather in Oklahoma City was windy and 21 degrees.

Chapter 23

Malcolm stepped out of the terminal at Will Rogers International on the bottom floor at the baggage claim. The wind and bitter cold made him turn his collar up on his lightweight Polo jacket. He spotted a waiting cab to his right and immediately sprinted towards it. When he opened the door and slid into the backseat, he startled the driver, who was of Middle Eastern ethnicity. He turned around in the driver's seat, facing the rear with a disgruntled look on his face.

"Sorry buddy, I have customer already...he is at baggage claim and will be on his way. You go!" The cab driver spoke while pointing at the running meter on the dash with his left hand.

Malcolm didn't bother to say a word. He twisted his face as he leaned to the side and pulled out a stack of money and peeled off two one-hundred-dollar bills. He dropped them over the seat across the cab driver's arm, getting his undivided attention, which caused his eyes to light up.

"Baptist Hospital homie, make it quick," Malcolm instructed with no plan of getting out of the cab while he stuck the stack of cash back into his pocket.

The cab driver turned around after noticing the white businessman coming towards the cab. The driver opened the door and jumped out and ran to the man wheeling his small bag and carrying his briefcase. Malcolm turned around in his seat to see what he was doing. The driver handed the man a twenty-dollar bill and ran back and hopped in the cab. They drove off, leaving the businessman looking for other transportation in the cold, cursing. Malcolm laughed as he sat back in the seat, pulling out his mobile phone from the inside of his jacket. He pressed the POWER button but couldn't get it to work; the battery was dead.

He slammed the phone down on the seat next to him then lifted his arm and peeled his right jacket sleeve back with his left hand to check the time on his watch; it was 6:22.

On the edge of downtown at the corner of Western and Sheridan, in the McDonald's drive-thru sat a hungover Sergeant Teresa Smits. She was running late for the shift briefing by the captain. She didn't give a damn because she needed something to put inside her body to calm her stomach and head down.

Last night, she went through with what she planned to be her last mission with Sergeant Eddie Sloan. He was the evening shift supervisor at the main evidence room for the Oklahoma City Police Department. The evidence room was an old train station, which was two blocks south of the downtown police station.

Teresa almost threw up in her lap when she thought about how she felt when Sloan was sliding inside of her. His body was covered in pimples, and he looked and smelled like a sweaty, fat pig. She detested the sight of him from the very beginning, when she was introduced to him by the captain when she was put on the evening shift. Instantly, Sloan was attracted to her olive skin, dark eyes, and brown hair, which she kept pulled back into a ponytail, showing all the perfect features and curves on her face. She was something to look at when she came around and was always a topic of discussion among all the men officers.

Her beauty was no doubt a gift from God. And she knew it,

but she didn't use it to her advantage, until it was needed by her lover. Because of him, she changed to the evening shift, and soon after her mission was accomplished, she changed back to mornings so she wouldn't have to see Eddie Sloan again.

Teresa got mixed up with Sloan outside of work by running her mouth at the wrong time. One night after she had gotten off of work, she met up with her lover at his low-key garage apartment in the upscale Heritage Hills neighborhood. It was the first rich neighborhood established in Oklahoma City, dating back to the late 1800s, sitting just north of downtown. The property where the garage apartment was located was owned by Cecelia's employers, who liked Malcolm. They rented it to him just so that it would be occupied, and he used it to stash drugs, guns, and money. The only woman other than the landlord and Cecelia who knew about his kickback spot was Teresa; in fact, they were the only three outside of him that knew of it at all. It was safe and in the cut; nobody would ever think of him having a place above a garage in the backyard of a nineteenth-century mansion.

That particular night, after Teresa got out of the shower and walked back into the small living room wearing nothing but one of Malcolm's T-shirts, she began to boast. She told about how this cop named Sloan offered her money if she let him eat her pussy. Malcolm was not the least bit disturbed by what she was saying, but still, he indulged with her in the conversation by finally asking her who Sloan was. When she opened her mouth and exposed Sloan as being the supervisor of OCPD's main property room, Malcolm's look made her get wet. In all actuality, he was turned on as well when he looked at the curvaceous, beautiful key standing in front of him. Teresa was the key to the jail cell that was going to set his homeboy Dollaz free.

GHETTO MERCHANTS

That night Malcolm pulled an all-nighter digging into Teresa's brain along with every hole she had that was fuckable. By the time the sun came up, Teresa had another agenda added to her plate besides just keeping him up on what the narcotics department was doing and who was snitching. She had to dig inside Sergeant Sloan's head so she could get the empty shell casing that had Dollaz's thumbprint on it. That alone could get him the death penalty at trial. When she left Malcolm's spot on her way home, she knew what she had to do, and nothing was too big for her man.

That evening, Teresa dropped by the evidence room and did some flirting with Sergeant Eddie Sloan. Two days later, they met up at the Flying J Truck stop at one o'clock in the morning for breakfast. That night inside Sloan's car in the dim yellow lighting of the parking lot, Teresa let him do some groping, and she gave him a hand job. He wanted more, but she assured him that if he was patient, he'd get all of her.

Ten days later, Teresa met up with Malcolm at his garage apartment for the first time since her instructions were given about Sloan. When Malcolm opened the door, Teresa had her million-dollar smile on, along with a clear plastic bag with EXHIBIT A (DEANTE PARKER). Inside the bag was an empty shell casing. She handed it to him like a dog retrieving a stick for its master.

From that point, Teresa began to ignore Sloan's pages, and she eliminated all her duties that would put her in the property room. She also changed back to the morning shift, which aggravated the captain. The game Teresa pulled on Sloan had him heated, but she didn't care; she didn't worry about him dropping by her place because he didn't know where she lived. One morning, Teresa was pulling her cruiser out from the motor pool; Sloan pulled into the exit, which blocked her in. He angrily jumped out of his car and approached her on the driver's side of her cruiser, where she frowned at his unprofessional behavior. The only thing he said was that he wanted five grand for his role in springing Parker when it was unveiled that the crucial evidence was gone.

That evening, she met up with Malcolm. He knew Sloan would eventually want something else after drawing the conclusion of being used as a pawn. Malcolm gave her the money, but was hesitant; he knew the cop would continue to come because he felt as if he had something to hold over Teresa's head. When Malcolm explained this to her, she insisted that Sloan was nothing more than a lovesick pervert who had his heart broken because he couldn't have her. For some reason, she was naive enough to think he would get over her and what he had done to taint the case against Deante Parker aka Dollaz.

Malcolm didn't like the way that she underestimated the cop because Malcolm seen what extent a man would go to get even with a bitch they couldn't have. He decided to give her the benefit of the doubt and let her handle Sloan on her own with the 5 g's. Besides, he wanted to keep it all cool because he was working with Dollaz's attorney on getting the preliminary hearing bumped up. Once Dollaz was out of jail he wouldn't give a fuck about Sergeant Sloan or Sergeant Smits either. They couldn't put him in the shit they did anyway, Sloan didn't know him and Teresa wouldn't fuck him around because she wanted to pursue her career and become a detective.

Dollaz's attorney managed to get the preliminary hearing moved up. The district attorney jumped all over it with joy until he found out the only evidence they had was missing in the high-profile case. The lack of evidence brought pressure on the OCPD's Chief for the lack of professionalism in his Evidence Department. This brought on an investigation by Internal Affairs. After months of questioning everyone who worked in the evidence and property department, especially the supervisors, Sergeant Sloan held strong. He was a third-generation Oklahoma City Police Officer, and he would die before he ratted out anyone, but Teresa didn't know that. She was going crazy, wondering if any day she would be called in for questioning because of Sloan. This made her vulnerable, and he knew it because he hadn't paged her in months, and he hadn't tried any other way to contact her.

Now he was going to make sure she played his game by getting twenty grand from her along with some pussy from her pretty ass. He was going to be sure to remind her about the time she told him to be patient, and he could have all of her. The time was now, and he wasn't going for any excuses, she was going to uphold her end of the deal, along with the money. Sloan didn't care where she got it from just as long as it fucked with her head.

Just like he did last time, he waited for her to leave out of the motor pool. There, he made her follow him to a parking lot in the old warehouse district on the eastern edge of downtown. At the meeting, Teresa's face revealed how rattled she was, with visible bags under her eyes. Sloan gave her his ultimatum, and in return, she would have the guarantee of not being implicated in the missing evidence scandal. She pondered on his wants, sex at the Embassy Suites out by the airport, and the twenty thousand dollars. Teresa didn't have the luxury of having Malcolm right next to her, and she had to give Sloan an answer right now. She closed her eyes for a moment and thought of what Malcolm would tell her to do; besides, this was all for him anyway. She agreed to meet him that night, but he would have to wait a few days for the money. But this would be the last time he and she would meet, and the debt would be paid.

That afternoon, Sloan paged her and put the room number in her pager. From that moment on she knew she had to get wasted to go through with the task of letting Eddie Sloan put his dick inside of her. That night, when she arrived at the Embassy Suites Hotel on South Meridian, Teresa had already consumed almost a fifth of Jack Daniels.

Now she was feeling like shit and looking like shit too. Her main objective was to get her food, hear the rest of the captain's briefings, and get in her cruiser. Once that happened, she'd park somewhere and watch traffic and try to get in contact with Malcolm. She'd let him know what she'd done last night, and he would take care of the rest.

"Welcome to McDonald's, can I help you?" The lady's voice coming from the speaker and through the small crack in the window snapped Teresa out of her thoughts.

Malcolm ran through the lobby of the hospital to the elevators and pressed all the up buttons and tried to wait. He turned around in a circle and saw STAIRS lit up; he ran to that door and leaped up the flight of steps to the second floor. When he pushed the door open on the second floor, he almost knocked himself out and dropped his phone from the impact of hitting the door that he was supposed to pull. He reached down and picked up his mobile and pushed the battery back in place until it snapped. When he made it out of the stairwell, he looked left and right until he found the nurse's station. There, he explained who he was, and a nurse escorted him to Deziree's delivery room. As soon as he entered the room, a nurse immediately helped him off with his jacket and helped him put on a smock because Deziree was about to deliver. Both Cecelia and Deziree's mother, Mrs. Holt, were already in the room wearing the same garb, and they both gave Malcolm a nod to coax him towards Deziree. He slowly edged to her side, there she was panting and groaning in pain with her eyes closed, gripping onto the side panel of the bed. Malcolm reached down and touched her hand softly, causing her to open her eyes, recognizing his touch. She smiled briefly until another contraction hit her before she could speak. After it passed along with the contorted facial expression, Malcolm used his open hand to wipe the beads of sweat from her forehead.

"I'm so glad that you could make it...I told your mother that if it were any way for you to get here, you'd finda way."

Deziree's OBGYN walked into the room and stepped to the bottom of the bed to look between Deziree's legs to check how much she had dilated. She is ready to deliver. Malcolm observed the doctor probing between her legs but tried to ignore it by turning his attention back to Deziree's statement.

"I wouldn't be able to forgive myself if I wasn't here, but I thought they were due on March fifth?" Malcolm asked.

"Young man, there is nothing to worry about. Sometimes babies are ready to come at thirty-six weeks. We've exhausted the option of trying to prolong the labor; it didn't work..." The doctor spoke after eavesdropping on Malcolm and Deziree's conversation.

Deziree squeezed Malcolm's hand and screamed at the top of her lungs. It was time, the twins were coming out. The delivery team got into position and within three minutes of Deziree pushing, screaming and squeezing Malcolm's hand, she delivered a little girl. One minute later, she delivered a boy. The only reason Malcolm let go of her hand was to cut the umbilical cords. Briefly after the nurses cleaned the crying babies, they let Deziree and Malcolm both hold them. Within minutes of the grandmother's oogling over their cuteness and Deziree being stitched up, the twins were taken to the NICU for observation.

They were all told that since the twins were premature, they would have to stay under strict observation and be inside incubators to help build up their lungs. They were always weak with preemies. While the OBGYN elaborated on the condition of the twins, along with giving Deziree a clean bill of health, Malcolm realized that Dr. Holt was not present. He figured that it must have been some bullshit that the good Dr. Holt was on for him not to be present when his grandchildren were born. Malcolm decided to wait until all the medical staff were out of the room before he asked.

"Where's Dr. Holt at?" Malcolm asked boldly, looking at all three women.

"His flight arrives at eleven. Well, congratulations to you two kids on our beautiful grand babies, but I'm ready to get me a shower and some breakfast. Cecelia, do you think you can take me to the house so I can get myself together? I think Malcolm is capable enough to look out for his family without us here." Mrs. Holt spoke as she stepped to Malcolm's side, giving him a hug and a kiss on the cheek. Then she gave her daughter a motherly kiss on the forehead.

"I'm tired as hell, too, girl, let's leave these two kids here. I'm sure they got lots to talk about since they got an early surprise." Cecelia removed her smock and prepared to exit, too.

GHETTO MERCHANTS

It was close to noon when Cecelia returned to Deziree's room with both of the Holt's in tow with her. Deziree and Malcolm were both sleeping. Dr. Holt quietly walked to his daughter's bedside, leaned over, and kissed her on the forehead, causing her to awaken. She smiled as soon as she opened her eyes, seeing her father, who grabbed her hand and squeezed.

"Hello, Dad," Deziree spoke with a scratchy voice.

"Hello to you, too, princess. I seen your brats and I must say that they are precious. Just so happened I had a chance to catch the pediatrician at the nursery. He said they will both be fine and more than likely able to go home within seven to ten days."

The conversation between Mrs. Holt and Cecelia, who sat beside one another on the small sofa by the window, and Dr. Holt speaking with Deziree woke Malcolm up. He made a loud noise as he stretched and yawned, which distracted Dr. Holt, who began to smirk before addressing him.

"Congratulations to you, young man." Dr. Holt voiced loudly as he took the appropriate steps around the bed to where Malcolm was sitting in the lounger.

Dr. Holt reached out and shook Malcolm's hand, then he looked over at Cecelia and his wife to make sure they saw him. He wanted them to know that he was man enough to put his dislikes of Malcolm aside to congratulate him on his grandchildren.

"I must know what plan you have in store for your life now that you are the father of my grandchildren. I refuse to have them raised around any type of riff raff that you may feel somewhat feasible?" Questioned Dr. Holt in a low tone, whereas only Malcolm could hear.

DRE LUV

Quickly, Malcolm rose to his feet, standing over Dr. Holt by almost a whole head. He looked down at his short, rotund frame, which was clothed in a houndstooth blazer with a sweater underneath and corduroy pants and penny loafers as he gritted his teeth.

"Let's step out to the lounge doc!" Malcolm snapped.

All three women heard the sound of Malcolm's voice and knew that he had been provoked by Dr. Holt. It was no secret that neither of the men saw eye to eye on any subject because Dr. Holt didn't think Malcolm was good enough for his daughter. These feelings began immediately after they were introduced to one another years ago at a Langston University function.

That same evening, when Deziree was alone with her parents, Dr. Holt forbade her to have any more dealings with the man he labeled as a street thug. The truth was that there was no man good enough for Dr. Holt's daughter, but he surely was not going to let her fall prey to someone like Malcolm.

Everything that her father said to her that night went in one ear and out the other because she had mad love for Malcolm. She didn't stop seeing him. Dr. Holt did some eavesdropping one night when Deziree was home for a weekend and heard her raving on the telephone in her bedroom to one of her friends about how her boyfriend Malcolm was so fine. Because she rebelled against him, he took her back to school the next afternoon, not allowing her to take her car, and cancelled her credit card. He gave a strict order for his wife to only give her a twenty-dollar-a-week allowance because she had a meal ticket in the university cafeteria. What Dr. Holt tried to do with tough love only pushed Deziree closer to Malcolm and further away from him.

GHETTO MERCHANTS

Although Deziree's heart was broken because of the tactics her father had used against her, Malcolm held her close and took up the slack. He moved her in with Cecelia and himself when Solo moved to their apartment, and he let her use his car. This allowed her to be able to continue to drive the forty-minute drive back and forth to the university.

It had been almost a year since Deziree and her father had spoken, and it was getting close to the fall semester of 1990. The feud between Deziree and her father was now affecting the Holt's marriage. Mrs. Holt disagreed with how her husband was handling the situation with their daughter and gave him an ultimatum. Either get Deziree back in our lives, or you're gonna lose both of us.

Dr. Holt debated with himself on just what he could do to possibly get his baby back from the street thug. The best thing he could think of was to beat Malcolm in the game of being a big shot. He knew Malcolm couldn't afford to give Deziree all the things she grew up accustomed to, besides, they were living with his mother. Dr. Holt, on the other hand, had credit and a legit bank account. Once he proved Deziree to be wrong about the slick-talking thug not having her best intentions in mind, he'd get her back. It was no secret that the two of them were having sex. But youngsters were wild and spontaneous and couldn't do what they wanted to do in their parents' houses. This was going to be the only way he could show his daughter that puppy love couldn't compare to real-life situations. Therefore, if Malcolm was serious about Deziree, Mr. Holt was going to show her that Malcolm wasn't Mr. Big Stuff after all.

He contacted RE/MAX Realty and found a nice twenty-four-hundred-square-foot foreclosure in a nice neighborhood for one hundred twenty thousand dollars. He knew that would be out of Malcolm's price range, and he laughed at the thought of how petty and small Malcolm would look in front of Deziree when he didn't have the money. Deziree would be begging him to come back home. It took only two weeks for Dr. Holt to get the paperwork drawn up for the unseen home. Just as soon as he got it, he told his wife he'd be back later. He headed north from their home in Plano, Texas, for a surprise visit to Oklahoma City, where his daughter resided with the Loves.

With Cecelia, Deziree, and Malcolm all present when he displayed the paperwork inside the den, Dr. Holt was getting ready for his trick shot. He let Malcolm know he needed fifteen thousand dollars towards the down payment, along with closing costs. He wasn't aware that Malcolm had just gone through the same thing almost two years ago when he gave Cecelia the same type of money to get into the house they were sitting in now. Immediately, Malcolm knew what Dr. Holt's game was. Deziree and Cecelia jumped to Malcolm's defense, but Malcolm quickly calmed them down, especially his mother. He let them know he could handle it without their assistance. Dr. Holt was enjoying every minute of confusion, waiting for Malcolm to ask him for some time or maybe even asking him if he would let him pay for it in rent until he got on his feet. What he didn't know was that Malcolm knew all along he would come running with some type of deal to buy his love back from Deziree.

Malcolm, who was sitting between his mother and Deziree on the black leather sofa, scooted up to the edge while looking at Deziree, who had tears in her eyes, shaking her head in disbelief. Malcolm patted her on her leg and assured her everything was going to work out and to trust him. When he looked to his right, Cecelia was staring at Dr. Holt with her arms crossed, forehead wrinkled, and lips twisted. She was thinking about getting up and going to her bedroom to get her Saturday night special 38 and slapping the shit out of Deziree's father. Cecelia hated a muthafucka that liked to flaunt with an ulterior motive. When Malcolm saw the look on his mama's face, he chuckled, telling her to chill out while he went to the back.

Malcolm got up, excusing himself to Dr. Holt and the ladies. When he returned from the bedroom area, he was holding a K-Swiss tennis shoe box that he sat down on the table in front of Dr. Holt. Malcolm calmly reclaimed his seat between his girl and his mother and leaned to the side and kissed Deziree on the cheek, causing Dr. Holt's bottom lip to tremble. He then smiled at his mother while lightly patting her on the knee. "There's twenty thousand in the box, if you're serious. If so, I want you to put Deziree's name on the paperwork, so she'll have her name on the mortgage. That way I know you ain't gonna pull no bullshit to fuck her credit up too. And don't worry...you can visit her whenever you like, but I ain't tryin' to see ya every mutha fuckin' weekend. Second of all, I don't want you to thank me for the extra five g's just yet. It ain't a bonus, it's for Deziree a down payment on a new car. I know her Escort GT is still sittin' in ya'll's driveway, trade that in and get her somethin' fresh. She deserves it after all the bullshit you put her through just cause she love a nigga like me. Take her home witcha tonight so she can see her mama..."

Malcolm looked over at Deziree, whose tears had dried up and was now looking surprised.

"How'd I do, baby?" Malcolm asked her while waiting for a reply from Dr. Holt.

Meanwhile, Cecelia was sitting next to Malcolm laughing her ass off thinking about how proud she was of how her son handled the snake.

Deziree was overwhelmed, feeling an unconditional love for Malcolm, who had just outwitted her father at his own game. From that point, she knew that Malcolm really loved her, regardless of what she would hear through the grapevine about him messing with other girls.

"Malcolm...are you sure you want to do this? This is different from just going out of town for a weekend or going to buy a new stereo for your car." Deziree spoke with a serious look on her face, showing sincere interest.
"Hey girl, listen to me. I love you and I ain't gotta problem with doin' my part in takin' care of you. You're in school tryin' to get your degree, when you get that we can pay bills together but right now I got this shit, don't trip. All you gotta do is continue to love me and stay pretty. I know what I want, and I know where I'm goin' and where I'm goin', you're comin' with me," Malcolm said proudly while putting his arm around Deziree's shoulders.

Thirty minutes later, Dr. Holt was headed back to Plano on the interstate with the K-Swiss shoe box in the backseat and Deziree in the passenger seat. She was staring out of the window, listening to Miles Davis coming through the speakers softly. Dr. Holt was wondering how he let Malcolm beat him at his game, then he glanced to his right and saw his little girl. I must be crazy, I won, I got my little girl back.

Back in the hospital, Malcolm told Deziree and Cecelia that he'd be back in a little while after taking a shower and handling some business. He grabbed his mobile and his jacket off the floor and waved Dr. Holt on.

GHETTO MERCHANTS

"Please be nice, baby," Deziree spoke softly as Malcolm and her father walked out of the room.

On the quick trip down the hall past the nurses' station to the lounge all Malcolm could think of was all the hateful shit Deziree's father had done and said. He was fed up and tired of being Mr. Nice Guy. Instead of going on into the lounge, Malcolm stopped at the elevator and pressed the down button. He decided he didn't need to go inside a private room to tell him what he thought of him; he already knew it because the feelings were mutual. Malcolm spun around and faced Dr. Holt's smug-looking face.

"Check this shit out man, I know you don't like me. I don't give a fuck cause I don't like you either. But I'm gonna tell ya this one time. Never again will you disrespect me in front of my mama, my girl or anybody. And if you was to do it in front of my kids I swear I'll kill you, ol' funny lookin' ass nigga. So just so we're clear...don't ever worry bout what the fuck my plans is cause I'ma grown ass man..."

At that point, the elevator chimed and opened up, and Malcolm stepped on.

"Now take ya penny loafer wearin' ass back down to the room. You got me fucked up homeboy..." Malcolm spoke until the elevator closed in Dr. Holt's face.

When Malcolm got downstairs, he reached into his pocket to make sure he still had his ring of keys, which contained all the house keys he had access to. He stepped off the elevator, disgusted, not knowing which way to go.

Back on the maternity floor, standing unnoticed by Malcolm at the nurse's station was Sergeant Hawkins. He was there visiting his sister-in-law, who had just given birth the night before. Hawkins had overheard part of the ass chewing Malcolm had given the aristocratic looking gentleman while he waited for the elevator. Hawkins saw Malcolm get in the elevator, and the older black man turned and walked in his direction and passed him, not knowing or caring who he was. Hawkins asked the operator at the nursing station to use a phone while he flashed her his badge. While she put the phone on the counter for him, he thumbed through his wallet for Agent Sharper's card. When he found it, he picked up the phone and punched in his office number. Upon calling the office, a secretary answered. She told Sergeant Hawkins that Agent Sharper was out. She suggested to him that he page him or allow her to forward him to his voicemail. Hawkins opted for the voicemail, leaving the message that Malcolm Love's old lady just dropped a set of twins up at Baptist Hospital.

After stepping out of the elevator, Malcolm caught a cab waiting outside the emergency room to his mama's house. As soon as he walked inside the house, he went straight to the kitchen and traded batteries from Cecelia's mobile phone that was on the kitchen island. After that was done, he darted to his bedroom where he sat down on the bed and called Big Tay on the house phone. After three rings, Big Tay answered.

"This Tay, who this?"

"Where you at nigga, I need to holla atcha?" Malcolm asked.

"In the projects on the east. You made it back my nigga?" Big Tay asked anxiously.

GHETTO MERCHANTS

"Yeah, I'll be that way as soon as I get outta the shower." Malcolm hung up the phone without saying another word or giving Big Tay a chance to answer.

After a much-needed ten-minute shower, Malcolm had the closet doors open. He decided on a Tommy Hilfiger hook-up, jeans, and a blue and burgundy plaid button-down. On his feet, he wore Polo boots, and he grabbed his heavy brown leather JR Riggins coat. He snapped on his gold Movado and splashed on some Polo cologne. He grabbed his jeans from the floor and pulled the money out of the pocket along with his wallet. He counted out seventeen hundred dollars and some change and stuck it in his front pocket and put his wallet in the back.

Then he went back to the closet and opened up the safe and pulled out his favorite Llama .45 along with an extra clip. He dropped them both in his right coat pocket, closed the safe, and headed for the kitchen. In the kitchen, he grabbed his mobile and his house keyring along with the keys to his truck, and he was out the door of the garage.

Fifteen minutes later, he was whipping into the parking lot of Red's Market on the corner of 26th and Kelly. He pulled over to the south side of the market and backed his truck in where it faced the projects. He was hoping to see Big Tay waiting.

Down the street at Kelly Mart which sat sandwiched between Springlake Drive, Kelly and N.E. 36th stood Hector screwing the gas cap back on after gassing up his Chevy. Meanwhile, Gilberto and Miguel sat in the back seat strapped with two Uzzis and they were still nervous because of the niggas staring at them. The only reason they were over there meeting up with the PCP hookup was because of Martha. After what she

brought them last night was gone, Hector told her to hook
back up with him and get a deal on an ounce.

Now she was sitting behind tint in the PCP dealer's Fleetwood
parked at the pump ahead of Hector's Chevy, making the
transaction. Hector looked around as he slowly walked to the
driver's door before getting in. When he got inside the car, he
turned around in the seat to face Gilberto and Miguel.

"I just seen the fuckin' baller Malcolm pass by in his truck...that's
the fucker I was tellin' you vatos about yesterday. The pinche
meyata has bread man, for real..."

"I wish Martha would hurry up, esse', it's fuckin' cold in your ride,
man." Gilberto cut Hector off.

Miguel started laughing after blowing into his hands to warm
them up from holding onto the cold Uzzi since they left the
southside.

"Fuck you esse', at least I have a ride," Hector replied as he
sneered at Gilberto and Miguel.

To make Hector's mood even worse, some gang bangers in a silver
Cutlass bucket were behind him, blowing the horn so he could
move out of the way. He started the engine up and pulled out,
barely missing the rear end of the Cadillac. Just as he pulled
beside the Fleetwood, Martha popped out of the passenger side
in a hurry, heading around the front of the Cadillac to get in the
Chevy.

Immediately, when Malcolm stepped out of his truck, he smelled
fried chicken coming from inside Red's. Hadn't nothing changed
there since the times that he used to go there with his daddy

when he was a little boy holding his hand. As Malcolm walked through the front door, he wished he had his daddy with him right now. Instead, he seen two of Big Tay's workers, Spanky and Lil T with a bunch of shit on the counter and Red looking pissed off. When they saw Malcolm, their faces lit up.

"Whassup, Malcolm, cuz?" They both asked together.
They reminded Malcolm of what Gooch and Solo would have been like if they had been raised in the same household. Malcolm gave both of them dap while Malcolm's daddy's friend Red was looking angrier and angrier by the second.

"Is you lil niggas gonna pay for the shit or not? I hate ringin' up shit when a mutha fucka know damn well they can't pay for hot shit with food stamps. Now come on, I got customers waitin' goddammit!" Red exploded with a vein protruding out of his forehead.

"Chill out, old man, how much is the chicken and potatas? We'll pay for the rest of the shit with stamps." Lil T spoke with a smile.

Malcolm laughed when Red started clearing his register while cussing to himself out loud.

"Just add their shit up with mine. Give me ten wings, four potato logs and a medium cherry slushy..." Malcolm gave his order as Red shook his head and walked away to prepare it.

"Good lookin' out cuz. Hey, I hope you bringin' Big Tay some work cause it's been dry around this muthafucka for the last few days except for niggas with that blow up." Spanky let Malcolm know after grabbing his stuff off the counter.

"Yeah, them smokers don't be likin' the shit them other niggas be bringin' in the projects."

DRE LUV

"Everybody know over here know Big Tay's spots got the cavy." Lil T cosigned right after his homeboy. All of a sudden, there was a loud bang on the counter. It was Red, he had slapped the counter with his club which he kept behind there with him.
"Y'all gotcha shit now get on!" Red yelled out.

"Hey, y'all go head and push on. Tell Big Tay I'm over here waitin' for him, and y'all need to be in school anyway. What's up with that shit?" Malcolm asked while putting a twenty-dollar bill on the countertop.

"School's for squares like my brother. He work at a restaurant washin' dishes and shit. Fuck that shit cuz, when I grow up I'm gonna be like you Malcolm. You got money, cars on Daytons, bitches..."

"And a killa team of niggas ready to ride for ya." Spanky cut in, finishing the sentence for Lil T.

"Holdem up, fellas. What ya brother is doin' by goin' to work every day is cool cause he ain't gotta worry bout goin' to jail. The shit I'm doin' can get me fucked off any day. I could walk out that door right now and somebody could be right there and blow my brains out cause they want my watch, my truck, my money...anythang. I realize y'all been kinda takin' care of yourselves for a while now, but if y'all don't make the right choices now, y'all just might regret it a few years from now. I know y'all don't like hearin' shit like that but it's the truth, shittt Mr. Red used to stay on our asses back in the day about fuckin' up but me and my niggas finished school. At least all the ones that ain't dead. Ya feel me?"

Malcolm looked at Spanky and Lil T and could tell that they were not the least bit interested in anything he had to say

338

about going to school. They were doing what they wanted to do, sell dope and set trip.

"Fuck it...go on then, tell Big Tay to come on," Malcolm ordered.

"Alright, cuz."

"Yeah, alright cuz, I'll tell em." Spanky left out following Lil T who was holding the door for him, and a couple of old ladies who just pulled up to the door in a new model Buick.

When Malcolm turned around to face Red, he was handing Malcolm's money back.

"It's on me today, Lil Chance. Ya daddy woulda been proud of ya for whatcha said to them lil fuckas. These youngstas nowadays is lost son, they's lost. You know what, outta all the kids I see come in an outta this place right here, you's probably one of the only ones I can see who's capable of makin' a change. I know it's been rough for ya since ya daddy left, hell you was knee high to a grasshopper and Kenny was bout them boys' age that just left outta here. Damn how time flies...it's been about ten, eleven years since Chance been gone?"

"Twelve years and a month. Don't trip though OG cause I gotta lawyer on his case right now that says he think they can get him up outta that bitch. If that happens, I plan on bein' in a position where all he gotta do is come home and kick back and live the rest of his life with my mama. I know they'll get they old thang back. Well, Red, it's been real, but I gotta go." Malcolm shook Red's hand and grabbed his bag of food and his drink.

"Watch out for them snakes, youngsta, they out there, and tell Cecelia I said come by and holla at me and the old lady one of these Saturdays. We still got the Tonk game goin'."

Malcolm shook his head up and down and walked out of the door, almost running into some people rushing inside for some of Red's famous fried chicken. When Malcolm got back behind the wheel of his truck, he immediately started it up to get the heat going. He placed his drink in the cupholder and began to chow down on his food. No sooner than he dusted off his second wing, he noticed Big Tay passing through the gate, leaving the projects. He was wearing all black from his beanie to his triple fat goose coat down to his jeans and boots. When he saw the vapors rising in the cold from the tailpipe of the 454 SS he sped up to get inside the all black beast minus the gold Daytons. When he got inside, he slammed the door and leaned over and reached inside Malcolm's bag. He pulled a wing out and began to munch.

"Damn homie, you tryin' to pull my shit off the hinges or somethin? This ain't that rattle trap K-5 that you got, my shit's new." Malcolm yelled after blowing his food.

"Stop cryin' nigga, this a truck. Goddamn this shit hot, he musta just pulled this shit outta the grease." Big Tay chewed the hot food as he spoke.

"Whatever nigga...anyway I want you to know that Deziree had the twins this mornin'. Second, we knee deep in the game now for real and the days are over for you postin' up across the street all day and night clockin' every nickel. From this point on we on some different shit. It's time to put some of the young homies in charge across the street while you got it on lock. Look, you got Lil T and Spanky both ready to take the reins. We got Dollaz ready to come through, drop and pick up..." Malcolm spoke until Big Tay interrupted.

"Dollaz? Why would I need Dollaz to come over here to pick

money up for me from my clientele?" Big Tay snapped in question.

"Chill my nigga while I lace ya up with some of this game. As of now, you's too big to be posted up across the street now. You on a whole nother level of the game. Let's just say your playin' field has expanded across state lines."

Big Tay looked at Malcolm, wondering what he was up to. He of all people knew just how cunning Malcolm could be when he wanted something to go his way.

"That's game nigga, what the fuck you mean by I'm too big for the projects and by the way, congratulations on the twins. Now back to the business, I got mad love for my nigga Dollaz, but I put in a ton of work to get that shit like I wanted it across the street. Ya feel me?" Big Tay explained.

"Listen...Paperboy and Hoodsta up in Minnesota right now layin' outta plan to get paid up there, birds goin' for like thirty g's up there. They gonna fuck with us on the work. Now peep this, Solo and Gooch on they way to Kansas City tomorrow to set up shop and to be a hub for Paperboy and Hoodsta. They slide down to KC from Minnesota to pick up work and drop off money, and we all get paid. I want you to go to KC with em so you can keep a watch on shit and make sho thangs go like it's supposed to. Come on my nigga, we been goin' strong for a while around here, it's time to give home a break. The best way to do that is for us to get our faces off the scene. As for Dollaz, he been in jail...he can take over our whole operation down here with me navigatin' him through traffic right from my crib. I'm gonna be chillin' at home with my girl and my kids while I help mama get her restaurant together. I'm tellin' ya the time is now if a nigga really wanna blow up cause we got the chance and we got the work to do it. I'm talkin' bout we should see that seven-figure mark by the end of summer."

Malcolm paused and opened the door. He slid out and brushed off the crumbs from the front of his clothes and out of his seat, leaving Big Tay a moment of silence to take in the information Malcolm showered him with.

"Where Dollaz at anyway?" Malcolm asked as he got back inside, leaving the door open for no apparent reason.

"He's somewhere around here flossin' in my 442 livin' up to the name Dollaz. I spent a bank at the Chevy dealer this mornin' when we picked up his Suburban. Then we dropped it off over at Mobile Sounds over on 63rd to get him some lightweight beats put in. I been fuckin' with that nigga since y'all been gone and believe me when I say that nigga crazy as hell..."

Suddenly, they both heard the throb of bass approaching fast. They both figured that it was Dollaz comin' in Big Tay's 442, but when the car came into view with the bass, it was an olive green '68 Chevy spinning on chrome. It was Hector and Martha in the front seat with two more Mexicans in the back. Malcolm slammed the door, pulled his .45 out of his coat pocket and dropped the truck in drive, and put his foot to the floor. They came out of Red's parking lot sideways all the way to Kelly Avenue. Malcolm had to drop his pistol to get control of the truck before almost crashing into two cars in the oncoming traffic. Big Tay finally got a chance to pull his Glock from his coat after getting his balance from being thrown all over the cab of the truck.

"What the fuck Malcolm?" Big Tay asked, trying to get the scoop on why they were spewing in the northbound lane going south, chasing Hector, who was in the far-right lane on the proper side.

"Say vato's, pinche Malcolm is coming up on us fast. If he comes up beside us be sure to light his black ass up. He's driving that black SS truck coming this way in the wrong lane." Hector quickly told Gilberto and Miguel. Martha turned around and looked over her left shoulder, seeing what was about to happen. Hector slowed down because of the cars in front of him slowing for the yellow light.

Martha grabbed the door handle and was getting ready to jump out in a panic.

Back inside Malcolm's truck, Big Tay put his hand on Malcolm's shoulder.

"Hey, cuz, stop trippin'. You know damn good and well them Mexicans got some heavy shit in the back seat of that Chevy if they over here. You bout to get us sprayed up, and all we got is two pistols. Look ahead, the left turn light just turned green my nigga. Make that mutha fucka then you can tell me what the beef is with Hector, and we can handle that shit later but not right now. This ain't the time or place." Big Tay explained while successfully coaxing Malcolm into taking the left turn. As they passed Hector's Chevy, Big Tay looked over in the car and could see the heat they were holding in the back seat, waiting to take them out.

"Stop at Dee's liquor so I can get some Remy. Fire this up, you need to relax my nigga." Big Tay handed Malcolm a joint from the roll of his beanie.

Cruising west, obeying the speed limit on 23rd, was Hector and his crew. The car had been quiet since the almost fatal incident that happened back on Kelly. Suddenly, Martha lost her cool and shoved Hector with both hands, causing him to swerve just as they passed a parked Capitol Patrol. Hector quickly corrected his steering, narrowly escaping the patrolman.

"I fucking told you I didn't need you to come with me to pick up the sherm. Then, when I get it you just couldn't wait to get home, you just had to smoke it right then. Then you almost get me involved in a drive-by shooting with whoever was in Malcolm's truck. I fucking hate you Hector, hurry and take me home!" Martha shouted the words out of fear, and without warning, she started throwing up on the floorboard of the car.

Just as soon as Hector felt he was out of sight of the lawman who was parked in front of the Governor's Mansion, he reached down and grabbed Martha by the hair. He snatched her back to where her back echoed from the impact of her hitting the seat, getting vomit all over her coat.

"You little bitch, you think you can raise your pinche voice at me punta... ehh? Don't you forget who el jefe is, comprende," Shouted Hector as spit flew out of his mouth with every word, and Martha's throat burned from the bile and vomit that she was forced to swallow. Hector pulled her closer to him and stared at her with the evilest stare she had ever seen, waiting for her to acknowledge what he said. When she nodded her head yes, big crocodile tears flowed down her pretty face. Hector then pushed her head towards the door, making her hit her face on the window. When he was done, he reached into his ashtray and put the half-burnt sherm stick between his lips and fired it up. Gilberto and Miguel sat in the backseat, clutching the Uzzi's still and never said a word. Back on the other end of 23rd, Big Tay hopped back into the

344

GHETTO MERCHANTS

passenger side of the truck, handing Malcolm the pint bottle of VSOP Remy Martin in exchange for the indo stick. Malcolm signaled, and they pulled off from the curb and continued eastbound. Big Tay took a couple of pulls while Malcolm cracked the top on the liquor and raised the console to get the lemon squeeze, causing his mobile to roll onto the floor. Big Tay reached down and picked it up.

"I'm not even gonna ask you what was up with that shit back there with Hector, but it's obvious it can't be too much since you been gone almost a week. You gotta get control of your temper my nigga, five minutes ago you talkin' bout us gettin' rich then you go and almost get us smoked. Here you go and tell me that I finally gotta chance to be a chicken hawk and within minutes I almost get shot outta the sky by some Mexicans that ain't got shit to do with us. Hey, cuz, you betta chill man, and I aint playin, and you just had some kids too. You trippin' for real. Pass the Remy."

"You right my nigga. There's just so much happenin' and it's like all the shit is happenin' all at once. Javon still missin' I guess since you ain't said nothin' bout em, Deziree havin' the twins a fuckin' month early. Oh yeah...that LA trip was so crazy that you wouldn't even believe," Malcolm explained while Big Tay took another hit of the indo and passed it back while holding in a cough.

"Let's roll over to Javon's mama and daddy house. If somethin' is up with the nigga they'll know by now and his mama will tell you cause she like your silly ass," Big Tay laughed as he spoke.

"That's a good idea, and after that, I need to go out to Mathis Brothers so I can get another baby bed and bassinet."

DRE LUV

Big Tay took another drink and passed the bottle back to Malcolm, and turned the music up a little, then Malcolm's mobile started ringing. Malcolm quickly passed the liquor back to Big Tay, then picked up his mobile and pressed SEND.

"What's up?" Malcolm asked.

"What up pops?" Asked Solo from the other end.

"Hittin' a few corners with Tay runnin' the game plan down. We gettin' reedy to slide over to Javon's mama's house right now to see if there's any news on him. Everythang cool with y'all?"

"We good. We just left Albuquerque gettin' some gas and food. So, how's Deziree and the twins?" Solo asked.

"She's cool, the twins is cool too, except they gotta stay at the hospital for maybe a week. Check this shit out though, a nigga seen Hector and Martha with two more esse's rollin' down Kelly and they was comin' the direction you and Gooch's crib is at. I could be trippin' and it ain't nothin' but I just don't trust them two, you feel me?"
Solo took a look in the rearview mirror at Gooch laying on the letdown bed watching TV.

"Check this shit out big cous, they pose no threat to us. We on some shit now that goes right over their head. Anyway, my nigga, fuck em...hey what y'all should be doin' is worryin' about what kinda minivan or station wagon to get Solo clowned.

"That's what type of time you on nigga, fuck ya...here talk to Tay cause we pullin' up to Javon's mama house and the

346

nigga's Range Rover out front."

Malcolm handed the mobile over to Big Tay as he parked behind the Range Rover. Seeing Javon's vehicle brought a sign of relief to Malcolm's mind. It was kind of crazy that Malcolm felt relieved because if it would not have been for Javon being on some bullshit Malcolm may never have had the opportunity that he and the rest of his crew had right now. Although there was a flip side to it as well, the trip to California could have cost all of them their lives. For days Malcolm toiled in thought about what he was going to do if he ever saw Javon again. He really wanted to knuckle up with him and then afterwards give him a brotherly hug, thank him for introducing him to Fats and never speak to him again. By the time he saw his face, his thoughts could change and right now he was reaching for the handle on the outer glass door. That was when Malcolm saw Mrs. Mims pulling the wooden door closed behind her. Quickly, Malcolm opened the glass door for her, allowing her to step out across the threshold.

"Thank you, sweetie." Mrs. Mims showed her appreciation with a smile on her face, then she gave Malcolm a tight hug and a peck on the cheek.

"How are ya today, Mrs. Mims?" He asked with a quick smile, then changed it to a frown as he glanced at the front door.

"I really hate it that you and Jazmin didn't get y'all's relationship back on track. You've grown up to be so handsome. Well, I heard you and your girlfriend were gonna have yourselves a set of twins. I'm happy for you two. Is it safe to say that you're looking for your friend?"

"Yes, ma'am."
"He's in jail way out in Las Vegas, and if you don't watch out,

so will you if you get pulled over. Sweetie, you smell like liquor..."

Mrs. Mims reached inside her purse and pulled out a pack of chewing gum and gave Malcolm a piece, then she continued, and Malcolm didn't interrupt.

"Anyway, something happened, and his truck ended up in the impound out there, and it's registered to me and his father, so he couldn't get it out. Instead of waiting for us to fly out there and pick it up when he called home, he wanted us to send him money to gamble. But, sweetie, let me tell you, that boy jumped the fence at the impound yard and busted out the glass on the rear driver side door and got caught. They charged him with trespassing and burglary. That was Saturday morning. Me and Mr. Mims made it out there around noon Saturday and found all this out. Javon was in jail, and that's where we left him and that is exactly where I want you to leave him at as well. He needs to take a time out and realize that life is serious, and you know Javon has been given everything he needed and wanted by me and his father. Well, now it's time for him to grow up. All he's done is gamble off every dollar he gets his hands on. Would you believe that over the last year, he's come by here and slowly gotten every dollar that he's had me keep for him? I'm talking well over two hundred thousand. I called out there and spoke to the judge and informed him that my baby has a gambling problem. I'll have you know that his clerk was courteous enough to call. They sentenced my baby to six months in the county jail this morning, so even if you tried, you wouldn't be able to get him."

"As for you, I know what you boys do for a living, but sweetie, please believe me when I tell you that all that seems good that's wrong will come to an end. I'm only telling you this because I love you, sweetie, and I don't want to see anything bad happen to you. Who knows, maybe Javon got off lucky by going to jail for something petty, perhaps it will open his eyes to see his path in a different direction."

Malcolm was beginning to feel like he was in church, the more Mrs. Mims spoke. He had to break this conversation up because he was ready to go on top of it being cold.

"I'm sorry to hear about Javon, but I assure ya that I had nothin' to do with his bad habits that led to his financial problems. In fact, I've constantly done my best to help him when he needs it. Well, anyway, if there is anything that I can do, don't hesitate to get in touch with my mama."

"There is a way. We own Javon's condo, as you know, and being that we just had it remodeled, we'd like to rent it out to someone. Do you have anyone in mind?"

Instantly, Malcolm thought about Dollaz, and he thought about Hector and Martha knowing where Solo and Gooch's pad was. It was no longer safe to stash anything over there. Besides, Dollaz was going to need his own place to live, and it had to be out of the way. At least with renting from the Mims, they wouldn't have to worry about any pop-in searches of the property. Lots of owners didn't like their property to be occupied by them for fear of drugs being sold there. When you have the opportunity to rent from someone who knows you, you have a certain advantage. If the police got a tip about someone on their property, they usually notify the owner's and that alone was the advantage of having a cordial relationship with them.

"It's funny you bring that up; my brother just made it back to town from the service, and he was telling me that he needed to find a place. I'm sure he would like Javon's crib, and I know he's responsible," Malcolm responded cheerfully.

Mrs. Mims quickly reached inside her purse feeling the cold air upon her now and pulled out a safety pin with two keys on it. She handed them over to Malcolm with a smile on her face.

"Here's the keys to the place, tomorrow me and Jazmin are going over there to box up all of Javon's personal belongings. We'll go ahead and leave the furniture and electronics since family will be staying there. You be sure to tell Kenny he can only stay for six months...okay. The rent is six hundred plus electric."

"Yes, ma'am, I'll be sure that he knows, and I'll be by in a day or two to drop off the thirty-six hundred. We'll handle the electric bill month to month, I suppose," Malcolm set the plan in motion, then turned towards his truck, seeing Big Tay waving at him through the dark front window. Malcolm raised his hand acknowledging that he saw him. That was when Malcolm dug inside his pocket and pulled out his money and counted out six hundred dollars and handed it to Mrs. Mims.

"This right here is for Javon's girls. Well, I've gotta run Mrs. Mims, love ya."

Malcolm opened the door on the Range Rover and gave Mrs. Mims a kiss on the cheek, then helped her up in the truck. They said their goodbyes and he closed the door for her. Then he trotted to his truck. When he got inside his truck, he turned the blower up to high and moved the heat control to make it blow out of the dash vent as well as the floor.

GHETTO MERCHANTS

"Goddamn it's cold as a mutha fucka out there. What was you wavin' at me for?" He asked Big Tay as he backed out on Kings Row Lane.

"Somebody kept callin' your phone back-to-back; I answered but they wouldn' t say shit. Fuck em, so what Ms. Mims say about Javon?"

"That nigga in jail out in Vegas."

"Damn! I didn't know that fool was hustlin' out there too."

Big Tay didn't hide his surprise as he tried to hand the liquor to Malcolm.

"Hell, naw that nigga wasn't hustlin' out there ... I'm cool on the drink my nigga. How bout the nigga in jail for tryin' to get his truck outta the impound yard? You got some money on ya?" Malcolm asked.

"Yeah, I got about thirteen hun on me. What's up?" Big Tay answered.

"Cause I'm gonna need some money at the furniture store, nigga." Malcolm voiced playfully as they hit the southbound ramp on I-35.

When Malcolm signaled to hop on the southbound I-35 ramp, he sped up to seventy miles per hour and set the cruise, and looked over towards Big Tay.

"Mrs. Mims dropped a dime on Javon tellin' me the nigga broke as a mutha fucka. He... " Malcolm's mobile began to ring, and he immediately stopped talking to Big Tay and picked up the phone and pressed SEND.

DRE LUV

"What's up?" he asked.

"I've been trying to get in touch with you since yesterday. What you don't answer your phone or your pager anymore? Listen here, I need to speak with you as soon as possible like yesterday. Where are you now?" Teresa asked nervously.

"I'm in my truck gettin' ready to hit the I-40 junction goin' west towards downtown on my way to May Avenue." Malcolm answered.

"Well, slow down, baby and I'll catch up with you," Teresa replied, then she hung up.

Malcolm looked at the phone and saw it flash LOW BATTERY. He reached down and grabbed the charging cord and plugged it in while wondering what was so important that Teresa needed to talk to him so urgently. The mobile phone beeped, signaling that the battery was low, then it rang again before he could sit it down. Big Tay looked at him and laughed, seeing the frustration as Malcolm pressed SEND again, then put the mobile to his face again.

"Hello!" he snapped into the mouthpiece.

"Are you still mad at me, baby?" asked Amber in a cheerful tone.

"I'm good. Hey, check this out...we'll get together late this evenin' or sometime tomorrow so we can discuss our situation. Alright." Malcolm quickly responded in a calmer voice this time.

352

GHETTO MERCHANTS

"I'm sorry for just springing that information on you over the telephone. I felt so silly later on that night. It's just that I hardly get to spend any time with you, and that'll be even less when Deziree has the twins."

"Amber, don't trip, believe me when I tell ya that without you, my life is not complete. You're the one that got me focused on some real business type shit. I'm always gonna have time for ya, and especially now. Believe me when I tell ya the time will come and we'll be able to spend more quality time together but for now I'm gonna need a little bit of space. Here in a few weeks or a month or somethin' we'll take us a getaway vacation, just me and you. Maybe we'll go to Cancun for spring break...Hey baby, I'm gonna have to call ya back cause this phone is almost dead and..."

"Okay, okay, before you go, I want you to tell Ms. Cecelia I've got the keys to her restaurant, but she needs to sign a few more papers. I hear a siren; are you being followed?"

"I'll tell..." Those were the last words Amber heard before Malcolm's mobile phone gave out. The battery Malcolm had exchanged from his mama's mobile phone had been almost dead as the one he had. In his rearview mirror, he could see that the police car that was approaching from behind had moved in on his bumper just as he passed the Villa exit.

Back at her desk, Amber was once again dreamy-eyed because she had gotten a chance to speak with Malcolm. She was kind of upset that she didn't get a reply from him about how he'd feel about her having his baby. The other news she wanted to see was how he'd feel when she told him that the mortgage company she worked for had just acquired the old Club Axis on Wilshire Court. Since their first date, he told her of how he dreamed of owning a big nightclub someday.

DRE LUV

Malcolm passed his Llama over to Big Tay as he pulled over on the shoulder of the interstate. He pushed the button for his flashers and let down the dark-tinted window. In his rearview mirror, Malcolm watched as the cop got out of the cruiser, approaching his truck and glancing back over her shoulder several times before making it to the cab of the truck.

"License and registration, sir...what seems to be the big rush?" asked the officer as Malcolm pulled his registration down from his visor and his driver's license from his wallet. He didn't bother answering; he just handed the two articles over.

The cop looked at them both briefly, then stepped over closer to the mirror.

"Step out of the vehicle, sir, and come back to my cruiser, please."

When they both got inside the cruiser Teresa called in Malcolm's tag number to cover both of their asses in case another cop stopped for assistance. She could always say she pulled him over for swerving if need be. Teresa took a deep breath as she cautiously reached down to rub Malcolm's leg while looking deep into his eyes.

"Baby, I got something to tell you...I I fucked Sloan last night, and you smell like liquor. Are you fucked up?" asked Teresa.

"What the fuck ya tellin' me for?" Malcolm snapped.

"I can't fucking believe you, you asshole! If it wasn't for you, I wouldn't have done it. I'm not a whore Malcolm; you are the

354

only man I've been with since we first started seeing one another. Don't fuck with my emotions, Malcolm Love, not now because I'm not in the mood. The reason I'm speaking to you right now on the side of the highway is to inform you that Sloan is under investigation by Internal Affairs. It's all in regards to the evidence he stole from the department, you know what I'm talking about. I really have no idea how deep this investigation goes, but I'm letting you know that we can't see each other for a while until I am sure Sloan hasn't turned on me. I don't want you to worry baby, because he knows nothing about you because I never told him why I wanted the shell casing. For all he knows I could have wanted it just to see if he would do it," Teresa explained.

"You never called him from your crib, did ya?" Malcolm asked.

"Of course not, Malcolm, I'm not stupid! I remember you telling me not to. You also told me that I wouldn't have to fuck him either, oh baby he made me feel so disgusting. Please don't let that change things between us, tell me it's not? I love you, Malcolm," Teresa confessed with sad eyes, with bags underneath.

At that point, the dispatcher came back to her over the radio, giving her the name Malcolm's truck was registered to, showing no hits. Teresa acknowledged the dispatcher and queued out, awaiting Malcolm's answer.

"Check it out, if you love me, it doesn't matter whatcha did since ya did it for me. So does any one of ya fellow officers know bout you and me?"

"Of course not, silly, you do think I'm stupid, don't you? Don't you dare answer that question asshole. But there's more, when I made it inside the briefing room this morning, I heard

DRE LUV

Lieutenant Hart talking with Sergeant Hawkins from Springlake Narcotics division. Hawkins was saying that he was getting help from the DEA to take you down along with your Ghetto Merchant Crew. I will do my best to keep you posted on what's really going on with that, but I can tell you they were talking to each other. I was eavesdropping, it wasn't for everybody to hear, so it may not be official business yet. You've got to do your part as well."

"My part, what the fuck you mean by my part?" Malcolm asked aggressively, displaying a scowl.

"You'd better take that frown off your face before I hop over there and rip your clothes off. You know I like that rough stuff, baby, but for now I need you to lay low. I want you to know the facts. If you guys get your files transferred from OCPD to the government, there'll be nothing I can do for you anymore as far as information. Now the last thing on the list is...Sloan wants twenty thousand dollars from me by tomorrow, baby. I swear I don't have it."

Malcolm quickly contemplated all that Teresa had told him. He tried to get his next words together for Teresa, but in reality, he wanted to go to the hospital and pick up Deziree and his kids and disappear.

"Okay, Teresa, that was some real investigative work you've done." Malcolm managed to say in a jovial voice, trying to show Teresa he wasn't fazed by her news.

"Investigative my ass. That's what you call it. I call it part of my duty as a prostitute on call for you, mutha fucka. That's the last time I'm going to give my pussy away to somebody I don't want to fuck. I went down that road in college, buddy, not now..."

"Stop it, Teresa, if you love me like you say, there's no limit to unconditional love. Besides, don't I do everythang you ask me to do?"

"No, you don't eat my pussy!"

"Enough woman...anyway, do ya have Sloan's address?"

"Yes," Teresa quickly grabbed her notepad from the seat and jotted down Sergeant Sloan's information and handed it to Malcolm. When she finished, Malcolm gave her a new set of instructions.

"You've gotta catch up with em face to face and say you'll have the money tomorrow evenin'. Be sure to tell him you'll meet em at a hotel for the drop. You've gotta jazz up the conversation to make that mutha fucka think ya wanna give em some more ass. I promise ya he's gonna think you think that if ya fuck his fat ass again you might not have to pay. He ain't that stupid either, believe me when I tell ya he knows that you got a way to get the money. That alone will make him drop his guard down all day thinkin' he's gonna get another chance to fuck. You in the game now, Teresa so that means ya gotta play the game to the fullest. So does he live by himself?"

"He lives by himself. Baby, please don't do anything crazy that'll put you in a position where I won't be able to see you again. I don't like him at all, and I have to admit I've had thoughts, but we'll get through this together, I promise. I'll never let him do anything to hurt you..."

Teresa was interrupted by the radio. The dispatcher

announced a 211 in progress with a hostage situation at Freemont Federal Savings on 25th and South Shields.

"Baby, I gotta go. I love you and don't forget about the money, and I'll take care of what you told me to do. Now get out of here and stay out of trouble."

Teresa blew Malcolm a kiss and flashed her beautiful smile at him as he opened the door and slid out of her patrol car. Upon Malcolm getting back to his truck, Teresa hollered out of the window letting him know she'd help him get on the highway. When he got inside his truck, she turned on her siren and edged out onto the highway, allowing him to get on and smash out. When Malcolm looked into the rearview mirror, he saw Teresa turn around in the median and head back eastbound. As he looked back one more time at the flashing lights going back the other way, he thought that Teresa might be the one who loved him more than anyone. He knew that love had limitations; it was conditional in most cases.

"Damn, my nigga, you was back there all that time and didn't get a ticket?"

"Naw, she ran my name and the plates. She was gettin' ready to run a nigga in because she smelled the liquor on me. Gotta keep readin' the street signs my nigga, a nigga gotta stop drinkin' and drivin'. Ya feel me?" Malcolm explained, then turned the music up as the May Avenue exit approached, and he got off.

There was no hiding that he was shook up from Teresa's news. Malcolm began to think of the night he met Teresa. He was hanging out with Javon on campus corner down in

GHETTO MERCHANTS

Norman.

Right then, Big Tay fired up another joint and tried to pass it to Malcolm, but he shook his head and continued with his previous thought. He and Javon stepped inside Boomer's; it was the only strip club in Norman. Teresa was working the door, and she was wearing her police uniform. She asked Malcolm for his ID, then she licked her lips. After seeing that he wasn't 21, she told him he could get in anyway if he'd call her later. He agreed as they talked for a moment while she wrote the number down. All the while, Malcolm didn't know she was a real police officer; he thought she was a stripper in costume.

One week passed and Javon asked him if he'd ever called the bitch from the strip club which jogged his memory. He dug inside his wallet and found her number and called. They hooked up that night at her apartment on S.E. 89th. When he made it to her bedroom, he found out that Teresa worked part-time at Boomer's as security. She was a real Oklahoma City Police Officer. From that point on, Malcolm and Teresa grew to have a decent relationship. She was busy trying to accelerate her career. And she did what she could to help him with information that could help Malcolm in the streets. Never did Teresa question him about what else he did with any other women, except for asking him not to bring her a disease. Now she had put herself out on a limb for him and Dollaz. She was in jeopardy of losing her job or even facing jail time. He had to figure out today how he was going to handle the situation with Sergeant Sloan. He wanted twenty g's now, last time it was five. Next time he'll want fifty. It would have to end sooner or later, as far as the outcome he didn't know yet, but it was serious.

Suddenly, Malcolm needed a drink. "Pass the yac, Tay,"

DRE LUV

Malcolm spoke in a flat tone.

Big Tay opened the glove box and pulled out the pint and unscrewed the top off and handed it to the left. He could tell that Malcolm's whole mood had changed.

"What's up my nigga, you supposed to be on top of the world right now. You just had twins, and your crew got chickens. We gettin' ready to be rich, why you lookin' so sad cuz?"

Malcolm took a drink of the Remy and passed it back to Big Tay. He paused after swallowing it, then he took a deep breath before speaking.

"The lady cop is my inside connection to OCPD. She's the reason we been lastin' in the streets. Ya know how we'll have a spot that's checkin' major chips then all of a sudden, I'll shut it down?"

Big Tay adjusted his weight so that his back was more against the door than the seat, and he was staring at Malcolm.

"Yeah." He answered.

"And how we'll sometimes drop everythang and take a road trip to Dallas and fuck off some money for a week or somethin'?" Malcolm asked.

"Yeah, I'm with ya homie, keep it comin'." Big Tay maintained eye contact with him.

"All the information was comin' from her. She'd get information at the shift briefings. All the sergeants on shift, whether they're narcotics, homicide, robbery or whatever.

They all get a heads up on what's goin' on in other divisions. Teresa would always give me the information along with givin' me heads up on the snitches, drug busts, and all. And she'd run warrant checks on all of us. That's my girl Tay; I trust her cause she ain't ever told me nothin' wrong. In fact, she just told me that she overheard Hawkins talkin' to this lieutenant in the briefings this mornin' about how he was gettin' some help from the DEA to get us off the streets."

"Goddamn! Pass me the liquor, I feel like gettin' fucked up for real. Oh yeah, I'm damn sho ready to slide up to Kansas City now. Fuck this shit down here my nigga, it's time for us to shake the spot. Hey, is she the reason Dollaz beat that murder case?" Big Tay asked before taking a drink.

"Hell yeah, along with a few g's. Now this mutha fucka that works in the evidence department that got the shit for her is tryin' to extort her for another twenty g's. He already played her outta some ass. So, what do you think of all this shit?"

"Fuck the DEA, the FBI and OCPD. As far as I'm concerned when it comes to all them mutha fuckas if they want us they'll have to come get us. I'm tellin' you right now that they'll never take me alive. If I see em comin' I'm holdin' my court in the streets. I ain't goin' back to the pen again, especially what level we on in the game now. We lookin' at time like your pops my nigga, and all our homies. Fuck waitin' on probation, parole, appeals and all that shit. I put this on the dead homies when I say I'd rather be dead." Big Tay expressed, then he pulled his gun from the glove box.

"I feel the same way homie. Fuck em all!" Malcolm yelled loudly."

"Exactly, we can't let that shit stop us now," Big Tay replied as

DRE LUV

he reached over and he and Malcolm knocked fists.

Chapter 24

Agent Sharper had been caught up inside the federal courthouse on N.W. 5th in downtown Oklahoma City since eleven a.m. His pager had been vibrating off and on for hours, displaying numbers along with his voicemail digits appearing.

He couldn't leave the courtroom because he was a witness. Finally, the judge adjourned for the day shortly after three p.m. He hated the fact that he was caught up in the high-profile Asian Heroin Trafficker's case; it had been taking up too much of his time. After having a quick conversation with two US Marshals who were present with him at the time of the bust, he got a chance to break to a phone booth downstairs to check his messages. When he got the message from his old friend Sergeant Hawkins, he hung up the phone and ran down the hall. He was on his way to Baptist Hospital.

After spending about thirty minutes inside the furniture store, Malcolm and Big Tay found a solid oak with cherry finish baby bed along with a bassinet. Big Tay paid for them, and Malcolm paid for the same-day delivery, in which he paid extra to have it delivered by six that evening. When they were walking out of the doors to the parking lot, Big Tay's mobile phone started ringing; he had been holding it in his hand. When he answered it, he found Dollaz on the other end. Big Tay informed him that they were on their way to the hospital to see Malcolm and Deziree's twins. Malcolm grabbed the phone from Big Tay and told Dollaz to meet them up there so they could talk business. Dollaz let him know he was ten minutes away and he'd meet them. In return, Malcolm instructed him to meet them in the lobby on the first floor and ended the call.

DRE LUV

Malcolm handed the mobile back to Big Tay. When they made it inside the '454, Malcolm grabbed his mobile off the seat and turned on the power. Luckily, it had charged up enough while they were inside the furniture store. He pressed in the hospital number and SEND and got transferred to Deziree's room. After a few rings, Cecelia answered the phone. She let him know Deziree had just fallen back asleep, also that the nurses had brought the twins in a little while ago and had let them feed them. She said that Dr. Holt had caught a cab over to the house to get some rest. Supposedly, he had been up for days with one of his patients who was terminally ill. That was why he was late getting to Oklahoma City and why he was leaving in the morning.

Malcolm told his mother to call Dr. Holt and make him aware that the furniture company would be delivering by six o'clock. She, in return, told Malcolm to hurry up and get there because she and Mrs. Holt were going to Quail Springs Mall to shop for the twins as soon as he got there. Malcolm told her he was on his way.

When he was pulling out of the parking lot, he pressed the gas and smoked the BF Goodrich tires as he came out sideways, pressing Big Tay against the door. They were en route to Baptist Hospital.

There was no sign of Dollaz when they made it to the hospital. After Malcolm explained to Big Tay about his mama and Deziree's mama waiting for him so they could go shopping, Big Tay chose to wait downstairs for Dollaz while Malcolm went upstairs. He wanted to grab some flowers and gifts from the gift shop anyway before he went upstairs.

As Malcolm walked around the nursing station towards

Deziree's room, he saw only one person standing in the hall, staring inside the nursery. As he got closer, Malcolm observed the Wrangler jean ensemble from his pants to his coat with the fuzzy white collar that matched his hair. He also wore cowboy boots, and he held a cowboy hat against his right leg with his right hand. It was something about him that looked familiar, the way he stood, his profile, what was it? As Malcolm passed up Deziree's room to get a closer look at the cowboy along with his twins, it appeared that his twins were who the cowboy was looking at.

Two nurses were inside, tending to the infants who had the names Love Girl and Love Boy on paper at the ends. Now Malcolm was standing inches from the stranger while they both gazed at the innocent babies that filled the nursery. Suddenly, the white-headed cowboy brushed Malcolm on the leg with his cowboy hat.

"Mr. Malcolm Love, that is quite a gift the Lord has blessed ya with. Are ya aware of the disadvantage a child has when growin' up in a single-parent household?"

The statement boggled Malcolm instantly, causing him to step away from the glass and try to focus on who the familiar-looking stranger was while clinching his fist.

"Who the fuck is you and how you know my name cowboy?" Malcolm angrily questioned the stranger while getting his footing together as he sized him up.
At the very moment when Malcolm was about to take a step forward and advance on the cowboy with force, he was distracted from behind. He cautiously turned around to see the distraction that was saying his name. It was a nurse with brown skin and glasses, short in stature, wearing a badge that read T. JAMISON LPN pinned to her top. She had extended

her arm with a shake, as well as displaying a smile. Suddenly, her smile changed with a puzzling look on her face as she noticed the scowl and clenched fist that Malcolm displayed.

"I don't know what happened, but I can assure you that I'm not responsible." T. Jamison joked, then she paused and leaned to the side to look around Malcolm.

"That's strange...well, I'm just letting you know that I'll be the one who will be tending to the Love twins this evening. Congratulations, sir, they are so adorable..."

After being sidetracked momentarily by the suspicious cowboy by T. Jamison, Malcolm turned back around, ignoring what she was saying. When he did, he was surprised; the cowboy was no longer standing there. There was another hallway that circled the nursery. Malcolm took off in a sprint, headed in that direction in order to catch the man, leaving T. Jamison to stand alone.

The hallway was short, around the corner, leading only to the left. When Malcolm made it to that turn, he saw the cowboy step into the elevator. He turned back around to face the opening, and that was when he saw Malcolm running towards him. Agent Sharper placed his hat on top of his head and tilted his brim towards Malcolm as the elevator doors closed, and the arrow lit up, showing down.
"Damn!" shouted Malcolm in a low roar as he pounded his fist against the door.

"Sir, what's going on?" asked T. Jamison, who had chased behind Malcolm.

"Who the hell is that cowboy?" Malcolm couldn't hide the

panic in his voice.

"Calm down, Mr. Love. I'm not sure of who he is, all I know is that I saw him get off the elevator about five minutes before you. Do I need to call security, cause if he threatened any one of those babies..."

Malcolm let the nurse jabber away as he thought about what Teresa had told him about the D.E.A. It had already started; the big boys were on him, and they were not discriminating against the fact that he was a brand-new father. The federal government didn't give a damn about that shit. He was a living witness to what they had seen them do to his father; now they were after him. But for now, he had to play it cool cause if Teresa's information was correct, they didn't have anything on him yet. Unless there was more to Javon being in jail, more than what Mrs. Mims claimed. He was definitely going to have to clip some loose ends.

"Ya know what, I don't think security will be needed. I just had him confused with someone else. So, how's your day so far?"

"It was great until you scared the living daylights outta me. Thank God that's over. You know, when you got off the elevator, I was reading through some of the charts, and that was when I ran across the Love twins. Nurse Jones pointed you out as being the father of them. That was why I introduced myself to you, letting you know they would be well taken care of. Well, now that we've gotten all of that out of the way, I'll let you get on with your evening. It was a pleasure to meet you."

"The pleasure's all mine, nurse...Jamison." Malcolm replied with a genuine smile and a handshake.

Then there was the distinct sound of the elevator chime again. Malcolm turned away from watching nurse Jamison walk away while playing with her stethoscope to face the elevator. Two minutes ago, he wouldn't have been a bit surprised if the feds had stepped off. Now that he had slowed his mind from racing, he sighed deeply and was pleased to see Big Tay appear. He was holding a floral arrangement in one hand and two gift bags in the other. Behind him were four nurse aids, all carrying floral arrangements as well. None of them paid Malcolm any mind as he leaned against the wall next to a fire extinguisher. Then the other elevator chimed and opened, and this time it revealed Dollaz. He had two stuffed bears tucked up under one arm and was being handed a piece of paper by a nurse of Indian descent with a skin color so beautiful it was indescribable.

All Malcolm heard her say was, call me tomorrow when Dollaz stepped out and she stayed on.

When Malcolm walked inside Deziree's room, all the young women who had been following Big Tay were leaving, and Cecelia was shedding tears of joy as she hugged Dollaz tightly. Big Tay already had his turn and was now standing over Deziree, laughing. After Cecelia let Dollaz go, she introduced them as Deante and Brandon, giving them titles as her nephews. After the two of them shook hands with Mrs. Holt, she and Cecelia gathered their coats and set out on their venture to the mall.

Deziree, Big Tay, and Dollaz all conversed while Malcolm stood at the window and stared at the traffic bustling down Northwest Expressway. Finally, after about five minutes, Deziree got his attention and asked him to join in with the rest of them in conversation. She noticed the stress in his face but decid-ed not to comment as he walked towards her, taking off his leather piece. He handed it to her to sit next to her on the bed because it held his pistol. She felt the weight of it as he handed it to her, and all she could do was shake her head and smile at him.

"Come on, baby, you brought your gun to the hospital? Who you gonna shoot you in the hospital?" Deziree joked, trying to get a laugh from Big Tay and Dollaz.

"Ya never know," Malcolm told her in a serious tone.

"Yeah, sis, it's mandatory to have your ghetto express witcha at all times if you's a ghetto merchant." Big Tay added.

"Whatever...anyways they're going to let me go home tomorrow. I don't wanna leave my babies up here all alone, how's that gonna make me look?"

"You can come and stay all day, stop stressin'. They'll be okay, girl," Malcolm stated.

"I'm goin' to take a look at 'em. They're right out there behind that glass, ain't they?" asked Dollaz as he stood up and stretched.

"Me too...what did y'all name them?" Big Tay inquired. Deziree giggled for a split moment while catching an eye-piercing stare from Malcolm.

"Me and Malcolm hadn't come to terms on what we were going to name them. We just knew we had a whole month to go before they arrived and look how all of that changed overnight. But hey, you can see them in the nursery, their little incubators have Love Girl and Love Boy on them."

"If it's not too much of an inconvenience for you guys, will you please go down the street to the Hunan House and get me some Chinese? I'm starving. That is of course, after you see my little sweeties."

"Don't trip, sis, we gotcha. Me and Tay'll roll and getcha some grub. What kind do ya want?" Dollaz reassured her as he waved Tay to come on.

While Deziree was putting her order together in her head, Malcolm stood up and got some money out of his pocket and attempted to hand it to Big Tay. Big Tay shook his head side to side.

"We got it, pops. Deziree, what is it that you want?" Big Tay asked.

"It doesn't matter, I'm not gonna be picky, Tay. Just make it fast," she laughed as she spoke.

I'll be right back, I'm just gonna walk with them down the hall. Okay," Malcolm told Deziree as he followed Big Tay and Dollaz out the door.

When Malcolm made it into the hallway, he looked in both directions searching for anything out of the ordinary as before, like another cowboy. Not seeing anyone that did not look as if they belonged, he stepped over to where Dollaz and Big Tay were looking through the glass of the nursery at the babies. He gave them a few minutes to clown about him being a daddy before he called a meeting to order in the lounge. Malcolm led off going in the direction he went when he was chasing after the cowboy, Big Tay and Dollaz followed him until they got to a lounge that was in the cut. It was just to the right of the elevators hidden from anyone not paying attention. Malcolm stood up with his back against a window by a pay phone. He urged Dollaz and Big Tay to take a seat, both were puzzled somewhat by the urgency although Big Tay felt he knew most of the details.

"This can't wait til we get back from gettin' the grub?" Dollaz asked with a confused look on his face.

"Holdem up my nigga, this ain't gonna take long. I just wanna put ya up on game real quick. It goes like this; I got this police broad that's been down with a nigga for a few years now. She lets me know about shit like who's workin' with the police, what the task force got in store for niggas like us. And it's because of her you're sittin' right here lookin' at me and Tay."

"Stop it! Tay...you hear this shit? This nigga got some soap opera shit goin' on in this mutha fucka." Dollaz busted out laughing while getting up and hugging Malcolm.

"Alright, alright, I love your crazy ass too but sit down so I can finish. Just today, she warned me that the local PD is supposed to be gettin' some help from the DEA to try and put a case on us. To me I think it's crazy cause it ain't like we some major mutha fuckas distributin' tons of shit. We local until the van pulls into this mutha fucka tonight. But I'll get back to that later. When I come up here and Big Tay was waitin downstairs, I seen this cowboy dude lookin' through the glass at the nursery. I walked up on em he called me by my name like he knew who I was. I mean the mutha fucka called me Malcolm Love..."

"I seen a cowboy gettin' off the elevator when we was comin' outta the gift shop. Ol' Marlboro man lookin' mutha fucka with a big ass hat..."

"All white with a white fur lookin' collar," Big Tay finished the sentence that Dollaz took over from Malcolm.

"Yeah, my niggas, that's him. Keepin' it real though they probably really want me, and they mad as hell downtown at you cause you got away with that murder. But check it out, though, the only way they'll be able to get me is through one of y'all. I know that ain't gonna happen, but Javon in jail accordin' to his mama. For all I know he can be someplace in federal custody tellin' them bitches everythang he know bout all us and the Cali plug that he owe. What I'm gonna do bout that is send Kenny to Vegas and see if he really in jail, and if so, what for. Regardless of what's goin' on we've gotta get all our shit strategically placed so we can get these birds pushed across these state lines. I just need to know if ya down or not Dollaz, Tay already said he's still in it to win it. If so, you'll be down here cleanin' up on all the clientele and if ya need help, BigTay gotta couple lil soldiers that's lightweight seasoned and ready to make some money. Big Tay goin' outta town to hustle in Kansas City with Solo and Gooch tomorrow so they can meet up with Paperboy and Hoodsta..."

"What Paperboy and Hoodsta gotta do with us?" interrupted Dollaz.

"Game done changed on ya Dollaz, we gettin' ready to be puttin' work all the way up I-35 from Oklahoma City, Kansas City to Minneapolis. That's what Paperboy and Hoodsta gotta do with us. They gonna help us push this mutha fuckin' cocaine and we gonna get filthy rich until the feds come and get us. But check it out, we gonna have Paperboy's sales down here. Remember when you was cryin' back in the day wantin' to do this and that, well now's ya chance. It's finally ya turn to be the man. I'm gonna have to show ya how to get down in the kitchen 'cause I'm not gonna be around that much. I'm gonna be busy orchestratin' all this shit from the sideline and changin' diapers and helpin' my mama with her restaurant..."

"Restaurant?" Dollaz questioned. "You goddamn right I'm ready my nigga. I want both of you niggas to hear this. Y'all is the only brothers I ever had and I wanna really apologize for the dumb shit I done by gettin'...well I'm just sorry for everythang. Thank y'all for givin' me a chance to get down with the new and improved Ghetto Merchants and givin' a shout out to the originatin' Mafioso Seven and the homies that's restin' in peace." Dollaz spoke, trying not to get emotional.

"We gotta send them niggas some money too. I ain't sent em nothin' in about three months." Big Tay changed the subject.

"I gave both them niggas girls two ounces of powder to take to them niggas last month. Believe me when I tell ya they ain't got no problem with tellin' a nigga when they need somethin', ya feel me?" Replied Malcolm.

Big Tay stood up and walked over to the other window in the lounge and stared out into the darkness, lit up by another wing of the hospital. He was thankful Malcolm had not spoken about all the information he revealed inside the truck. Big Tay knew how Malcolm and Dollaz analyzed things. If Malcolm had said something about the crooked cop who was extorting the policewoman, Dollaz would want to end that before it went any further. They all knew Dollaz was trigger-happy; he was known for that well before the case he just got out of jail on. He was also greedy, and that alone would keep him in check of pushing any issues of getting rid of Malcolm's policewoman without Malcolm bringing it up first. Now that Malcolm had let him come back inside their circle and put him in the position to really get paid there was no way he would want to fuck that up.

Big Tay felt confident in Malcolm's decisions that he had made for their crew. He knew that Malcolm wouldn't let anyone with a badge dictate the way he stacked his paper. Therefore, if the policewoman was a threat, Malcolm would make certain she kept her mouth shut. After Big Tay let those thoughts run through his head, he turned around to face Malcolm and Dollaz still talking. "Yeah man...you got vision the average drug dealer lacks. You care about people who care about you. What I'm sayin' is this; the average drug dealer would be hundreds of miles away by now if he heard news that the alphabet boys of any kind was on his trail. But you still plottin' and plannin' shit so that all ya niggas can still get paid..." Dollaz finally took a breath.

"Come on Dollaz, so we can get Deziree somethin' to eat before it gets too late. We'll bring you somethin' back too pops," Big Tay spoke quickly after interrupting him.

"Yo Dollaz check this shit out. I'll get out in traffic witcha to make it all official. When niggas see us two together, they gonna know you back in." Malcolm smiled and shook his hand before he walked out towards the elevator.

Chapter 25

When Big Tay and Dollaz made it back to the hospital room with the Chinese takeout, the head nurse came in and told them it was time to leave. Visiting hours were over. Malcolm told Big Tay that he would make sure he had the rundown on how they were to get around in KC by the time they hit the road. As for Dollaz, he simply told him to come by Cecelia's house around one o'clock tomorrow afternoon.

Shortly after Malcolm's homeboys left and he and Deziree finished eating, he dropped a bomb on her by saying it was a possibility that he, she, and the twins would be moving. When she asked him why, he simply told her not to worry about it, and there was no more discussion about the topic. It didn't take Malcolm long to doze off in the chair, and Deziree got up and covered him with a blanket.

What seemed like all night turned out to be just a few hours when Malcolm heard his mobile phone ringing. Feeling somewhat incoherent from the absence of rest over the past week, Malcolm reached down on the side of the chair and grabbed his mobile. After pressing SEND and putting the phone to his ear, Malcolm heard Solo's voice. He was informing him they made it to the Oklahoma City city limits. He wanted to know what Malcolm wanted them to do and where to go. Malcolm slid his right sleeve up and took a look at his Movado. It was ten minutes after nine and there was no time to waste. Malcolm instructed them to come to the hospital and meet him in the cafeteria on the bottom floor.

Sitting in a dimly lit corner facing the cafeteria entrance was Malcolm. When he saw Kenny walk through the door with Solo and Gooch, it was nine thirty-three. All of them reached the table to see Malcolm playing with a plastic spoon inside a small Styrofoam cup with hot coffee. He could see the sign of victory lighting up all their faces, signifying that they made it. Kenny was sitting to his left, Solo on his right, and Gooch sat straight across. Malcolm casually pushed the cup filled with hot liquid forward enough to give him room to put his elbows on the table and cross his arms. Nobody said one word; they waited to see what Malcolm had to say, which was so important.

"I actually prayed to God for y'all to make it home safe, here ya are. Unfortunately, I've got some bad news..."

"Is it Deziree and the twins?" Kenny asked, not giving Malcolm time to finish his statement.

"Deziree is cool, in fact, she'll be getting outta here tomorrow. The twins are in the NICU, but they'll be alright. Their doctor says they'll probably be home in seven to ten days. I'd take y'all upstairs, but visitin' hours is over. Check game while I lay this shit out real quick and then y'all can get on so ya can get some rest."

"We just holla'd at Big Tay and Dollaz, he said they was up at Harold's Supper Club fuckin' with some ho's and havin' some drinks. I see ya told him about the trip we plannin' up to K.C." Solo responded quickly, looking anxious to leave.

"Like I was gonna say...I got this broad that's OCPD. This afternoon, she laced me up on game that the local NARCs are reachin' out to the DEA to try and throw a monkey wrench in our program," Malcolm spoke slowly, then paused and pulled the piece of paper out of his pocket that Teresa gave him earlier in the day. He flagged it in the air for everybody to see, then he dropped it on the table.

"On top of that I got a crooked cop on this piece of paper that's bribin my bitch for twenty g's. She told me that Internal Affairs is crawling up in his ass cause he's the one that took the evidence outta the station that got Dollaz free. Now I don't know if he's gonna knock my bitch if he get knocked, but one thang is fa sho and that is he wants that money. I already gave her five g's to give his bitch ass not too long ago. I'm gonna keep it real, I'm shook-up cause I don't know if or when this shit is gonna come back and fuck a nigga off. One thang is for real and that is all y'all is safe as long as ya get outta town and do ya thang like we talked about in Cali..."

While Malcolm was talking, Kenny picked the paper up from the table and began analyzing it.

"So, keep the van parked at ya mama's house, Solo. She ain't trippin' bout that shit, she down. Is Paperboy still online?"

"Hell, yeah, he on online. I got at him earlier this evenin', he said as soon as we make it up there to give him a call so he can slide down. So how many do ya wanna give em since they gettin' it on front?" Solo inquired, looking more focused since Malcolm's story.

"Go ahead and give them niggas four of 'em. If it's jumpin' like they say it is, they'll probably be back atcha before the weekend is over. At first, I want y'all to charge them niggas twenty-seven. When it starts to roll, we'll drop the price. Make sure y'all find a cool house close to the highway with a nice garage. Mutha fuckas be nosey, I don't care what kinda neighbors ya got. I'm sayin that so y'all know a nigga can't be unloadin' birds in the front yard or in the driveway. Ya feel me. When it starts rollin' with Kansas City sales that's when

y'all need to get another crib to lay back in when nothin' ain't happenin'. Also, a nigga gonna have to get some cool wheels, nothin' too flashy but tight so a nigga can get around in the snow up there and roll that bitch outta town."
"Like a Grand Wagoneer or a four-wheel drive Suburban?" Gooch suggested.

"Somethin' like that. It's gonna cost some g's but a nigga can't be rollin' around in some shit that's gonna break down. A nigga can't be rollin' around in a Range Rover droppin' off work either. Speakin' of Range Rovers, how bout Mrs. Mims got Javon's Range Rover at the house. She said the nigga in jail in Vegas for burglary and tresspassin', and the nigga already got sentenced to six months. The whole thang sounds fucked up to me and I wanna find out if it's true cause for all we know the nigga could be across town posted up in a safe house with the feds. So, Kenny, this is where I need ya again. I want you to roll out to Vegas and visit the nigga in the county jail. If he there let em know he gotta spot on the Ghetto Merchant team when he get out. If he ain't there I'm gonna shake the town cause he know enough to get a nigga a life sentence. But I'ma take Mrs. Mims word that he is there. If so, and everythang is all good with em I need ya to take the 454 on to LA to Xavier so he can put the super tank stash in that mutha fucka. We'll make that the bird runna. By the way, don't say shit to Javon about us goin' to LA fuckin with Fats. It's gonna rack his brain to figure out how we stayin' up out here without him. Hopefully everythang'll go accordin' to plan. Oh yeah, Solo, Gooch, be sure to give Dollaz all of y'all's weight contacts. We gonna try to get rich around this mutha fucka too. Dollaz ain't hot in the streets for sellin' dope right now. He can push full steam ahead with some help from me and some of Big Tay's lil niggas like Lil T and Spanky. Them lil niggas ain't tryin to do nothin' but come up and buy a Cutlass or a Regal and put it on some Daytons. Them lil niggas wanna get it. " Malcolm explained fully.

"Just how many birds is we takin' to Kansas City?" Solo asked.

"I think ten is cool. Make damn sho y'all keep the count right too. I'm gonna get up in the mornin' and meet y'all over to Mama's to give y'all twenty g's. That'll be enough to give Auntie a few dollas to help y'all find a crib, put a little bit of furniture in there, and a down payment on a truck. Solo, the rest is up to you. You know how to eat outta that Pyrex. Whip up some crack and that'll give y'all some spendin' money. Remember, just like we did when Dollaz fuck'd off the money and we grinded all winter and flossed hard as a mutha fucka all summer. You best believe I'm gonna be down here gettin' extras up outta Javon's kitchen. By the way, we got that niggas condo for six months. His mama rented it to Kenny until Javon get home. As bad as I hate to say it but I hope that nigga in jail for real for that little bullshit his mama said he in there for."

"So, you've taken it upon yourself to get me a place so you can eat from Pyrex? That doesn't make any sense." Kenny finally spoke, not understanding what Malcolm meant. This caused everybody to laugh except for him.

"Damn Kenny, you's square as a mutha fucka for real aint cha. He's talkin' bout droppin' cocaine in some glassware and whippin' up some crack. Damn." Gooch added because he was finally happy that he knew more than somebody about the game.

"Chill bro, I gotta get minez too. Believe me, when I tell ya if I start to see thangs lookin' shaky around here, I'll be shakin' OKC headed somewhere. All I need you to do is drive the work from Cali to here and sometimes Kansas City.' We gonna make damn sho you getcha money, we gotta, you's the driver now."

Kenny listened to Malcolm as he talked and tried to make everyone feel as if he was calm and collected. He wasn't, regardless of the time that he spent away from his little brother, he still knew his character. Kenny could tell that Malcolm was uneasy and he should be from all the things he was telling them. God forbid the things he was keeping to himself. At that very moment, Kenny decided to do what he could to help, although he also knew he may be crossing the line with old friends. He didn't give a damn though, let the truth be known, they actually owed him dearly.

"I have a few friends in DC that I'll give a call tomorrow. Discreetly, I will have them look into a few things just to see if any federal agency actually has an eye on you Malcolm. If they do, no doubt they'll be looking at all of you so, until I find out anything be careful. As for me, right now I'm just about ready to lay down in my bed." Kenny said, butting in.

"Go ahead and take the van over to mama's. Gooch and Solo can use my truck, it's outside. By the way, I seen ya bitch today, Gooch. If it wasn't for Tay I woulda smoked her and Hector's bitch ass. They was rollin' down Kelly comin' from the same direction as you and Solo's crib...". Malcolm switched the conversation back to Solo, not paying Kenny any mind, regardless of him being ready to leave.

Gooch, on the other hand, was already thinking about Martha before Malcolm brought her name up. Just a few hours ago, he spoke with her on his mobile. She told him about the situation that happened on Kelly when she went to cop the

PCP with Hector. He could tell that she had been crying, but she wouldn't tell him what for. Whatever the reason, he would find out soon enough because he was going to see her tonight. Gooch knew things about Martha's past; she told him about things. He didn't care because as far as he was concerned everybody had some kind of bullshit in their past, they wanted hidden. One thing he knew for sure was that Martha was a hustler and all she needed was a break. Gooch was determined to be the one to give her that break, but he needed some help. He was gonna have to rap with Dollaz one on one and tell him to look out for Martha on the work when he was up in Kansas City.

Solo was also at a crossroads. He felt it was his duty to let Malcolm know how he felt, and he believed the time was now, in front of family.

"I appreciate the responsibility of puttin' the reigns in my hands on this outta town plan. Still yet there's somethin' botherin' me."

"Spit it out then," Malcolm spoke out curiously. The comment grasped Gooch and Kenny's attention, too.

"It's Dollaz."

"Ahh, Dollaz. Okay, whatsup?" Malcolm asked.

"Do ya think it's a good move to put him in such an important position already? I mean, goddamn my nigga we earned the right to sell weight, we spent countless days and nights to make this happen. I'm gonna keep it real witcha, I don't think he deserves it handed to him without havin' to put in any work. Don't get me wrong, I wanna see my nigga get paid but...fuck it, it's whatever."

DRE LUV

"I see where ya comin' from, Solo, but don't forget we gotta have somebody around here to collect the money right here at home. It ain't no way I'm gonna just let some lame ass niggas catch all the sells we built. I'm gonna control the sack, Solo, not Dollaz. He gotta come to me to get the work, and work is just what he gonna do. You damn right, he don't deserve to just come into the circle without puttin' somethin' down but you betta believe he's gonna get it in now. He owes all of us and he knows it and he's ready, and he ain't scared to get out there. And right now, in front of all three of y'all I swear that if Dollaz make me look bad again I'll kill em myself. I put that on my mama."

"I need to be sure you can focus on keepin' the business straight in Kansas City by not gettin' shot. Nobody else either, as far as that's concerned. Do me a favor and let me worry about Dollaz and what goes on down here. And just in case them hoes gotta secret agenda and they come pick me up from this hospital tonight. Go on and execute my plan...I'm goin' back upstairs. C'ya in the mornin'."

Everybody could see the look on Solo's face. He was pissed off and he did not care what they thought about it. He got up and headed out of the cafeteria without saying anything else. Gooch quickly jumped to Solo's defense after pick-ing up Malcolm's truck keys from the table, which diverted his attention. Kenny noticed that and cuffed the paper with the crooked cop's information on it.

"Don't worry bout Solo, Malcolm, he's only sayin' those things to try and protect you. We all knew how fucked up you was when Dollaz burned out on ya. Solo respects Dollaz for lotsa things, even the fact of when he left for the reason of y'all two havin' disagreements on money. Solo just hates the fact we all had to

382

suffer behind him. Alright then, we need to get our bags outta the van, Kenny," Gooch spoke quietly while he, Malcolm and Kenny stepped into the hallway.

They watched Solo push through the exit doors leading to the parking lot, where the van was parked a few spaces away from Malcolm's truck.

"You ain't gonna say nothin' are ya? Fuck it, if y'all both gonna be on some bullshit, so be it. I'll be outside waitin', Kenny!" Gooch told them both as he walked away.

Malcolm just looked at him like he was crazy. Gooch shook his head and went after Solo while Kenny stayed back.

"I'll see you in the morning, Malcolm. Don't worry yourself too much because all things tend to work out sooner or later. Go get some sleep and watch over my little nephew and niece and let them know I love them and their mother."

The elevator chimed, and Malcolm peeked that way and proceeded to get on it.

After waiting momentarily for Kenny, Gooch and Solo got their bags from the van. They put them in the back of the truck, and they got inside and drove out of the parking lot. Kenny turned on the map light while sitting behind the wheel of the van and pulled the paper out of his pocket that Malcolm had left on the table. He looked at it then he looked at the time on his black and stainless-steel Breitling timepiece on his wrist. Kenny had come home to get away from problems and found himself caught up in the middle of a critical situation. He had to do whatever he could to keep his family together, even if it meant breaking the law again. Kenny neatly folded the paper and placed it in the cupholder and put the van in gear and drove off.

DRE LUV

Sitting at the light in the turning lane to get on Lake Hefner Parkway was the 454 with Gooch behind the wheel and Solo on the right listening to Ice Cube. Solo still hadn't said a word since he was speaking to Malcolm inside the cafeteria. Gooch turned the music down, causing Solo to stare at him through the dim yellow lighting seeping through the tint from the streetlights hovering overhead.

"I don't know why ya mad. Right now, we in a position better than anybody else we know on the streets. At least the niggas we fuck with. Let's just do our part and go on with Malcolm's plan. True enough, he's hardheaded and don't wanna listen to nobody and he thinks he's always right. One thang is real, he usually is. Stop trippin' and get ready to show a nigga how to do it Kansas City style cause we on now and it ain't no holdin' us back," Gooch elaborated with a smile.

Solo remained quiet for a moment after soaking up Gooch's words. He was going home, and suddenly his anger began to subside. Malcolm was right; he'd concentrate on Kansas City business. There he'd be the boss. The thought made him grin with the new hidden agenda of possibly branching out on his own when shit started flipping.

"Fuck all this shit that's goin' on down here with the DEA, FBI's, Internal Affairs and police bitches. You goddamn right Gooch, I'm gonna do my part by gettin' away from this shit. Malcolm is a smart mutha fucka after all, by givin' us an out. Now that I think about it, I'm gonna find my nigga Dooney and take him all the way to the top with us. I owe him that cause he went to the pen tryin' to get me outta jail. You know what happened to me when I tried to return the favor. It's all kinda strange how when I left from up there three years ago, I was a minor figure. Now a nigga returnin' havin birds."

GHETTO MERCHANTS

"Now that's what I'm talkin' bout. Hey, check this out...I aint tryin' to be hangin' out at Harold's all night gettin' drunk with them niggas. All I'm gonna do is change my voicemail on my beeper and have Dollaz's number on there. Tonight, I got somethin' to do," Gooch declared.

"Alright, ya goin' to go fuck on Martha aintcha? Fuck it, might as well ol fool ass nigga. That's on you. I got somethin' to do too, just drop me off at the house and I'll see ya in the mornin'. I ain't goin' up to Harold's either, Malcolm and Dollaz got all this shit handled down here, you heard em,"

Solo looked over at Gooch, then he exploded in a horrific laugh.

Chapter 26

In route to his home in the middle-class neighborhood of Greenbriar was Sergeant Sloan. He sped west on South 104th, not caring about being pulled over for speeding, he had a police shield on his license plate. The only thing on his mind was making it home to get a quick shower and clean up his place a little before Teresa showed up. There was no way he was going to let her see his place in disarray for fear that she would not return. Right now, he had to hurry up because he was pushing the clock close. She was due to show up somewhere in the midnight hour. It was almost twelve. He never dreamed the day would come for her to want to see him, but his plan worked. Twenty grand and some ass were really going to have him sitting on top. She was so dumb she had no idea the Internal Affairs investigation was over, still, he led her on to think they would pull her in too. It wasn't like she could go to their office and ask if they were investigating her for the missing evidence in a triple homicide case that sprung a known killer. Not even the biggest fool in Oklahoma City would do that; it would be career suicide.

Wearing a grin ear to ear, Sloan turned the Fleetwood Mack tape up on his factory deck as he wished he had come up with the scheme months ago. By now, he would've been watching Teresa walk around his house naked at will. Oh well, better now than never. Besides, it was her fault that she was in this situation. She came to him with the scheme, choosing to get involved with Deante Parker's case that ended up making OCPD and the Oklahoma County District Attorney's office look bad. After doing some digging into Parker's background, aka (Dollaz), Sloan found out he was a member of a crew that had been involved in several unsolved murders. That was when he came across the name Malcolm Love; he was a known drug dealer in Oklahoma City. Sloan connected the dots that fingered Teresa as capable of getting the cash from the gangster. She had allowed herself to be used and who knows what else by some street thugs, which made her damaged goods to some. To Sloan she was a goddess, and every time he saw her, his dick got hard which led to him stalking her. He knew everything about her except who she would see in the garage apartment behind the mansion in Heritage Hills. At this point, he didn't care.

When Internal Affairs began investigating his department, he already had all his tracks covered. Sloan knew all the ins and outs of the property room because he'd seen it his whole life. He'd gone there as a child when his father held the same position; therefore, he was a pro at altering paperwork. The only way for him to get caught would be for him to tell on himself or for Teresa Smits to become self-righteous and rat them both out. Sloan knew she would never do that because she dreamed of becoming a robbery homicide detective one day. She knew that if she were to expose what she and Sloan did, she wouldn't make detective. She would make it to Mabel Bassett Women's Maximum-Security Prison. Little did she know the investigation had been called off because the high-ranking brass in OCPD, along with the head Oklahoma County DA, didn't want the media to get hold of their fiasco. It was election year, and the public wouldn't take too kindly to the fact of a gang member/drug dealer getting away with murder, especially because of missing evidence. And the reason for the missing evidence was because of the mishandling by public servants paid with taxpayers' money. Therefore, the chief, the mayor, and the hopeful to be reelected district attorney all got together and decided to sweep the whole incident under the rug. They all knew that too much bullshit brought out of the closet could start a federal investigation, and nobody wanted that. Besides, they figured that three drug dealers from out of state were not such a bad thing after all. As far as the accused murderer, Deante Parker, he would slip up again.

Then there was Sergeant Sloan, who was merely issued an informal demerit along with a promise to be terminated if another incident occurred on his watch. That would never happen again because Sloan had everything he wanted with Teresa.

Turning right into Greenbriar, he drove two blocks down and turned left at his median-separated cul-de-sac. As he accelerated down the curved street with the green spray-painted winter lawns and the floodlight-lined driveways, he found something odd. When his driveway appeared around the bend, he noticed his flood lights that lined the driveway weren't lit. As he got a little closer, he hit the button on his garage door, and it opened, but the motion detector light above the door didn't come on. He thought it was probably a tripped breaker because the inside light came on inside the garage. He slowed down as he pulled into the driveway, scraping the front scoop on his Ford Taurus. Suddenly, he was overwhelmed with relief because he wouldn't have been able to entertain Teresa if something was wrong with his electricity indoors. Although it really didn't matter because he was going to have twenty thousand free dollars tomorrow, maybe even tonight.

As Sloan pulled further into his garage, the more his mind raced, his testosterone level began to rise. He pulled to a stop and hit the button on the garage opener, causing it to lower. Sloan opened the car door and attempted to get out but was surprised when the Taurus kept moving forward. He took his foot off the brake without putting the car in park or shutting off the engine.

While he was occupied with that small task, he didn't pay attention to what was going on behind him. Little did he know that in the shrubbery on the side of his garage, someone was waiting for him. When Sloan pulled into the garage and it started to lower, the figure dressed in all black crept around the corner. They stepped over the trip beam just in time to get right behind the Taurus to see and hear Sloan almost crash the car into the wall. As Sloan got out of the car, he looked at the clock on the radio; it was 11:42. His eyes grew as big as golf balls when he saw the intruder rise from behind the car with an arm extended and a pistol pointed at Sloan's head. Before he could say a word, he shit and pissed on himself.

Epilogue

Without hesitation, J.R. ducked back into his room wearing nothing but his boxers and put on his clothes while Dooney banged on the door, hollering for JR and Menace.

Menace was dressed, wearing only plaid pajamas and house shoes, holding a Mossberg. JR approached him, and the hardwood floor creaked loudly. Out front, Dooney yelled out that he could hear somebody in there and to just open the door so they could talk.

"Them niggas didn't come to talk, dog. What's up?" Questioned JR in a whisper, nodding his head towards the front door.

Just as Menace was about to answer him, the back door came crashing in, causing both JR and Menace to wrench their necks back to see the kitchen door hanging together by splinters and Gunna gripping a Desert Eagle with both hands, walking towards them. Menace immediately dropped the Mossberg because there was no need to try to swing it around towards Gunna. But in a split second after he let it go, he wished he had used it as leverage by pointing it at the front door where Gunna knew his little brother stood.

One shot through the door with the double odd shot would have laid Dooney to rest on the front porch.

"Where the fuck you nigga's think y'all goin' and where the fuck is my bread?" Gunna asked angrily as he walked up on Menace and JR.

Gunna didn't see JR had a Ruger by his side because he was still halfway concealed behind the door jamb of his bedroom. JR felt like he had nothing to lose, he stepped back inside the room and opened fire through the wall, firing blindly, hitting Gunna in his left arm. Gunna grunted from the heat of the bullet that went in and out of his forearm. Not knowing whether his wound was clean through or not, or whether he or Dooney would get killed, Gunna gritted his teeth, shotgun at Menace's face as he looked up while on all fours. Gunna pulled the trigger, but nothing happened.

"You fucked with the wrong nigga's money!"

Gunna shouted, then he racked the slide back on the Mossberg, putting one in the chamber. Menace knew there was nothing else to do. He closed his eyes, and Gunna pulled the trigger as soon as Dooney stepped aside. When Menace's body fell over it no longer had a head. Gunna walked into the bedroom and cleared the chamber. JR scooted over trying to get under the bed.

"Nooo!!!" He pleaded at the top of his lungs.

Gunna gave him the same mercy he gave Menace; he blew his head off as well.

"Go turn on the kitchen stove; be sure to blow out the pilots. I'll push the back door shut!" Gunna commanded.

Dooney did as he was told in a hurry, Gunna on his heels to do his part of his plan. Dooney was acting nervous; he couldn't get the top up on the stove to blow out the pilot flame. Angrily, Gunna shoved him to the side and snatched the stove away from the wall, breaking it free from the gas line that immediately filled the room with the smell of natural gas. Rushing out of the kitchen, Gunna saw a candle jar along with a Kansas City Call paper, both sitting on the table. Gunna reached into his pocket, pulled out his lighter, and lit the candle and the newspaper.

DRE LUV

"Go start up the truck and wait for me!" Gunna shouted.

Dooney jetted out the door as told, Gunna put the slow-burning newspaper under the old curtains, which went up in flames as if they were drenched with gasoline. He then pulled out the Desert Eagle and tossed it on the floor while thinking his Houston connect sold him that pistol. It would never be traced back to him anyway, no prints left because this old stick house was about to go up in flames and explode. Gunna walked out and closed the door behind him. He wasn't worried about who may have seen his truck; people in that area knew how to mind their business. Besides, he knew if someone did tell, they would never have the courage to testify against him. They'd be signing their death certificate the day they signed a statement. Gunna hopped up in the passenger seat with help from Dooney, who already had the door open. He closed the door, and Dooney backed out of the drive, not knowing where to go.

"Take me over to Big Mama's house so she can look at this shit," Gunna instructed.

When Dooney pulled up to the light on Brush Creek, they heard the booming sound of an explosion. The light turned green, and they crossed the light heading north. When they made it to the top of the hill on Elmwood, Gunna turned around and looked back through the rear glass, seeing dark smoke rising in the sky from a distance. Dooney gripped the wheel tightly while taking a deep breath, thinking that Gunna was serious when it came to his money. He'd just killed two niggas he'd known most of his life over five grand. He hated to think of what might happen if there was ever a serious disagreement with him, Solo, or any of the guys in his crew. Hopefully, that would never happen because he hated the thought of having to kill somebody since he had never had to. As for his brother, he just witnessed that it was no problem for him. When it came to Solo it was rumored all through the streets, he was seen driving out of the parking of the Church's Chicken the night the niggas who shot him were gunned down.

www.ingramcontent.com/pod-product-compliance
Lightning Source LLC
Chambersburg PA
CBHW072022020726
47501CB00006B/1911